The shining splendor **Y0-CDK-308**
*the cover of this book reflects the glittering excellence of
the story inside. Look for the Zebra Lovegram whenever
you buy a historical romance. It's a trademark that guar-
antees the very best in quality and reading entertainment.*

"Take one spunky heroine, one virile rancher, a cattle drive,
add danger and romance, and you have Martha Hix at her
sizzling best!"

— *Romantic Times*

"WHY DON'T YOU WANT TO BE MY WIFE . . . IN MORE THAN NAME?" ASKED GIL.

"You . . . you promised you wouldn't force yourself
on me," said Lisette.

"Am I doing that?" Gil changed positions and eased
himself closer, settling against her. "Have I tossed you
to the ground and ripped your clothes off?"

Lisette felt his hands moving along her body, stroking her curves. "I know that you want me," he whispered. "I can see it in your eyes. It excites me every
time."

His caresses began to melt her resistance. She
yearned for him, yet . . . she wanted all of him, not
just his passion. "You're embarrassing me," she protested.

"I don't mean to. If you'd rather, I won't say anything. We'll just spend the rest of our lives doing
what's natural."

A lifetime together. What a beautiful idea. She
yearned to meet *all* his needs. Yet she lacked the courage to confess her sin. She needed more time; and
when his hand began an even more intimate caress,
she propelled herself forward, grappling for footing.
Once again, Lisette was running away from her husband. . . .

Martha Hix

CARESS OF FIRE

ZEBRA BOOKS
KENSINGTON PUBLISHING CORP.

*To the beautiful German girl
who goes the distance—
my mother-in-law,
Ann Uhr Hix*

ZEBRA BOOKS

are published by

Kensington Publishing Corp.
475 Park Avenue South
New York, NY 10016

First printing: April, 1992

Printed in the United States of America

Chapter One

February, 1869

She needed what he could offer.

Twice, she had set out to speak with him. Twice, courage had deserted her as she neared the entrance to the Vereinskirche building, where he stood talking with a trio of men. Twice up and down Main Street, and nothing to show for it.

Backbone, that was what she needed to approach the rancher less than a block away. A few steps meaning the difference between drudgery and freedom.

Lisette Keller took a deep breath and walked toward Gil McLoughlin. She prayed nothing would go wrong.

A rotund farmer, one of the few locals on the street this morning, sidled up to her. He scratched his reddened nose and said in German, the language spoken by most of Fredericksburg, Texas's populace, "It's a fine day, is it not? Balmy even for this climate."

Lisette didn't wish to discuss the weather, yet she wouldn't be rude. "It is."

Otto Kapp's expression veered, curious. "What are you doing in town? I thought your brother was

5

planting those peach saplings he imported."

She was supposed to be planting that orchard, not Adolf, and *if* she returned to the farm, there would be hell to pay. She stole a look at the distant form of Gil McLoughlin. Return to her brother's farm she would not, and the rancher would be the instrument of her escape.

"Fräulein Keller," Otto Kapp said, "there is something I have been intending to discuss. Marriage. I mean to speak with Adolf about you."

She hid a shudder. Several times the widower Kapp had made his intentions clear, but she would rather be dragged naked down this very street than marry him. Her feelings weren't necessarily a result of his lack of physical appeal. She simply didn't like him, and wouldn't spend the rest of her life being his *Hausfrau.*

Mumbling a nonspecific reply and an *auf Wiedersehen,* Lisette adjusted her handmade, eagle-feather-trimmed fedora and sidestepped the farmer. A wagon rolled by, blocking her view of her key to freedom. She cut around the vehicle and stepped to the street corner. No more than a quarter block separated her from the dark-haired, lanky McLoughlin.

"Lisette."

Recognizing Anna Uhr's voice, Lisette stopped and turned to the one person who knew about her plans. Nonetheless, they nettled her, all these interruptions.

"Are you going to do it?" Anna asked, wide-eyed.

Lisette scanned the surroundings to make certain no one could overhear. Die Biergarten's proprietor strode outside to pour a bucket of slop into a trough for his pigs; Otto Kapp greeted him, the pair disappearing into the saloon. Gil McLoughlin and his companions weren't within hearing range.

Assured of privacy, Lisette finally replied, "Yes."

"Herr McLoughlin will never agree."

"He will. He will."

"He'll think you loose for asking." Anna batted a fly buzzing her nose. "It is not proper, what you're wanting from the Yankee."

"Scotsman," Lisette corrected.

"I doubt he's as in need as you'd like to think."

"He'll let me have my way." Lisette spoke bravely, not feeling half as courageous as her words. "He's a newcomer around here, and from where he hails, they probably don't have as strict a code of propriety."

"I wouldn't count on that. Ladies are ladies in Illinois and Scotland — or wherever he's from. Even if what has been said about him is true . . ." Anna moved away from a stray pig that had waddled up to her. "I imagine a proposition such as yours would be frowned on anywhere."

"You have a point," Lisette conceded, "but there's no other way out."

"There might be no need for the unseemly if you'd flirt a bit. He might offer for your hand, then you wouldn't be forced into disgrace." Anna's teeth tugged on one side of her bottom lip. "Is it you don't wish to be wooed by a man with scandal attached to his name?"

"Anna Uhr, bite your tongue."

Though her own disgrace was mostly a secret, Lisette felt a certain kinship with the cattleman she would meet today. According to gossip, he, too, had been hurt by life. Though he wasn't openly shunned by the townfolk, he hadn't been welcomed to the community, and Lisette sympathized with his situation.

Anna, unaware of her friend's past heartbreak, continued her attempt at matchmaking. "He's well fixed — I've heard his Four Aces Ranch is an isle of profit in the sea of our local poverty. And surely you don't think he's homely."

Lisette, flushing, looked in the rancher's direction. She'd never seen him up close, but even from afar, he emitted a virile aura that a woman would have to be cold as a February day not to notice.

More advice came her way. "The Yankee, er, Scotsman will be driving his cattle to Kansas shortly, and if you work fast, you'll have a ring on your finger, and —"

"Marriage isn't what I want from him. It'll take money and lots of it for me to get to Chicago, and he can provide it."

"In all the years I've known you, Lisette Keller, I've never known you for a conniver."

Lisette studied the toes of her worn shoes. As a rule she didn't scheme to achieve her purposes, but why feel guilty? She would give more than she took from Herr McLoughlin, so he had everything to gain and nothing to lose from accepting her deal.

She met Anna's skeptical gaze. "No one will hire me — not for any job, much less at my hatmaking trade — without my brother's permission. And Adolf would never approve. Herr McLoughlin is my last hope."

"Oh, Lisette, I wish there were some way Egon and I could help. We've had such a time, trying to catch up on our taxes and keeping food on the table. But I worry about you."

8

"I know." Appreciative of her friend's concern, she touched Anna's arm, and her voice softened. "I do need to 'work fast.' Or he'll be gone before I—"

"Fine. Go on." Exasperated now, the married woman warned, "Remember something. If he takes you up on your bargain, you'll still be an unmarried woman once you reach Chicago."

Instead of replying, Lisette fingered her hat, reminding herself of the trade that would finance her freedom . . . once she reached the shores of Lake Michigan.

"You are the prettiest woman I've ever seen," Anna went on, and her remark drew a mien of disbelief from Lisette, who had always considered herself rather ordinary.

Anna was saying, "But you're not getting any younger. Twenty-two doesn't make for a prime matrimonial prospect even if so many eligible men hadn't been lost in the war." She paused for emphasis. "Twenty-two or fifteen, you wouldn't be able to count on any man taking you to wife, if your name is sullied. Even the desperate, such as Herr Kapp, would think twice. Men have too much pride to marry unrespectable women."

Lisette swallowed. The Civil War had shattered many lives, including her own. No longer was she young. No longer was she above reproach, if the truth were known. Along the course of reaching her advanced age, she'd erred in judgment and given her trust to the untrustworthy, only to be jilted.

No man would want another's reject, should he discover her shameful secret. No man? Well, if such an understanding man existed, he didn't live in this narrow-minded community.

Since she was penniless, she had to depend on her wits, had to use any resource available to escape her brother and his wife. She wouldn't lose sleep over sacrificing the reputation she had guarded like a miser did a penny, nor would she be swayed by capricious courtship ploys, nor by vague Scottish virility.

Gil McLoughlin was a means to an end. Nothing more, nothing less.

Once more her eyes found the Scotsman.

Oh, no! He made the motions of leaving, was untying his sorrel stallion from the hitching post as his companions disappeared into the Vereinskirche building. Lisette rushed forward, the hem of her best of two dresses dragging through the street's dust. In her agitation, she called to him in German.

Correcting herself, she said in English as he put his foot in the stirrup, "Mister McLoughlin, hold up, please."

His booted foot returned to the ground, and when he turned to her, the first thing she noticed was the startling contrast of his silver-banded blue eyes to his tanned and now-smiling face.

Her study latched on to black eyebrows—straight across his eyes, winged at the temples. "May I have a moment of your time, sir?"

"I reckon I might have a minute to spare, little lady."

Strange, she'd expected him to speak with a Scottish burr, and she found herself taken aback that he'd call her a little lady. At five-eight, small didn't describe her in the least. Be that as it may, she enjoyed the appellation and the Western inflection.

He doffed his Stetson. Forgetting all her vows to keep romance out of her yet-to-be-proposed deal, Li-

10

sette had the sudden urge to fluff the loose raven-black waves adhering to his head where the hatband had been.

He pitched his hat atop the saddlehorn. At that same moment, the sorrel — his powerful muscles swelling and ebbing beneath a glistening coat — reared his head, snorted, and tried to pull away from the reins. His master's "Behave, Big Red," murmured in an authoritative yet calming manner, quietened the fitful stallion.

Gil McLoughlin ambled over to the hitching post and wound the reins around it, and Lisette made a few observations. She supposed most men who drove Longhorn cattle all the way to Abilene could use gentle persuasion on a single majestic beast, but she was impressed with this particular man.

His features had character, from the faint lines radiating at the corners of his blue-gray eyes to the determined set of his clefted chin. He was dark and lean, though not skinny by any stretch of the imagination, and he appeared powerful enough to coerce even the most ornery beast into line.

None of which had any bearing whatsoever on her purpose.

And he was gazing expectantly at her.

"*Ich bin* — I mean, I am Lisette Keller."

Those arresting eyes welded to her lips. "I know."

The meeting's purpose drifted away like smoke fanned by a breeze. Never had she imagined him giving a single thought to her. "How did you know who I am?" she queried, and a grin tugged at her mouth.

"You'd be surprised at the things I know about you."

"Oh? What, for instance?"

11

He stepped closer. No telling how he would smell a few days into his cattle drive, but at the moment Gil McLoughlin smelled nice, like bay rum and soap all mixed up with sun and man. She ought not to let all this Scottish virility affect her, but to act on her own counsel was like asking the earth to stop turning.

The back of her hand at her waist, she said, "I'm waiting for an answer."

"Standing in the street is no place for explanations." He winked before hitching a thumb in the beer garden's direction. "How about I treat you to a nice cold glass of sarsaparilla?"

"That won't do." She shouldn't be objecting to any offer. There were limits, though. "It wouldn't be proper, my visiting Die Biergarten."

"I'd never take a lady to a saloon." This time he motioned to an area of trees fronting the Gillespie County courthouse. "If you'll do me the honor of having a seat under that big oak, ma'am, I'll fetch us a couple of cool drinks."

How mannerly he seemed, such a gentleman. In light of Gil McLoughlin's knowing some things about her, Lisette wanted to know everything about him. Was it true, she wondered, the gossip about his past?

The rancher ran his fingertips across the swirls of ebony chest hair visible above the opening of his shirt, and Lisette wondered why he didn't keep his shirt buttoned right up to the throat, as other men did. Apparently he didn't adhere to many social strictures, and she found this oddly charming.

"May I interest you in a refreshment, Miss Keller?"

"*Danke*—I mean, thank you." An urge came over her, totally improper, wholly diverse to her purpose:

she wanted to acquaint her own fingers with the feel of his chest. "Uh, um, that would be lovely."

His spur rowels pinged as he crossed the street to enter Die Biergarten. Lisette decided he wore his Levis much too tight—which must be uncomfortable when he rode that horse. She chuckled at her thought. Those britches did look nice on him, what with broad shoulders emphasizing narrow hips and long legs.

Stop it, she chided herself. She needed money, his money; nothing else. And everything was going smoothly.

She hastened to seat herself on a bench on the courthouse lawn. Mockingbirds sang. Lifting her face toward their leafy perch, she smiled again. This was truly a lovely day in spring.

Two glasses in hand, Gil McLoughlin strode toward the comely Lisette Keller. According to Matthias Gruene, his strawboss for the upcoming cattle drive, she was a true lady.

Hence Gil was pleased as a pup unearthing a dried-up old steak bone when she'd approached him. Apparently the young German had gotten word to Lisette: Gil wanted to meet her.

She was as pretty as any sweet little filly he'd ever laid his thirty-year-old eyes on. Big boned and well-proportioned, Lisette Keller was wrapped in the allure of innocence and vulnerability. He liked that.

Good gracious, Old Son, look at those cornflower-blue eyes, he thought as she turned those beauties on him.

"Sorry," he said, handing over a foam-flecked glass. "They were out of sarsaparilla. Coffee, too, and—"

"No apology needed, sir," she cut in, her English incredibly melodic, even with the accents of her native language and her occasional lapse into it. A smile brightened her face even before she added, "We Germans prefer beer to root beer any day."

She held the glass between two roughened hands. Gil knew she worked hard. Time and again he had passed by her brother's farm, had seen Lisette in the fields. She was much too lovely for such labors.

"You know," she said, "when I lived in San Antonio, I met a Scotsman or two, but you don't sound like them."

He hitched a booted foot up onto the bench, and her attention went to the crotch of his Levis; quick as a wink, she forced her line of sight upward . . . and blushed.

Realizing his vulgarity, Gil put his boot back to earth. He tended to be crude. Spending most of his time with cowpokes and longhorns, he'd gotten out of the habit of polite behavior. Maisie McLoughlin would have given him both sides of her tongue, had she witnessed her grandson treating a lady with anything but the utmost respect.

"Why don't I sound like a Scot?" he said, eager to ship over his breach of decorum. "I left Inverness when I was a boy. Grew up in Illinois, then joined the Union Army when the war broke out. I've been in the West since late '65." Lisette listened closely, leaned forward to catch his every word. "Guess I speak like a lot of the men here in Texas, this town excluded." He shrugged. "Doesn't mean I've completely lost my Scot's ways, though."

"What made you come south?"

14

All this interest had a marked effect on Gil, and a smile broadened his face as he scanned the fair-complected Miss Keller. He admired her hair. It was tucked under a silly-looking bonnet, but Gil knew those locks were long and pale.

She'd asked a question. What was it? Oh, he remembered. "I came south for the want of land. And for the want of money."

"Now you have both."

"Not quite. Land, yes—money, no. Don't get me wrong, I'm not destitute. By money, I mean gold in the bank for the Four Aces."

Why was he being candid? It wasn't in his nature to talk freely about his business, but he decided, with Lisette, he wanted matters out in the open.

"Once my cattle drive is finished," he went on, "my land and all on it will be on solid footing. Everything depends on getting those cows over to the feeder route and up the Chisholm Trail—safely. And I'll do it."

"You're quite a determined man," she observed, her admiration shining. But her next statement caught him off guard: "I understand you're not married, Mister McLoughlin."

Gil jacked up a brow. This was one bold lass. Very bold. He liked that in a lady. Liked her manner so much he winked—*boldly*, to be sure—and answered, "Not at the moment."

Again she blushed from the roots of her blond, blond hair to the collar of her dress. Dropping her chin, she admitted, "I wanted to meet you. My brother wouldn't introduce us."

"Or allow us to be introduced."

Her head shot up. "I don't understand."

15

Gil had had his eye on her for all six months of his ownership of the Four Aces and had tried for an introduction a dozen times. "Matt Gruene talked to your brother." *Who's a narrow-minded ass.* "I tried to go through proper channels."

"I never dreamed."

"Yet you took introductions into your own hands." Pride adding an extra inch of height to his six-two, he shoved a thumb behind his gunbelt. "There've been a couple of times I thought you were on the verge of approaching me."

"Das ist richtig. I mean, that's true."

"If you hadn't made the first move, I would've. And soon. I like your spunk, Miss Keller. Like it a lot."

His grin became a grimace. Would she be interested in him once she learned the truth? There was one way to find out.

He took a swallow from his glass before speaking. "A couple of minutes ago you spoke of—you mentioned my—" This wasn't easy, yet honesty was important to him. "I have been married, ma'am. I'm divorced."

She took a taste of beer, yet uttered nary a word.

"I reckon you did hear me, Miss Keller?"

"I did. And I've heard about your divorce." She removed her hat, set it on the bench, then smoothed the edges of her coronet of braids. "There's been gossip to that effect."

Breaking up with a spouse wasn't socially acceptable, not in this enclave of German immigrants. That fool Adolf Keller . . .

"It was your brother's excuse to keep us apart."

"He's funny that way."

"I run into a lot of that. Being a grass widower wasn't acceptable back in Illinois, either."

Divorce had been Gil's only choice. It had taken a long time for him to get over the hurt his former wife had inflicted, and he'd given up trying to define the meaning of what the poets called "love," but Elizabeth Dobbs McLoughlin was the past, and he had been lonely long enough. Now he was ready to take another chance. And this time he'd be choosing a woman worthy of his respect.

Gil looked Lisette steady in the eye before saying, "I am divorced. If that's a problem, I'll be on my way."

"Oh, I—I . . . it's not a problem. None. None at all. Please don't leave."

She licked her lips; her hand shook when she set her glass on the lawn; beer sloshed on the hem of her skirts. Gil grabbed his bandana and bent to sop up the liquid. He got a whiff of lilac water laced with hops and an ample view of a shapely ankle. Now it was his hand's turn to shake.

A darned nice feeling eased through him. The woman of his many fantasies hadn't turned away from his tarnished name, and she didn't want him leaving right away. She, a good and upstanding lady.

This was the beginning of a beautiful courtship.

Cutting his eyes to the Vereinskirche, an idea came to him. The Germans would hold a dance tonight, and Matthias had told him Lisette loved to dance, so why not ask her . . .

"There's something I'm wanting," she said, and beat him to the punch. A slight breeze ruffled a wisp of her hair and the sleeves of her faded calico dress when she stood. Something in her demeanor shouted determi-

17

nation. "I understand you're in need of a cook for the trip to Kansas."

"I am." He'd had an easy enough time hiring cowpokes, but good cooks were scarce as hen's teeth. Cook or no cook, though, the Four Aces crew would leave in a week. "Do you know someone who might be interested in work?"

"Me."

His glass dropped.

Matthias Gruene had lied. Lisette Keller was no lady. Her suggestion was the most preposterous, most *improper* thing Gil had heard in a long, long time.

And what was worse, he had been a fool, believing she might be interested in *him*.

Chapter Two

Her nerves jumping like frogs around a pond, Lisette stepped over the dropped glass. "I'd be a credit to your cattle drive, Mister McLoughlin. I'm a fine cook, and—"

"An attractive young woman in company with a bunch of love-starved cowboys?" he roared. "Absolutely not."

His voice cleared the courthouse lawn. A pair of mockingbirds flew from the oak tree, the county clerk slammed shut his window, and Lisette all but quailed under the tempered steel of Gil McLoughlin's angry eyes.

"Let me prepare a meal for you—at your ranch." She compelled a smile. "I'd like to prove my cooking skills."

"You'd do that, wouldn't you?" Disgust written all over his face, he said, "You'd sashay out to the Four Aces and be damned about what your fellow Fredericksburgers would say."

"If you're worried about your reputation—"

"Gossip doesn't bother *me* in the least. But you ought to think about your name. Cooking unchaperoned at a man's house? You'd never live it down."

He sounded very like Anna. And if she weren't desperate, Lisette would have adhered to social mores. After all, she'd spent four years concealing her broken engagement and fearing public ridicule. But she had to escape Adolf and Monika, and the rewards would more than compensate for the sacrifice.

"Let me worry about my reputation." Studying a broad shoulder instead of his face, she said, "I truly need a job, sir, and yours would answer all my prayers. You see, if I worked for you, I'd be earning my keep. As far as Kansas, anyway."

"That so?" he said, a restrained thread to his tone. "It's a mere train ride from there to Chicago."

"How nice. You figure I'll be useful . . . 'as far as Kansas, anyway.' I'm charmed," he added facetiously.

Puzzled by his reaction and now-tight expression, she asked, "Why are you upset?"

"A cattle drive isn't a Sunday school social."

"I never figured it would be."

"Boy, was I wrong about you. You introduced yourself just to get a job, when I thought you were interested in me."

Her stomach dropped. Before she'd asked for the job, she'd become aware of his interest, but all her nosy questions had been taken as flirtation. Of course she was interested in him — too interested in him! — but what a foolish, foolish *Tropf* she'd been, hurting his feelings.

Her hand going to his sleeve, she said in German, "I do like you, but —"

"I don't understand your language. But I'll tell you this — I've heard enough." With military precision, he

20

wheeled around. Marching across the street, he collected his hat and mount. And he didn't look back.

His refusal rang in her head like the noonday peals from the spire of the Lutheran Church. Going into this, she'd known the dangers, but his upbraiding hurt more than she could have expected. Once more she'd been rejected.

But she had rejected him first. And her sympathies lay more with him. Would it help to apologize?

If only she hadn't encouraged his attention, he might have been more receptive. All she wanted was a chance to prove herself worthy. *Liar.* She'd been as interested in him as he'd been in her, but romance had no place . . . *Then why did your pulse race each time you looked at him?*

She ached to chase after him, to do something— anything—to make amends. Impossible. In a cart approaching the courthouse, whipping his ox forward, Brother Adolf had found her.

"You have work to do," he called from his seat. "I am here to collect you."

Lisette trudged over to him and got in the cart.

She spent the next six days fretting over the miserable end of her meeting with the handsome trail boss. She considered calling on Matthias Gruene to see if her old school chum would intercede on her behalf, but her brother and his wife kept a sharp eye on her. There were no more forays into town, much less another chance to try to convince Gil McLoughlin of her worth.

Now, as she prepared for bed in the barn loft that served as her bedroom, Lisette felt her shoulders sag. Weariness from physical labor had a lot to do with it,

21

but she was accustomed to hard work. All that toil, coupled with mental exhaustion, made her more than ready for the blessing of sleep. She felt twice her age.

She pulled on her heavy cotton nightgown, then unfastened her braids. Picking up her sister-in-law's handed-down hairbrush, she heard the barn door creak open. Lisette didn't wonder about the caller's identity. This sort of thing happened all the time.

Adolf's wife huffed up the ladder to the hayloft.

"The sheets on our bed are filthy." Mean, tiny eyes skewered Lisette. "Why didn't you wash them?"

Lisette counted to ten. Losing patience with Monika would be more trouble than the satisfaction was worth, so there was no use pointing out that the linens had been changed yesterday. How could they be filthy?

"Monika, it was nightfall when I finished in the fields; then I had dinner to prepare — and clean up after." She placed the hairbrush on a crate. "I dressed the children for bed. Karl and Viktor wanted bedtime stories."

Lisette smiled, thinking of her elder nephews along with their younger brother. She adored them. The thought she'd tried to suppress surfaced: Would she ever have her own children?

She wanted babies. She wanted a husband, too, despite her whistling in the dark. If a dream man were to come along, he'd be more important than freedom or obscure visions of Chicago.

Cautioning herself not to dream impossible dreams, she inhaled. Chicago and a millinery shop of her own were in the realm of possibility . . . provided she could get to Illinois.

"You aren't listening to me." Monika cupped her fingers under her protruding stomach. "If I were in good health, *I* could handle all your chores . . . with my hands tied behind my back."

Lisette scowled at the unkind comparison. *Try to be tolerant.* Pregnancy probably wasn't the easiest condition to weather. She extorted a smile. "It's awfully late. Why don't I change your sheets in the morning, before breakfast?"

"Do it now."

"But I'd have to dress." Any excuse was worth something, she reasoned, then added a valid one. "And it would disturb the children, my getting fresh linen out of their room."

"Laggard." Monika dropped down on the bed and curled her lip. "I assume you're wanting to turn in so you'll be plenty rested tomorrow. Perhaps for ducking into town. Again."

"Monika, please . . ."

"You were seen speaking with that Yankee McLoughlin. You aren't planning another—"

"We've been over this before. Yes, I spoke with him. He offered me a refreshment, that's all," Lisette lied.

"Is that what your Confederate soldier in San Antonio offered you? *Refreshment?*"

It was as if a blast of winter wind hit Lisette, but her chill melted to the heat of anger. "Adolf told you not to speak of him again!"

She might as well have saved her breath.

"We certainly won't allow you the liberties you enjoyed during the war, when you were living in that wicked San Antonio with *Onkel* August and that English wife of his, and—"

23

"God rest their souls," Lisette interrupted. "Leave them out of this."

Monika sniffed. "When it comes to propriety, we must be careful what could be said about those in our family. And this time, if you're jilted, we won't be able to keep it quiet."

May the devil take you. And may he take Adolf, too.

She had been foolish to confide in her brother upon his return from the Civil War. And he'd been heartless, going straight to his vengeful wife and betraying his own flesh and blood. Thom Childress was best forgotten, but no way would Adolf's *Frau* allow it.

Was there a chance some miracle would set her free from Adolf and this wife of his? If only she had a job and the funds it would provide, she could make her own miracles.

Lisette started down the ladder. "I'll get those sheets changed now."

She took care not to awaken her nephews while gathering linen. Within ten minutes she had Monika and Adolf's bed changed. Her brother, yawning and tugging on his yellow beard, offered a curt "Good night" before he limped over to settle on the clean sheets.

"Before you go back to the barn, fix *mein Mann* and me a cup of chocolate," Monika ordered. "And don't make it so hot this time. You nearly boiled our tongues last night!"

"Leave her alone," Adolf bellowed; he didn't object to the hot drink.

A few minutes later, Lisette again entered the bedroom.

Propped up in bed, her brother reached for the cup.

24

"Otto Kapp spoke with me this afternoon. I've given my permission for your marriage. You *will* wed him as soon as arrangements can—"

"I will not."

"Oh yes, you will." Monika crossed her arms under her bosom, and her marble-like scrutiny went to Lisette. "And you'd better be thinking of an excuse for your wedding night. I've been told chicken blood works well. You may take one of our hens as a wedding gift."

"Monika, you've no right to imply my sister isn't chaste." Bending a skeptical eye at his sister, Adolf said, "If you are in need of the hen—"

"*Ruhig!* I have heard enough." Lisette whirled around, ran from their bedroom, and slammed the door.

Unfortunately, the noise awakened her eldest nephew.

Karl howled, and Lisette appeased him with a promise of cocoa. But his cries roused his brothers, so Lisette took baby Ludolf to his mother for nursing, then comforted the older boys with a song about the spring fires that turned nearby Cross Mountain into a kettle for "boiling Easter eggs." Her melody made no mention of the true sources of those blazes: the Comanche. Afterward, she warmed more chocolate for Karl and Viktor.

Somewhere between the lullaby and the cookstove, Lisette made a decision. Gil McLoughlin *would* hire her as his cook. And that was all there was to it.

The Four Aces outfit left Fredericksburg a day early,

Gil McLoughlin being itchy to get on the trail. Unfortunately they left without a cook. Gil had hired one a couple of days after Lisette Keller's preposterous offer, but the fellow hadn't shown up the morning they'd set out. And Gil saw no value in tarrying.

Oscar Yates, a grizzled and cantankerous cowpoke, got conscripted to the chuck wagon. Trouble was, Yates's chow didn't even suit Gil's collie cowdog, Sadie Lou.

Two days into the trip, the men threatened mutiny.

By the third morning, six of his crew of eighteen saddled up and headed south. The remaining dozen refused to speak to their trail boss. It bothered him, as the sun set and Yates toiled at the cookfire, that his second-in-charge for the drive still sided with the others. A strawboss ought to be loyal to the man paying his salary.

Of course he ought to be furious with Matthias Gruene for lying, for saying Lisette Keller was a lady. Matt probably didn't know any better, for he was as green as his name when it came to females. Besides, even life-seasoned men had been fooled by women since Adam took a bite of that apple, so Gil didn't fault him.

Anyway, quit thinking about that Keller woman.

Gil grabbed a cup of coffee and downed the watery brew. He glanced around the camp. Not so much as a single cowpoke lounged around the fire, which, outside of a saloon or a whorehouse, was a cowboy's favorite gathering place at day's end. Even Sadie Lou had abandoned her favorite spot under the worktable that opened by hinges from the top of the chuck box.

The collie had seen fit to follow Matthias, the duo

26

nowhere to be seen in the fading light.

"Damn 'em," Gil muttered under his breath.

The cook, a smoke dangling from the corner of his whiskered mouth, reached for a Dutch oven. "Ye got a burr under yer saddle, cap'n?"

"Tend to your cooking, Yates."

"I'd rather be tendin' cows, I would. And that's what ye hired me to do. It ain't right, I say. It just ain't right, yer makin' me cook. Why, ye're makin' a steer outta me. Did I ever tell you about the time my Susie—"

"Oh, please," Gil broke in, thoroughly versed in Yates's revered departed wife.

He'd tried to do Yates a favor, putting him in charge of the cook fire. The cowpuncher was getting too far along in years for the rigors of herding, and it was the natural course for older men to take over chuck wagons. It was also natural for cookies to be grumpy. "Never mess with a mule, a skunk, or a cook" was a widely used expression in the West—so Gil tried to be patient.

"You're earning top pay," he reminded him.

"It ain't money I be needin', cap'n. I be needin' to get back with the dogies." Yates squinted at him. "Ye shoulda taken time to hire a cook whilst we be in Fred'icksburg."

Gil had enough on his mind, worrying over the possible problems of driving three thousand longhorns between the jagged hills of Indian country and beyond; he didn't need to fret over cowhands and their palates. They would have to accept Yates's culinary misadventures, and Yates would have to accept his lot.

The reluctant cook's pride had bruises all over it,

27

though, and Gil attempted to placate him. "This early spring we're having could signal a blistering summer. We have to make tracks while the making is good."

Oscar Yates muttered a base oath. Slapping eating irons on his worktable, the wiry cowboy-cook announced sourly, "Chow's 'bout ready. Where's yer men?"

"I have no idea."

Gil dug in his saddlebag for the piece of wood he'd been whittling at home and sat in front of the fire to lose himself in his hobby; his knife gouged a chunk from the oaken bluejay. He tossed the half-finished piece into the orange glow.

The bowlegged cookie advanced on the triangle suspended from the chuck wagon, then rang it. The sound pounded in Gil's head like a hammer against a nailhead.

He listened in vain for the approach of feet.

Yates groused, "Ungrateful varmints. Ain't a one of them hasn't complained about having a meal set under their ugly noses. I just don't know about people," he spat. "Wish I'd stayed in Missoura, that's what I wish. Folks, they be civilized in that part o' the country."

"The men will get used to your cooking."

"They sure better." Again Oscar Yates rang the dinner bell, getting no response.

All of a sudden, Gil had had enough. He charged from the ground, stomped over to the bell, and rang the damned thing for a solid minute. The cowboys began to appear, yet to a man they kept their distance — including the turncoat Sadie Lou.

As was his right as sultan of the chuck wagon, Yates hollered, "Come and get it."

They didn't.

Gil hoisted his voice to where it could probably be heard all the way to Abilene. "If you intend to be part of the Four Aces outfit, line up and fill your plates. And I do mean now, God damn it!"

Matthias and the collie were the first to reach the chuck fire, and it consoled Gil, his strawboss's show of loyalty, forced though it was. Yet the big German didn't speak as he spooned food onto a tin plate. Yates offered Sadie Lou a piece of charred beef which she dropped as if it were a hot potato.

"Ungrateful bitch," Yates bellyached. "I oughta skin ya and serve ya up for breakfast."

Her chin hanging almost as low as her tail, Sadie Lou whimpered and curled up at Gil's side.

The other men fetched their food. Each ate about as much as a whiny three-year-old. Gil frowned in disgust. He had never expected grown men to act like children. In turn, he glanced at Ernst Dietert, Dinky Peele, and Wink Tannington.

These men had been with him for the last three years, since Gil had made his first trip between San Antonio and the Rio Grande to round up the unbranded cattle which thickened that largely unpopulated area of Texas.

"I vould not feed tis zlop to zvine," Ernst Dietert said.

"Slop, Ernst? I seem to recall you've a hankering for pickled pig's feet and blood sausage. And you're calling good red beef—slop?"

"Richtig! Zlop."

Gil shook his head in disgust. He'd made Ernst's acquaintance in San Antonio, had cottoned to the immigrant from Nassau-Hesse. This time last year, Ernst had been the one to suggest that Matthias be hired as strawboss, then he'd pointed out the For Sale sign on the Four Aces.

For all three years, Ernst Dietert had been the epitome of loyalty and acceptance—until now.

"It be right awful," Dinky added, scratching his nappy crop of hair. "Makes these ole bones pine for plantation food."

Gil's face clouded. As for the diminutive Dinky, he had known him even longer than Ernst. Back in Natchez, when Dinky Peele had been under the yoke of slavery, his ribs had been the first thing a person noticed. On the day Gil and his company of Union soldiers had freed him, Dinky had grabbed a half-raw pork shoulder right from a cookfire and had gobbled the meat down in less than a couple of minutes.

And he was pining for plantation chow.

Wink Tannington poured his fare into the fire. "I ain't hungry."

Besides Matthias, Wink was the best cowpuncher Gil had ever met. And the Mississippian did his job without the left arm he'd lost at Shiloh. When he reached his home in Biloxi, Wink had learned that each of his four brothers had given their life for the Confederacy and that his missus had run off to a crib in New Orleans. Tannington knew about pain and suffering.

Never had Gil figured these men for scrubby schoolboys.

Then there was Preacher Wilson. Rather than sustain himself after a hard day of punching cows, Eli added the contents of his plate to Tannington's. You'd

30

think a man of the cloth would be above that sort of thing. Weren't preachers supposed to be godly? When he'd hired on, Eli Wilson gnashed at the bit to work his way to his family and a pulpit in Kansas.

Right now, the only thing gnashing about the preacher was his teeth.

Gil didn't bother to observe the other men.

He took a bite of flattened cornbread, then chugged too-damned-weak coffee to wet his abruptly insulted gullet. When he bit into the burnt steak, the act of chewing went all haywire; he sliced the inside of his cheek. Swallowing the clump of beef and a taste of his own blood, he had a hard time staying angry with his men, especially after he swallowed an eating iron of nearly raw pinto beans.

What were they going to do between here and Lampasas? With any luck, he'd find a proper cook there. But it would take weeks to reach town. Furthermore, Gil had no desire to make a trip with a bunch of cowhands who might desert over dessert.

The strangest thought popped into his mind: he wondered what Lisette Keller's cooking would taste like.

Damn.

His food joined the growing pile on the campfire, and Gil stomped over to his bedroll. That fool woman. Whatever possessed her, thinking she could go along on a trail drive?

"No lady would ever so much as consider such a thing," he muttered under his breath.

Sadie Lou barked twice. Gil glanced first at the chuck wagon, where the dog stood next to Matthias, then toward the cattle grazing and resting alongside the cottonwood-lined creek. He listened to the night. Beyond the sounds of cattle, the gentle movement of water, and the chorus of a thousand crickets, he heard nothing. Yet Sadie Lou pulled back her lip and growled.

A voice floated from the vicinity of a copse of oaks: "Hello there!"

A woman.

A woman? What was some female doing in the thick of Comanche country? Or was this some redskin trick?

Gil's hand went to his gunbelt to clutch the six-shooter he long ago and for no particular reason had dubbed Thelma. By now, all the cowpunchers, fire-arms drawn, were edging closer to the intruder.

"Who goes there?" Gil shouted into the dark of night, and advanced in the intruder's direction.

"A friend from Fredericksburg."

That couldn't be . . . of course not. The night was playing tricks. Gil cocked Thelma's hammer. "Raise your hands and make yourself seen."

Two figures appeared, walking side by side. One was human, the other a mule. They were about twenty feet away. Sadie Lou rushed around a prickly pear en route to protecting her interests. The human bent down, and Gil heard the woman say something in German.

The collie wagged her tail.

Gil lowered the barrel. "Just as I suspected. Damn you, what are *you* doing here?"

Chapter Three

Gil waited for a response from Lisette Keller. But his men were closing in, and dealing with *her* was something he preferred to face alone. He called over his shoulder, "Keep your distance. I'll handle this."

At their retreat, he stepped forward. Rather than let loose a barrage of obscenities, Gil honed in on the mule. The thing was a pitiable sight, swaybacked and loaded down with packs. It looked as unhappy as the Four Aces crew.

The mule reached down to nip at the circling Sadie Lou. Stalking with teeth bared and hackles raised, the collie clipped around to the beast of burden's rear, and for that lapse in strategy, she got a kick to her brisket.

"Willensstark, bad boy," Lisette admonished her traveling companion as the cowdog yapped and beat for camp.

Gil couldn't help chuckling. It was an unusual day when Sadie Lou found herself bested. But he mustn't ignore the trouble standing in front of him.

Lisette worried a strand of blond hair peeking from beneath a man's horrible and aged hat, and Gil recalled the way sunlight could dance through her blond braids. Remembering the way he'd felt upon sopping up that spilt beer—

Right, Old Son. And don't forget how you felt when she asked for a job instead of a man.

"What are you doing here?" he repeated.

"I want to be your cook."

Admonitions about a lot of things scattered like roaches at first light when he studied her somber face and her absurd attire: a man's shirt, ill-fitting, and—by the Holyrood!—*trousers*.

"What're you doing in that getup? If you're thinking to pass yourself off as a man, think again. You wouldn't fool a village idiot." Gil eyed her prominent breasts. "After few days on the trail, you'd look like a goddess to my hungry-eyed men."

Lisette tugged at the waistcoat's hem. "I didn't intend to fool anyone. I wanted to downplay my femininity."

"Downplay it somewhere else."

"You don't need a cook?"

The taste of Oscar Yates' burnt steak lingering on his tongue, Gil's mind flooded with images of all those disheartened, hungry cowboys. Yet pride and prejudice were mean bedfellows.

"I have a cook."

"Oh."

He couldn't help responding to her final, simple sound of defeat. "I'm having a hard time understanding what you're about, Lisette." This was the first time Gil had addressed her in the familiar; he wasn't concerned about his gaffe. "Why is hiring on with me important to you?"

"Because . . ."

34

She grappled for something, was it English or an explanation? Her shaking hand moved to rub one of her eyes, and Gil felt his heart melting now that he'd begun to recover from the shock of her appearing here. This was a woman in trouble.

As if they had minds of their own, his feet stepped toward her and his hands went to her elbows in a comforting fashion. "Honey, what's wrong?"

"E-e-e-everything."

He warned his body not to take heed of her closeness. A tough warning, yet Gil McLoughlin was mostly a tough man. The edge of his thumb lifted to dry one of a dozen of her tears. She sniffled a "Thank you." There were a dozen reasons why he ought to step back, none of which popped to mind.

Cradling her head against his chest, he asked, "What's this 'everything'?"

"I cannot abide living in another woman's home— not even a day longer. I had to get away."

He said nothing, knowing intuitively that more would come.

"I stole my brother's mule and a lot of Adolf's provisions and I took Monika's sewing kit—even though she's never used it—and I can't go back. I just can't."

What could he do to help?

He could be gallant, could take her home. The trip would take upwards of a week, even if they encountered no trouble along the way, and given the black moods of his cowpunchers, Gil could see no smarts in leaving them alone for as much as an hour.

He *could* ask Matthias or the preacher to escort her back to Fredericksburg, but why should he cut loose one of his men, when he needed each

35

and every one on the trail?

José Vasquez, his remaining Mexican *vaquero*, called out from around the chuck wagon, *"Mi jefe*, do you need help?"

"No!"

"Everything all right, boss?" asked Wink Tannington.

"Nothing I can't handle." He didn't doubt his words, and if anything was right about this situation, it was that Lisette Keller felt right fine in his arms.

She pulled away. "Please tell me. I'm curious who you chose for a cook."

"No one, really."

"Would you let me fix a meal?" she asked. "As a try-out?"

Responding to the desperation in her voice, he conceded, "Maybe just this once."

Tomorrow she'd have to go. Yet her eyes, those guileless eyes, haunted him. A man ought to protect all that innocence. She was innocent — and vulnerable and desperate. She might be lacking in judgment, stealing her brother's effects and taking off after a pack of men, but Matthias had told him she was a lady, and Gil decided against all reason and judgment that Matthias hadn't lied.

Lisette Keller *was* a lady.

A lady in need of rescue.

"Girl, ye be born to a chuck wagon," Oscar Yates announced a few minutes after he'd begun to show Lisette around the domain he was eager to abandon.

While his words sounded nice, supper had yet to be

started. Thus his praise was premature at best. Looking about, Lisette saw shovels and axes, ammunition and firearms, plus a huge pile of bedrolls. The wagon had but one entrance, up by the spring seat. Directly behind the seat, in a corner, was an upright wooden trunk.

After stepping over those bedrolls, the conscripted cook led his prospective replacement outside, to the rear of the wagon. Cowboys not guarding the herd waited for another supper. Six men, sitting cross-legged, circled the fire trench while Yates rambled on. They were a youthful group. Even the whiskered cookie seemed more spry than his years. Lisette guessed he was sixty or more.

Matthias Gruene wasn't among the group; she supposed he was on night patrol. Although she knew Jakob Lindemann and Ernst Dietert through church, she wasn't close to either, and she'd be glad when Matthias appeared. Maybe she could talk him into having a word on her behalf with the absent Gil McLoughlin.

"This here's where ye do most o' yer work," Yates explained, calling her attention to the drop-leaf table. "Ye'll find ever'thing in easy reach, girl. This wagon has nearabouts all the conven'nces of a real kitchen. Now, the cap'n, he's gone to a lotta expense, he has, to stock it right nice. Cowboys be grateful for that sorta respect. And we got ever' kinda staple a good dough-boy—'scuse me, girl, I mean cook—could want. Ye won't need a durned thing."

Except for the job.

Yates had told her to call him by his given name, so she replied, "Thank you, Oscar."

With bowlegged strides, Yates went over to the youngest of the group, Willie Gaines. "Nighthawk, she be ready to fix us a tasty meal, so ye need to dig another fire pit."

Jakob Lindemann scratched his armpit. "What does she need with another fire?"

"Ye dimwit, for extry cooking pans."

Lindemann nodded, and Willie set to digging.

"*Fräulein,* do you know how to make son-of-a-bitch stew?" asked Lindemann.

"Gawddammit, Lindyman, watch yer lang'ge." Yates rushed over to thump the man's head. "I ain't havin' ye yammerin' nasty to the lady." He flushed beneath his whiskered face. "Pardon me, girl, I didn't mean to take the Lawd's name in vain."

"I don't expect special treatment because I'm a woman."

"Welp, I be glad o' that, 'cause me and the boys 're about beyond redem'tion." Yates returned to the tour. "Ain't amiss for no medicines, neither, girl. Quineen. Turpinteen. Here be calomel—case one o' the boys gets stopped up—and this here's horse linnymint." He whispered, "We got snakebite medicine, but the boys ain't supposed to have it less'n they gets bit."

"He's talking about Scotch whisky," Johns—not John, she'd quickly learned—Clark explained while snickering.

"Aw, shut up." Yates shook a finger. "It ain't nice overlistenin' to what other people be sayin'."

"Didn't your precious Susie ever tell you it's not nice to whisper?" was Clark's comeback.

"Leave that sainted lady outta this." Yates returned to his style of inducement. "I always did like a wuman

38

what be handy with a skillet. That why I marr'd my Susie. May she rest in peace. She could whip up a meal like nobody's business."

After imagining the poor woman hobbled to a cook-stove, Lisette told herself not to make judgments. Besides, she rather liked Oscar. She poked through drawers of coffee, sugar, baking powder, and decided that while the trail boss might not want her along on this drive, Oscar certainly did.

"There ain't nothin' finer, I always says, than a good pan o' biscuits and a purty lady to fix 'em," Yates continued as Lisette began a Dutch oven of braised beef.

"Say, Yates." Wink Tannington adroitly lit a cigarette with his single hand. "You're doing such a fine job of selling, you ought to hire on with a general store. Why, I bet you could even sell liquor to redskins."

The cowhands roared with laughter, urging Tannington to go on. "Why don't you leave the lady alone, Yates?"

Yates huffed over to the cowboy. "Shut up, ye one-armed scalawag. All what's been outta yer mealy mouth's been gripe about my chow, and I be gettin' us a cook."

Tannington poured a cup of coffee and propped his maimed arm on a saddle. "Why don't you show a little mercy, and get out of her way? Your breath would run off a skunk."

Lisette almost added a protest in defense of Oscar Yates, but she mixed sourdough biscuits instead. There was a good-natured air to the awful things these men said to each other. The cowboys were enjoying themselves. Lisette enjoyed them, too, and she was thankful no one complained about the length of time it was taking to prepare a meal. But where was the trail boss?

By the time she'd peeled potatoes and onions, a Mexican *vaquero* appeared, carrying a guitar. He sported a wide smile and an even wider sombrero.

"Give us a song, José," Johns Clark prompted.

The *vaquero* proved an excellent guitar picker, and Lisette delighted in the romantic sounds of his Spanish melodies.

The main course simmering on a rack above the extra fire, she said, "Oscar, I can't find any dried fruit."

"Apples be in that there drawer to the right o' the tobacco. Or is it the left?" He lifted his short arms to study each hand. "I never can fig're out which be which."

"That's cause you're as stupid as a Four Aces cow," Johns Clark teased.

"Stupid? If I's so stupid, how come I can out rope the likes o' ye, Mister Smarty Pants?"

"Two bits says you can't."

"Ye're on." The bowlegged cowpoke went for his lariat and the two men got on with their contest.

Realizing how warm she'd become standing over these fires, Lisette took off the waistcoat and rolled up her shirtsleeves. She set about making turnovers.

"Anything I can do to help, miss?" Willie Gaines tried to flatten the carrot-red hair sticking straight up from his head.

"You can bring those jars of turnip greens from my packs, and open them." At the mention of turnip greens, Lisette felt guilty; she'd stolen them from the Keller larder.

40

When Willie returned with the jars, he admitted shyly, "I hope you stay on, miss. You remind me of my sister. Pearlie's real sweet and nice, and she's real cotton-headed, too."

Lisette hoped he referred to hair color rather than lack of good judgment. She smiled, figuring the youth meant it as a compliment. "Thank you, but I'm not always 'sweet and nice.' "

"I think you are." His face turned the hue of a ripe beet. "Uh, um, this wagon's a sight to behold, ain't it?"

"It's bigger and wider than any wagon I've ever seen."

"Did you know it takes six draught horses to pull it? Got lots of weight to pack, miss, what with all that water and molasses and sugar and flour and lard and kerosene."

"It is well stocked."

"Oh, yes, miss. It's got extra steel reinforcing the undercarriage, too. Never have to worry about breaking an axle."

She'd never driven anything heavier than Adolf's cart. Could she handle this monstrosity? *Don't get the cart before the horse.*

Please don't let anything go wrong, she prayed. When she'd purloined Adolf's provisions and his mule, Lisette had feared nothing except for Gil McLoughlin's turning her away, but leading Willensstark through miles of open country had given her a sharp dose of fright. Wild beasts and even wilder Indians were never far away, yet nothing or no one had accosted her. Had she imagined them?

Don't be ridiculous. They are hiding out there. Her own sister had fallen victim to Comanches. Poor, sweet

41

Olga, who had lived hell in her death. Lisette sucked in her breath, gaining control over her sorrow of eight years' standing.

She could do nothing for her adored sister, but she must look out for herself—if nothing else, in Olga's memory.

After she slathered the apple turnovers with boiled sugar, she rang the dinner bell. The collie dog, the same one Willensstark had kicked, came limping up to the campfire.

"Her name is Sadie Lou," Willie Gaines explained. "She's a cowdog, case you didn't know. And she's right nice."

The canine wagged her bushy white tail.

"Hello, *Liebling.*"

The greeting barely out, a trio of cowhands rode into camp. The friendliest one was ebony-skinned Dinky Peele. Eli Wilson didn't hide his disapproval at finding a woman in their midst. It bothered Lisette, having a minister's censure, but she was more bothered by the last of the three.

Blade Sharp was about forty and had a mean, shifty-eyed look. The jagged scar extending from an ear to the corner of his paper-thin mouth probably lent that sinister appearance.

"Lise!"

Recognizing Matthias's voice calling her girlhood nickname, she turned and waved. Shock was written all over his face, she noted as he walked up to her.

"I never expected to see you here," he said. "If Gil hadn't warned me, I might have had an apoplexy."

"Sorry. Maybe we can talk about it later?"

"Ja."

42

Gil McLoughlin appeared, his gunbelt riding on leather chaps shiny from wear. A black mat of swirled hair peeped from a shirt unfastened to the middle of his chest. His Stetson pulled low over his dark brow, he stared at her from the opposite side of the original fire. The flames limned his long, lean body in golden relief.

Her mouth went dry. Whether it was from his impassive stare or from the fear of being sent away, she didn't know, but it pleased her that he hadn't stayed gone.

She stepped around the fire. None but a few paces separated them now. She was struck by the hue of his eyes, no longer impassive. While they were more blue in daylight, at night they were like quicksilver, shiny and gray.

"Looks like you've made yourself at home," he drawled.

"I want to please you."

"You could please me," he murmured too low for his men to hear.

What did he mean by that? Don't be a *Tropf*, she warned herself. His words had nothing to do with her domestic skills. He wanted a woman, not a cook. And as far as Lisette was concerned, he was the only man in the world. Betrayed by her feelings as well as by her body, she felt her nipples tighten beneath the chambray shirt.

Stop it. She quelled the urge to cover herself. If she had put her hand to her bosom, she would have drawn attention to her femininity. Maybe he wouldn't notice her reaction.

He noticed.

His eyes moved from her chest, and he quirked an eyebrow.

Unwittingly falling to German, knowingly breaking the spell, she asked, "May I fix you a plate of supper?"

"Speak English."

She repeated the question.

"I'll get my own chow." He pushed a thumb behind his gunbelt. "If you want the men to eat, you'll have to give your permission. That's etiquette."

She turned to the cowboys. "Please, help yourselves."

Like a pack of rabid wolves, the men lit into the fare.

The trail boss, on the other hand, took his time filling his plate. Obviously he had no intention of gathering with the others to eat; he disappeared around the chuck wagon.

That wouldn't do.

She followed him, catching up a dozen yards from the campsite. "If you see my cooking has pleased your men, surely you'll think twice before turning me out."

"Honey, back off. I won't be pushed."

Thoroughly put in her place but determined not to agonize over it, Lisette returned to the eaters. Soon the cooking pots were empty. The collie, her tongue lolling in expectation, barked for the smidgen or two of remaining turnip greens, but Lindemann grabbed and licked the bowl. Lisette put Sadie Lou to work — or was it dog's Valhalla? — dispensing with beef bones.

"Mighty fine grub, ma'am," complimented Wink Tannington.

Again, Willie Gaines attempted to flatten his ornery

hair. "Miss, I can see myself eating like that all the way to Kansas."

Oscar Yates scratched his whiskered chin. "Girl, I ain't et such a tasty meal since before Susie—God rest her soul—fell dead over a wreck pan."

The young man in charge of the horses—she'd learned he was called the wrangler—belched and smiled. *"Schönen dank!"*

All around the campfire, praise echoed. Even the preacher, who had had more than a word or two to say about an unmarried woman in the company of men, tipped his hat.

Without a gesture of praise, Gil McLoughlin returned his plate only to disappear again. She would have traded all the cowboys' compliments for one smile from their boss.

Blade Sharp sidled up to her. "Seems I oughta give a little treat, seeing how you filled my belly so nice." He clamped his hand on her hip. "Meet me later, and—"

She retreated from his disgusting touch.

"Let me help with these dishes." Matthias pulled her even farther from the leering, overbearing cowboy. "Sharp, take another turn at night guard."

The two men glared at each other. For a moment Lisette feared they would fight, yet Sharp backed down, saying, "Whatever suits you, Mister Bigshot Strawboss."

She was relieved at Matthias's thwarting the hard-eyed Sharp. She liked Matthias, always had. As children they had sailed on the same schooner across the Atlantic, and he had given comfort when her mother had died during the voyage. Upon reaching Freder-

45

icksburg, they had attended classes in the *Vereinskirche*, and Lisette remembered many a time when he'd yanked her braids. And then the war had come along.

Matthias, like many of the local boys, had sided with the North. Her own male kin had gone along with Texas's secession, had fought, mostly to the death, for the South. And Lisette had been sent off to San Antonio—where she faced her own disaster.

She gathered a pile of dishes and started toward the creek. Matthias, similarly loaded down, walked behind her. Neither spoke until the chore was almost done.

"You worry me, Lise," Matthias finally said in German, his dark-brown eyebrows knitted. "You shouldn't be here."

"But I am." She rinsed a plate. "Will you talk with Herr McLoughlin about keeping me on?"

"No." Matthias placed forks in the wreck pan. "If you were wanting a job, why didn't you strike out for San Antonio?"

"Adolf would have found me there. Or anywhere else in Texas, eventually."

Furthermore, San Antonio wasn't for her. That town held too many memories as well as the source of those recollections, Thom Childress.

"Chicago is the place for a fresh start," she said. "And I'm certain I'll find plenty of work. I've mentioned the lady who taught me the millinery trade, haven't I? Agnes was from there, and she told me all about the wonders of her hometown. I'm going to experience them for myself."

"It gets awfully cold up in Illinois, *meine Liebe*."

"Then it should be like our birthplace, Dillenburg."

46

Matthias shook his head. "Your memory's grown sketchy in the dozen years since we left the duchy. Chicago and a hamlet in Nassau-Hesse are two different places. Chicago is a rough city."

"I'm not worried."

A sigh expanded Matthias's chest. "I don't think McLoughlin will allow you to follow along. He's a fair man when he sees he's in the wrong, but I don't think he'll see the right in keeping a woman in his camp. And he's stubborn — stubborn as that old mule of Adolf's. When he's set on something, McLoughlin would cut off his roping hand rather than back down."

That was exactly the impression she'd gotten, but she couldn't give up. And didn't want to. It was crazy and foolish, but she wanted to be around Gil McLoughlin . . . and not just as his cook. She had to stop such thoughts.

"In this instance *I* am going to be more mule-headed than your mule-headed trail boss," she said. "Wait and see."

"I wouldn't want to place a bet on that." Laughing, Matthias hugged Lisette. "On second thought, knowing you . . ."

He didn't know her, not really. Not a hint did he have about her romantic fiasco, and she intended to keep it that way.

From the left Lisette spotted the trail boss stomping her way. Starlight reflected from his eyes . . . or was it rage?

"Shove off, Gruene. Now."

Matthias did as told, and his boss ground to a halt in front of Lisette. Now that she got a good look at his eyes, she knew it was rage, even before

47

he pointed a finger at her nose.

"Damn it to hell, woman, I won't have you charming my men. Not even for the *one night* you're in my camp."

Lisette would have defended herself against this unfair accusation, but she needed another chance, just one more chance at that job. Thus, she latched on to his "one night."

She coerced a smile, hoping it was as bright as the fire in his eyes. "Does this mean I can stay until tomorrow and prepare breakfast?"

Chapter Four

"I'm waiting," Lisette announced, her bravado as apparent as fireflies in a night sky. "Are you going to let me prepare breakfast tomorrow? And maybe the midday meal as well?"

Gil scowled. How could she stand here, right by the creek where she'd let Matthias cuddle her, and act as if he'd interrupted nothing more than a quilting bee?

He grabbed her elbow to march her even farther away from his men's big ears. Short of the resting cattle, he released his hold, stepped back, and planted his feet wide apart. Arms akimbo, he demanded, "Before I make any promises, I want to know why you allowed that big German liberties."

"Liberties? No, no. You misunderstand. Matthias is an old friend. He was comforting me, nothing else."

Comforting her? Gil had to think on that. Her excuse sounded reasonable, especially since Matthias, back at the Four Aces, had told him Lisette was like a sister. An apology might be in order, but the Stars and Stripes would wave over Inverness before he'd do it. He was set that way.

"You still haven't told me *why* you left home," he

said gruffly, "beyond some excuse about not wanting to live under another woman's roof, that is."

"Another woman's roof *is* the problem, Mister McLoughlin. I have no home." Her lovely mouth became pinched, her innocent eyes clouding with indignation, yet she stood taller. "Before the war I considered the farm my home. By the time it was over, my brother had inherited the land. My father expected I would marry, so he made no provision for me beyond a small dowry—which my brother felt would be better used to enrich the property."

"He spent your dowry?" Gil asked, astounded but not totally surprised.

"Yes. And I became a slave in his wife's household."

She told him about her lack of options; how no one would hire her in Fredericksburg; how she believed no settlement in Texas would be far enough away to keep her out of her brother's reach. Her explanations made sense.

"I need help," she said.

He thought about those roughened hands, recalled seeing her in the fields. Hers had been a miserable situation, comparable to slavery which anyone would want to escape. He had fought a war to free human beings from the yoke of servitude.

Outside of the belles of the beleaguered Deep South, he had never known women to face Lisette's hardships. It took guts to break away from such hell.

Trouble was, he couldn't be her deliverance. If there were some way to help without inviting trouble from his men—or running short of them—he'd latch on to it.

"You could marry," he suggested, conjuring up im-

50

ages of white satin and lace, and him in a dark suit and starched collar. That thought got severed, quick-like.

"I'm not a young woman. I'm a spinster of twenty-two."

He had the sudden urge to see if she possessed a sense of humor. "Hmm, twenty-two changes every-thing." He winked. "I understand why you've given up on marriage."

She grinned, and he couldn't take his eyes off the alluring curve of her mouth as she said, "My teeth aren't so long or so many that it's time to put me to pasture."

"Let me count 'em. Gotta see for myself."

"Not for marbles, money, or salt," she came back, laughing and showing perfectly beautiful teeth. But she quit laughing. "We've gotten way off the subject. I do need employment."

"Living around a campfire isn't home and hearth," he replied sternly. "It's sleeping under the stars. And the men tend to be profane, including myself."

"It wouldn't be a cozy life. But I'm not accustomed to coziness. I've been around my brother and his boys. I'm not overly delicate about the differences between men and women."

"That's a plus as far as credentials go, but a lady in company with a pack of crude males? I don't think so."

As a youth, he had had his mouth soaped out more than once over foul language, and his curses had grown bluer with age. Asking his men to curb their behavior didn't seem right, since the trail boss was be-yond help. Anyway, he was wasting thought. This cat-tle drive was no place for a lady.

51

Trying to disregard the pearly blond of her hair as the moonlight made a halo around it, he said, "I'm talking about more than a mere indelicate situation."

"I told you I can handle indelicate."

"Are you saying you aren't a lady?" He held his breath.

"I am a lady, sir." Setting her head at a proud tilt, she looked him in the eye. "But I'm a lady in difficulty. I have plans for the future, and they all rest on reaching Chicago."

"Such as?"

"Such as a home of my own. And my own millinery shop. I've always been good with my hands."

Right then Gil could think of a lot of things she could do with her hands, none of them involved hat-making. As for his own hands, he'd enjoy skimming his thumbs across the taut peaks he'd witnessed earlier tonight.

He got serious. "Being cookie isn't whipping up bonnets. It's long hours, lost sleep, and hungry cow-punchers demanding food, rain or shine, dust or wind. It's gathering fuel and building fires with no help whatsoever." He was exaggerating on the no-help part, but she needed scaring. "It's flies and varmints. Nuisance animals, too. And the men would expect you to be barber and doctor, sympathizer and scape-goat."

"How much does the job pay?"

"Sixty bucks a month."

"That much? My. I'd have a tidy nest egg." Her face lit up with enthusiasm. "Be assured, hard work doesn't frighten me. I can handle the job. I can do anything, once I set my mind to it. And my mind is set."

52

"I'm beginning to get the picture. There's something you've got to know, though: I won't get you to Chicago."

"Once you pay me for my work, I'll take a train there from Abilene."

A fist clamped his chest, his pride taking the pressure's full force. Again, she'd reminded him he was nothing beyond a meal ticket to her dreams.

Change her dreams.

Dismissing his thought, he said, "You cannot, absolutely cannot, have the job."

Disheartened, she turned her back.

He couldn't stand all that dejection. And he considered himself. For too long he'd been lonely, had spent unending nights with nothing but stars above, or four empty walls. For the past half year, though, he'd spent a lot of time thinking about Lisette sharing his bed. Of course, meeting her had been a disappointment, but he was now convinced . . .

"The only way it would work is if you're a married woman."

"Out of the question." She spun around. "Besides, you're forgetting something: it takes two to make matrimony."

Jangling spurs cut through the night to draw their attention.

Preacher Wilson called out, "I must have a word with you two." The clergyman, his right hand holding a Bible, huffed up to the creek. "Mister McLoughlin," he shouted with his superior tone, "when I signed on to assist you to Kansas, I had no idea you meant to make a Sodom and Gomorrah of our journey."

"Now hold up there, preacher!"

"I, as a man of God, as a minister of the Gospel, will not hold my tongue. I believe you intend to hire this . . ." He wagged a finger at Lisette. "This Jezebel. I shouldn't have to remind you dallying with an unmarried woman will bring you to hellfire and damnation."

"Listen here, preacher man, you're making an unfair judgment about a decent young woman, and I won't have it. If you intend to stay on, you'll apologize to Miss Keller. Right now."

"I answer only to God."

"Fine. Then pack your duds and be gone at first light."

The preacher nodded. "That will be more than fine with me." He huffed off toward the campsite.

"Thank you for defending my honor, Mister McLoughlin," Lisette said, her voice quiet.

Weariness getting to him, Gil knelt down to pitch a pebble into the stream. He glanced at the stars, assessing the hour as midnight. What Lisette needed, what he needed, was a decent night's sleep. Tomorrow he'd decide what to do about her.

In the chuck wagon temporarily vacated by Oscar Yates, Lisette settled into a bedroll. Tired beyond imagination, she slept, but not for more than a couple of hours. She awoke to darkness. A coyote howled. She trembled, thinking about her prospects. Would she be the next night's dinner for some wild beast?

More frightening—would she meet Olga's fate?

Lisette jolted up from the hard bed.

Pulling the stolen trousers up over her hips and

tucking her shirt into the waistband, she leaned to the right, where she knew Matthias Gruene was nearby, guarding the wagon. She cupped her fingers around her mouth and pressed them against the canvas wall. "Are you asleep?"

"Nein."

She grabbed the waistcoat, put it on, then pulled on her boots. Hopping to the ground, she said, "I must talk with you."

"Shhh," Matthias whispered. "You'll wake everyone."

"Let's go over there." She motioned toward the creek where Gil McLoughlin had scotched her dreams.

A couple of minutes later she and Matthias were sitting by the water's edge, Sadie Lou at their side. Nearby, a cow lowed. Lisette turned to the sound. She saw nothing but cattle.

"They're huge, Matthias, especially the bulls."

"There're not—never mind."

Lisette continued to gaze at the herd. There was no set design to their hides; browns and rusts and blacks mixed with white in a myriad of patterns. Their horns—in no way did these descendants of Spain resemble their German milk cow cousins. The longhorns had a formidable spread to their horns, horns capable of ripping another cow to bits—or a person. Yet she didn't fear them. In fact, earlier tonight, it had been a welcome sight, the head upon head of wide horns. The stink, now *that* was another proposition altogether.

Again the coyote howled.

Lisette shivered in the warm night. "I'm scared."

"Don't be. The coyote is far away."

"It isn't the wild animals, nor even the fear of Indians. Well, that's not exactly so. Oh, Matthias, your boss is going to send me away."

"You mustn't create your own problems. Life gives us all enough worry without our searching it out." Matthias sighed. "It breaks my heart to see you unhappy. I know life's been unfair, what with you losing all your family but Adolf."

"You know we've never been close," she said sadly. "But I do miss his boys."

She missed them along with all the departed Kellers. Mostly, she missed her mother and Olga. After these many years, she should have stopped, but . . .

"You need someone of your own to love, Lise."

"That's not what I need." For some odd reason, she recalled Gil McLoughlin and his words about being married. *What a peculiar thought.* She gathered her wits. "Matthias, do you have any money?"

"Five dollars."

"Would you lend it to me? I haven't a cent, and five dollars would keep me from starving . . . if I make it to town."

"I said don't create your own problems. Gil will make a wise decision about you. I don't know what, you understand, but wise men don't leave women stranded in the wild."

"Do you really think so?"

"I suppose he'll have one of us take you to Lampasas." As she breathed a sigh of relief, Matthias broke a blade of grass. "Tell me, *meine Liebe,* what do you think of the Scotsman?"

Suddenly warm, she recalled the morning in Fredericksburg when he'd admitted wanting to meet her. And she recalled how she'd responded —

then as well as tonight. Her heart did a flip-flop.

The defenses she'd spent years building had taken a battering.

"Answer my question," Matthias pressed. "What do you think of Gil McLoughlin?"

"He doesn't smell as bad as you do."

"I beg your pardon, naughty girl. I spent yesterday with the drag-riders, while the boss was way ahead of the herd." He reached to thump her shoulder. "I'll not have you making disparaging remarks."

She started to appease him, but her shoulders stiffened at a night sound. An owl, perhaps? Sadie Lou, who had been sleeping at Matthias' ankle, roused up and sniffed the air. A covey of birds scattered from their roosts, a score of cows lumbering to their hooves.

Several growls intermingled with Lisette's "What is it? Do you think the horses got out of the remuda?"

"No." Pulling a revolver from his gunbelt, Matthias surged to his feet. "It's Comanches."

Her limbs stiffened.

"Be still," her friend whispered.

She opened her mouth, intent on shouting to the others, but he clamped his hand over her lips and cautioned against her calling attention to them. They rushed back to camp, Matthias guarding the perimeter, Lisette heading for the chuck wagon.

She shook the trail boss awake. "Indians."

It didn't take saying it twice. He charged from the bedroll, his cowboys abandoning their beds as well. All gathered guns. By now she heard war cries, dozens of them, plus exploding gunfire and thundering horse hooves.

Cattle ran pell-mell.

The night was lit orange with the flare of rifle and pistol fire as about a score of Indians circled and attacked. Cowmen defended them. Though frightened, Lisette wouldn't run.

She'd never fired a gun in her life, so she grabbed a butcher knife. Beside her, Gil yelled, "Get under the wagon," but she didn't. She was determined to do her part.

A painted, vicious face came toward her. She swung the knife as he leaned down from his pony, but the bullet from Gil's repeater rifle slammed into the Comanche's chest. He fell not three feet from her.

The Indian's pony cut to the side, galloped away.

Gil yelled, "Get under the wagon, and I mean *now*."

This time she got beneath the wagon.

The attack lasted another five, maybe ten minutes before she heard retreating horses. Pain grabbed her ribs when she forced air from her lungs. It was then she realized she had been holding her breath for quite some time. Worried about the trail boss and Matthias and the others, Lisette called out, "Are you all right?"

"Some of us are."

Recognizing her friend's voice, she scrambled from her place of safety. "What about Mister McLoughlin?"

"I'm okay."

There was an uncharacteristic gruffness in his voice, and when she studied him, she knew why. Shoulders drooping, he stood over the still body of Willie Gaines. Willie, poor Willie. He'd said she reminded him of his sister . . . and he'd wanted to eat her cooking all the way to Kansas.

Lisette had to force back tears. To cry would be a show of weakness in character with her gender.

And there were more tears to stifle. Two more men were dead. Ernst Dietert and the guitar player, José; both had been on night patrol. Ernst had been a good, honest, hardworking man, José a fine musician. *Those poor, poor men.*

But no one said a word.

Lisette, also silent, stoked the embers of last night's fire and made a pot of good, strong coffee. Johns Clark and Oscar Yates carried off the seven dead Comanches. She didn't know where they were taken. And didn't care.

It did matter about the men of the Four Aces. She watched as the trail boss carried Willie to the crest of a hill. The wrangler, Fritz Fischer, toted Ernst; Matthias carried José.

With shovels from the chuck wagon, Fritz and Matthias began to dig the hard-packed earth. The other men rode out to round up the cattle that had scattered during the attack. Stone-faced, Gil McLoughlin set to work fashioning three wooden crosses from oak limbs.

At daybreak, ten mourners and a seemingly unruffled Blade Sharp laid the three cowhands to rest.

Preacher Wilson said the proper words over their creekside graves, concluding with ". . . in the name of God Almighty, Amen."

They backed away from their fallen colleagues, all but the trail boss; hat in hand, he lingered. Lisette knew his grief was deep. Not knowing what else to do, she patted his arm. Turning troubled eyes to her, he settled his palm over her hand.

"I—I'd better get breakfast," she said, embarrassed by the intimacy.

Lisette returned to the wagon and set about making

breakfast. She had no desire to eat, and doubted the men did, but all would need sustenance for whatever lay ahead.

The salt pork fried, she set the pieces on a platter. There were no eggs, of course. She made flour-and-water gravy; milk would have given it better flavor, but even she was aware that longhorns were notoriously poor milk-givers. Lifting biscuits from the Dutch oven, she looked up and saw Gil McLoughlin speaking with the preacher. The clergyman nodded every once in a while. Hopefully Eli Wilson wouldn't leave, as he'd threatened during last evening's tirade.

When Lisette rang the triangle-bell, Sadie Lou wagged her tail and sat up on her haunches. "You'll be fed, *Liebling.*" Within a half minute, the Four Aces crew assembled. Gil McLoughlin stood close by. As the men filled their plates, she couldn't help but notice the trail boss staring at her. Each time he caught her watching him, he flushed beneath his tan.

Unnerved, she hastened to set a food dish on the ground for Sadie Lou.

When she stood, she met the trail boss's gaze.

"Lisette, if you're not too hungry, I'd like a word with you." He gestured to a score of cattle. "Let's . . . let's walk over there."

"*Ja.*"

By the time they reached the appointed place, Lisette was a bundle of nerves. Her eyes shifted to the left . . . and she screamed. A tonsil-vibrating, high-pitched scream.

A bull, his nostrils dilated, was charging her. His massive thews, his twitching tail, his horns — wide as the beast's body was long, and capable of great destruction—all of this was coming at her, from no more than fifty feet away. She whirled to flee, but Gil stepped in front of her and put a restricting hand on her forearm.

"Settle down, it's okay," he said softly. "He won't hurt you. It's a handout he's after. Yates'll take care of him."

For some reason, she trusted his word.

The bowlegged cowboy appeared, whistled to draw the bull's attention, and led the enormous animal away. Lisette heard the tinkling of a cowbell; when she ventured a look at the bull, she noted a bell attached to an end of one horn.

She could have died of embarrassment.

"He's one of your lead bulls, isn't he?" she uttered in a tone very like a child's.

"My best. He's Tecumseh Billy. We call him T-Bill for short. Couldn't do without the lad. He guides the other leaders, and they keep the herd headed up the cowpath. This drive would be lost without him. He's been with me for all three trips to Abilene." The trail boss shuffled his boots. "He's almost a pet."

She stepped to the side and mustered as much dignity as the situation allowed. "Adolf had only one milk cow, so I'm not accustomed to bulls."

"Uh, Lisette, there aren't any bulls on this drive. T-Bill's a steer. Do you know the difference? A steer's harmless. But a bull can make it 'round the bend, and force his partner there . . . if need be."

The trail boss spoke with a double meaning, and Lisette sucked in her breath. *He* was no steer, if looks were any indication. Gil McLoughlin was all virility and potent vitality.

She turned all red and flustered.

At last she found a voice. "I've a lot to learn. And I apologize for overreacting." *Since you'll never hire me now.*

Blue-gray eyes assessed her face. "Don't be apologizing. You didn't know."

"But I am a quick study." She forced a confident stance as she met the doubt written in the trail boss's features. "And I've got something on my side that you'll find to your liking—the will to persevere."

"You did recover quick-like."

His doubt turned to something akin to admiration, yet he didn't utter another word for interminable seconds. Lisette became worried again.

"Lisette," he said at last, "I've done a lot of thinking over the past few hours."

This didn't sound good.

"I'm in a terrible fix. I really have no option."

This sounded even worse.

"It's a long way into town, and your reputation would suffer. I've got to think about my men, one in particular. I understand Blade Sharp was talking with you last night." A long-fingered hand rubbed the back of his neck. "He's an acceptable cowpuncher, but he's no gentleman."

Oh, just spit it out.

"Another thing," he said. "I know you and Matt are friends, but a man's a man. You distract him. And you do yourself a disservice, inviting trouble with your forwardness."

She did not admire his bent toward the judgmental, and defended herself with, "I am what I am."

"Yeah, but you agitate the others, too, in that man-noticing-woman way. Well, maybe not the preacher." He mopped his brow with his bandana. "Lisette, the men need to keep their minds on cattle and the elements and Comanche attacks. Each'll be doing the work of two now."

"I know what you're trying to say, and—"

"No," he broke in, "I don't think you have any idea."

She looked at him. Doffing his Stetson, he exhaled and ran his fingers through that thick crop of curling, raven-black hair. Oh, *Gott in Himmel*, why did she have to think about his handsomeness? And why did she recall how refreshing it had been, his teasing? More than anything, she couldn't stop figuring that he would prove no steer . . .

"Lisette," he murmured, "I'm not going to send you away."

"Danke." Rushing forward, she threw her arms around his neck. He was warm, solid—all strength and power. "Thank you, thank you, thank you."

Despite the horrors of predawn and the scare of Tecumseh Billy, this was a fine, fine day. The sky had never looked so blue. The birds had never sung this sweetly. Gil McLoughlin had answered all her prayers.

Chapter Five

He dislodged Lisette's arms from around his neck; her relief turned to apprehension, especially when the trail boss glanced across the stream, back at her, and scowled. She didn't breathe. Surely he wouldn't renege on the job offer still fresh in her ears. Would he?

Of course he wouldn't. He didn't strike her as a man who made empty promises.

"Excuse me." He strode to the halfway point between the creek and camp. "Herd 'em up, boys," he shouted. "Yates, leave the chuck wagon be. We'll catch up with you."

The *"we"* confirmed her confidence in him.

His men began to make a ten-wide column of longhorns, with Tecumseh Billy leading the pack. The boss, striding along the cactus- and cottonwood-lined path, returned to Lisette's side. He kept a distance of three or four feet.

"I need to ask some questions," he said gravely. "They're on the personal side, but a lot rides on this. You're not a woman to . . . you don't . . . I couldn't have — it's like this." He ran his hand down his mouth in a nervous gesture. "A loose woman could turn this drive into more trouble than any redskin could wreak on us. I can't have that."

She could certainly assure him on this score. "No one shares my bed, Mister McLoughlin. No one."

"I thought so." He expelled a sigh. "You've got to understand, it was a question that had to be asked."

"I understand."

"Lisette, it won't be socials and teas, not here and not anywhere between here and Kansas."

The calm assurance in his gaze wrapped around her like a warm cloak on a winter's day when he added, "Don't worry, I'll cushion you from the brunt of the hardships. And the work."

"I neither ask for, nor will I accept, special treatment." She glanced at the herd disappearing over a rise. "You won't find me screaming at the likes of Tecumseh Billy again, if that's what you're concerned about."

"That's not what bothers me." Turning his hat around in his hand, he said, "Lisette, your hiring on has a stipulation. The only way it'll work is for you to get yourself a husband."

"You've been unfair, leading me on." Frustration and the edge of defeat wilted her shoulders. "It takes two to make a marriage."

"True. But what I'm suggesting has nothing to do with tradition. You're needing the kind of union that doesn't ask too much of you."

Confused, she whispered, "Pardon me, but I thought the only reason men and women married was for love, and with the hopes of raising a family."

"In this instance all you need is the protection of a

65

man's name. I'm referring to a marriage of convenience."

Her mouth dropped. No wonder his own marriage
hadn't worked out, what with his attitude. "You seem
to hold a low opinion of the sanctity of matrimony."

He studied the ground before elevating his jutted,
clefted chin. "You know I've been divorced, so it goes
without saying that I've had trouble in the past."

She wanted to ask the source of the problem. She
knew some things from gossip. He'd been married
during the war but was divorced by the time he
reached Texas. Anything more was none of her business, just as her past was none of his.

Yet the hurt issuing from his heart and soul compelled her to step forward to offer comfort. In-
stinctively she took his hand to give warmth. *He's as
lonely as I've been,* she realized.

"I'm so sorry, Gil," she murmured, half realizing
she'd called him by his given name. "Please forgive me
for calling attention to your heartache."

Like butter on fresh toast, his frown melted into a
smile. "You make me feel good," he murmured. "I
need that."

He needed her, and she needed him to need her.

These realizations were a powerful aphrodisiac.
Nothing remained but the need to assuage a corner of
his pain.

She lifted a palm to his face, feeling the firm set of
his jaw, the whisper of day-old whiskers. Beneath her
thumb, he swallowed, and then his arms were around
her, hers around him, his Stetson toppling behind
him. The strong beat of his heart tapped against her
breasts as his mouth descended to take hers. And she

responded to him, responded as she never had with Thom Childress.

When Gil lifted his lips—his wonderfully warm and evocative lips—she smiled at the contentment and desire illuminating his features. Or was she smiling at her own passion, the emotion she'd long tried to quell?

"I've spent six months, dreaming about kissing you," he admitted in a voice soaked in sensuality. "And I'm not disappointed in the reality of it."

She blushed, lowering her eyes. He had been dreaming about her . . . when she'd been lonely, so lonely, and had yearned for attention. While she'd known rejection along with solitude of the heart, she hadn't realized the extent of it until this moment.

"Do you ever think of me—more as a man than an employer?"

She shouldn't admit it. If she did, she'd be placing her trust in him. "I'd be lying if I said I haven't thought of you. As a man."

"You don't know how that pleases me, because I'd come to the conclusion you wanted only the job." His hands at her waist, he squeezed gently. "And it makes it easier to say what I'm wanting to express. *I* want to marry you."

"What?" She flinched as if stung by a bee. "Are you up to some sort of tomfoolery, like snipe-hunting?"

With a look of hurt, he answered, "No."

It wasn't a joke; he was serious. Her inner defenses slammed down to surround her heart again. "M-marry me? Mister McLoughlin, you don't even know me."

"I know enough—and I know my mind." Solemnly,

he gazed into her eyes. "We could be good together. Give us a chance."

"I—I can't accept. Why, we don't love each other."

"I'm not a great believer in that love nonsense. That could change in time, of course. For both of us."

"But it might not. And I won't take the chance. Marriage is sacred. *Promises* are sacred to me. I wouldn't vow to love you if I didn't mean it."

"Can't you find something to love about me? Then you wouldn't be lying."

Was there anything to love about him? She searched his eyes. She loved the way he looked at her. She loved the way he looked to her. She loved the way he made her pulse race and her limbs quiver.

Deep trouble. She was in it.

"I'm not looking for anything that even resembles love," she finally replied.

He turned toward the creek. The spring breeze ruffled his hair, and despite herself, she longed to pat those tousled black strands into place. *Stop it!* she warned herself.

Pitching a pebble into the water, he said, "You may not be looking for love, but you are wanting safe passage to the railhead. Therefore you need the protection of my name. It's a matter of practicality. If you're my wife, my men will keep their distance out of respect for both of us."

His offer was tempting, so utterly tempting: a name to protect her against attentions such as Blade Sharp's, plus an avenue to her dreams. Strangely, all that freedom didn't hold its former appeal. And it all had to do with the tall, virile cattleman who was beseeching her with his words and kindness as well as with his mesmerizing eyes and all-too-handsome face.

If San Antonio hadn't happened. If only . . . Since she couldn't in good faith accept his offer, Lisette realized she had to make a decision—and now.

"I am flattered and honored you'd go to such lengths to make your proposal appealing," she said earnestly. "My only choice is to be on my way. But I do thank you for not turning me out. I bid you a heartfelt *auf Wiedersehen.*"

"Don't be hasty." His hand took her forearm, forestalling her departure. His thumb made circles on her wrist, stoking the fires she kept trying to dampen. "Lisette, maybe I haven't made myself clear. If you aren't attached to me by the time we reach Kansas, we'll get an annulment. In the meantime, I'm not asking for husbandly rights."

Oddly disappointed that he wouldn't demand such license, she cautioned herself not to be weak.

"I am not going to marry you."

The faint lines radiating from his eyes deepened; a frown bracketed his lips. "You showed a lack of judgment, tearing off after my cattle drive in the first place. Now you're ready to jump into hot water, when I'm willing to protect you."

Wary, she studied him. "If there's one thing I've learned, it's that nothing is given freely. You would expect something in return." Just as she'd expected Thom not to break their engagement by marrying another woman. "And, no matter what you say, I imagine that something is bedroom privileges."

"My bedroom is back in Fredericksburg."

"You know what I mean! I am *not* willing to trade my body for passage to Chicago."

"I'm glad to hear that, cause I wouldn't want to give my name to a woman who would. Let's give this marriage scheme a try. And on my oath, I'll respect your chastity." Winking boldly, seductively, he grinned. "Unless you don't want me to. Then we'll have a real marriage. Till death parts us."

If only she could give him the one thing he expected. She couldn't; it wasn't there.

"You asked what I want in return," he said. "I'd expect you to cook for the Four Aces outfit. My men have a right to the best I can give them, and honey, they're dreamy-eyed over your cooking skills. *I'm* dreamy-eyed over it. That supper you fixed was the best I've ever eaten. If you'll help me, I'll help you."

Chewing her lip, she stared downward. Just as when he'd told her not to be frightened of Tecumseh Billy, she trusted his word. Matthias trusted his word, too. "He's a good man, Lise," he'd said. He was a good man, this Gil McLoughlin. And she drew comfort from giving her trust . . . without fearing it was misplaced.

And he did *need* her.

Evidently he took her hesitation as an affront, because he asked, "Why are you stalling? Would you rather not sully your name with mine, since I've got the taint of a first marriage attached to it?"

"The stigma of divorce? I do not hold that against you, rest assured. I—"

"Thank God."

She'd started to confess everything, but his interruption lowered her courage. In no way could his disgrace match hers, for Monika had been right. She would need chicken blood to fool a husband into thinking her

70

pure. To deceive this wonderful man thus would be a sin she couldn't live with.

But it would be a marriage of convenience.

How long would that last? She wanted him — wanted the comfort of his companionship, needed his arms around her, yearned to explore the passions he roused. If she allowed her heart to rule her head, though, he would know her dreadful secret.

Maybe he'd accept her as she was. Maybe he wouldn't. She turned; she ran — toward Willensstark, and away from facing up to her lack of judgment in 1865.

Women. Gil McLoughlin had never understood them. Probably never would. He had offered Lisette all he thought she wanted, but she had turned him down flat. Scratching his jaw, he took a look at her. She was fitting that damned old mule for her sashay into the wilds.

All and all, Gil's mood was black. Beyond the Lisette debacle, three good men had lost their lives to the frigging Comanches. This was not a good day.

He gave himself a mental kick for trying to bend this willful German girl. He had had to try, nonetheless. His grandmother used to say, "The worst someone can say is 'no.'" Lisette had said no. Then another of Maisie McLoughlin's pearls came to her grandson's mind: If they don't answer the front door, knock on the back one.

As Lisette continued to load her pitiable traveling companion, Gil checked the harnesses on the draught horses. He called to her, "Ready to go?"

"Yes." She didn't appear any too ready or eager, yet she yanked on the mule's lead-rope; Willensstark dug in his hooves.

Gil ambled over to them, gave the beast of burden a pat. *Thank you, old lad. I need all the help I can get.*

"My men near about cleaned out your food supply," Gil said. "What are you planning to eat along the way? Dandelions?"

"You could compensate me for my stores."

He tsked. "Lisette Keller, that would make you an Indian giver, taking back what you gave of your own free will. Now tell me, what are you planning to eat?"

"None of your business."

"Funny, I never heard of such a dish. Is it a German specialty, like sauerkraut?"

She shoved an empty canning jar into the mule's packs. "Mister McLoughlin, if you keep talking like that, I'll leave here with a bad impression of you."

She was not leaving here, not unless his ploy failed, and if that were to come to pass, she'd leave with money, food, and an escort even though he would regret having to lose another cowhand for days on end. Mostly he'd regret losing Lisette.

Leaning his elbow on Willensstark, he crossed his ankles. "Say, do you know how to shoot a rifle?"

"No."

"Then I guess there's no use in giving you one. 'Course, you need some sort of protection against redskins and coyotes and predators like them, you being in the middle of nowhere. Excuse me. You're at a gravesite, if you wanna count that. Middle of Comanche country, too. I've tried to be hard-hearted about burying good men along the way, but it still hurts." Gil grimaced. "This is my third trip up this cowpath, and Ernst and José and Willie make the eighth, ninth, and tenth casualties."

He watched the fear she tried to hide. Pleased for getting to her but regretful for his means of persuasion, Gil offered, "Maybe you ought to take a rifle anyway. I'll load it for you. Who knows? You might get a lucky shot."

Her fingers tightened on Willensstark's lead. "I—I'll hide during the day. I did it before, and I'll do it again."

He fingered a blond braid lying over her breast. "Boy howdy, would those redskins love to get their hands on this. It'd be quite a coup for some hatchet-faced brave, having a blond scalp decorating his tepee."

Her face ridden with fright, she pulled up her shoulders. "You're trying to s-scare me."

"Maybe I am getting carried away. They'd think first before scalping you. No doubt they'd find a better use for all this blond bounty." He gave Willensstark another pat. "Why don't you tell me which route you're taking? If Adolf Keller never sees the whites of your eyes again, I can tell him where to search. In which redskin camp, that is. You ever gotten a whiff of a tepee? Phew."

"Cows smell, too."

He chose not to reply to her statement. "Comanche men like being waited on hand and foot, so it's a good thing you don't mind hard work. Squaws do everything but the hunting and warring. Well, sometimes they do those, too. Whatever keeps them occupied— outside of keeping the buffalo hides warm on a cold night—they've got a papoose strapped on their back and a passel of younguns squalling at their feet."

"If a woman is looking out for her own husband and children and home, I doubt she resents the work."

Damn, his schemes weren't working. Yet he replied, "See, you're already thinking like a squaw."

"No, I'm thinking like a woman."

"Glad to hear you don't make a distinction. It'll make life easier. I hear the Injuns are fine ones for needlework, what with their beading and so on. Those braves, why, I bet they'll let you keep your needles to stitching, though I don't think they hanker for ribbons and lace and frou-frou on their headbands."

If looks could have stitched Gil McLoughlin, he would have been tattooed with embroidery.

"It'll be tough, Lisette, breaking the news to Adolf."

"You won't be needing to tell him anything. I'll write from Chicago."

"How you gonna get there? Not on that, I hope." He gestured at Willensstark, who brayed.

"He got me here. He'll get me away."

"Right. Say, one more thing. When the Comanches capture you, better not try to escape. They don't take to that sorta stuff. I've heard they're not as bad about cutting off women's noses as they used to be. 'Course, you can never trust gossip."

Her face whitened during his oration; he was glad for it. "I saw a couple of noseless white women toting breeds around San Antonio. White folks usually shun the women, which I think is an abomination, since it wasn't their fault they got captured and pregnant and maimed."

Lisette's chin trembled. Again, Gil leaned against

74

Willensstark's scrawny, pack-laden back, else he would
have drawn his frightened quarry into his arms to assure her that no harm would befall her . . . as long as
he drew a breath.

"You ever seen a woman after Comanches are done
with her?"

Shaking like a leaf, she murmured raggedly, *"Ja,
meine Schwester."*

A multitude of emotions skipped over her face, indecision and consternation and agony among them. It
was then that she buried her face in her hands and
sobbed. He didn't know what she'd answered, but
whatever it was, it was bad.

He took her into his arms, pressing her face to his
chest and whispering, "Shhh, it'll be okay, honey. I
promise."

She cried against his shirt, wetting it, and his fingers held her there. Her arms locked around his back,
holding on as if he were a lifeline.

What had she said a moment ago? He asked her to
speak slowly, and she did.

"My sister Olga was captured by the Comanches.
We found her . . . dead at the foot of Cross Mountain. She was only twelve years old."

"Damn."

He groaned, feeling awful. Matthias had told him
Lisette had lost a sister, but he'd figured the girl had
died of natural causes, just as the mother had during
the trip from Germany. What else had the strawboss
neglected to tell him?

"Lisette, forgive me for scaring you."

Her reddened eyes lifted. "I am so frightened of being abandoned."

"I'll take care of you. If anyone leaves, it'll have to be you, because I'll *never* leave you."

"You mean that? You won't make me go away?"

"I stand by my word."

"Oh, Mister McLoughlin, you are such a good man."

"Keep spoiling me with your praise." *I love it.*

A tentative smile softened her ravaged face, and the devil within him lowered his mouth to hers. He tasted her salty lips; his arms wrapped around her. With a sigh, she opened to him, her hands climbing to his shoulders, and he took more than he ought to, considering she was overset with fear.

Yet as the moments wore on, she continued responding to his kisses, to his caresses, to his gently spoken endearments.

Their first kiss had been great; these were even greater. She was more than he'd ever expected, was warm and responsive, all innocence and awakening passion.

If he didn't stop kissing and cuddling her, he might get carried away. He wanted a virgin bride, not a virgin lover. For once, marriage would start on the right foot.

Through wedlock, he would cultivate her feelings and they would celebrate the act of love.

Pulling away, his heart slamming against his breastbone, his blood having centered in his groin, Gil cut around to the far side of Willensstark. He exhaled heavily. *Behave, Old Son.*

"We'd better talk," he said. "When we're married, you'll get my protection and the freedom to do as you please, as long as you go along with the pretense of being a loving and devoted wife. We mustn't bring suspicion on ourselves and let the men think it's only a sham."

"That would be wise."

"You'll decide whether we keep it as a marriage in name only, or make it a real one. You'll have the option of getting on that train for Chicago . . . or returning to the Four Aces with me." He leaned across the mule to touch Lisette's cheek. "I do, however, reserve the right to change your mind about the convenience part of the marriage."

Her eyes closed. "I—I can't marry you. I'm not a—"

Here we go again. "Shhh. Don't say anything but yes."

"You don't understand," she murmured. "There is something you need to—"

"Enough talk. 'Yes' is *all* I'll accept."

Again he cut around Willensstark and brought Lisette into his arms, this time to hush her protests. He would do everything in his power to make theirs a real marriage. Furthermore, he was *not* going to lollygag in making it real.

Chapter Six

At dusk, the Four Aces outfit made camp about eight miles northeast of the site of the predawn Comanche raid. Matthias Gruene chose not to appear at supper, and his decision had little to do with anxieties over having watched Lisette struggle all day with the chuck wagon and its team.

Being a loner by nature and especially by present circumstance, the strawboss plodded across the open range and tried to collect his wits. Impossible. He felt as if a tomahawk had rent his chest. McLoughlin was going to take Lisette to wife — tonight.

Behaving like a *Dummkopf* instead of a man of twenty-three, he hadn't protested when the Scotsman had asked for help in gaining Lisette's acquaintance. Matthias had figured nothing would come of the situation, Adolf being the way he was.

He should have known McLoughlin wouldn't stop until he got what he wanted.

Right now Matthias could have smashed the trail boss's face . . . and might before the wedding even began. He had always been fond of Lisette — overly fond of Lisette — and her happiness meant a lot.

How could he stop her foolishness?

He hurried back to camp. His fellow cowboys weren't crowded around the fire. Maybe they too were shocked at the upcoming marriage. *They couldn't be as surprised as I am.* Maybe his colleagues weren't shocked in the least, since they were eager for a good cook; so eager, in fact, that the cowherds had been on their good behavior. Probably McLoughlin ordered them away.

He was good at shouting commands.

The trail boss, Matthias noted, stood away from camp, huddled with the preacher. He quelled the urge to provoke a fight; Lisette was the one he needed to convince not to go through with the plans.

Matthias sought her out. The supper dishes washed and put away, she was tidying up the chuck box, acting as if nothing out of the ordinary would occur in the next few minutes.

Her hair flowing freely down her back; she wore the dead Willie Gaines's britches and shirt. Matthias recalled how, as a boy, he used to yank on her braids. As a man, he'd always wanted to touch those silky strands, but he hadn't been brave enough to make a bid for her hand.

Matthias didn't stand on ceremony when he reached her side. "Rather an abrupt courtship, wouldn't you say?"

"Desperate times lead to desperate measures."

He studied her. From the grim set of her mouth, from the rigidity of her back, he knew she'd go through with the marriage. Which didn't mean he shouldn't show some courage.

"You aren't in dire enough straits to sell out on your

dream." He stepped closer. "Lise, you don't have to marry the Scotsman. I'll take you away from here."

"If you'd offered yesterday, I would have accepted."

"I didn't think it would come to this."

"Matthias, you know he wanted to court me. I've accepted his proposal, and I won't look back."

If he'd known she wanted marriage, he would have offered it; thus, there would have been no need for her to take flight from Fredericksburg.

Take flight . . .

He could abscond with her . . .

But what could he offer except protection? His worldly goods filled less than one duffel bag, his pocket held nothing but five measly dollars. Even his horse held the Four Aces brand. At a time he should have been collecting wealth, he'd been fighting Mister Lincoln's war. When it was over, he'd returned to a state struggling for economic survival. And the laughing blonde hadn't been the same girl he'd left in 1863. The laugh had gone out of her.

"Why is this marriage important to you?" he asked. "Why, after all these years of spurning admirers, do you want to mark yourself with a divorced stranger?"

Her shoulders drooped; she didn't reply.

"Do you love him, Lise?" he asked, hoping she'd deny it.

She slammed closed a cupboard drawer. "Enough to pledge my troth."

"Enough to make you happy?"

"Ja."

He didn't believe her. He had heard of love at first sight, had never thought it existed, and still didn't. Yet Lisette wasn't a woman to lie.

"If there's even a slight chance you'll be happy, who am I to stand in the way?" he asked rhetorically, pitying himself for not being more aggressive *before* she'd met McLoughlin. His voice hollow, he said, "You have my best wishes."

He made for the bridegroom. Ignoring the curled-lipped minister, he told McLoughlin in no uncertain terms, "You had better be good to the *Mädchen*, or you'll answer to me."

McLoughlin, smooth and arrogant, gave his assurance.

Lisette watched Matthias as he went to her fiancé. She hadn't been completely frank with her friend, and it hurt to see him worried. She couldn't confess she'd had no choice but to accept Gil McLoughlin's proposal.

Saying yes to the bargain was a matter of survival. He had frightened her witless, evoking horrible memories of her sister. Lisette's eyes squeezed closed. As if it were yesterday she remembered that dry creekbed of eight years ago and the mutilated body beside it. Her thick, blond hair gone, there had been a grotesque, petrified cast to that precious, dead face. For Olga, Lisette had cried—then, and again today.

And Matthias' offer of help had come too late.

She'd promised the trail boss she'd be his cook, and she wouldn't renege on her word. If she had, she'd be as much of a lowlife as a certain male in San Antonio.

Moreover, she had faith in Gil McLoughlin. From the way he carried himself to the strong set of his jaw, his appearance bespoke trust. And as each moment passed, each time they conversed, her faith in him grew. He had promised to protect her from harm, and he would. He had promised not to abandon her; he wouldn't.

And the latter was the more important to Lisette.

The most significant aspect of their relationship, though, was: they needed each other.

He wouldn't regret giving her his name. She'd play the roll of affectionate wife without a lack of feeling on her part, and she'd please his men with her best culinary efforts, which would make the trail easier for everyone. He would find her a devoted and sincere partner in his enterprise.

Her all was what she would give . . . all but her body.

She glanced at the man who would give her his protection. He was walking toward her, his gait loose and relaxed. He appeared pleased at entering this travesty of marriage. *He did reserve the right to change my mind about the name-only part.* She could never, ever, allow their marriage to become anything more than a simple arrangement.

Her bridegroom was near her now, wearing a clean flannel shirt and twill britches. Gone were his hat, chaps, and gunbelt. He smelled of bay rum and fresh air. She enjoyed this scent, but she liked the manly, plain aroma of him as well. For once his hair was somewhat under control. The urge to tousle those loose black curls was as real as the canopy of stars above, the warmth of this evening, and the beaming smile of her soon-to-be husband.

"These are for you." He lifted his hand, and his voice was as tight with emotion as the strings of her heart. "A bride can't get married without a bouquet."

Her heart thrumming, she accepted the bluebonnets and buttercups. This wasn't a church, nor was the marriage for real, but never had such a sweet gesture affected her so deeply; she wanted to cry.

"Thank you," she whispered. "I—I never expected . . ."

"It's only appropriate." His palm settled on her upper arm, his fingers curving. "Expect the unexpected."

The preacher made a noise from his throat to call attention to their dawdling.

"Honey, let's get married."

Gil McLoughlin offered his hand, and she laced her fingers with his. They took their places before the preacher.

Eli Wilson yelled, "We need witnesses."

Seven cowboys appeared and lined up between the chuck wagon and the campfire. Sadie Lou, under the worktable, roused from sleep to sit up and watch the happenings. As if he were an invited guest, Tecumseh Billy trotted to the camp's perimeter, then stood by, his great horns turned in their direction.

Ashen-faced, Matthias walked up. His expression read, "I've given my best wishes, but I want you to think twice."

She had done her thinking and deciding.

Nonetheless, the wildflowers began to shake, and trying to get a grip on them as well as on herself, she glanced upward. Clouds moved across the moon.

Preacher Wilson, the Good Book cradled in his palm, cleared his throat. "Let me repeat. Will you take this man to be your wedded husband?"

Her gaze flew to the man at her right, and she gained strength from his steadfastness. There was no other she'd want for her own. "I will."

Gil squeezed her hand.

"Will you take this woman to be your wedded wife?"

"I will," was the strong, sure reply.

Preacher Wilson turned back to Lisette. "Will you love, honor . . .

I will honor him. And I do love him in untold ways.

". . . forsaking all others, for as long as ye both shall live?"

"I — I will."

"Will you love, honor, and keep her, forsaking all others, for as long as ye both shall live?"

"I will."

The sacred vows continued. Gil slipped a gold band on her finger, and it carried the warmth of his hand. For a fleeting moment she wondered where he'd gotten it and why it fit.

"In the presence of God and these witnesses, I now pronounce you man and wife." The minister smiled at the couple. It was his first expression of approval since Lisette had joined the Four Aces outfit. "You may kiss your bride."

Gil's hand went to her waist, and it felt warm and protective . . . and provocative. He smiled his seductive smile that made mush of her insides. His lips parted to kiss her. Hers did not part. The bouquet fluttered from her fingers, yet she grabbed the cherished flowers from the ground . . . and accepted that her tall, strong partner would seal their vows with a deep kiss.

This was a wedding — their wedding — and she allowed herself to be weak. Just this once . . . no, once again.

Her fingers flattened against his nape as his lips met hers. His tongue moved inside, and she tasted the pure flavor of his mouth. *Mmmm. so nice.* His arms were around her, his hands pulling her close to the hard strength of his warm body. *Mmmm. nicer.*

"Oh, Mister McLoughlin," she murmured breathily. "You won't regret this. I promise with all my heart."

This, she pledged meaningfully — to her husband and to God.

The witnesses cheered; the dog chased Tecumseh Billy from camp; Matthias drifted away from the celebration.

And Lisette wished her marriage could be different. If only she could accept all he'd offered . . . But theirs would be a good arrangement, she vowed. Somehow she'd keep her distance.

Once more, she whispered, "Oh, Mister McLoughlin."

"Darlin', you'd better call me Gil."

Chapter Seven

All the bridegroom wanted was to dispense with his bride's virginity, and *now*. Yet Gil had promised himself to cultivate and celebrate their loving, and he wouldn't pounce upon her. He'd done enough pouncing in his life. He didn't want sexual release; he wanted everything. The everything he'd never had, but would . . . with Lisette.

An hour had passed since his men had finally called it quits on the nuptial celebration. Out of respect, they had spread their bedrolls well away from this chuck wagon, where Gil and his bride were spending their first night as man and wife.

Sitting on his upright trunk, his back to the spring seat, he watched her. She stood at the rear and brushed her long, flowing locks in the dim light, and he knew her hand wasn't shaking in anticipation of marital pleasure.

Since the moment they had climbed into the wagon, she'd been trying to ignore him. He hadn't let her. Okay, they had conversed about trivialities, about the cattle drive, about the weather — all the things that were least on his mind — but he hadn't allowed her silence.

They ought to be making love. This was their wedding night, damn it. But theirs wasn't a real marriage, not as far as she was concerned. Not a garment had she discarded, despite the wagon's warmth. He, too, remained buttoned up in wedding attire, such as it was.

He wanted her to notice him as a man rather than as an employer who shared the same last name.

"Wouldn't you be more comfortable if you shucked a few of those clothes?"

She continued to brush her hair.

"At least loosen the top buttons of your shirt," he said. "It's hot as Hades in here."

The brush stilled. "I am *kalt* . . . I mean, cold."

Never would he believe that. Already she'd shown her passionate nature. Each time they had kissed, he'd got the impression that fire burned within his innocent Lisette. He damned sure hoped so.

"You looked beautiful tonight, standing there in front of the preacher."

He yearned to stand, to close the distance between them. He wanted to acquaint himself with the womanly lines of her body . . . and acquaint her with the manly lines of his. Cultivate, celebrate.

"You look even more beautiful right now. I wish the lantern were lit. I'd love to look at you, really look at you."

She set the brush aside. "Gil, do you mind if I ask a question?"

"Shoot."

"Where did you get this wedding ring?" She held her left hand aloft, looking at the gold band.

"It belonged to my grandmother."

"Has she . . . Is she deceased?"

"Maisie? Not by a long shot."

87

"Why isn't she wearing this ring?"

"Because she gave it to me. With a stipulation or two. I was in pretty bad shape when I left Illinois, what with the divorce and all," he explained. "For the first time in her life, Maisie took off her ring. She told me, 'Lad, by the ghost o' Bonny Prince Charlie, I have faith in you. I know you'll pull yourself together and find happiness again. Put this ring on the lass you're sure you'll spend the rest o' your days with.' "

"Gott in Himmel. You shouldn't have given it to *me."*

"Darlin', the next time I see the Four Aces Ranch, you're going to be at my side."

"Gil," she said quietly, "can't we talk some more about my duties? Now, as I understand it, I'm the first person awake in the mornings, and when I have breakfast ready, I call the men. While they're eating, I start the midday meal. Then you guide the chuck wagon to the noon rest stop, and I finish lunch. As soon as the dishes are washed, you lead me to our evening camp. And—"

"Mind if I loosen a few of my shirt buttons?" he asked, watching her profile from the length of the wagonbed. He unfastened his shirt to the midway point. He was still hot, and not necessarily from the warm night. "Mind if I take off my boots?"

"I fix enough bread at breakfast to do for the midday meal, I believe you told me."

"Lisette . . . I could use your help. And I don't mean as cookie." When she turned to face him, he explained, "I have a helluva time getting my boots off."

"Then you should buy larger boots."

"You're right. But how's that going help now?" She trembled; he felt it all the way over here. "Will you help me, Lisette?"

"Gil, you've had *dreissig*—I . . . I m-mean, th-th-thirty years to learn to take off your boots."

Her accent was thicker than pea soup. Again she attacked her hair with the brush. Nervously she braided the waist-length mass. Again. This was a night for agains. Probably it wasn't a night for lovemaking, but he had to keeping trying.

"Nobody ever told me to buy my boots bigger. See how much you've helped me already? And we haven't been married three hours."

"*Ich*—I . . . I think it would be better if you didn't refer to our agreement as m-marriage. I must think of my duties as cook, and you should . . . should preserve your energies for your cattle drive."

"Honey, I've got plenty of energy." He levered himself to stand, then angled his trunk down to sit again. "Come on. I'm making boot removal one of your responsibilities."

Without a word she walked to him. Yet her demure regard wouldn't meet the open need of his. When she started to kneel at his feet, he stopped her.

"I know a better method." He took her hand. "Straddle me. Backward. Then pull up. It's much easier that way."

It took a while—probably five or six minutes—to convince her, and he doubted the convincing was necessarily over the best way to remove boots.

At last, though, she was sitting on his knees, her back to him. His fingers clamped around her waist to "keep you steady." Damn, she felt good to him. And he was getting harder and harder.

She yanked on a boot; it flew from his foot. Quickly, much too quickly, she had the other off

89

and was standing again.

"Don't you think it's time for you to take your bedroll outside?" she asked, her face averted.

"That's not how I want to spend my wedding night, and I don't think that's how you want to spend yours."

"Are you not a man of your word? You promised to move outdoors, once your men were safely asleep. I'm sure they're safely asleep."

If he rushed his reluctant bride, he'd have trouble in his hands rather than a fistful of willing flesh. *Cultivate, celebrate.* He collected his bedroll.

For hours he tossed and rolled on the ground, gazing at the north star. Giving up any notion of sleep, he folded his bedding and ambled around the campsite, Sadie Lou at his side.

"Think I'll write some letters," he said to the dog. "Busy work'll keep my mind off my lusts . . . I hope."

He got paper and pen from the chuck box, stuck the lot of it in his pocket, then collected firewood from the chuck wagon's underbelly store — the cooney. Deciding on a location far from his men and even farther from the temptations of Lisette McLoughlin, he made a fire and sat down in front of the blaze, his cowdog beside him.

He addressed the first letter to his grandmother. In glowing terms he told her about the new Mrs. McLoughlin. Since he'd never been one for subterfuge, especially with the silver-haired, Junoesque matriarch of the family, he admitted the marriage was for show. For now. He intended to make her a great-grandmother, and he told her so.

"Maisie will love that part," he told his canine confidante, who settled her chin on one of his crossed legs. "My old granny may be a stickler for manners, but she's a lusty

90

wench, seventy years young. She speaks her mind about the birds and the bees, expects the same from others. And no one loves babes, especially McLoughlin bairns, more than the indomitable Maisie."

Limpid, understanding brown eyes looked up at him. Would that Lisette gazed at him with that same adoration . . .

"You know, Sade, in a way, Lisette reminds me of Maisie. Neither one of them would ever say die." He remembered his scare tactics in getting Lisette to agree to the marriage. It had taken a lot of scaring. He chuckled. "Yep, it was underhanded of me, scaring her like that, but a man's gotta do what a man's gotta do."

Sadie Lou had her own gotta-do. She craned away to scratch her ear. Appeased, she settled her chin on Gil's knee again, and a long tongue snaked out to rake the heel of his hand. He gave her a pat of reassurance.

He folded and addressed Maisie's letter. "Better write that gimp Adolf Keller, too."

Sadie Lou yawned.

In brief terms he informed the German, "I've taken your sister to wife."

Signing his name, he said to the dog, "I'd best send some money with this. Gotta pay for the stuff Lisette brought here." He considered sending funds to pay for Willensstark but decided against it. "He's going back to his owner. This drive doesn't need any obstinate mules along, that's for certain."

The animal, money, and letter could be shipped from Lampasas.

Gil wrote two more letters. One was for Ernst Dietert's wife, the other for Willie Gaines' sister. He didn't know how to get in touch with José's family. The

91

vaquero had never given information about himself beyond his name.

He rubbed Sadie Lou's scruff. "If a person doesn't offer details, one doesn't pry. This is the way it is in the West."

Gil folded the notes. He thought about those three graves, and it haunted him to think José's family would never know the good-natured Mexican's resting place.

He had the urge to talk about it. Would Lisette listen? Definitely; she was that kind of woman—at least when conversation didn't concern making more of their marriage than she was ready to accept.

He tucked the letters into his pocket, gave Sadie Lou another pat, and got to his feet. Needing a safe place for his letters, he stuck them in his saddlebag.

And then he eased into the chuck wagon, stepping over the seat and leaving the flap up to allow moonlight in. His gaze slid down to the floorboard, to Lisette's sleeping form. She hadn't undressed. She still wore those britches and shirt. His eyes welding to the thrust of her breasts, he sucked in his breath. *If you don't stop gawking, there won't be any talking.*

He forced his eyes to her recumbent face. Her braids were in disarray, and he ached to loosen them completely and twine his fingers around those locks.

Her lashes, dark brown despite her fair coloring, fanned her creamy cheeks. He loved the way those lashes could drop demurely or frame her big eyes when they widened in surprise.

Her nose was neither too big nor too little. It had a faint rise at the bridge and was halfway between thin and wide. Pert it wasn't, which wouldn't have fit her anyhow. Pert was for women who lazed about the manor when not attending lavish balls and glittering cotillions. Lisette's nose showed the heritage of her forebears—good, strong Teutonic stock. Her nose was a superb one to pass down to descendants.

Leaning against his upright trunk, he smiled. His mind's eye concocted a passel of wee McLoughlins, all of them looking like their mother.

Aw, hell, what was the matter with him? He didn't even know if she liked children. She had all those ideas about hatmaking, but surely stitchery wouldn't hold a candle to motherhood.

He hadn't an inkling of her preferences, save for a love of the dance—plus her millinery intentions and her quest to see the city of Chicago. Would she like listening to rain beat down on the ranchhouse's tin roof?

Would she be as passionate as he suspected her of being?

He had a lot to learn about the new Mrs. McLoughlin . . . and he intended to be a devoted student. And he would be a tireless *teacher* in the art of lovemaking.

He knew how to get a woman warmed up, he'd had a lot of experience along that line, but never had he known satisfaction of the soul. He had damned sure known hell.

Betty—damn her—had played him for a patsy, had come to the marriage bed broken to a man's saddle. And the bitch had laughed in his face, recounting her sexual escapades.

It wouldn't be that way with Lisette. Lisette McLoughlin was a paragon.

He pushed away from the trunk and gazed down at his bride. Her alluring mouth parted slightly; she took short breaths as she slept. Should he awaken her? If he did, it wouldn't be to converse about the subject that had prompted him back to the chuck wagon: leaving three men in their graves.

And she needed time to celebrate and be cultivated. Gil wouldn't push the issue, unless he just couldn't take the heat anymore.

Tonight, he could take the heat.

He crept out of the chuck wagon to make himself yet another rotten bed in the woods. He didn't get a wink of sleep, for his mind was crowded with Lisette and his groin was in critical need of a cold-water dousing. Way before daybreak, he snuck back to his wife.

Her hair was braided anew and wound around her head in a coronet, and she was dressed in clean shirt and trousers, eager to make breakfast. There would be no reveling today. He did work on the cultivating part, though, to no success.

The second day of their married life proceeded the same as the first. Gil was approaching the end of his patience.

On the third day, just after the midday rest and food stop, Big Red threw a shoe. Collecting it, Gil fastened his eyes on the approaching chuck wagon, and most particularly on its driver.

Hmm, Old Son. What do you think?

He made a survey of the situation. At the time of the sorrel's bad luck, the herd was lumbering along without protest, the cowboys half asleep in their saddles, no doubt hankering for an hour's siesta to settle the latest delicious meal prepared by Miz Good Biscuits—the nickname his men had given her the day after the wedding.

Patiently, Gil walked the limping stallion toward the

chuck wagon. Where Lisette was concerned, his patience had ended. He wanted her. Here. Now.

Though the locale was fine for his skills as smithy, it wasn't particularly conducive to lovemaking, not with three thousand sets of horns plus their punchers in attendance. Plus, he figured Lisette herself would throw a shoe if he made motions to stop longer than it took to shoe Big Red. She expected to reach the night camp ahead of the herd so that the beans would be just right and the roast just so. And his men deserved her best efforts. The hell with it.

She was spoiling every man jack in the company, including Tecumseh Billy. Only this morning she'd had that steer eating carrots out of her hand. "T-Bill" could move on ahead — and eat grass for a change. The men could sup on steak and fries tonight. There was leftover vinegar pie — boy howdy, was it good, tasted just like lemon pie. No one would suffer.

Still guiding the limping stallion along, Gil motioned for the longhorns and their escorts to move ahead. "Matt, you know the way to Slick Rock Creek. We'll meet you there."

Right here, in this deep green meadow, Gil would make Lisette his wife in fact, rather than merely in name.

There was no time to waste.

Chapter Eight

"Hold up, honey."

Bent on making Lisette his woman today, Gil brought the limping Big Red abreast of the chuck wagon. She reined in the draught horses and turned her covered head his way.

"What is wrong?" she asked in that German accent which never failed to excite him.

Gil pointed to the sorrel's left front leg. "I need to fetch the smithy tools."

"No need. I'll get them while you hobble him."

Gil watched her climb into the wagon. Good gracious, she was pretty, even with her usual men's clothes and that peculiar headpiece. The man's hat was gone, replaced by the fedora he'd seen her wear in Fredericksburg, and it was a mess after the past days, all flattened feathers and road dust. No matter, she still looked pretty to him. He'd bet she'd be a helluva lot prettier without a stitch of clothing.

Trail dust swirled as the mooing herd continued on, over an incline. Thankfully Sadie Lou was doing her job, wasn't paying mind to him and the sorrel. By the time Lisette had fetched the collection of nails and a hammer—what the hell was keeping her?—the drag riders were in sight.

It took massive resolve for Gil not to grab Lisette into his arms when she handed over those implements. *Remember, Old Son, she's skittish as a doe and innocent as a newborn. Don't rush her.*

Nonetheless, Gil wasn't above stripping off his vest and shirt to attack the horseshoeing. Hell, he wasn't kidding himself. He intended to capture his little doe's attention and give her a lesson in becoming a woman.

Yet, to be honest with himself, he'd turned a mite scared. If he didn't make the first time right for her, it might turn her off him forever. He'd make certain it was right.

Sun rays beat on his back as he raised the sorrel's front cannon. "Honey, wanna give me a hand?"

"S-sure."

Since their wedding night, when he'd browbeaten her into helping him with his boots, Gil hadn't asked for anything special, and it pleased him no end that she hadn't fallen to her usual brand of objections. Maybe she was more ready than he had figured. *You'd like to think so.*

She set the bonnet aside, thank goodness; it was all he could do not to snicker at the silly thing.

"Take hold of his leg, honey. That's right . . . just like that."

He put nails in his mouth and took the hammer in his right hand. She leaned over to keep the horse's knee immobile. Around the iron nails, Gil inhaled the womanly scent of Lisette, drawing her musk through his nostrils, letting it seep through his senses.

While her aura spread like the gentle lap of water

97

against a shore, he stole a glimpse at her breasts. They were so close to his mouth . . . so close. He considered himself fortunate not to swallow the nails, and Big Red was lucky to get a good shoeing.

The last nail in place, he gave the stallion a pat, tied him to the chuck wagon, and fetched some hay. Gil's back was to his wife, and if she saw the testament to his arousal, he figured she'd take flight. He yearned for her to see and appreciate all of him, but . . . *cultivate*.

"I could use something. To drink," he said hoarsely.

"It's . . . the lunch coffee . . . I—I kept the pot in the sun, so it should be warm, at least. Would you like a cup?" she asked, her voice catching.

Right now, he could use one of those beers she and her countrymen were so fond of. "Yeah, that'd be nice."

She returned to the chuck wagon to fetch the coffee, and he willed himself into decent enough shape to turn around. Ambling over to the chuck box, he took the cup between his hands. He did not look at Lisette. If he had, sheer will wouldn't have been enough.

He settled on the ground, resting his naked back against a wagon wheel and extending one leg in front of him. As he sipped the tepid coffee, he watched Lisette seat herself a couple of yards to his left. She drew her knees up to rest her chin on them.

"Gil." With a demure tilt to her head she studied his bare torso. "H-how did you get those scars?"

"From wars."

"Wars? Not war?"

"Wars. Comanche arrowheads made a couple of holes in my arms." He pointed to the silvery indention

98

on his shoulder. "A Johnny Reb in Georgia got me here."

She looked away, but not before he caught her startled expression.

"Lisette, you know I served in the Union Army." This wasn't where he wanted the conversation to lead. If there was a problem, though, they needed to get it out in the open. "Why do I get the impression it bothers you?"

"It doesn't bother me. But I thought you knew Adolf . . . and my father . . . and my uncle were all Confederates."

He hadn't known anything of the kind. Most of the German-Texans had sided with the Union. While he didn't hold with Confederate beliefs, he respected any man's right to fight for his own beliefs.

"Adolf was wounded at Gettysburg." A tear rolled down her cheek; she swiped it away. "Thank God he didn't die."

Gil could tell by the emotions issuing from Lisette that while she resented her brother and the hell he and his wife had put her through, she loved him. Such loyalty was a precious gift. Too bad Adolf Keller hadn't appreciated it.

She said, "General Hood himself lost the use of his arm at Gettysburg, but he was kind enough to send Adolf back to Monika. I—I suppose you've noticed how my brother limps."

"I have."

"My father and uncle were with the general, too— in Georgia."

Her admission caught Gil in the gut, like the force of a minié ball. "They were valiant fighters," he uttered. Suddenly he wished for a smoke, a habit he'd given up.

"Yes, valiant to the death."

"I wish they could've returned to you." Gil meant this.

"That would have answered my prayers." Tilting her head, her eyes growing suspicious, she asked, "How do you know about their bravery?"

Gil was tempted to skate over the truth, but he wouldn't delve into deceit, even if the price was his wife's admiration. "I fought in Georgia. I was an attaché to General Sherman."

Two of her fingers lifted to press against her temple, as if a pain had suddenly struck.

"Do you hate me for being a Yankee, Lisette?" he asked then.

"No." She dropped her hand. "I haven't let the war rage on in my heart. But I won't lie and say your allegiance to Sherman doesn't stun me, because it does. From what I've heard of his assault against the people of Georgia as well as the soldiers of the Confederacy, I think it was an abomination."

"Honey, war isn't a picnic. Each side has to use every weapon in the arsenal."

"I suppose." She hesitated. "Gil, if you had it to do over again, would you torch your way to the Atlantic?"

"I never left Atlanta. I never burned anything except for a hellhole of a plantation, and as an officer in charge of a brigade, I never fired at shot—in Georgia, anyway. I might've had to, but I was wounded in the initial battle. General Sherman put me in charge of a captured precinct after I left the field hospital."

She wasn't saying a word; he got to the point of the

question still evident in her set features. "I gave my best efforts to *win*. I fought to free human beings from the same sort of hell you experienced in your brother's household. Only true slavery is much worse than being in company with a demanding sister-in-law. Ask Dinky Peele, if you don't believe me."

"Let's clear up your misconception. I *never* condoned slavery. My family didn't, either. Adolf and *Onkel* — I mean, Uncle — August and my father fought for the Lone Star." She spread her arms. "The state opened its arms to us, gave us shelter when we needed it. When my kinsmen were conscripted, they didn't turn their backs. They answered the call."

She got to her feet, rubbing her temple, and asked, "If you don't mind, can we change the subject?"

"I'd welcome it. Why don't you let me rub your temples?"

"Nein!"

His eyes moved down her curvaceous form, then back up to her face. He intended to get closer to his wife — a helluva lot closer. Closing the distance between them, he said, "Come here, honey. I'm going to give you a good rubbing."

Chapter Nine

"Nein!" she repeated. Her English had left her, as it always did at times of greatest stress. Lisette scrambled away from her advancing husband. "I do not want you to rub anything. Go on to your herd. And put on your shirt!"

Ever since he had starting shoeing Big Red, Gil had been driving her to distraction. Their days of so-called married life had driven her to headaches, period. And now, with the two of them alone, his men and cattle north of the meadow, and she feared letting down her guard.

As never before.

His forehead creased with concern as he halted three paces in front of her. "You *do* resent my service in the Union Army."

Once more she kneaded her throbbing temple, collecting her English to answer honestly, "No, I do not."

"Well and good." Gil's brow flattened, then concern marked his features anew. "But you've got a headache from something, and if it's not from Adolf's stories, why won't you let me massage away your pain?"

"Because I . . . because I'm so confused I don't

know what to do or which way to turn."

It didn't help to center her attention on the picture of male perfection he presented, standing there shirtless, the sun kissing his muscle-bound, scarred shoulders and shining through the ink-hued, crinkled hair dusting his arms and chest. And why was it that she lacked enough will to turn her eyes from the network of veins above all that arm brawn and those strong, capable hands?

Her gaze dropped—but not to the ground.

Below his bare torso, the gunbelt still rode on his hips. And those chaps—they shone with the patina of years of working cattle. At the top of them, at the front of him, denim caught her eye, denim worn smooth with the outline of a formidable bulge of male virility.

"Still confused?" he asked.

Not about one thing. A *Tropf*, that's what she'd been for not realizing that there might be no retreat from this meadow, not without experiencing everything he offered. Was that so horrible? No! She wanted him, wanted to be his wife *in fact*.

He murmured, "Let me rub your temples."

"You've got to keep your distance. If you don't, you'll be taking your husbandly rights." On a shake of her head, she cringed at her honesty.

"If that's not an invitation, your name isn't Mrs. Gil McLoughlin."

A smile eased across his features, lit the eyes more blue in the sunlight than argentine under the moon and stars. Just one of his gazes had the power to mesmerize her, and he had welded many of them to her. This one had an intensity the others lacked.

Her face contorted as her headache intensified.

"Lisette, you are going to sit down." His tone brooked no debate. "And you are going to let me at what ails you."

"I . . . I don't know."

"I do. Let's get out of the sunshine." He gestured to an ancient oak of low-reaching limbs. "It looks pleasant over there. No cattle tracks, just a quiet, soft place to sit down."

It appeared so. Ankle-high grass carpeted the land between here and there. An early spring breeze rippled through the trees. Leaves clattered together, and many fluttering to the ground, making a carpet of umber and green. She heard mockingbirds exchange a call of *sooddy, sooddy*. A bee buzzed by, another following; the two danced in the air to flirt with each other.

It was a perfect place for relieving a headache — and much, much more. Therein lay the problem. She knew what he was after; she knew what she wanted.

"Lisette." He drawled her name. "Let's go."

Having had a wealth of experience with his determination, she let him take her hand. She expected he'd sit next to her under the canopy of the oak, on the leafy glade. But he didn't. Turning her head, she saw him kneeling behind her, his hands reaching upward.

His black hair, tousled as ever, gleamed blue in the daylight. As always, she had the urge to pat it into place. Don't even think about it, she warned herself.

"Turn your head, darlin'." When she obeyed, he crooned, "Just relax, just relax."

How could she be at ease with Gil so close? Yet his fingers had magic in them. They made deep, lingering circles on her temple and forehead, and she began to droop as the pain left her head.

"*So schön* . . . feels so good," she whispered.

"Yeah, beats a sharp stick in the eye, doesn't it?" he joked.

"Oh, Gil, you are so silly," she murmured.

"Silly over you."

Massaging a trail to her neck, he kneaded the tension out of her shoulders. Then his lips touched her nape . . . In thrall, she shivered.

"Relax, my sweet. Open your senses. Smell our surroundings. Inhale the scent of the leaves, the green of the grass, the sweet fragrance of bluebonnets. And the sun, smell the sun. Think about how it moves through your nose, the sun on flesh. Let the tension flow out of your fingers and toes."

She was adrift with the scent of him. The warm sun on his skin, the faint traces of horse, the oil of the coffee she'd fixed him, his own musky scent . . . she found all of it endlessly appealing in her husband.

Yet, she could almost smell her own misgivings.

He was seducing her, and if she didn't do something—anything!—she had no one to blame but herself.

"There aren't any bluebonnets around here."

"Pretend there are."

"I think your senses are sharper than mine."

He sighed. "I'm beginning to think there's not a romantic bone in your body."

"I wouldn't agree," she replied, and wished she

hadn't, for he took it as invitation.

His voice laden with meaning, he said, "If your brother had allowed it, I'd have courted you properly. I'd have given you flowers, and you'd have seen me all slicked up."

"You gave me flowers. They're pressed in a Bible I found," she answered softly, again under his spell. "And you look fine the way you are." *More than merely fine,* she thought.

Gil picked a twig that had drifted to her shoulder. "But it would've been enjoyable, getting polished up for you. Like, wearing the necktie my grandmother gave me."

"The grandmother who gave you her wedding ring?"

"Your wedding ring now. But she's one and the same. Maisie—that's short for Margaret—Mc-Loughlin. I don't want to talk about her. I want to talk about us."

The day before, Matthias had told her Gil had two brothers, that the parents were deceased, and Lisette wanted to ask questions. One was at the forefront of her mind: What about his former wife? What caused her to quit on their marriage?

Lisette had a word with herself. This union was for show, and his past was not her business.

Lightly, he placed a kiss on her shoulder. "I'd have been proud to escort you to church and to those dances you Germans are so fond of. If the Fredericksburgers would have allowed a divorced man in," he added on a chuckle.

"Don't be harsh on yourself. The Lord's house is for everyone. As far as the dances, no one would've

106

turned you away. I imagine they'd have been eager for the gossip."

"Gossip? Who cares about it. What's that old saying, 'Sticks and stones . . .'?" Not one caustic syllable edged his words. "Besides, while they'd have been yammering about me, they'd've left someone else alone."

"That's one way to think about it." She, on the other hand, had done everything in her power to avoid the tongues of scandalmongers. The gossip theme had to be avoided, thus she turned the topic. "Gil, it was nice of you to say those things about courting me. I've never known a fraction of your kindness."

"As pretty as you are? I'm surprised a thousand fellows haven't fallen at your feet. Or are you just being modest?"

Thankfully, he didn't give her a chance to answer.

"Forgive me, Lisette. What was I thinking of? The war made for lonely hearts . . . made many young women widows and spinsters. And your brother being a mother hen . . ."

"Yes, Adolf was persnickety," she replied in truth, yet not delving into the war years.

"To hell with him. He's out of the picture now." Gil looped his hands under her arms, raising and expanding his fingers across her jaw. His touch elicited a shiver, and she was almost lost when he whispered, "Why don't you want to be my wife . . . in more than name?"

"You . . . you promised you wouldn't force yourself on me."

"Am I doing that, Lisette?" His fingers exerted a

slight pressure. "Have I tossed you to the ground and ripped your clothes off?"

"No." She needed something—anything!—to latch on to. "But you're trying to pry me away from my dreams. I . . . I want my own hatshop. I want to see Chicago." She still wanted these things almost as much as she yearned for her husband.

"Stifling your dreams, honey, isn't what I'm about. If you've a mind to do nothing more than stitch millinery, do it. Open a shop in Fredericksburg—I'll finance it."

"That town is too close to Monika."

"Just thumb your nose and tell her to go to hell."

Lisette couldn't help but laugh. "It would be infinitely satisfying."

"Since you're set on Chicago," he said smoothly, "we'll make a honeymoon trip up there. By train, of course, from Abilene."

"You offer too much."

Doggedly, he went on. "I'm not stingy, despite my Scottish blood. And I'd spend my last penny just to be with you. I fancy the way you smile, I adore the way you walk, I near about pass out over your accent. Did you know it gets thicker when you get worked up?"

"And sometimes I speak German instead of English."

"Yeah, and I love it." One hand moved to her head, his fingers making designs on her scalp and loosening the hairpins. "All I think about is spending the rest of my life with you and your enchanting accent. I want to watch you sewing hats, and I want to be there when you open your shop.

Proud as punch, I'll be."

Gil would hand her the world. He needn't have suggested anything but himself.

And then he was changing positions, easing his legs around the outside of her thighs, settling her against him. Powerless to protest, she felt his fingers press her midriff. She yearned for the hardness insinuated against her derrière. No . . . she wanted all of him, not just his passion.

His hand moved up to cup her breast, his fingers stroking the shirt-covered fullness. It bloomed under his caress, and heightened desire braided the core of her being.

His breath feathered against her neck as he said, "I've seen the way your nipples pucker when you look at me." Gently, he worked one between his thumb and forefinger. "I get excited every time."

Nervously, she protested, "You're embarrassing me."

He touched her sleeve. "I don't mean to offend your sensibilities. If you'd rather, I won't say anything. We'll just spend the rest of our lives doing what's natural."

A lifetime together . . . what a beautiful concept. She yearned to give and share, and meet all his needs, yet she lacked the courage to confess her sin. She needed more time, and if she didn't break away from his seductive touch and voice . . .

His hand moved to caress her inner thigh. Her thoughts a jumble, she propelled herself forward, grappled for footing. Once more she began to run away from her husband.

Lisette was running from him — again.

Sun rays glinted off her white-blond hair like the sparks of St. Elmo's fire as she raced toward the chuck wagon. Her braids came loose from the corona, were flying behind her as the remaining hairpins flew to the ground. To Gil she had never appeared so innocent nor so frightened. It was time for him to make peace with her.

But he was out of blandishments, which hadn't worked anyway. Just as when he'd had to scare her into accepting his proposal, it was time to get tough. The cultivating was over. It was time for celebrating.

He chased after his wife and caught her as she ran through the grass. Grabbing her arm, he tightened his fingers, whirling her around. Her eyes were wild with alarm.

He pressed her against his thighs. "We are married, woman — married. It's no sin to sleep with your husband. It *is* going to happen. Sooner is better than later."

"Du machst mich ganz verrückt!"

He had no idea what she said. But he figured it probably wasn't, "Yes, my darling, precious husband, do carry me to our lair and ravish me until my eyes are glazed, until I can take no more of your ardent aggression."

She opened her mouth, but he clamped his fingers over her lips. "I'm going to kiss you, and I'm going to touch you, and I'm going to make love to you. And you're going to let me."

She fought him. "You promised not to force me!"

"There'll be no force. You are going to yield."

Her balled fists beat against his bare shoulder; she tried to twist out of his reach. Out of control, he swooped his mouth to hers, his tongue prying her lips apart. The inside was ice and heat. His hands cupped her squirming backside. When he terminated the kiss, he didn't let go his grip.

Chest heaving, he gazed into her teary eyes. "Say you don't want me, and I'll leave you alone."

She said something—several things—in German, none of which he understood except for "pretzel." He decided she was admitting her own needs. Of course, she might be expressing an intention to twist his arms into pretzels if he didn't leave her alone, but he doubted it.

Better make it a simple question. "Do you want me?" He pressed her to his blatant need. "Just say yes or no."

"*Ja!*" Hiding her face against his chest, she grasped his upper arm. And he felt her tears as well as the heaving of her shoulders. "Gil! *Du musst verstehen—ich bin keine Jungfrau!*"

"Hush!" He would have no more of her protests, be they English or German. "Nothing you can say will stop me from making you my woman."

She grew still.

Her accent became thicker than ever. "You mean it?"

"Take a cat-o'-nines to me, honey, if I ever lie to you."

The fight in her vanished. Her arms went around his waist. She reared her head, looking into his eyes, as she laughed for the joy of it. There was no doubting her joy.

111

He beamed. The minx had wanted the chase, had asked for the fight. His innocent Lisette . . . all fire and the promise of a wanton. Well, the chase was over.

Without a word he swept her into his arms and carried her to the oak tree. He set her to her feet, unfastened her braids. His blushing bride's face radiant, he finger-combed the hair cascading to her waist.

"You wore your hair down for the wedding. I like it this way," he said, his voice rough with admiration. He corded the silvery mass around his fingers, letting it slide across the palm. "You don't know how much I wanted to do this."

She smiled shyly. "And I've always wanted to pat your hair into place."

"We black Celts have lots of hair. Too curly to control."

"Black Celt?"

"That's what I am. Black as the Douglass himself."

"I don't know about any Douglass . . ."

He unbuttoned her shirt, parting the chambray. "The only black Celt you need concern yourself with is right here."

He held her away to gaze at those proud, coral-crested breasts. She tried to cover herself, but he wouldn't allow it. In a frenzy to see all his Lisette, he stripped her. As each garment floated to the leaves below, he caressed her exquisite flesh. He felt her trembles of modesty.

"Unbuckle my gunbelt," he ordered in a husk.

Her fingers worked the buckle, and he was dying a thousand beautiful deaths at the feel of her clumsiness. Or was she being all that awkward? He could only hope.

Taking her hand, he guided her to the leaves. Yet she turned on her side and pulled her hair across a shoulder.

"Don't hide from me, Lisette. Look at me. Allow me to look at you."

She pivoted her head, taking in his six-foot-two frame as he rid himself of chaps, then shucked his footwear. With an arched brow, she teased, "I notice you didn't have trouble getting free of your boots."

"It's, uh, well, I . . . You know, you're right." He could have gotten them off if they had been much, much tighter, but he didn't point this out. At this moment he had superhuman strength. "But you wouldn't be a harridan and make too much of it, would you?"

She smiled and replied, "Of course not."

"Good."

He rid himself of his britches, and quickly, demurely, she averted her eyes again. *She's gonna need some tutoring, Old Son. Take your time, don't pounce on her.*

Hence he allowed himself a stare. She was lovely from her head to her toes. Her feet were slim, her ankles narrow. A ray of sun cutting through the tree caught those long, long legs, the gentle curve of her hip, the indention of her waist, and her flat belly. He dropped down to the deep pillow of leaves, easing against her. His hand shook as he traced the fine ivory down on her arm. He grew hotter, both from the sun and from her nearness.

He trailed his lips to the arched length of her neck, and her trembles enticed him to greater exploration.

113

Rolling her to her back, he captured a nipple between his lips to draw on the peak. She moaned. The arms that had lain limp on the leaves lifted, and she laced her fingers in his hair. The wonder of her response shot through his every muscle, his every nerve, and invaded the marrow of his bones to settle in his already aroused groin. This was how lovemaking ought to be, how it had never been before for him.

His mouth withdrew from her breast, moving toward the other. Yet he paused to nestle his face between the cleft. "My precious maiden, how I adore you."

She tensed.

"It's okay, it's okay," he crooned, and dislodged a twig from her hair. "All I want is to make you happy." His words seemed to soothe her. "I promise to take enough time."

It would have been easier having his fingernails ripped from their roots. Her breasts teased his jaw, her crisp thatch his abdomen. Moving upward, he nestled his shaft against her belly.

At her quick intake of breath, he explained, "It means I want you, my getting all stiff like this."

Her brow quirked, as if he had said something she didn't understand.

"I want to be inside you, my darlin'—deep inside you. That's the way it is with husbands and wives."

Her voice barely audible, she said, "Such coupling could bring a child."

"I hope so."

Not any time soon, he thought but didn't add. For the next half year, give or take a few weeks, they

114

would be on the trail, and then there was Chicago and the journey home. No, now was not the time for progeny. Though if one came, who could regret it?

More than a quarter minute passed before he added, "I don't even know if you like children."

"I like them."

The idea of Lisette bearing his child brought a sweet — a bittersweet — vision to Gil. Once before a child had borne the name McLoughlin. *Don't think about the boy.*

"Do you like children?" she whispered.

"If they are ours, I'll adore them."

She smiled.

Again his lips moved to her enticing flesh. On instinct, her leg curved around him. He yearned to plunge into the depth beckoning him. Instead he let his fingers bask again in the sensation of her long, gossamer hair. He felt her tremble when he caressed her shoulder and the underside of her chin. He knew he had nearly reached his limit of restraint.

"Oh, Gil," she murmured as his lips descended to the dip below her collarbone.

Tears sprang to her eyes, and he almost disliked himself for what he intended to — no, what he *would* — do to her. His fingers moved to the apex of her thighs. His thumb furrowed into her pubic hair, his middle finger . . . She was wet, wet and hot. Innocence and heat.

Old Son, you are damned lucky.

She bucked against his hand, a hum of appreciation vibrating from her throat. Her fingers dug into his back. She murmured something in German, and her flesh warmed even more as he continued to stroke her. It pleasured him, his bride turning into a furnace of heat.

"Am I hurting you?" he asked tenderly.

"No," was her moan.

Placated, he played her as if she were a smooth, cherished instrument. Which she was. Yet, as the moments wore on, he had the strangest thought as his finger explored her dampness. He didn't feel a maidenhead. Having experienced only one virgin, though, how could he be an expert?

He settled between her thighs. His aching-to-bursting lance at her womanly portal, Gil's restraint was at an end. "Lisette, my darling, it will hurt you the first time, but never again."

Chapter Ten

She felt the racing of his heart along with the pressure of his urgency as he told her it would hurt the first time but never again. Hadn't he been listening when she'd said she wasn't a virgin? Or had the confession been only in her mind?

"Please stop," Lisette implored.

With the leaves at her back and her husband above her, she pushed his shoulders, forcing him away, yet she wanted to hold him closely, lift her hips in invitation, and allow his entry.

"You mustn't," she pleaded.

"I *can't* stop. It's too late."

She cried.

Her tears stopped him. The tips of his fingers brushed the moisture from her cheeks; he kissed her eyelid. Though he had forced her to accept him, he was so tender and dear! She squeezed her eyes against the sun's glare, and the glare of her own shortcomings.

"I . . . I'm sorry," she whispered, her fingers crushing oak leaves instead of caressing him.

"I know you're frightened, but . . . I'll make it good for you. Touch me. Just touch me. Put your arms around my neck. Don't turn away. Please trust me," he murmured against her lips. "We should be part of each other."

Her hands found his taut shoulders. Each muscle, every bone — all his perfections and imperfections — called out to her, demanding she do his bidding. Gil kissed her, his lips vital with passion, and once again she was drawn into the ardor that had expanded since the moment of his first touch.

But she had to tell him again — before it was too late!

Before she could say a word, Gil thrust deeply into her. His length and width filled her, his heat raising her temperature to the flash point of pleasure.

Yet he didn't move, and he was so still he didn't even breathe.

"Tell me it's not true," he uttered.

Her heart stopped. "I — I did."

"Liar," he growled raggedly, his disappointment knifing through her. "Damn you."

"I did not lie," she choked out, her eyes going moist again with damnable tears. "When you ran after me, when you demanded to know my feelings, I told you — I was no virgin."

Or had she said, *Ich bin keine Jungfrau*? Dear Lord, had she spoken in German?

Still, her husband didn't move. Frantic to please him, she twisted her pelvis. Her legs went around his narrow hips. To allow him to leave her was more than she could abide; she held tightly. She needed intimacy . . . and understanding . . . and acceptance.

Yet she felt him pulling away.

"Don't leave me, Gil." Her nails dug into his flesh. "Please don't leave me."

But he did, and his abandonment sent chills to dampen the fire he had stoked. She wanted to roll into a ball, wanted to hide from him and from herself, yet she wouldn't. She mustn't let him leave her!

Her eyes lifted. She sucked in her breath at the sight of him. He stood above her, magnificent yet half flaccid, and stared at the sky. Her desire renewed. She hungered for the joining he had forced her into accepting, and was ravenous for fulfillment.

She wouldn't let him reject her! This was her greatest fear—to be rebuffed.

"I want you," she whispered. "I want you to be inside me, like you said you wanted to be. I have a throbbing for you. Please do something about it."

He shuddered, yet she saw that he was no longer soft. Her fingers wound around his ankle. She turned to her side, a breast touching his foot, as her forefinger moved upward to experience the richness of his bristly calf. He cursed and tried to move his foot, but she pressed her lips against his ankle.

"Wanton hussy," rumbled from his throat.

And then he was bending down, spreading her legs. Her arms lifted to him. Pinning them above her head, he stretched atop her and gave a ragged cry as he entered her once more.

There was no tenderness in the mating. He lunged into her again and again and again. The earth beneath the oak leaves dug into her back as

Gil continued to forge into her. She deserved the pain for disappointing him. But as he pummeled her body, as he shouted an oath, she met his hard thrusts, and the pain turned to something altogether different from agony. Her breath shallowed, her pulse raced. A spasm — one she'd never felt before — overtook her. She screamed her husband's name.

His movements quickened. "Damn you," he cried out and spilled himself in her. He didn't withdraw.

She felt somewhat soothed. He *knew* about her shame, yet he had taken his husbandly rights.

"Satisfied?" he asked sourly.

How could she answer? Although she'd experienced bodily gratification, she wanted something she couldn't name. With her husband, it had been different from her previous experience. Back in San Antonio, she'd expected nothing and received her expectations.

Gil had taken the time to arouse her spirit, had taken the time to warm her blood, and she had welcomed and enjoyed the hard thrusts, but something was lacking.

She shouldn't expect too much, yet . . .

"You should be happy." Gil let go her wrists. "You got what you wanted."

"All I want is you. And your understanding."

"I'll just bet you do." He slid out of her, standing once more and grabbing his Levis. "Damn you, I bet you haven't been a virgin in a long, long time."

He spoke the truth; how it hurt her — much more than his harsh touch. "I want to please you."

"Get dressed."

She turned her head, burying her face in the

120

earthy bedding and closing the thighs still warm and wet from their coupling.

She expressed her regret that she hadn't been chaste, that she wished she could have been, for his happiness meant everything to her.

"Speak English. You're in an English-speaking country. Quit talking like a damn Hun!"

Earlier, he had said he loved her voice, but obviously that was no longer so. "I said . . . I'm sorry I wasn't pure."

" 'Sorry' won't work with me, sweetheart." The endearment was spoken with a blade of disgust. "Look at me, God damn it. At least have the guts to face me."

His toe slid under her cheek, raising her face. He wore his britches, but his chest remained bare, and her heartbeat quickened. Looking into his closed face, she whispered earnestly, "I wish I could have been what you wanted."

"That makes two of us." He paused. "Why did you deceive me, Lisette?"

"I didn't. When you ran after me — I told you!"

"You could've said anything, but the fact remains, you lied. Before I fell for your line of bull, I asked you if you were loose, and you replied clear as a bell, 'No.' And I, by damn, took that to mean you hadn't been spreading your *dubious* charms all over the State of Texas."

His words, his tone were like a whiplash. She shot up hurt, her anger building. "I am not promiscuous. And as for my 'dubious charms,' there's only been one other man. I —"

"Shut up," Gil cut in, his eyes hard as steel. "I

121

won't tolerate a replay of your conquests."

"There have been no conquests."

"I said, shut up." He drilled another scathing look into her before pushing an arm through the sleeve of his shirt. "I thought you were a decent woman."

"I *am* a decent woman. And I'll do everything in my power to make you a good wife."

"Don't flatter yourself into thinking you've trapped me into some web, 'cause frankly, you weren't that good."

Once, as a child, she had been kicked in the stomach by a mule, and had nearly died from the injury. But that pain was nothing compared to the one Gil had inflicted. God in heaven, she knew something was lacking, but had she failed completely as a woman?

Obviously so.

Maybe her lackings were why Thom had gone to the arms of another and had given her the Childress name.

Lisette observed the man who'd given her the McLoughlin name. Loathing issued from his eyes, from the hard set of his mouth, from his stance. She had hurt him, and he had hurt her.

She wished the earth would open to swallow her.

Too angered to think straight, Gil McLoughlin walked purposely away from Lisette. He was itching to beat the living hell out of the miscreant who'd led him to believe she was the epitome of respectable. His anger wasn't necessarily directed at Matthias Gruene. He was furious with himself for being a chump.

Once before he'd been gullible, and now history had repeated itself. When most men took a woman to wife, she was pure, and her loyalty lasted until death parted them. Why was it that he, Gil McLoughlin, had twice chosen a wife with a past? *Twice.*

Lisette had wanted to explain. But he hadn't taken it, and he never would. History would not repeat itself on that score.

He collected Big Red, leaving Lisette in his dusty wake as he rode to catch up with the herd. Ten minutes into the ride, he halted the stallion. If he tore into Gruene, the cowboys would put two and two together—nothing was right with the newlyweds. The trouble between husband and wife was his and Lisette's business and no one else's.

Besides, his men needed to think everything was smooth between their boss and his bride, and Gil meant to keep it that way. Keep it that way? Why keep anything *any* way? It would be easy enough to send Lisette packing.

Lisette. He'd left her alone in the woods, his humiliations reverberating through the air. *Damn you, you didn't have to say some of those things. When you said she wasn't all that good, you were lying just as baldly as she'd lied to you.*

No, he hadn't lied. But he refused to consider exactly what had gone on under that oak tree.

Lisette hugged her arms as she sat shivering on the chuck wagon seat. Leaning forward, with the sun bearing down on her head, she buried her face in her hands. Never could she be what he needed.

He'd hurt her with his cruel condemnation, but the issue lay in the fact he had expected a virgin, and she should have been one. She could never be what she was not. She hadn't been chaste and she wasn't woman enough for her husband.

He hadn't received complete fulfillment, but she had everything else to give. And her faith in Gil was such that she felt he would be understanding, once he recovered from his shock.

Lisette lifted her head. All she could do was try to make the best of a bad situation, try to bring him some measure of peace and happiness. Her shaking hands reached for the team's reins. Gil must understand that she had tried to be honest.

She intended to beard the lion.

Lisette quit the meadow.

She tried to set a steady pace for the draught horses. Four days as a part of the Four Aces outfit hadn't given her a wealth of experience at handling the heavy chuck wagon and its team, though.

Fifteen minutes after she'd vowed to beard the lion, uneasiness washed over her and it had nothing to do with her ineptitude as a driver. Where was Gil?

Surely he wasn't furious enough to abandon her. He wasn't—of course he wasn't. Gil McLoughlin wouldn't do that to his wife.

She studied the sky and read the sun's position. A couple of hours had passed since he had pulled her over to shoe Big Red. The sorrel could catch the herd easily, but with the weight of the chuck wagon, hers wouldn't be such an easy feat.

And what would she say upon facing the cowboys' curiosity about her whereabouts? What would her husband tell them before she reached them? For the second time in her life, she wouldn't deliberate over other people's reactions, not when making peace with Gil was the most important consideration.

She tapped the reins, picking up speed. A javelina raced across the horses' path. The team balked, the wagon wheels swaying, and her heart thumped in a staccato beat as she brought the wagon to rights.

If the wagon were to lose a wheel or worse . . . Anything could happen. Fear skittered unfettered — the Comanches might find her.

Her grip on reason lost, she stood. Picking up the long whip, she reached to give the lead horses her command. Under their response, the chuck wagon shot forward, pulling her back to the seat. Her hair, loosened by her husband's fingers, blew into her face; half the reins dropped from her clutch. She bounced from the rutted pathway, from the wagon's wobble, and her backside took a beating as the wagon veered off the trail and into the woods.

Chapter Eleven

The chuck wagon's canvas top clipped a tree branch as it careened into the woods. Lisette tried to curb the horses, but their momentum proved too great for her meager skill. A barrel fell from its mooring, crashing and breaking.

Hazily, she spied Gil and his mount charging toward her. Thank God! He had come back for her.

Big Red, his mane flying, his hooves eating up the ground, hove with his rider to the team. Gil swung his lariat and caught the lead gray's neck. He jumped from the saddle, grabbing the gray by rope and by the neck. As the riderless Big Red slowed and circled back, Gil dug his heels in the ground. Dust and his hat flying, he held on tightly. The draught horses whickered and whinnied, then skidded to a stop, the metal of traces and harnesses clanging. Gil righted himself.

Lisette set the brake, and he hobbled the leaders.

He yanked the bandana from his neck and jerked it across his dust-covered face as he stomped toward Lisette. "What the hell did you think you were doing?"

Sweeping her hair out of her face and leaning toward her husband, she asked, "Are you all right?"

"No thanks to you." He brushed his sleeves. "You could have killed my horses and wrecked my wagon."

And gotten both of us killed in the process, she thought. Evidently he wasn't concerned about her fate. Should she explain that fear had compelled her into driving the team out of control and off the path? No . . . she must not show frailty . . .

"I didn't mean to hurt them. I was pushing ahead to—"

"For all I know, you were trying to steal my team and wagon."

Unable to restrain herself, she flinched as if struck. "I . . . I was not. I wouldn't have."

"Tell that to your brother." Gil tied Big Red to the chuck wagon, then backtracked to glare at his wife. Hatless under the Texas sun, he stood below her. "You didn't think twice about stealing his stuff."

She did feel guilty over purloining Adolf's property, yet he'd had years of her free labor and he'd taken her dowry money. Neither had anything to do with the here-and-now. Her husband considered her an abuser of animals, a thief, a speaker of damnable tongues, a liar, and a deceiver.

So much had happened this afternoon. Earlier, he'd revered her, had wanted her body, and now . . .

Warily she met his rank disgust. Yearning to plead his understanding and acceptance, too prideful to do it, she straightened her shoulders. "If I were intent on taking what isn't mine, why would I have been traveling north?"

"Looks like you were headed to Austin."

127

His charge, she realized, was just too ridiculous to address. *"Ich—"* *Don't let me start that again,* she prayed. Climbing down from the seat, she pulled up to her full height. "I'll rub down the horses."

"Your concern touches me. But it's not necessary." He kicked a rock, sending it flying. "As soon as we catch up with Preacher Wilson, I'm ordering him to take you to Lampasas."

"You can't mean that."

One hand flattened on the floorboard. "Why wouldn't I?"

When he'd proposed to her, she'd accused him of having a less-than-sublime view of marriage, but her opinion had since changed. She replied, "You're too honorable to quit on me."

"Don't make me into something I'm not."

"Don't make yourself into something you're not." She looked him in the eye. "I may not be what you expected, but you're too good a man to turn your back on your marriage vows."

"You'd like to think so."

"I know so."

"Give it up, Lisette. You and I weren't meant to be. Other men's leavings don't interest me."

If she'd held a smidgen of doubt over his hurtful remark regarding her ability to please him, it vanished. Her heart broke all over again, and despite the warm afternoon, she felt cold and exposed. She wasn't woman enough for him.

Again she peered at the man she had trusted above anyone else. His arms crossed over his chest, he perused her with a holier-than-thou countenance.

"You expected me to be pure," she said, "yet *you* weren't."

"I'm a man."

There was no doubt about his masculine attributes, and she damned herself for gazing upon the male who had brought her such satisfaction . . . yet had received but a trifle in return. "So?"

"So a man sows his wild oats."

She laughed bitterly. Why was it right for men to take what they wanted, when women had to pay and pay for even one mistake in trust? Here she had spent four agonizing years paying for her lack in judgment with Thom Childress, while she was to him as the "wild oats" were to her husband: nothing.

What did it matter, though, how Thom had perceived her? The only feeling she had about it was regret — regret that he had swindled her out of her chastity.

She had lived through Thom's rejection. She could live through Gil's. But why did it hurt so deeply this time?

Past her closed throat, she asked, "Where do we go from here?"

"I don't know about you, but I'm going to Kansas."

"Why does that sound as if I won't be going with you?"

"Why don't you cease with the wounded-innocent performance? You didn't lose anything from our tumble in the leaves. But I feel like I owe you something. You are my legally wedded and bedded wife."

How could he think she'd lost nothing? Didn't hope count for anything? When she'd left Fredericksburg, it had been to follow an ambiguous dream of Chicago and hatmaking. Gil McLoughlin had changed all that . . . she had begun to dream the impossible.

"You're right. I lost nothing. But I believe I have earned something." She paused. "I've earned the right to the truth. Were you coming back for me?"

He shook his head slowly.

The headache that had precipitated all this hell returned. "Is impurity sufficient cause to forsake a wife?"

"What the hell does that mean?"

"Maybe I'm not making myself clear," she cut in. "I often don't make myself clear. Being a *Hun*, I have difficulty at times with the language of this country, so please bear with me. As you pointed out, we are legally wedded and bedded. Is my lack of virginity enough to turn your back on our marriage?"

Dead quiet. A muscle ticked in his jaw. At last he admitted, "I got shut of one wife. I suppose I'm capable of doing it again."

She staggered, then stood petrified with dread. All along she'd assumed the first Mrs. McLoughlin had been the one to do the leaving. Wrong. Moreover, he'd said he was capable of abandoning a second wife.

Her greatest fear was coming true.

Where was her faith in him? He wouldn't leave her . . . he *wouldn't*. She couldn't be *that* wrong about him. Maybe she'd mistaken his meaning. Hoping and praying this was the case, she asked, "What . . . what do you mean?"

"It means I've married my second piece of goods. I divorced the first one after she bore another man's child."

Lisette sucked in her breath. Now she understood his unyielding resistance. What a horrible, horrible disservice she'd done by not being courageous enough for total honesty—*before* the wedding.

"Oh, Gil, how awful," she murmured sincerely, her self-pity gone. She yearned to give comfort; his face was dark with hurt past and present. "I will never be unfaithful."

She reached to touch his shoulder; he deflected her fingers, and his eyes like ice-coated tin, he said, "I've heard enough. I've wasted enough time for an afternoon."

God, help us both. But the Lord helped those who helped themselves. Yes, she was in the wrong, but Gil had been the one to demand marriage as well as her body. She would not abide veiled threats, nor would she live in fear of being deserted.

Advancing on her husband, Lisette said, "I may have been less than you expected, but you're less than I expected, too."

Brushing the Stetson that had fallen from his head when he'd stopped the horses, he imparted yet another glare. "In what way?"

"I never took you for a maker of empty promises."

He shoved the crumpled hat atop his head of black hair. "If you've concocted something to manipulate me, forget it. It won't work."

"I've concocted nothing. You promised to escort me to Kansas, and you promised to protect me all the way there. Likewise, you promised not to leave me. Furthermore, we made vows before God, and I don't intend to let you forsake them."

Obviously taken aback, he swallowed and stared at the ground. His thumbs tucked behind his gunbelt, he half turned to squint at the sun, then back to the chuck wagon.

"I did make promises." His voice was slow and measured. "I won't renege."

"Good," she said with the courage that had failed her so many times. "I expect as much."

He removed his thumbs from his gunbelt and stepped forward to grab a hank of her hair. "Don't think you've pulled some sort of coup, Lisette. As I said, I got shut of one piece of baggage, and I'll do it again, if you don't toe the mark. You will honor the deal you made. You're going to cook your way to Kansas." He freed his fingers as if he'd been scalded. "Do whatever it takes—and women know a few methods—to keep your lusts to yourself."

Flabbergasted and offended, she mocked his crushing words of earlier that afternoon. "Don't flatter yourself."

"With you, I don't."

"Believe me, I will never, ever grab your ankle again."

"I mean, keep your lusts away from my *men*."

"I've given you *no call* for a remark such as that. And if this venture is to be successful, you must never say such things again."

He blinked. "I suppose we do need to save face in front of my men. Be warned, Lisette. I expect you to act as if you're a happy, *faithful* wife."

"Faithful will be no problem. As for happy, I'll do

it. Somehow. And you might want to work on your own expression. You look like you've just eaten a sour pickle."

That night, Lisette tried to ease the tension between herself and Gil by making amends in her own way. She did her best to repair his crumpled Stetson.

He tossed it in the campfire and told her, "When I want extra from you, I'll tell you. For now, I want nothing but your cooking."

"Fair enough," she replied, watching the hat draw up and disintegrate like the shreds of her hopes.

In the days following the calamity of the meadow, Lisette gave everything to Gil's demand: she did her job and left him alone.

From way before sunrise to way after sundown, she toiled at each and every duty ascribed to a trail cook—and more. She allowed no one to assist her. At night she made certain she didn't touch his ankle, but she was well aware of each moment he carried his bedroll outdoors. Every night she cried into the floorboard.

For a week this went on.

And the same seven days began again.

Fifteen days passed from that awful day in the meadow. She began to accept that she'd never win her husband's understanding, yet her spirit could not be crushed. That evening she went about her chores, and tried once more for his attention.

Following him as he left the campsite, she said, "If you've got a minute . . ."

"What do you want?"

"I've noticed, well, your hair could use a trim. And I believe you told me barbering is part of my duties."

"I'll get a haircut in Lampasas."

He stomped away, leaving her frustrated anew.

Damn her, using a haircut as a ploy to get on a man's good side. Gil stomped into the woods, relieved himself, and crammed the part of him that wanted attention back into his britches. Buttoning up was no mean feat, since he stayed half-hard despite his anger and disgust. All he had to do was look at Lisette and the old passions roused. But it would be a cold day in hell before he'd act on them.

Taking his time, he made his way back to camp. A quartet of cowhands circled the fire. Johns Clark played the French harp; Fritz Fischer finished off an apple turnover, licked his fingers, and left. Stretched out, Blade Sharp rested his head on his saddle, his hands laced across his stomach. And Wink Tannington was talking to Lisette.

"I hate to trouble you, ma'am," Gil heard Tannington say, "but I've got a smarting shoulder. Wrenched it this afternoon. Do you reckon you could rub some liniment on it?"

"Certainly, Wink." She pointed to an empty, upturned barrel. "Have a seat over there, and I'll be right with you."

Gil didn't cotton to her rubbing anything into anyone, but a cookie was expected to be an amateur doctor, so he simply frowned and scissored to the ground. He retrieved his whittling knife, picked up a

134

piece of oak. His line of sight was aimed at Tannington.

The one-armed cowpoke doffed his shirt. Lisette, a bottle in hand, poured from it. Tannington sighed as the liniment touched his right shoulder. The fingers that had touched Gil McLoughlin in passion now stroked the arm and shoulder of his employee. Tannington's eyes rolled back. His legs spread, and Gil saw that the Mississippian was getting aroused.

Christ. Tannington wasn't the only one. Gil wanted her hands touching the flesh a wife ought to be caressing.

The piece of oak dropped from his grip; he started to put a halt to Tannington's lusts, but the cowpoke brought his legs together and blushed.

"Thank you, ma'am. That'll be enough."

It better be. Gil picked up the oak piece again. Weeks on the road were getting to the entire company, he knew. It would be a good thing, reaching Lampasas and its whore. Trouble was, what the devil was he going to do, once they got there? He couldn't visit the doxies, and he wouldn't seek Lisette out.

At that moment Blade Sharp raised up from his nap. "Say, Miz Good Biscuits, since ya're of a mind to doctoring, think I could talk ya outta a little barbering?"

Not replying, Lisette replaced the cap on the liniment bottle.

Johns Clark took the harmonica from his mouth and studied the goings-on. Gil kept an eye on it all, too.

Sharp rolled a cigarette and lit it. Taking the sto-

135

gie from his mouth, he picked a piece of tobacco from the tip of his tongue to examine it. "You ain't gonna help me out, gal?"

Gil did the answering. "See the barber in Lampasas."

While he trusted Tannington and the others to keep their lusts to themselves, he held no such respect for Blade Sharp. *Best keep an eye on that one.*

The morning after Blade Sharp had asked for a haircut, Lisette set the breakfast dishes to rights, then picked up the ax. Dawn was sending ribbons of orange across the eastern horizon as she split firewood. The only man left in camp was Matthias Gruene.

He walked up to her and took the ax out of her hand. His brown eyes troubled, he said, "You have a right to help, Lise."

Since her wedding, he'd tried to speak with her, but she had avoided him, thanks to his criticism of the union. Today, though, she replied, "I ask no favors for being a woman."

"Being a woman has nothing to do with it." Aggravation dented Matthias's mouth. "As nighthawk, Willie Gaines would be doubling as cook's louse, were he alive. Besides that, the cowpokes are supposed to pitch in and help you."

"That wasn't what I was given to understand," she replied, and could have bitten her tongue.

"Gil said you're supposed to do everything?"

"He said nothing of the kind."

But Gil *had* spelled out a cook's duties. The day

136

he'd asked for marriage, he had been clear about her responsibilities. Why had he lied?

Common sense had a word with her suspicious mind: *Think about what you'd accuse him of.* He wasn't a liar. And he *was* the boss. It was within his right to set any conditions, any responsibilities for his underlings. If he expected her to work alone, then fine. She would continue to do so.

Since she had no wish to discuss her husband, she switched the topic. "I understand we're to reach Lampasas tomorrow."

"Right."

"The men have been talking nonstop about it," she said. "They all seem to have plans. You, on the other hand, haven't said a word on the subject."

He didn't comment, and she scrutinized her brown-haired friend. Matthias was tall, hale, robust, and even-featured—the attributes young ladies found attractive. Yet she'd never known him to have an affair of the heart. Of course he was young—twenty-three wasn't old for a bachelor—but wasn't it a shame he'd never found someone to love and make marriage and a home with, rather than taking to the lonely life of a cowboy?

"What about you, Matthias? Will you seek out the Lampasas ladies?"

An odd look crossed his square-jawed face. "Ladies don't interest me."

"Matthias!" A vision from the past burst forth. "Surely you aren't like Rudolf Klein!"

He chuckled. "No, Lise, I am not like our old schoolmate. I *do* have an interest in the fair sex. I

137

said *ladies* don't interest me. I am interested in one lady."

"Who, Matthias? Tell me. I want to hear all about her."

"Frau Busybody, I will not tolerate your prying." He shook a finger. "I came over to chop wood. Will you allow me?"

She shook her head. "No."

"You're too pigheaded for your own good," he said, exasperated.

"Work, Matthias—it awaits you. But not *my* work."

As he walked away to collect his hat and lariat, she wondered about him. She had been prying, but why didn't he wish to discuss his lady friend? He rode out of camp. And Lisette hoped everything would turn out well for him.

You've turned into a romantic, just like Anna Uhr. Given the hopeless situation with Gil, Lisette supposed she'd lost the last grip on sanity.

Ten minutes later, she rubbed her brow with the back of a hand . . . and caught sight of Blade Sharp. A shiver of revulsion went through her. Every man in the outfit had been cordial and nice, except him. For the past week—and always away from the others—he had made a nuisance of himself. Last night had been his closest to showing his true colors in front of her husband.

Forget any more firewood. She tossed what she had in the cooney, then rushed to finish harnessing the draught horses. But she wasn't quick enough to deflect Blade Sharp.

Running an overlong nail down the scar on his face, he asked, "Got any more coffee, gal?"

"You'll have to wait for the midday break." She hurried with the harnessing.

"Don't want no coffee, noways."

"Aren't you supposed to be herding up the mother cows?"

At her own question, she grimaced. The practice of leaving newborn calves behind was an abomination which no one seemed to mind . . . except for Lisette.

With Blade Sharp advancing on her, this was no time to be thinking of cows.

"Ya sure are purty, gal. I been hankering for ya since the first night ya showed up. Figgered ya'd set sights on McLoughlin, him being the nabob boss, but I been biding my time."

"Go away."

He cupped his private parts, jiggling them. "The two of ya ain't been getting along, I can tell by the way he's been sneering at ya. So I'm going to show ya what it's like to have a real man betwixt yar legs."

"Get away from me." She hurried toward the wagon step.

"I like the ones that fight. Makes me get real hard."

He insinuated his reeking bulk between her and the chuck wagon. She shrank from his presence and the stink of his liquored breath and ducked away.

She put her foot on the wagon step, but he grabbed her from behind, forcing the air from her diaphragm, and snapped her against his damnable body. She tried to scream but found no voice.

The buckle of his gunbelt dug into her spine. She kicked his shin and tried to elbow his side as he

139

rasped, "I'm wantin' me a piece of something tart. Like a big piece of Miz Good Biscuits."

He threw her to the ground. She tried to roll away. But he was on her before she could move. His greasy hand clamped over her mouth. "Ya're a good fighter, girl. Hope it don't get so rough I have to kill ya. But I will if I have to."

The other hand loosened his gunbelt as well as the buttons of his trousers. She continued to fight him, yet he managed to rip Willie Gaines's britches from her waist. When he did, she hoisted a hand to gouge his eye, drawing blood but missing her target. He hauled back his fist, connecting it with her jaw. Dazed from the pain, she went limp.

Again he hit her face, this time with the flat of his hand. Reds, blues, and whites flashed in her eyelids. She tried to fight him — tried. With the last strength she had, Lisette clamped her thighs against his invasion.

And then he went still . . . as a gun barrel clicked above their heads.

"Get off my wife," Gil demanded.

Oh, God in heaven, he'll think I invited this.

Chapter Twelve

Gil shoved the six-shooter's barrel against the back of Blade Sharp's head, morning light glinting off the steel. It had been naive of him to think such a jackass as Sharp would leave Lisette be, simply because she carried the McLoughlin name.

"Unless you want your brains scattered all over the State of Texas, you'd better get off my wife."

Sharp rolled away from Lisette. She clutched the tatters of her clothes as her molester grappled for footing. Sharp's breeches collected at his feet; he pulled them up fast.

"Lisette, get back." Gil reached for Sharp's discarded gunbelt. "Way back."

She scrambled to huddle behind a wagon wheel at the same moment that Sharp challenged, "If ya think ya're man enough, McLoughlin, come on. Fight for yar woman." His fingers crooked in invitation, and his eyes went to the hand holding his gunbelt. "Let's make it a fair fight, though. Gimme my gun."

Gil was at the point of murder, thinking about those paws on Lisette, yet he was done with killing, thanks to the war.

He replaced his gun, Thelma, in her holster, then tossed Sharp's gunbelt across Big Red's saddlehorn. His hand made a fist as he stepped closer. "Frankly, Sharp, you're not worth a bullet."

Sharp laughed. "Ya're yellow, McLoughlin."

As Gil reared back to punch him, he said, "I never said anything about not defending my lady."

His fist connected with Sharp's nose; he heard the bone pop. Blood splattered. Sharp tumbled backward; he righted himself to advance again. Gil caught the fist with his arm before landing another punch on the cowhand's jaw. The man roared in anger, bending forward to thrust his elbow into Gil's stomach. Gil feinted away from the blow.

A punch from Sharp ripped the skin under his left eye. He wasn't down. Both his arms flipped upward; Sharp crouched to grab Gil's shoulder. After kicking a knee into his opponent's stomach, Gil pounded his fist into the jackass's face.

At last, the cowpuncher fell to the dirt, clutching his gut and face simultaneously.

"Whew." Gil rubbed his brow.

Sharp slithered toward the chuck wagon, reached to the underbelly, and plucked an ax from the cooney. Gil kicked his wrist. The ax whirled out of reach.

With his head, Gil motioned southward. "Collect your gear, Sharp." Panting, he rubbed his injured cheekbone with his bandana. "Your services are no longer required."

Sharp spat blood while wiping the back of his hand across his mouth; he turned his eyes to the gunbelt laying on Big Red's saddlehorn. "I ain't leaving without my revolver."

"Yes, you are."

Evidently Sharp knew Gil was serious. He said, "I'll get ya for this, McLoughlin."

"The only thing you'll get is packing. Do it, Sharp. I want you gone in five minutes."

It took less than three.

As Blade Sharp dug his spurs into his horse's flanks and headed out, Gil turned to his wife. Huddled under the wagon, her shoulders hunched, she had buried her face in the crook of her elbow. Instinct shouted to him to give her comfort. Yet the only words forming were rough: "Lisette, you can get up now."

He heard her muffle a German reply against her forearm. "I'm sorry for speaking as a Hun." Shaking her head, she peeked between the spokes. Anguish written in each line of her lovely face, she said, "Believe me, I did *nothing* to invite his advances, and I — Gil!"

She crawled from beneath the wagon; a shaking hand reached up to him. "Your face! You're bleeding. Oh, God in heaven, let me help you."

He barely noticed his injury. All he saw was the start of two bruises, one on her cheek, the other on her jaw. And he warmed to his wife's tenderness and consideration. After nearly being raped, she was more concerned for him than for herself.

"I must get you stitched," she said worriedly.

He crouched beside her, closing his fingers around her hand. "Don't worry about me. I'm worried about you."

"I . . . I'm all right." She tore a strip from her apron, dabbed it against his cut. "It would take more than the likes of Blade Sharp to ruffle me."

"You mean it?"

143

She eyed him squarely. "I have never lied to you, not openly . . . and I don't intend to start now."

He believed her. He thought back on all that had transpired between them. Except for the lie of omission about her lack of virginity—she could have actually told him, since she had spoken in German the day they had had sex, when he'd provoked her into it—there had always been a certain honesty to Lisette.

Maybe he ought to hear what she had to say about herself. Trouble was, she didn't need any more emotional upsets. *You're looking for a way out,* he told himself. Maybe. It was tough, trying to break a vow never to allow a woman to discuss her sexual conquests.

Suddenly he realized how tough it must have been for Lisette, owning up to her past. How very difficult it must have been. How should he handle the here-and-now? Until he could gather his courage, he would quit being so damned mean.

Swallowing, he watched as she collected needle and thread to sew up his wound. *Give her a chance. She'll put the whole of you back together.*

Thinking back on something she'd said, he squeezed her arm and offered, "Lisette, I want you to know something. Never for a moment did I think you made a play for Blade Sharp."

Relief made her lift and drop her shoulders, and her beguiling eyes moistened. "Thank you. Thank you for believing me."

An ill wind that blows good.

This was how Lisette viewed Sharp's attack. It had brought a modicum of peace to her relationship with Gil, and for this she was thankful. Maybe there *was* hope for them.

144

And she was glad to be free of the dastardly cow-hand.

No one seemed to notice he was no longer a part of the outfit. To a man the cowboys were indignant over Sharp's attack. Dinky Peele, Preacher Wilson, and Johns Clark offered to go after him, but the boss put the halters on their idea.

"He's gone," Gil said, "and that's the end of it."

It ended another habit as well. The cowboys quit calling her Miz Good Biscuits, since it reminded her of Sharp. The visual reminders remained: Lisette's bruised face and the stitched skin over her husband's cheekbone.

Life went on.

The Four Aces outfit reached the cedar-flecked out-skirts of Lampasas the next day at noon and corralled the longhorns there. The cowboys were more than ready to partake of all the town had to offer, and Gil advanced them their pay.

They drew lots to see who would be the first ones into town. Oscar Yates and the brawny, slow-talking boy in charge of the remuda, Fritz Fischer, lost out and were left to guard the herd. Fritz was crestfallen.

The grizzled former cookie took it better, saying, "Aw, shucks, I be too old fer antics, anyhoo. I'll keep an eye on the dogies and Her Majesty Sadie Lou, here." He patted the dog's head and received a snap for his efforts. "Ye boys have a good time. And pinch some gal's rear fer me."

Wink and Dinky headed out to do Oscar's bidding. Jakob Lindemann, a man of few words and a large appetite, set a course for the local bakery.

Johns Clark left, but not before smiling and an-nouncing, "Seems to me there's a gal named Jean

145

Dodson lives over by the springs. Think I'll see if she's still got an itch I can scratch."

Matthias departed without a word.

Now, with no one else around, Gil having taken him off to tally the herd, Preacher Wilson called Lisette aside.

The Good Book tucked under an arm, he said, "There's something I've been meaning to talk with you about."

"I'm listening."

His eyes moved upward. " 'Defraud ye not one the other, except it be with consent for a time, that ye may give yourselves to fasting and prayer; and come together again, that Satan tempt you not for your incontinency.' "

"Please, please. Don't quote the New Testament."

"Are you not a believer, child?"

"I believe I've heard enough."

She began to turn, but he caught her arm. "Forget religion, then. The law says I must file a marriage license for you and the mister. That will make your marriage legal. But, Mrs. McLoughlin, I'm not blind. I can tell you and your husband aren't married in the spirit of Canaan. Just by the looks on your faces I see this."

Embarrassed that their private life read like an open book, Lisette wished to be far, far away. Yet she wouldn't turn from the reed-thin preacher, nor from his wise hazel eyes. Never before had she really looked at the man.

He was on the down side of thirty, and had thinning hair and an air of reason. Of course, he had once called her a harlot, but why wouldn't he think such? No wife of Caesar would have stalked a trail drive, would have agreed to a marriage less than sublime. Lisette McLoughlin wasn't above reproach, but she did have her pride, and she said, "Mind your own business, sir."

"I am a man of God . . . but I am also just one of the flock. You are a good woman, you are young, and you could have your choice of husband. I also see that you are unhappy. I could . . . I could neglect to file that license."

Though appreciative of his sacrifice, she could not give an immediate response. Still, she wouldn't lie. "You wed Gil and me in the eyes of God, for better or for worse. And the marriage is real, though it isn't without its flaws. We have consented to disagree."

Lisette spotted a carefree pair of bees flitting above a cedar bush; would that life could be so simple! But it wasn't. She addressed the preacher as well as her marital problem. "I think you should speak with my husband before making a decision on filing the license."

"I did, three days ago. He told me to forget it."

Why would such an answer shock her? She should have expected as much, yet a dagger of regret lanced her heart. Her eyes snapped to the source of her hurt. Gil was handing his sorrel over to the wrangler.

He wanted to end their marriage. Well, why make it easy for him? All right, she hadn't come to the marriage a virgin, but *he* had been the one to pester her into submission. Pester? From the beginning, her desires had superseded all reason. Whatever the case, Gil was bound by God; why not let him be bound by law? Marriage had been his idea.

"Reverend, we are married under God's ordinance. I have given myself to him. And we have agreed not to agree. But it's a long way to Kansas, and there could be a child. God wouldn't want me to name such a babe a bastard. File the license."

Eli Wilson smiled. "God will be merciful."

"I hope so."

He bowed and took himself off.

Remembering her husband's admission that she hadn't satisfied him as a woman, Lisette was rocked by what she had asked Eli Wilson to do.

There was no backing out; the preacher had mounted a mare from the remuda and was gone.

Now what should she do?

It would be best to take matters as they happened, and deal with them as needed. Which didn't mean she had to slink away. After all, the preacher had spoken to her husband three days ago, before the Blade Sharp incident, and Gil had been civil since. Civil, and almost husbandly. Hope wasn't dead—it merely slept.

And when he ambled over to her, she asked, "Will you drive me into Lampasas?"

"I'd figured to."

Within minutes she was sitting beside him on the spring seat and they were on Main Street. Leaving the team and wagon at the livery stable, he set off to make arrangements for Willensstark's return to Adolf and to post some letters.

"Would you mind posting this one, too?" Lisette asked, handing him an envelope for Anna Uhr.

In a veiled report, Lisette told Anna about the wedding, about the bouquet pressed in Gil's Bible, and about the wonders of travel over the trail. Pride had kept her from apprising her friend of anything negative.

Lisette did, however, caution Anna against making any mention to Adolf of her plans or proposed where-

148

abouts. She didn't feel safe from her brother's clutches, even though she wore Gil McLoughlin's ring.

While she had no wish to inform Adolf and Monika of her whereabouts, she wondered about them. Had the peach saplings taken root? Who would butcher the hogs this spring? Would Adolf's bad leg get worse from bending over to plant the cabbage garden? How was Monika enduring her pregnancy? Most importantly, how were the boys?

Lisette's chest tightened as she recalled baby Ludolf. Soon he would be walking, and she'd miss that significant event. And Karl and Viktor. She chuckled, remembering their pranks, their scruffy faces, their unruly caps of blond hair. Right then, she wished she could be brushing their hair.

"Don't be ridiculous," she muttered.

Glancing around as she waited on the courthouse lawn for her husband, Lisette saw oak and pecan trees, a multitude of low-growing cedar, plus a few native stone buildings among the clapboard ones. Lampasas was a pretty town, for Texas. The edge of town wasn't so winsome, she recalled. There, the feeder to the Chisholm Trail had cut a deep groove into the sea of grass, and there hung in the air a dust smelling of cattle, cattle, cattle. She'd grown accustomed to the sharp aroma over the past weeks. Nonetheless she yearned for a real bath and a real bed.

Lisette eyed a general store nearby. Shop, shop, shop, a voice in her brain intoned. That store would sell the makings for bonnets, plus the ready-made clothes which would free her from britches and men's shirts.

She had three twenty-dollar gold pieces in her pocket. Gil had told her to use them for anything she wanted, but she hesitated. She wouldn't spend a penny of his money, not when so much remained unsettled between them.

Instead of careening through Litton's General Store as if she were set on buying out their wares, and especially their hats, Lisette glanced down the street, to the Lusty Lady Saloon. Tinny piano music blared from its swinging doors. A painted woman, plumes in her hair and red satin draping her voluptuous body, emerged from the establishment, her arm around Matthias.

"Your lady would be ashamed of you," Lisette scolded him *sotto voce,* certainly out of earshot.

"Afternoon, ma'am."

She turned to the strange voice holding a Southern drawl considerably softer than a Texan's accent. A nattily dressed gentleman approached Lisette and tipped his hat. He looked to be in his early thirties and had a refined air about him.

"Excuse my forward — good heavens, ma'am, you've been injured."

"I had an unfortunate accident. That's all."

"Is there anything I can do to help? I've heard a cold steak helps bruises." Concern in his dark eyes, the stranger went on. "Why don't you let me fetch one?"

"Please don't bother. I truly am fine." And she was — a bit beat up, but fine. "My husband is taking wonderful care of me," she overstated.

"Where I come from . . . well, you don't want to hear all that." He took a step forward. "May I present myself? I am Charles Franklin Hatch. And you are . . .?"

"Lisette Kel — McLoughlin."

"McLoughlin." A muscle ticked above his eye as he

smiled. "Nice to meet you, Mrs. McLoughlin."

"The pleasure is all mine, sir."

"Your husband . . . Where is the fine man?"

While she considered Mr. Hatch a gentleman, she was beginning to think him much too nosy. And she was somewhat suspicious of his intentions. "Mister Hatch, I really think it wrong, my speaking to you without proper introductions."

Gallantly, he nodded. "You're right, Mrs. McLoughlin. Where were my manners? As a gentleman of Georgia, I apologize for putting you in a delicate position." He began a retreat, then stopped. "Perhaps we'll meet again, when your husband is present. I'd be honored to buy supper for the two of you."

He tipped his hat and went on his way, and he dropped from Lisette's thoughts.

She scanned the surroundings again. Once before she had waited on a courthouse lawn for Gil McLoughlin. Was it mere weeks ago she had been so filled with hope for the future?

At present she had no idea of what it would hold.

"Lisette."

She straightened and turned to her husband. He stood a couple of yards in the distance, near the street, his brow shaded by a new, wide-brimmed straw Stetson. He held a cigar, the first she'd ever seen him smoke.

Of course he wore his usual attire—gunbelt and Thelma, bandana, denim shirt, doeskin vest, close-fitting britches—but the leather chaps had been left in the chuck wagon. She noticed his feet. New boots, those were new boots, larger ones. They made a statement. As did his fresh haircut.

151

She yearned to make peace with her handsome, unhappy husband.

"Did you buy dresses and hats?" When she shook her head, he said, "We'd better rectify that. You can't go on wearing Willie Gaines' gear forever." He took off in the direction of Litton's. In the middle of the street, he turned back to her. "What's keeping you?"

An hour later, they checked into the Keystone Hotel, two boxes hanging from strings in Lisette's hands and a hat tugged down over her brow to shade her bruises. Three boxes were tucked under Gil's arm as he signed the registry.

An odd realization was that they would be sharing one room. She had suspected Gil would ask for two.

"We have baths," the desk clerk pointed out, leaning back to get away from the clientele's odor. "Hot springs baths. They're extra, of course. Fifty cents. You interested?"

"We're interested."

"That'll be a buck-fifty for the room and the baths."

Gil handed over the appropriate sum and took the skeleton key from the bespectacled clerk. He dug in his pocket, extracted a coin to flip it across the counter. "Get someone to fetch my trunk. And send up some food, will you?"

"Of course." Smiling and revealing a gold tooth, the clerk pocketed the extra specie. "Anything else, sir?"

"Leave us alone after you've done as I requested."

Lisette's heart tripped. Gil wanted to be alone with her. *Why?*

152

Chapter Thirteen

If Gil had expectations of bathing with her, or even talking with her, he didn't act on either, and Lisette swallowed a large dollop of disappointment. Disappointment was made to be swallowed.

Outside the Keystone Hotel dusk came and went while she twiddled her thumbs and waited for her husband to join her. She knew he had entered the bathing area; she'd been with him at the time. When she'd waited in the corridor, fully dressed and smelling of lilac-scented soap, he had yelled out, "Go on to the room. I'll be there after a bit."

Hours had passed since the wooden trunk was delivered. The meal sent up by the desk clerk had grown cold and congealed. Right now, as the clock on the bedside table struck eight, the fried chicken had withered to petrified proportions and the potato salad probably had enough sickness in it to fell the entire Prussian Army.

She paced the room. Her eyes kept catching on the five boxes. Litton's General Store sported a large selection of dry goods. Gil had picked out five dresses

153

and the proper underpinnings, though Lisette had es-chewed a corset.

"I refuse to lace myself into one of those contrap-tions, fashion or no fashion," she had announced vehe-mently. *Even if I could afford one,* she added silently.

"I don't blame you," he'd said. "What about this bonnet? Your face is getting brown. Like it?"

It was a hideous thing of calico, though in vogue for most pioneer women, and Lisette hated it. Yet the beast nestled among the pile of purchases.

And Gil had insisted on purchasing lanolin "because your hands are rough," plus ribbons and hairpins "since you lost yours a while back."

"I don't want these things," she protested in a small voice, not wishing to be beholden to him. She dug in her pocket and turned to the proprietor. "I'll have this cake of lilac soap, and that will be it."

"Wrap it all up, and add some lilac water."

Lisette's chin was not perhaps as jutted as Gil's, but she thrust it upward. "All I want is the soap."

"Tally up the clothes, man, and be quick about it."

The proprietor rushed to do the cattleman's bid-ding, and Gil said to Lisette, "I won't have you smell-ing like the wrath of God or looking like Willie Gaines' ghost."

"Aren't I fortunate?" she said breezily, not feeling her sarcasm at all.

Now, as the hours passed in a second-floor room of the Keystone Hotel, she was especially glad for not go-ing wild in the emporium.

Plainly, Gil had no use for a browned woman with rough hands who reminded him of a man, dead or otherwise, least of all the same woman he didn't want to be legally wed to. A woman who was used goods.

154

Her eyes went to the iron bed built for two. Already she knew the sheets were clean as a whistle and smelled of the sun. The bed had a snowy white crocheted spread and four plump pillows, and it invited more than sleep. Therein lay the obstacle. Even if Gil were to charge into this room right now, saying he'd forgiven her, and even though their marriage was duly recorded, she would shy away from disrobing.

Frankly, you weren't that good.

Why hadn't she thought about that while speaking with the preacher?

Gil's reprove tumbled over and over and over again in her head and heart. In his words, "Damn."

Dressed in a robin's-egg-blue dress of corded silk — totally frivolous for the upcoming days on the trail but insisted upon by her husband — Lisette sat down on a hard-backed chair facing the window. From the Lusty Lady Saloon below, piano music blared. Was Gil there? Had he sought out a woman trained in the art of giving pleasure?

Lisette shivered. With his passions, he couldn't go on forever without relieving the pressure. Was her husband releasing his seed . . . and smiling?

If she had an ounce of pride, she'd leave this hotel room. Instead, she slammed closed the window and cut out the sounds of the Lusty Lady.

Another hour passed before he rattled the knob and opened the creaking door.

"You didn't eat your dinner," Gil said, and she heard him walk across the room.

"I wasn't hungry."

"You'll get skinny if you don't eat."

"As long as I can do my work — thin, brown-faced, rough-handed — why would you care?"

155

He chuckled. "You have all the makings of a shrew."

"You won't get an argument there. I *am* a shrew." She studied the worn rug. "I used to be somewhat more amenable—before I encountered your ugly face."

"Do you think my face is ugly, Lisette?"

Her muscles tensed. She refused to answer, would not turn to him. He cut around the chair to halt in front of her. At last she turned her face up to him.

He wasn't tousled nor did he appear sex-spent; his look was as fresh as a man just returned from a bath. Although they had lain together but once, she could tell when he didn't have the look—or smell—of sex. No, he hadn't spent the past hours in some strumpet's arms.

Gil repeated his question.

Ugly? No, he wasn't. Despite the new wound under his eye, which was reddened and puffed, he was still as attractive as ever. His hair needed smoothing, and she yearned—despite any rhyme or reason—to touch the indention on his chin. All around, he looked magnificent, wearing fresh clothes and those provocative boots. And she remembered exactly how he'd looked, naked.

Desire, cursed desire began to build in Lisette.

Replying to his question, she said, "You're about as attractive as a cake of lye soap."

"And you are as beautiful as heather on the hillside."

She hadn't expected his tone to be soft, nor his eyes to gaze tenderly at her. For once his inflection held the tone of his homeland. Back in Fredericksburg, she'd wanted to know everything about him. She still did. While she knew many things about this man she'd taken to husband, Lisette realized there were many facets yet to discover—among them, what did he want besides a woman untouched by another man.

And where *had* he been?

She voiced her question, and he replied, "Taking care of business. Hiring more cowpokes." He paused. "And mulling the question of you and me. I found Eli Wilson, told him to file our marriage license. I want to settle this trouble between us."

Relieved that he had spoken with the preacher, she was nonetheless unconvinced of their long-range potential for marital success. "I can't be what I was not."

"I know." He crossed to the bed and sat on its edge. Dropping his wrists between his spread legs, his head ducking, he said, "Yesterday morning I decided . . . I never thought I'd be asking, but I got to thinking about something you said. You told me there'd been but one man in your life besides me. I want you to tell me what happened."

Back in San Antonio, when Lisette learned Thom Childress had made vacant promises, Aunt Ernestine had warned her never to speak of him to another man. *Onkel* August's English wife had said no man enjoys hearing tales of another. Lisette believed his wise counsel.

She abandoned the seat, walked to the window, and stared down with unfocused eyes. The room took on the quiet of a crypt. She could feel Gil's gaze on her back, and she heard his breathing as well as the rasp of a match striking. Even before a ribbon of smoke waved toward the ceiling, she smelled the sweet scent of expensive tobacco.

"Lisette . . . how many other men have known your body?"

"I told you: one."

"Just one?" he asked slowly.

157

"I said one."

"Tell me what happened."

"I'd rather not dredge up the past."

"We'll get nowhere with lies of omission between us."

"Lies of omission? Seems to me you left out a few details about your former wife."

"I'm not here to talk about Elizabeth."

Lisette almost laughed at the irony of the woman's name. "Elizabeth, you say? Do you know the German forms of her name?"

"No, Lisette, I don't."

"One is Lisette."

Another tendril of smoke curled through the room, and she moved to open the window. She heard Gil as he tamped the smoke into a dish. "That's where the similarity ends," he replied at last. "I recognize you're not Betty."

"The similarity ends with our names?" She disliked herself for being so cynical, but why not? "I was under the impression she and I had another similarity—our both disappointing you."

A moment passed. "Lisette, we can spend this evening arguing, or we can get on with the conversation. Which do you choose?"

"Getting on with the conversation."

"Then tell me why you didn't come to me a virgin."

If this was the sole way to air their problems, so be it.

She closed the window and turned away from it. Speaking as if she were narrating someone else's life, she answered, "I met him in San Antonio. I'd gone there to wait out the war. My uncle and his wife took me in. A neighbor had a millinery shop, and she offered to teach me the trade. A young man delivered

158

supplies for the shop, and we became friendly. When Uncle August left to join my father's regiment, Thom asked my aunt for permission to court me. I thought I was in love with him."

Gil rose from the bed. "Go on."

"Thom was conscripted into the army. He was to leave for training on the first of February. The day before he left, we received word my father and Uncle August had died in battle. I was . . . I was grief-stricken. And Thom preyed on it—on that, and on his own leaving. He said he might not return from battle, and he didn't wish to leave this earth without having known what it was like to hold me in his arms."

"His was one of the oldest ploys in the world, Lisette."

She wasn't schooled in ploys, but the past four years had versed her in reality. "Tell that to a girl of eighteen. Anyway, he asked me to be his wife, and I said yes. Of course, there was no time to marry. He left the next morning."

"Did he die in combat?"

"He's not dead. On the battlefield, he got a case of—" She laughed dryly. "Dysentery sent him to the infirmary. One of the doctors had a daughter helping out, and Thom and the woman . . ." Lisette sighed. "They were married within a couple of months. The war ended before he returned to his regiment. He brought his wife back to San Antonio."

"The guy must have been crazy not to wait for you."

Perplexed, she gazed at Gil. There was nothing in his eyes, nothing in his expression to indicate he had been less than honest. Yet . . . *Frankly, you weren't that good.*

Gil walked across the room to pull her against his

159

chest. She couldn't let him do this. It was unfair, his holding her as if he meant to be her lover . . . for forever. But how long were his forevers?

She stepped back.

"Do you still love Thom, Lisette?"

Shaking her head, she gave an honest reply. "I do not. I'm not certain I ever did. I was a girl craving affection. That's all."

"Then let's put him in the past."

That was more than fine with Lisette, but just exactly what would happen if they—

Her eyes cut to the bed. If she went with her passions, if he received more satisfaction than the first time, would theirs be a lasting union?

Don't be a Tropf.

Weariness sluiced through her, confession and uncertainty having sapped her strength. Tonight she couldn't deal with the present. Her attention turning to the bed once more, she yearned for its comfort, its solitary comfort. And she almost laughed. For hours she had ached for Gil's appearance; now she wished he would leave.

"Leave me alone," she said.

"Impossible." The tips of his fingers moved lightly across her bruises, and his silver-banded blue eyes became soft as velvet. "I want to cherish and protect and love you till—"

"Love? You told me once it was a foolish notion."

"I expect to—"

"I expect nothing from you, Gil." *Except an honest chance* . . .

"As I told you the night we wed, you can expect the unexpected." His lips moving to her ear, his hand stroking the rise of her breast, he murmured, "Expect

160

to be made love to."

She tensed.

His tongue making circles behind her earlobe, he asked, "Don't you want me?"

That wasn't the issue. Last time it had started this way, Gil's touching and seducing her, and where had it led?

Her eyes heavy with fatigue, she stepped away from his arms and made for the bed. Fully dressed, she lay down on the covers and turned her face to the pillow. She was simply too weary to make a decision she might regret later.

Or maybe she needed to hide one more time.

"I'll have to think about it, Gil."

She's out like a light, Gil thought as he spread her braids across the pillow. Not a muscle did she move as he stripped her of shoes and dress and undergarments. Somehow he got the covers pulled back and her naked form on the bottom sheet. Pulling off his own clothes, he gazed at her. Her beauty held him captive.

She appeared somewhat plumper than the last time he'd gazed at her unclothed body. Not much, just a couple of pounds. Despite her hard work, the trail seemed to be agreeing with her. She was one helluva pioneer woman.

Unlike his former wife, she was molded of good stuff—determined, courageous, and accepting. Never would she try to control. He'd had a problem with Betty trying to run the show. *Put her out of your mind,* he told himself.

As he stretched out next to Lisette, his hand molded to his new wife's breast and his thumb flicked across the coral peak. In her sleep she smiled.

His Lisette was more than any man should expect.

His Lisette?

Nothing like jumping to a conclusion.

Her "I'll have to think about it" left their marriage up in the air. After the events between their wedding and now, he should have expected nothing more. Well, he wasn't going to tuck his tail between his legs and run away.

He would make the loving good this time.

But she was drained, emotionally and physically. She worked hard, too hard, and never complained about the privations of life on the trail. And he, her husband, had given her hell over one lapse in judgment. He, who had a scroll-long list of mistakes in his past.

He doused the hurricane lamp and slid into bed. Pulling her into the cradle of his arms, he held her while she slept. When they made love, would she be as hot as before? He hoped so. He prayed so. This time he wanted to make it right for both of them — before, during, and afterward.

His fingers caressed her jaw, her chin, her temple, and he feathered a kiss on her eyebrow. It was wicked of him, wanting to waken her, but he had a growing desire to make love to her.

Nonetheless, it took Gil another twenty minutes to rouse her from sleep.

Chapter Fourteen

Lisette awoke to moonlight streaming through the hotel window to make shadowy patterns on the bed. And a long-fingered hand was making patterns on her flesh.

Womanly needs coursed through her unclothed body, as if her husband had been touching her intimately for quite some time. His arms were around her. His tongue made circles on her throat, his fingers canvassed the dip of her waist, then between her legs; his toes slid up and down her calf. It took her a moment to realize there was no hostility in his actions.

It took but one more to recall the situation.

"Stop," she moaned.

"Why?"

"Because I don't want to disappoint you."

He reared his head. "Disappoint me? What in hell are you talking about?"

"Don't you remember what you said in the meadow? 'Frankly, you weren't that good.'"

"Oh, my darlin' Lisette, you *are* an innocent." He cuddled her against his broad chest. "You don't even know the difference between good and bad loving."

She gazed into the eyes that watched her closely. "You're making fun of me."

"I'm not. I'm wanting to show you what good loving is all about. Hell, I need to know myself."

Confused by his words, she said, "I don't understand. You've been married before, and surely you've known other women."

"All that is true. But I want to make ours a marriage for keeps."

"You're absolutely sure?"

"Absolutely, positively."

Was he lying? *Trust your instincts*. Instincts? They'd done her wrong, but should she let yesterday's foul up tonight? Going on her feminine desires, she answered, "I like that idea."

"You'll like this one even better."

He rolled to his back, pulling her atop him. She flattened her forearms on the sheet and raised up to study his expression, but his aroused sex, long and thick, pressed against her stomach, rendering her incapable of clear thought.

The hair on his thighs tickled her legs, that on his chest doing the same to her breasts. Her insides were warm and heavy, and those senses sharpened as he whispered, "My angel, let's start all over again."

Once more, she worried. She could accept his offer and take a chance of not satisfying him. Or she could hold on to her pride, and keep a distance between them. But since they were abed, both nude, and he was doing his best to arouse her by touching her most intimately, she decided there might be a chance of giving him a modicum of pleasure.

"All right, husband. Let's start anew."

A grin eased across his face. "Thank you."

His hand abandoned the top of her thighs to stroke her hip, but she scooted back. "G-Gil, I do want you to enjoy yourself. I do not want to make you unhappy. If I do anything you disapprove of, please tell me."

"You are an innocent."

"Not totally. When we did this l-last time, I was going on my instincts."

"Don't quit." He winked boldly. "On second thought . . . give us a kiss."

"Us? Who's this us?"

"Don't get too literal on me." His hands swept down her back. "What about that kiss?"

Her disarrayed braids falling forward, she leaned to plant a kiss on his whisker-shadowed jaw. His "Not good enough" moved her lips to the sensual ones half parted in expectation. What was left of her braids became clouds of hair as he fiddled with the mass. His tongue slid into her mouth, and the rhythm of loving was in his every movement.

She felt the shape of him, turgid and eager, at the portal of the place he had denounced in the meadow.

Yet . . . her body heated further as she wiggled against him. The kiss ended. Her breasts touched his hair-swirled chest, the sensation sending tendrils of heat to the center of her being, and he smiled as she drew in a deep breath of anticipation.

"Will we make love like this?" she asked, raising her head and moving her fingers to the thick mat of hair enticing her.

"If you're willing to give it a try."

"I'd be willing . . . if you think you might like it."

He laughed. "Ah, Lisette, you are some woman. Bold as brass, innocent as a lamb. I like you like this." He reached up to nuzzle her throat. "And I'm so hot I don't know if I can wait too long to have all of you."

Apparently not waiting too long would make it good for him. Last time he had spent a long time warming her up. "It feels as if I've been ready for hours," she admitted in all honesty.

"I've been trying—you can bet I've been trying to get you this way."

Scooting his fingers between their naked bodies, he captured her nipples to touch them gently, then with more pressure. She grimaced, wondering why her breasts were more sensitive than before.

Her concerns subsided as he asked silkily, "Do you still think I'm ugly?"

"No, you vain devil . . . no."

"Then move up a bit, honey." He blew a stream of arousing air across first one nipple, then the other. "Old Son's wanting to pay you a visit."

Levering above him and bracing her palms on his chest, she questioned, "Old Son?"

"Yeah. *This*." He lunged upward and deeply.

Impaled on his shaft, she inhaled deeply and quivered, her muscles tightening around him. "Oh, my."

He didn't move beyond framing her face with his hands and saying, "I'm glad we're together again. And not just this way."

"S-so . . . am . . . I."

"Lisette, my sweet, do you want it slow and deliberate, or do you want it hard and fast?" he whispered, bending his knees and bringing her against his chest. "You set the pace. Show me how you want me to love you."

"But I want to please *you*."

"Do as I say, Lisette. Do it now."

She rocked her hips; he growled with pleasure.

"Touch me," he urged, his thumb grazing her nipples. "Do whatever feels right."

Lowering her face, she pressed her lips to his. And then she was kissing him as he had kissed her in the past, her tongue sliding into his mouth. His flavor was slightly of tobacco and whiskey, but mostly it was what she preferred—the slick, pure taste of Gil.

She pulled back far enough to ask, "Do you like that?"

"Do it again."

Their tongues cavorted, mated; and then his tongue was in her mouth, moving fast and hard. She knew he wanted this from her. She moved her hips against his long, filling length, and a flurry of eagerness if not impatience built within her. He'd told her to set the tempo, and she would. She fancied the idea.

Her hair flying around her, fanning him, she rode him . . . rode him as if he were a stallion. He growled, prodding her on. The springs sang beneath them. Perspiration moistened the cleft between her breasts as his hands cupped her backside, keeping the unwavering rhythm going. She moaned, then cried out as needles of awareness pricked her nerves. How could she have thought the last time was good when this was so much better?

And it got even better. He turned her to her back, his long fingers spreading behind her ears, his hands cupping her jaw. "Now it's my turn, my love," he said in a rasp. "Put your legs around my waist . . . and hold on tight."

She held him. He drove, drove, drove. Her eyes glazed at the intensity of his loving strokes. As the moments turned to minute upon minute, her reasoning became unclear. All she knew in her mindless ecstasy

167

was, that mindless or not, this was *ecstasy*.

"Lisette," he uttered, drawing out her name, reaching the pinnacle of satisfaction at the moment of hers.

Both breathing heavily, they lay contented in each other's arms. Moonlight from the nearby window limned his features as he brought her fingers to his lips and kissed each tip. When he finished, she spread her hand across his emery-like jaw and settled her thumb in the dimple of his chin. She felt reborn, felt as if life had given her another chance. And it had: this was the finest moment of her life.

"Was it better this time?" she asked with bated breath.

A warm growl rolled from his throat. "Do I have to tell you?"

"Yes."

"It wasn't good, darlin'. It was like floating above the clouds, flying to the stars, capturing heaven."

"I guess that means it was good."

"I guess it means we were great together. You, me . . . Old Son." His voice tender and dear, he asked, "Am I making too much of your feelings? How do you feel?"

I think I'm in love. "I feel wonderful!"

"Good."

Nestled close, she curled her fingers around his shoulder. When she'd set out from Fredericksburg, it had been to follow a nebulous dream of freedom. Now she had an anchor. His ambitions would be hers, and she would do everything in her power to see them to fruition.

He needed a partner, a helpmate. She was that person.

And then he shook, shook with laughter.

168

"What are you doing?" she asked, angling back slightly.

"Thinking about you."

The lines radiating from his eyes were deep with mirth, but she'd yet to see the humor. Maybe she hadn't given as much pleasure as she'd thought. Oh, no . . .

"What's so funny?" she asked hesitantly.

"Remember that first morning in camp? I'll never forget the look on your face when you thought Tecumseh Billy was charging you."

Her palm tapped Gil's forearm. "You are not funny. That bull—"

"Steer, honey—steer. Don't forget there's a difference."

"—had me scared half to death."

"But you were cute as a bug, standing there in that god-awful getup, your eyes wide as the Texas sky." His mirth changed to the tightness of promise. "I wanted to haul you into my arms and kiss you till you couldn't see straight."

She smiled, caught up in his mood. "Mmm, I rather like the idea of your doing those things to me. Now."

"Something could be arranged," he drawled, his eyes filled with greater promise. "If you don't mind having a real bull after you."

"If Old Son's the bull, *Liebster*, I'm more than willing."

He pulled her back into his arms, kissed her until she couldn't see straight, and loved her till she was beyond breathless.

In the aftermath of their second coupling, Gil implored, "Tell me something. What does it mean,

'Liebster'?"

She hadn't meant to speak German, but there was no reproach in his question, and she answered, "Beloved."

"Thank God for that. It sorta sounded like 'teamster.' "

They both laughed. "Now you know what my endearment means," she said, feeling his hardness receding within her. "Maybe you'll answer a question for me. I've been wondering for weeks . . . What's in that trunk?"

"I'll show you."

He left the bed. Striking a match, he lit the hurricane lamp.

She grinned at him. "You know, Gil, I think your scars make you all the more handsome."

With feigned exasperation he shook a finger at her. "Woman, keep that up and you'll not be satisfying your curiosity about my trunk."

"I suppose I can wait a few minutes . . ."

"Fine. You go ahead with your gawking." Her face went scarlet, yet he assured her. "Honey, I like your staring at me."

In that case . . . She continued her perusal. Her gaze welded to his slim buttocks, enjoying the muscular view. All fluid motion, he traversed the room. Turning to the side, he flipped open the trunk lid and dug through the contents to extract a plaid garment. It looked like a . . . No, it couldn't be.

"My kilt," he announced, standing once more and holding the red and blue material in front of his midsection.

"Gott in Himmel, it is a skirt. A very short skirt." Her brows furrowing, she asked, "What are you doing with

170

an abbreviated skirt?"

"I wear it." He lowered the garment in question. "And it's not a skirt, it's a kilt."

All skepticism, she commented, "It looks like a skirt to me. I never knew a man to wear such a thing. Of course, there was some talk about Rudolf Klein. Everyone knew he was a bit strange, and—"

"Lisette, all men in Scotland wear kilts."

"You're joking."

"I am not."

"Imagine, a country filled with Rudolf Kleins." It was not a beautiful image.

"Don't worry yourself unnecessarily, wife. It's a tradition, that's all." Standing gloriously naked, he said, "It certainly doesn't mean Scotsmen are less than masculine."

In this case, she thought not. She boosted a brow and wet her lips, wanting to touch all his manly glory. *Ach du meine Güte,* was their no end to his appeal? Even in a *skirt?* There must be something wrong with her.

He winked before arranging the horrid garment around his narrow waist. "You don't think I'm less than a man, do you?"

"Well, I *didn't.*" Her eyes dropped to glue to the knees below the hem and the hairy, muscular calves. Then she laughed. "I hate to say it, Gil, but you're rather knock-kneed. And you look funny standing there naked except for that skirt."

"Kilt, Lisette. *Kilt.*" He bent to pull a weird contraption from the trunk. "Do you know what this is?"

"No."

"These are my bagpipes."

"I have heard of those, vaguely. Why don't you ever play them around the campfire?"

"Because I've been wanting to play for you alone." His eyes took in her form. "And I'll play for no one but you."

She smirked, then pulled her mouth into a moue of alarm when he lifted the mouthpiece toward his face. "Gil, you can't play that thing tonight."

"Whose army says I can't?"

"Gil McLoughlin, you annoying Scotsman, it's after midnight. You'll disturb the other guests."

"They're probably at the Lusty Lady, having a drink and chatting up the doxies."

"I wouldn't count on that."

Gil made himself comfortable on the edge of the bed. Despite her skepticism, despite her stewing over whether he'd blow that piped thing and awaken every roomer in this hotel, she wasn't unappreciative of her husband's beauty; she smiled at the picture he presented. He looked rather charming, sitting there in nothing but that plaid skirt.

He fiddled with the bagpipes, arranging them just so on his left shoulder.

Lisette jumped out of bed. "Don't you dare play that thing."

"It isn't a thing. These are bagpipes."

She grabbed the rumpled sheet and wrapped it under her arms. "Put it away. I'll listen to it tomorrow."

He blew into the mouthpiece, and the sound was so horrid, she covered her ears. The sheet dropped. She wilted into the chair she'd abandoned earlier in the evening and shook her head in dismay. When he blew into that contraption again, though, she smiled. It was a beautiful tune, mournful and filled of something she couldn't explain, and she said as much.

"It's the sound of the Highlands, lass."

172

Enjoying the plaintive sound and the wonder of their reunion, she whispered, "Then I think I should like to see your country for myself."

"Someday, my darlin'. Someday."

A series of loud bangs sounded against one wall. A voice yelled through it, "Wasn't it enough, your screeching and shouting and putting those springs to bouncing? Decent folks are trying to sleep."

Gil took the mouthpiece from his lips. Shrugging at Lisette, he said, "I guess you were right."

"Will you play it again for me?" She winked saucily. "Tomorrow?"

"Aye, my darlin'." His smile was as broad as her wink had been saucy. "After I rent the adjoining rooms."

Chapter Fifteen

Charles Franklin Hatch, gently born and reared in the state of Georgia, sat in the Lusty Lady Saloon and swilled rotgut whiskey. Midnight had come and gone. Piano music played on.

Hatch was a little drunk, but not so inebriated he wasn't revolted. Which wasn't necessarily a result of the whore who sat on his lap and coiled her fat, grease-smelling self around his shoulders.

"Sugar," the prostitute crooned—her breath would have offended a buzzard—"my room's not far from here, and I've got a jug of corn likker. We can have another drink, then you can stick your peckerwood in my sweet little honeypot. It'll only cost you a greenback. How about it, hmm?"

"Get up, Lucy, and get me another drink."

"Name's Lacy. Give me a kiss and I'll get that drink."

He pushed her away at the moment her hairy chin touched his face. "Get it now."

The whore shrugged, then waddled over to the bar. Hatch was thankful she'd had the grace to go. All that fat had obstructed his view of the room.

174

Smoke curled toward the ceiling, giving the place a cloudy cast. The smells of dirty sawdust, stale beer, and rancid breath were everywhere. And the clientele . . . by the Bonny Blue, had a one of these twenty or so women, or the forty or so men, *ever* taken a bath?

Since the time he had spent in a Yankee prisoner-of-war camp, Charles Franklin Hatch had had a thing about cleanliness.

Again, he curled his lip at Lucy. What a swine she was, and never would he accept her lewd invitation. He liked his women clean. Fastidiousness was the reason he had been attracted to Cactus Blossom. At least his squaw kept herself washed.

Damn the heathen for—

He pushed aside thoughts of that Comanche's immorality; he got back to the situation at hand.

A voice at the bar, pitched high and with a northern accent, shouted, "All right, already."

Hatch's hand tightened around his empty glass. He hated Yankees, and one in particular—the one called Gil McLoughlin. And McLoughlin was in Lampasas. Right here, earlier tonight, in the Lusty Lady.

Arrogant as ever, McLoughlin had ambled into the place and sashayed over to the clutch of men propping up the bar. Several of them had greeted him warmly.

A darkie—Hatch didn't understand why they'd let him in the establishment—smiled at McLoughlin.

"Mister Mack, let ole Dink buy ya a drink."

"No thanks, Dinky. I'll do the buying, you do the enjoying. I've got hiring to attend to."

A particularly ugly fellow, thin as a stick, opened his mouth of bucked teeth. "Are you Dinky's boss? If you are, I'm looking for work. Pigweed Martin at your service, mister."

175

Hatch shivered, almost feeling the slobber as it dribbled from beneath that overbite. Apparently McLoughlin wasn't as selective; he accepted the drooler's bid. Then he hitched the heel of his boot on the bar rail and glanced around the room, taking no note of Hatch.

Why should he?

When Captain Hatch of the Fourth Georgia Regiment had escaped Yankee imprisonment, his hair and beard were long and scraggly, and he had been thin and pale and as ugly as the one named Pigweed Martin. By the time he'd reached Georgia and had the misfortune to encounter Major Gil McLoughlin and the other firestarters aligned with William Tecumseh Sherman, Charles Franklin Hatch had been in worse shape.

That was no longer the case.

Bile rose in his throat as he thought of Georgia. The Morgan plantation, owned by his mother but his by rights, was no more. And Mother and Mary Joan had disgraced themselves in the minds of the community. Enough of that. Better keep his thoughts free of the charges against them that had brought shame on the Morgan and Hatch names, and had forced him to —

Again he stared at McLoughlin, who was scanning the barroom and saying, "I'm looking for drovers. Any of you men interested?"

Not a soul stepped forward. Apparently they were more discriminating than Martin.

The pint-sized darkie spoke up. "Mister Mack's chuck wagon, why, it be fit for a king. Take six big-feeted horses to pull it." Several pairs of eyes turned to the speaker, who rubbed his stomach and smacked his lips. "And, lawdy, the victuals be good. Mmm, mmm!"

A bear of a man, wearing buckskins and sporting a beard to the middle of his chest, put down his jug. Addressing McLoughlin, he asked, "You've got a good, dependable cook?"

"I do."

"I hired on with a commission outfit," commented a man in baggy britches. "They near starved us to death."

"You won't go hungry in the Four Aces camp." McLoughlin smiled with pride. "My wife's in charge of the chuck wagon. And she's the world's best cook."

"Ain't so," protested Baggy Pants. "My ma be the best cook in the world."

"Since I'm not acquainted with the fine lady's skills, I won't argue," McLoughlin replied. "But I can guarantee you'll find the best eating on the trail in the Four Aces outfit."

Several men clambered to McLoughlin, ready to accept his offer.

Using a forefinger, Hatch drew a line down his jaw. As he had suspected, the britches-clad woman he'd seen at the courthouse had been passing as McLoughlin's wife. Lisa, or whatever her name was, had looked as if she would clean up to a more than acceptable level.

But what happened to the real Mrs. McLoughlin? Now *there* had been a clean one—clean and wicked. Hatch had caught her in the slave quarters at Charlwood, spreading her thighs for his former overseer. Her big green eyes had watched Hatch the entire time Elmo Whittle had been pumping her. After sending Elmo on his way and bathing between her legs, she offered Hatch seconds. He had declined. Never would he be hard up enough to consort with a Yankee.

Hatch picked up his glass and emptied his thoughts of that green-eyed tart. He watched the goings-on in the Lusty Lady Saloon. McLoughlin appeared pleased at hiring several drovers. When the lot of them receded to swill the drinks their new employer had purchased, McLoughlin made another scan of the room. His eyes settled on Hatch. Again, there wasn't a flicker of recognition.

Hatch pushed to his feet and ambled over to the bar. Careful not to touch the sticky bar top, he said, "Quite a successful night, I take it."

"I've seen better." McLoughlin turned his flat, cold stare to Hatch. "Are you looking for work, pahdner?"

"I might be." That was a lie, but why not bait the Yankee dog? "Though you should be able to tell I'm a gentleman, not a drover."

"I meant no insult, fellow."

"None taken." An ash floated from a patron's cigarillo and landed on the sleeve of Hatch's white frock coat; he flicked the particle in the Yankee's direction. "Tell me more about your cattle drive. On your way to Kansas, are you?"

"Right."

"Funny, I'm on my way there myself."

Kansas had never entered his mind, but that changed and a plan formed. Hatch would find out *why* McLoughlin didn't remember Charlwood, and his strategy didn't include quick revenge. It would take consorting with his enemy, on a full-time basis.

Naturally, it would be dirty on the cowpath. Hatch had been dirty before. He could handle it again, since

178

he aimed to make McLoughlin pay for his transgressions.

"Perhaps I could give you a hand, sir."

"It's no job for a dandy."

"True, true. But I find"—he forced a sheepish look—"I'm a bit low on funds. It might behoove me to accept your offer."

McLoughlin shrugged a shoulder. "It's up to you. The pay is good, the food exceptional. And I could use the help."

"Then we're in agreement."

"Have you got a name, fellow?" McLoughlin asked.

"Of course. It's Hatch. Charles Franklin Hatch. Some folks back home in Atlanta call me Frank."

The Yankee major still didn't place him. Why should he? The name Morgan, not Hatch, was attached to Charlwood, and Frank Hatch decided this could work in his favor.

That interchange had happened hours ago.

Now, as Charles Franklin Hatch clutched his empty glass, he scowled. How could a man, even a disciple of that son-of-a-bitch Abraham Lincoln, ruin another man's life, and recall neither his victim's face nor his name?

The saloon doors banged open and a sorry-looking so-and-so stomped inside. "Where's McLoughlin?" he bellowed, obviously in his cups.

The piano player's fingers stilled on the keys. The din of whores and their prey settled to whispers. The bartender, wiping a filthy rag across the countertop, answered, "He left hours ago."

The drunk mumbled something to himself.

Hatch called to him, "Do you have a problem, sir?"

The ruffian weaved over to him. Hatch got a good

179

look at the scar gouging the hard-eyed face and the evidence of a recently broken nose, and it was all he could do not to curl his lip at the menace as well as the filth.

Bending closer and exhaling an ale-fortified gust of air, the sot inquired, "Do ya know McLoughlin?"

"I do."

"Where's he at?"

It didn't take a genius to figure out that retaliation for something was written on the scarred crags of this face, and Hatch asked, "Did McLoughlin do that to your nose?"

"Damned right. And he stolt my gun. I'm gonna get him for it."

"Who could blame you for wanting to get even?" Hatch almost felt a kinship with the sufferer. Almost. "Why, I feel it's my duty as a gentleman to take you to him." He got to his feet and patted his britches pocket. "Follow me, my friend."

The fool did as he suggested, stumbling in his drunken state and mumbling something about, "I warned 'im Blade Sharp would come after 'im."

"Where are you going, sugar?" the whore asked, lumbering after her quarry.

Hatch pitched her a dollar; she, thank the Bonny Blue, abandoned interest.

There were several men loitering on the street; he led the ruffian in a westward direction, toward the darkened seclusion of the edge of town. As they neared a shack — Hatch knew it was deserted — situated between town and the cowpath, the drunk asked, "How much further, mister?"

"Why, we're here already. You'll find him in that house."

"Whuz he doin' there?"

"Sleeping, I should imagine—with his pretty blond wife."

"Near abouts had me a piece o' that." Blade Sharp scratched his behind. "Where'd ya say she's at?"

"Right here. In this house." Hatch motioned toward the shack's pitiful excuse for a door, then slipped his hand into his pocket. "Go on. Go, go. Go get your revenge."

Idiot that he was, the dirty drunk fell for the trick. Letting the cur get a trio of paces ahead of him, Hatch pulled his hand out of his pocket, poised the knife, and let it fly. A garbled noise, not too loud, emitted from Sharp before he pitched face forward onto the ground.

While he divested his victim of a handful of coins, then dragged the corpse into the shack, Hatch gave mental thanks his squaw had schooled him in the art of the knife.

Breaking a kerosene lamp, he poured fuel over the dead man's body. At the door, he tossed a lit match into the interior. He wiped his hands and pitched the handkerchief into the inferno. Yet he lingered, watching the flames lick the weathered boards of the house and hearing the crackle and pop of it all. Hatch drew great satisfaction from his deed. No one would get revenge against the damnyankee—no one but the beleaguered son of Charlwood.

Once in his newly rented boardinghouse quarters, he shucked his clothing, hung them in the armoire, and scrubbed away any traces of Lucy and that ruffian.

Pulling back the crisp sheets, he chuckled.

"Vengeance will be mine. I will be the one to go

after McLoughlin. First, I'll gain his trust, then I'll undermine him. I'll wreak havoc on his livelihood. When I'm certain he has suffered greatly, he'll know my name and face, and why he must pay for putting the torch to Charlwood Plantation. Then I'll kill him . . . just as I did you, Mister Blade Sharp."

At least I'll remember my victim's name and face.

As the Four Aces outfit prepared to pull out of Lampasas three days after arrival, Lisette, radiantly happy and contented, packed the chuck box and noted the buzz of activity around her. A full accompaniment of drovers and supplies were assembled.

She'd added a lot to those supplies. A wealth of goods both edible and not, including several bonnets and the makings for more, had been purchased. She felt somewhat guilty that Gil was obliged to purchase a hoodlum wagon to haul all the supplementaries plus a pair of oxen to pull it. Pigweed Martin, deemed the least robust of the crew, had been assigned to the extra wagon.

There were more additions to the crew. Attitude Powell, a bearded Tennessee mountaineer come west after the war. A polite young man from Virginia, Jackson Bell. Toad Face Walker, who spat tobacco juice wherever he went. A couple of Mexican men, one tagged simply Ochoa and the other a guitar picker named Cencero Leal, had appeared this morning to ask for a job. Already, Cencero Leal had advised her on the making of a fiery stew dish called chili.

One man, from New Hampshire, appeared to be a loner. Deep Eddy Roland kept to himself.

The final addition surprised Lisette. Mister Hatch

of Georgia had hired on.

The seasoned members of the Four Aces outfit took their places in the herd, Dinky Peele, Johns Clark, Preacher Wilson, and Wink Tannington at forward flank. Sadie Lou whipped around the herd's fringe.

Gil called the new drovers together to advise them on what he expected—and what he would not put up with. Each man voiced agreement to the terms, then rode out, leaving Lisette alone with her husband.

He strode over to harness the draught horses, and for once she didn't protest having help. For some odd reason, she wasn't feeling up to par.

Inhaling, she asked, "Did I mention I met Mister Hatch the other day?"

Gil nodded. "Peculiar fellow, isn't he?"

"I'll say. Do you figure he knows enough about the business to make a valuable contribution?"

"He sits a horse well," Gil answered with a shrug. "The rest he can learn by trial and error. And Hatch seems eager to be of help."

"That's true. But he's such a particular man about his appearance. I can't imagine him covered in dust."

"He accepted the job. He's not too good for it." Gil patted a horse's neck. Smiling, he winked at his wife. "Speaking of drovers, now that we're flush with help, I want to spend more time with you."

Her heart skipped a beat. "I'd like that. It's been wonderful, our time in Lampasas."

"Now that you've gotten accustomed to bagpipes and kilt," he commented wryly.

"Oh, now, you. I only objected once to the skirt and that thing of yours."

After making certain the crew had departed, he shot her a look that was filled with teasing. "I didn't notice you objecting to my thing, Lisette." Striding up to her, he pulled her close and cupped her buttocks with his hands. "Matter of fact, you seem to have a great regard for Old Son."

"I was referring to your bagpipes."

"I was referring to this, my sweet." He pulled her even closer. "What do you think about our Old Son?"

Her hands smoothed up his shirt to curl into his hair. His hat slid lower on his brow as she answered, "I think, *Liebster*, if you don't cease and desist, you'll find yourself kidnapped for the rest of the day." On tiptoe, she touched her lips to his. "And the herd will have to go on without us."

"Not a bad idea," was his low growl.

Practicality won out, though, and Lisette broke the embrace. "We can't. Not now. But later . . . oh, yes."

"I'll hold you to it, angel."

"As long as you're doing the holding, Gilliegorm, I—"

"What did you call me?" He whitened beneath his tan.

"Gilliegorm. That's your name, isn't it?"

One hand went to his forehead so fast that his hat tumbled to the ground. "How did you know?"

"When I opened your Bible today to record our marriage"—she smiled, recalling seeing her bridal bouquet pressed between those sacred pages—"I found an entry for your birth. Naturally, it had your full name written there . . . Gilliegorm."

"Don't ever call me that again."

"Why not? I like the name."

"I do not."

"Why?" she asked.

"Because it sounds silly."

"You're being silly." She pressed the tip of her forefinger into the dimple of his chin. "I intend to name our first son after his father."

"Over my dead body. I've gone to a lot of trouble to keep my name quiet."

She cuddled against his solid chest. "Your dead body would do me no good. I want you alive—for at least fifty years. We'll have to think of another name for a future son."

"How about Angus, after my father?"

"How about Hermann, after mine?"

"I think, Mrs. McLoughlin, we should come up with different names. When the time is right." He dropped a kiss on the crown of her bonnet. "For now we'd better head out, honey, or our cattle drive will be a failure and we'll starve to death. Way before any fifty years is up."

When she went to take the reins of the draught horses, Gil slid on the seat beside her and took the straps from her hands. "I'm driving, and you're going to sit right here and do nothing but enjoy the ride."

"Gil, you'll spoil me."

"I certainly hope so."

Chapter Sixteen

The cedars and rolling hills of central Texas flattened to sparser terrain as the longhorns and their herders moved onward. The Four Aces enterprise crossed the Lampasas River, bypassed the settlement of Hamilton, and forded the river Leon, migrating toward the cowtown of Fort Worth. During their three weeks of travel from the Keystone Hotel, Gil spent a majority of the daylight hours driving the chuck wagon up the cowpath, and Lisette enjoyed every moment of their time together.

Those twenty-one days went without problems, basically. The weather warmed even further, though summer's heat wasn't on them yet. There was an abundance of rain which slowed the procession at times, but the creeks were swollen with the water that kept the grasses high and the herd healthy. Naturally all that rain made for an interesting experience, cooking-wise, but Lisette accepted quickly, if somewhat crossly, to the ordeal of keeping the pots boiling.

The new drovers did their jobs well, including the wraithlike Pigweed and the fastidious Hatch.

The only real blight on the trail drive was a concern

which had worried her since joining the company: baby calves.

One afternoon, the longhorns several miles to their rear, Gil stopped the chuck wagon to scout a creek for a possible night camp, and Lisette put pen to paper.

April 13, 1869

Dear Anna,

You'll think me a ninny, complaining after I've written glowing reports each day since we were in Lampasas, but, Anna dear, there's a situation I don't know how to handle, and if I speak to my husband, I fear he'll find me unworthy to continue our journey to Kansas. You see, I've learned I am quite sentimental when it comes to newborn calves.

They come into this world on wobbly little legs, needing their mothers. It is awful — my husband orders they be left behind as their mothers are herded north. Oh, how the mothers bawl for their babies, and they try to go back for them. Try to, Anna. Try to. Even Matthias goes along with Herr McLoughlin's orders. Can you imagine this of our gentle Matthias? Be that as it may, I am at my wit's end, fretting over the youngsters.

I wish I had another woman to talk with. I've even missed my mother. Oh, Anna, I miss you, too. Goodness, look at the teardrop staining this letter. What a ninny I am. To tell the truth, I've been acting strangely for days now. And I've eaten a crock of pickles — you know how I hate them! But all that overeating explains my new plumpness. And I'm overly sentimental about everything. Even the sunsets bring tears to my eyes. It must be the wonders of love.

If you'd like to write, send it in care of the Abilene

187

*post office. I'm sure your correspondence will gather
dust by the time we reach the place, but I'm most eager
to hear from you.*

*Oh, my goodness, I almost forgot to tell you, I've
been so busy and happy here lately, but there was an
awful fire in Lampasas. A house burned, and a former
drover of ours died in it. He was a horrid man, but
we are shocked by the news.*

> *Your friend,*
> *Lisette McLoughlin*

Lisette sealed the letter the moment her husband returned.

Dusting his hands, he said, "I don't like the looks of
here. Let's see if we can find a better night-camp."
Again, he took the reins of the draught horses.

For a good thirty minutes they rode along without
conversing. Sadie Lou, who usually worked cattle, was
taking an infrequent furlough by sleeping atop the
bedrolls behind her master. The pungent scent of in-
secticide—the cowboys, opposed to anything that grew
wool, wouldn't allow anyone to call it *"sheep* dip"—
wafted from Sadie Lou's nest. Lisette had insisted the
dog be bathed and deloused before sharing quarters
with them.

The only sounds above the singing of birds and the
dog's snores were the jingle of harnesses, the clop of
hooves striking rocks, the gentle neighing from the
team of six.

Gil turned to Lisette. "You're being quiet this afternoon. Not feeling well?"

"I'm fine," she hedged and patted his muscled thigh;
she felt him tense beneath her touch. It didn't take

much to heat her husband's blood. She smiled, thinking how true her thought. And she decided not to mull over calves and the like. She nudged her shoulder against his. "I'll be glad when night falls."

"Why's that?" he teased, his handsome profile drawing much of Lisette's attention. "Are you wanting to take advantage of my body again?"

"Could be. I like all the sneaking away from camp we've been doing. At night, of course."

"I miss our nights and *days* at the Keystone Hotel," he said, his voice rough with passionate recollections. "God, how I miss them. I can't wait for this drive to be over, honey. Then we'll have that honeymoon I promised you. Walking hand in hand along Lake Michigan has more than an air of romance to it, don't you think?"

"It does sound nice," she returned breathily. "Does your grandmother live on the lake?"

"No, honey, she's on the Mississippi. Chicago is on the lake."

"I knew that." She paused. "But there are a lot of things I don't know about you. I know you're mad for your grandmother, your parents are deceased, and I—"

"Been checking up on me?"

"You've told me about your brothers. Andrew and Robert, aren't they? And they've scattered from Illinois."

"That's right."

"I hope someday to meet the entire family."

"Clan, Lisette. Clan."

"Why did the McLoughlins leave Scotland?"

"To make a better life."

A wagon wheel hit a rut, bouncing the occupants,

189

cutting into the conversation. It did nothing for her somewhat queasy stomach. She clutched her midsection.

"What's wrong?" was Gil's worried inquiry.

"Breakfast didn't settle quite right."

"Breakfast, Lisette? We've had *lunch* already." He looked her up and down. "Anyhow, you've been this way for days."

"Perhaps it's some sort of malady coming on."

"Honey, I'm wondering if it's a 'malady.' Your breasts have been tender, I've noticed. Have you had your flux?"

She blushed. Though it had been easy to talk with Gil lately, she didn't feel comfortable discussing such things as monthlies, yet she wouldn't be dishonest. "I haven't."

"It's been over a month, right at six weeks, since . . . Maybe your flow will come in a few days."

She was beginning to doubt it, since her cycles had been as regular as the changing moon. Too, after being around Monika and experiencing the tribulations of her sister-in-law's pregnancies, Lisette concluded her queasy stomach and sentimental mood swings could well be attributed to a child growing in her womb. It was a joyous thought, the idea of bearing Gilliegorm McLoughlin's child.

So joyous, in fact, that her stomach settled down, leaving her feeling moderately robust.

Gil popped the reins. "You're probably catching a bug."

"What if it's a baby?"

"Then we'll become parents, Mrs. McLoughlin."

"Will that suit you?" she asked and held her breath.

"Absolutely." Taking the leather lashes in one hand,

he reached to hug her to him with the other. "Positively." He dropped a kiss on the top of her bonnet. "I'll be the proudest papa in the world."

Lisette had never dreamed she could be this happy. Again she studied her husband's profile. Though he seemed pleased at the prospects, she couldn't help wondering . . . "Gil, a while back, you told me your former wife bore a child. Do you feel comfortable enough to tell me what happened?"

His shoulders stiffened. "Comfortable enough? It's a sordid chapter in my life I'd rather forget."

"And leave me forever curious?"

He settled a booted foot on the splashboard, and from under the brim of his hat, peered at the ragged plains of north central Texas.

At last he turned his face to Lisette and said, "Let's go for a walk."

He helped her down from the chuck wagon, leaving Sadie Lou to her nap, and held Lisette's hand as they negotiated the hard ground. When she saw the tension in his fingers and in his expression, she regretted asking her question.

"Maybe we should forget it," she suggested.

"No. You asked, and I can't and won't skate around my past, since it's obviously on your mind." Stopping near a ridge, he let go of her hand and walked to the shade of an elm tree. He stood under its shade and ran a hand down his mouth. "You'd better sit down, honey. This may take a while."

In the form of all cowboys, he scissored smoothly to the ground; he sat about a yard in front of her. His hand grasping the brim of his hat, he set it aside, then peered at the sky, as if the action might lend strength to his words.

"I guess I should start at the beginning." Drawing up a knee and dropping a forearm to it, he spoke slowly. "Sherman granted me leave after the Vicksburg campaign. Went home to Rock Island. Maisie had been having a time of it, working the farm. Had to get her hands on money, you see. Maisie's wild for it, and stingy with its parting. Anyway, she was supplying apples for the prisoner-of-war camp close to Rock Island," he explained, "on the banks of the Mississippi."

"Go on," she prompted. "Tell me more about your marriage."

He stood, relocating to grip the elm's lowest branch. "My heart beat between my legs. And Betty was beautiful."

Jealousy snaked through Lisette. She didn't want her husband thinking any woman beautiful except her. Only once, when he'd seduced her under the oak tree, had he remarked on her looks.

Always, others had commented on her "beauty," yet she had never basked in their praise, since she considered herself rather ordinary, and she'd never thought herself vain until this moment. She wanted Gil to think her beautiful, though.

But she was brown-faced and disheveled, despite the Lampasas purchases. She glanced at her hands. Lanolin had done little for their coarse texture. Moreover, she feared she was getting to fat. Could she attribute her weight gain to a baby? Surely not . . . it was too early for extra poundage.

"She wasn't as beautiful as you, understand. My splendid wife, have I ever told you how I feel about your looks?"

As much as his words placated her jealousy, this wasn't the moment for dwelling on herself. "I'd rather you tell me about Elizabeth . . . I mean, Betty . . . and the child she bore."

A moment stretched before Gil answered, "I met her through her father. Major Dobbs was in charge of procuring rations for the prisoners. Anyhow, I was randy, and Betty was full of wiles. I guess I was smitten."

You're smitten with me. What about love?

In the beginning he had scoffed at the concept, but she felt confident it was only a matter of time before he spoke those words. And shouldn't actions count more than words? Gil had been wonderful to her here. She corrected her thoughts. Except for the hell between their first mating and the Keystone Hotel, he had always been wonderful. Stubborn, yes, when he had refused to hire her, both in Fredericksburg and at the encampment where she'd found him, and he had wanted to keep her away from the trail drive. But he was indulgent, caring, and protective. Protective, such as he'd been when that awful Blade Sharp had accosted her.

She said, "You went home, met a girl, and married."

"Showed myself to be a gullible fool is what I did. I'd assumed Betty was pure."

Lisette went to her beloved husband. She put her hand on his arm, the warmth of her loving concern going into her action. It seemed to give him the strength to go on.

Lacing the fingers of his free hand with the ones grasping his arm, he squeezed gently. "She knew which strings to pull, knew how to keep me in line. Betty held out for marriage. But she'd been spreading her legs for every available male in Rock Island

193

County. I didn't find out till the wedding night."

God in heaven, that's why he was so unnerved upon discovering my *impurity!*

"She took special delight in mocking me with tales of her escapades."

Her heart going out to his pain, Lisette ached for his battered pride. And she understood his reluctance to hear her explanations about Thom.

"Damn her for hurting you." Lisette spoke vehemently. "You're too good to be hurt."

"Your trust never ceases to amaze me." Gil smiled. "But I wonder why you have such faith in me?"

Because I love you. Now wasn't the time to express her sentiments. She decided such an announcement would be proper when or if she confirmed her suspicions about their child.

She whispered, "Please go on."

"I married her. Our time together was a pit of perdition. Never slept together unless I was in my cups and in desperate need of physical release." Gil kicked at a loose stone, sending the pebble flying against the tree trunk. "General Sherman called me back to duty for the Atlanta campaign. I caught enemy fire in my leg. I wasn't in danger of dying, unless infection set in, of course," he went on. "Betty showed up at the field hospital. By then I was on the mend. My defenses were weak, though. I didn't stop to think on why she'd traveled from Illinois to be at my side or put herself in the middle of battle. She was carrying on real sweet-like. I should've gotten a clue right there."

His bitterness arced through the air, hit Lisette full force as he squeezed the tree limb with such emotion that the leaves shook. He claimed not to care about the woman, yet why was he so visibly unnerved after these many years?

He was saying, "She'd cajoled the general into letting her take over Charlwood Plantation—the owners, an old lady and her daughter, had been arrested for atrocities I won't go into—and Betty insisted I stay with her 'for a couple of nights.' To 'tend me.' I wasn't strong enough to stay out of her clutches. General Sherman had put me in charge of a captured area, so she stayed around. It wasn't long before she announced we were going to be parents."

"You said the child wasn't yours," Lisette pointed out.

"He wasn't." Gil searched in his vest pocket for a cigar. Blowing out the match, he took a puff, then bent low to crush the glowing end into the earth. "She delivered seven months after our reconciliation. It was a ten-pound male child. There was no question of paternity." His eyes closed. Agony encased his features. "The boy couldn't have been mine."

"My poor darling," Lisette whispered. "How you must hurt."

"I'm over it."

She sensed he wasn't over anything, not after the way he'd reacted to her state of impurity and her so-called deceit. Growing wary, she asked, "What happened to the boy?"

"He died a couple of days after his birth."

Lisette tried to make sense of the horrible situation, yet in her sentimental state, she murmured, "How awful for Betty."

Gil's face hardened to granite, and his stance took on that same immobility. "Why do you defend that harlot? She couldn't even *guess* the father's name."

"I'm sorry, my beloved," Lisette whispered, but the

damage was done. Her utterance in defense of his first wife caused Gil to grab his hat and return to the chuck wagon, where he took Big Red's reins and said, "I can hear the longhorns. And it's getting on eventide. My men will be hungry. I'd better ride ahead of the wagon, and find a decent night-camp."

"All right. But, Gil, I didn't mean to offend you."

"Damn it, let's go."

Despite her misspent sentiment toward the first Mrs. McLoughlin, it pleased Lisette, her husband being so candid. Married folk needed to be open with each other. And she warned her insecure self away from making too much of Gil's feelings for his former *Frau*. If he'd loved Betty enough, he wouldn't have left her.

As she approached the wagon step, Lisette saw her husband untying Big Red. "Gil, I didn't mean to offend you."

"I know you didn't. You're just overly sentimental right now." He smiled. "And I think I know why."

She did too. Yet the child wasn't at the forefront of her thoughts. "I wonder," she said, "how our lives would have been different . . . if the war had never happened."

"Honey, some things happen for the best. For some folks, anyhow. In our case . . ." He led the stallion forward, and reached to hug his wife. "I think we got lucky. Circumstance brought me to Texas . . . to you."

"I brought myself to you."

"Don't argue, woman." After swatting her backside, he swung into the saddle and motioned to the north. "Keep to the path, honey. I'll double back when I find a good spot."

She nodded, appreciative that he hadn't remained

angry and that circumstance had brought them together.

Gil rode away, and Lisette put the chuck wagon in motion. A cold, wet nose nudged her sleeve, and turning her head, she saw limpid brown eyes staring at her. The collie settled her paw on the seat back and whimpered.

"What's the matter, *Liebling?*"

Again, Sadie Lou whimpered, then jumped to the seat. Wagging her bushy white tail, she eyed the human.

"You're wanting to get off this wagon, aren't you?" Lisette asked in German. "You aren't happy unless you're with your master." The dog barked as if she understood. "You're really loyal to him, *Liebling,* and I think that's tremendous of you. I think you're a grand *hund.*" Lisette halted the team. "All right, you can go to him. And I myself could use a stop. Nature calls, you see."

But Sadie Lou didn't run after Gil. She followed at heel as Lisette searched out the privacy of a tall bush, and by the time the two females had relieved themselves, Gil found them.

Concern marked his expression. "Lisette, you've got to be more careful. Call me when you need to take care of things, and I'll guard you."

"Don't be a fussbudget," she chided gently. "I'm fine. And I had Sadie Lou on the lookout."

The collie loped deeper into the woods, darn her.

"See, you can't depend on our canine friend." He whistled, then did again. "Where the hell has she gone?"

Chapter Seventeen

"Here, puppy, puppy."

Cactus Blossom, daughter of Comanches, woman to a Georgian, fluent in the white man's language, hungry beyond a growling stomach, scrunched her shoulders and closed in on dinner. The dog stood beneath a cottonwood tree, its body curled in defense, one paw poised for flight.

"Come here, Dinner," Cactus Blossom chanted in her native language and clicked her tongue three times. "Come and make me a nice roast."

She drew a knife from the sash of her buckskin sheath. For the past hour, her ears had detected the faint sounds of moving cattle to her east, south of here. The noise had scared game away. And even if it hadn't, she especially liked the taste of dog.

Her moccasin-shod feet moved forward—slowly, lightly.

"Sadie Lou!"

Cactus Blossom cursed the male voice. When she got a look at him, stomping through the woods with Dinner rushing to him and a woman at his side, she frowned. Long Legs—there was no better name for the man, she decided—looked straight at her.

He said something which rang like a curse, then put a protective arm around his woman, who reminded Cactus Blossom of Fish Belly, a Comanche of no color. Fish Belly was paler than the white woman; Hatch had called him an albino. Long Legs' woman was a blonde, she knew. During the past two of her twenty summers—ever since taking up with Hatch—she had seen blondes, but she had never gotten used to their lack of coloring. They reminded her of Fish Belly.

"We come in peace," Long Legs called in halting Comanche.

The white man always spoke with a forked tongue before drawing his long knife to slay her people and steal their land. She'd gotten accustomed to killing and stealing, though—so used to it, in fact, she had taken one of the enemy as her own. Of course, Hatch didn't seek blood. All he wanted was to steal gold, and make trouble for his enemies from the white man's war against his own kind.

"I am Cactus Blossom of the Comanche, and I am hungry," she announced in English before raising her knife. "I will have that dog for a nice roast."

"No," cried Albino.

White people and their strange abhorrence to dog meat! They had no sense of survival.

Long Legs pulled his Iron of Exploding Furies. "Be on your way."

"You would kill a woman over her empty belly?" Cactus Blossom asked, standing bravely.

"There's no need for that." The albino pulled away from her man's protection. "We have food. Plenty of it. And we'll be more than happy to share."

199

"Lisette, don't." Long Legs grabbed her arm and scolded, as if reprimanding a defiant papoose, "Watch what you say."

Dinner cut in front of the man and woman, giving Cactus Blossom clear aim.

The albino proved defiant of her man. "Please put away your knife. There's no need for you to go hungry. Our wagon is over there." She pointed toward the east. "Come with us."

"Damn it, Lisette, have you lost your mind? She's a redskin. The same sort killed your sister, not to mention Ernst and José and Willie."

"Gil, I won't have anyone going hungry."

For the stretch of a minute, Long Legs scowled at Albino. He shook his head, then said to Cactus Blossom, "If you'll toss your knife over here, you're welcome to eat."

I probably shouldn't trust these people, she thought. But an Iron of Exploding Furies stood between her and Dinner. And Long Leg's woman seemed pliable enough toward her. Cactus Blossom trusted her instincts.

Handle forward, she tossed the knife between herself and Long Legs.

Lisette McLoughlin had no reason to like Indians, yet as she had said, she wouldn't allow anyone to go hungry. And Cactus Blossom had put her fate in their hands; Lisette wouldn't betray that trust.

After the black-haired, petite woman had devoured two strings of jerked beef and a plate of cold beans, she asked for a ride to town. "My horse died seven sunsets ago, and I must reach Fort Worth to do trading . . . and to make powwow," Cactus Blossom explained.

Lisette — over Gil's strong objection — promised a ride.

She drove the chuck wagon up the cowpath, the Indian woman sitting beside her. With Sadie Lou flanking Big Red, Gil rode alongside the chuck wagon. He wouldn't stray from Lisette, since he "wanted to keep an eye on that redskin." He kept one hand on Thelma's butt.

"Your man is possessive of you," Cactus Blossom observed.

"He's worried you'll do something to me. It worries me as well."

"You've befriended me, Albino, and a woman of honor doesn't put a knife in a person who is kind to her."

Lisette glanced at the beautiful Indian woman. Her cheekbones were high, her complexion with a patina like bronze, her features all Indian — proud and noble. Sunlight danced through her black braids, giving them a bluish cast as they lay along her firm bosom. She wore a buckskin dress embellished with beadwork, lovely beadwork to Lisette, who admired the handicraft. Even though Cactus Blossom had wanted Sadie Lou for meal purposes, Lisette had a hard time equating the woman with warring Comanches.

"Why do you stare at me?"

"I'm thinking how pretty you are."

Cactus Blossom laughed. "I was thinking the same of you. From a distance, you're much too colorless. Up close, though, you are fine. You have nice blue

201

eyes, Albino." She paused. "Why are you so colorless?"

"The people in my homeland tend to be fair."

"Hmm. All those yellow scalps, they would look nice decorating a tepee. Where is this land of yours?"

"It's a German duchy, Nassau-Hesse." Lisette snapped the reins. "I hope you're not planning to take a few scalps along our way . . ."

"That is men's work, mostly."

"You don't have a man in the vicinity, do you?" Lisette asked and tightened her fingers around the leather strips until pain shot up her arm.

"I do."

This answer drew a frisson of fear, and Lisette was glad her husband rode close by, Thelma at his ready.

"Cactus Blossom, you aren't leading us into some sort of trap, are you?"

"I am not. I'm looking for my man. I searched in Lampasas, but he had left. Then my horse's medicine went bad, and I had to leave her by the wide waters the white man calls Leon. I've spent the last week running after my man." Cactus Blossom lifted her moccasined feet to the seat and rubbed each foot in turn. "It makes for sore feet, running after a man."

"I can imagine," Lisette murmured, remembering the hard walk between Fredericksburg and the man who had become her husband.

"I hope to find him in Fort Worth, if not sooner," Cactus Blossom said. "Maybe you have seen my man? He is known to the white man as Hatch."

"I know a Frank Hatch."

The Indian woman settled an elbow on the top of her thigh and rested her chin in her hand. "Some call him that."

Lisette's mouth dropped; she spat road dust and fastened her lips. Though Cactus Blossom was comely and young, she was Frank Hatch's woman? Somehow Lisette couldn't imagine the two together. She told herself not to be prejudiced. The pretty Comanche was clean and neat, despite her trek, and that sort of thing seemed to appeal to Mister Hatch.

Gil rode closer. "We'll camp here tonight."

The women debarked from the wagon. Lisette began to unharness the draught horses, and Cactus Blossom offered, "I am good at making cookfires. I will make one."

Gil stomped over to the woman. "We don't need your help, Injun. I want you gone—and *now*."

The back of Lisette's knuckles went to her waist. "You promised she could accompany us as far as Fort Worth, and as it turns out, she's Mister—"

"You promised her, I didn't."

"Well, husband, I don't make empty promises."

He glared, yet a trace of a smile edged a corner of his mouth. "Looks like your integrity has worked against me."

Lisette delighted in his subdued stance. "Gil, do you think you could water the horses? I need to get supper started."

He went for the animals, yet his eyes didn't drop their guard.

Cactus Blossom took the shovel and began to dig the fire trench. "Albino, since you know my man's name, do you know where I can find him?"

"I do. He's one of our drovers."

Cactus Blossom, propping up the shovel and resting her wrist on it, shook her head. "No. It couldn't be my

Dung Eyes. He never works; it would dirty his hands."

"Dung Eyes?"

"His eyes are the color of dung. It angers him when I call him thus. But his name fits. That is the Comanche way of naming."

"Mister Hatch's eyes are brown. And he's rather a dandy. We may be referring to the same man."

Cactus Blossom arranged wood in the pit, then leaned back on her heels. "I wonder why my man is driving cattle."

"He needed money."

"He had much wampum when he was with me." She extracted flint from her pouch, then struck the wood. "I am a good hunter, a good cook, and an excellent trader."

"What do you trade?"

"Myself. For the white man's wampum."

Lisette had never met a prostitute, and her face turned scarlet. All she could answer to the announcement was, "Oh."

A finger going to her upper lip, Cactus Blossom squinted at the dying sun. "His medicine must have gone bad, if Hatch is desperate enough to work for his living."

By now, the longhorns were approaching, Tecumseh Billy at the lead. Lisette pointed to a flank rider. "There's your man."

The squaw stood up and emitted a cry sounding much like the Comanche war cries that Lisette had heard the night Willie Gaines and the others had perished.

"Dung Eyes!"

Cactus Blossom ran, lithe and sure-footed, to Frank

Hatch. "I have searched long and hard for you."

Gil stomped toward the duo. "What is going on here?"

Grim-faced, Hatch glanced down at Cactus Blossom before turning his regard to the trail boss. "It looks as if my squaw has found me."

"No more couples on this drive," Gil said, slicing his hand through the air.

"You needn't worry, McLoughlin." Hatch tried to kick the woman away from her hold. "She'll be going back the way she came."

"Good." Gil doffed his straw hat to rub his brow with a forearm. "I'm glad to know you're on my side in this."

Yet Cactus Blossom didn't leave. She shared dinner with the Four Aces outfit, Cencero Leal serenading the group, and hand-fed her husband during it. Hatch didn't act as if he enjoyed the treatment. When the supper dishes were washed and put away, she was still in camp.

Lisette noticed Matthias watching the woman with open curiosity. As for the other men, a couple were straightforward in their dislike for the "Injun," but most didn't seem to mind her presence. Deep Eddy Roland, as usual, didn't express an opinion, which was his way.

Preacher Wilson, whom Lisette had grown to like as well as respect, said a prayer.

"Do you know how to make son-of-a-bitch stew?" Fritz Fischer asked slowly, and received a pop on the back of his head from Oscar Yates.

"Mind yer manners, boy. Don't be talkin' ugly in front o' women."

"But, Oscar, Frau McLoughlin is familiar with it, and I was just wondering about—"

"Now, my Susie could sure fix up a pot o' the stew in question, lickety-split." Yates continued with a long-winded tale about his much-revered departed wife and favorite cook. At the yarn's climax, several cowhands were yawning. ". . . 'Course, our girl Lisetty, she be the only woman what could hold a candle to my Susie. Did I ever tell you 'bout the time Susie . . ." He was once more on the oratory.

Dinky Peele, Wink Tannington, and Johns Clark emitted a collective groan and unfurled their bedrolls. Cactus Blossom stood up, extending her hand to Hatch. "We will sleep now." Brooking no argument, she grabbed Hatch's bedding.

"Going with her, squaw man?" asked Attitude Powell.

Hatch ignored the bearded man from Tennessee and swept his attention to the trail boss. "McLoughlin, I'd best talk some sense into the woman."

"You'd better, Hatch. You'd damned sure better."

The Georgian followed after his wife, and Gil turned to the men surrounding the campfire. "She will be gone on the morrow," he said, his nostrils flaring. "The only female on this drive is my wife, and it's going to stay that way."

It was all Lisette could do to cajole him to a hide-away place of their own.

He took the strongbox that had been hidden in the chuck wagon against "thieving redskins."

Lisette spread their pallet. At this point she didn't know how to feel about Cactus Blossom's presence in camp, since it seemed strange to have a prostitute

206

among the men. Surely Mr. Hatch wouldn't allow her to ply her trade.

If Gil were to discover her occupation, he wouldn't allow it, of this Lisette was certain, she thought as she watched him unbuckle Thelma's belt.

Tugging the shirttail from his Levis, he turned to Lisette; he rubbed the scar under his eye. "I get antsy when you get quiet. You're not thinking about keeping that squaw around, I hope."

Lisette elevated her chin. "I like Cactus Blossom."

"Get it out of your head. This drive isn't gonna turn into a paradise for women. And that's that."

Maybe it would be for the best if Cactus Blossom did say her good-byes. Yet Lisette had enjoyed having another woman to talk with. Cactus Blossom was as different from Anna Uhr as dawn was to midnight — Anna would never sell her body, for goodness' sake — but Lisette and the Comanche woman shared the camaraderie of women.

And to send the woman on her lonely way brought back memories to Lisette . . . memories of being alone and uncertain. She didn't wish for anyone to suffer that fate.

"Lisette," Gil said, stretching out her name, "I hope you heard what I said."

"You haven't fared badly having a woman along."

"A woman. One, not two." He pitched his boots to the ground and grabbed a cigar. He lit it, puffed in two quick draughts of smoke, then blew them out. "Get something straight, Lisette. I make the rules around here."

"Cactus Blossom is to be turned out, and there's no arguing?"

"As I said, *I* make the rules around here."

From his adamant tone, from the fierceness in his quicksilver eyes, Lisette knew there would be no arguing with Gil. It didn't mean she had to like it.

Chapter Eighteen

Frank Hatch didn't need this complication.

He cut a look of annoyance at Cactus Blossom as she spread his bedroll beside the shelter of a head-high precipice. Damn her. Why did she have to show up when everything was going so well for him and his plans for retaliation?

She turned and said, "We must powwow."

"All I want is for you to leave," he replied harshly.

Her big black eyes looked squarely at him. "I would not be here if I didn't think danger was upon you."

"You and your stupid heathen notions."

She shucked her buckskin sheath and stood naked under the moonlight. At one time Hatch would have been interested in the sight, but not anymore. And his revulsion wasn't totally a result of the self-inflicted scars that crisscrossed her belly.

She might be clean enough, but she was too sinful for his contradicting reasons and tastes.

She walked over to him, thrusting her tits upward, and he reached to twist a nipple. "I see your milk has dried up."

She slapped his hand, answering, "It has."

"Nothing's left of our daughter."

"I will never forget Weeping Willow."

"That I doubt. I don't think you give a care that she's dead." Hatch cared, for all the good it did him. He ordered sourly, "Put your clothes on."

"I am in need of a man."

"Then go back to camp. I'm sure you'll find one there. You usually can, wherever there's a hard cock. Try the bearded one — Powell. He should be a challenge, since you seem to disgust him almost as much as you disgust me."

"Would you like to watch . . . again?" was her languid response.

"I might." Ever since the real Mrs. McLoughlin had let him watch her with Elmo Whittle, Hatch had enjoyed the perversion. He cut a glance at Cactus Blossom. "It'd be the only satisfaction I could get from you."

"Then you will have to go unhappy. I will only trade my body to those I am interested in."

"Gotten persnickety, eh?" She nodded, and he scowled as she made herself comfortable in his bedroll. "Get out of there."

"No. I will sleep now."

Goddamn annoying heathen. "Then sleep on the ground. I need my rest for tomorrow."

"Why do you work, Dung Eyes?"

"Don't call me that."

He huffed over to kick her buttock. Meaning to scare him and scooting away before his foot connected, she gave him one of those mean Indian looks.

"You didn't answer me. Why do you work, Dung Eyes? I feel you have evil designs on something here."

"You do too much thinking."

She stilled, and he knew her ears were pricking. Slowly she went for her knife, then lunged out from the ground to decapitate a rattlesnake — that had been slithering toward him!

"Well, you're still good for something," he allowed as she sliced off the snake's tail and deposited the rattles in her pouch which held a score of this and that, most of it as detestable as the possessor. "At least I can depend on you to protect me from danger."

"That is why I am here. The silver star in Lampasas is looking for a murderer. A man died in a fire, and you are known as one who sets fires."

"No one knows that but you."

"You are wrong, Dung Eyes." She pointed the blade in his direction, no doubt to ward off another kick in the butt. "Word has reached the law that you are wanted in several towns for starting fires."

"Yankee houses. I just burn carpetbaggers' houses."

"If you send me away, I can tell the law in Fort Worth where to find you."

"Bitch, I ought to slit your throat."

"You won't, Dung Eyes. If you had been capable of killing me, you would have done it when the sun was rising over Dead Buffalo Bluff."

"Don't remind me," he bit out, closing his thoughts on her morning of ultimate sin. "I'd just like to know why the hell you're interested in staying with me."

"I have no interest in staying with you." Cactus Blossom put away her knife. "I am interested only in making certain you do no harm to the nice albino lady."

"If that's all you're worried about, then you can leave. I have nothing against the"—he clipped off "new," since it would be best to keep the squaw in the dark. "I've nothing against Mrs. McLoughlin."

"But you have something against her man. I can see it in the dirty brown of your eyes."

The damned squaw knew him too well. She knew he wouldn't kill her, and bring trouble on himself in the McLoughlin camp.

"If you hurt Long Legs, you hurt Albino," Cactus Blossom said. "I will not allow you to work your evil."

"I doubt you'll get the chance for anything but moving on. McLoughlin won't let you stay in his camp."

Cactus Blossom settled back in the bedroll. "His woman will not make me leave, and you should not try to keep me away. Don't forget, Dung Eyes, I can protect you from danger . . . or I can tell the silver star where to find you."

Hatch had to think on this a while. No way would McLoughlin allow Cactus Blossom to stay, but if he did, Hatch decided her presence might work in his favor, which was another reason to keep her alive.

Already he'd sensed that Lisette had a soft spot for the squaw, and Hatch wouldn't have anyone thinking him ungentlemanly by sending her on her way. Why not use it to best advantage?

Fingers of dawn touched Lisette's eyelids. She lay
in her husband's arms, not wanting to start another
day. Already she was late with breakfast, but leaving
the cradle Gil provided was as simple as pulling
teeth. Of course, she ought to be angry, what with
his refusal to allow Cactus Blossom to stay with Mr.
Hatch, but she understood his misgivings.

A pitiful bawling opened her eyes.

As she raised her head, nausea roiled. Taking a
deep breath to quell it, she saw a mother cow and
her newborn. The pair were about twenty feet from
this pallet, the cow licking the birth-wet face. Lisette's heart tugged; she knew the calf would be left
behind once the drive headed out.

Pulling away from her husband and picking up a
canteen of water, she turned her back on the pitiable
sight of *Mutter* and *Kleinkind* and went behind a bush
to vomit up the contents of her stomach.

Finished with that and with a modicum of ablutions, she accepted her condition. She smiled. A
babe was growing.

What would happen now? The trail drive was a
long way from the railhead. Could she, would she,
should she continue the trip? Of course she could
and would. She wasn't some delicate flower in need
of pampering. She was pioneering the trail, healthy
as a horse, and babes had been incubated under far
worse conditions.

She returned to the spot where she and her husband had slept. He was dressed, his forefingers

213

grasping the mule-ears of his boot as he pulled it on.

"Good morning," he said, and smiled at Lisette.

The newborn calf, a dozen paces to Gil's rear, captured Lisette's attention again. The mite was suckling an udder, his mother standing quietly with a look of pride and accomplishment on her shaggy, bovine face.

"Oh, Gil," Lisette murmured, "aren't they wonderful?"

"Huh?"

And then she spied Cactus Blossom, a knife in her raised hand, stealing toward the animals.

"Don't you dare!" Lisette rushed forward. "Cactus Blossom, don't!"

Shaking her head, the Comanche woman sheathed her knife. "What is wrong now, albino? Don't you eat calf? It makes for tender eating. Even the toothless of my tribe can enjoy it."

"We aren't interested in hearing stories of your damned tribe," Gil said. "What are *you* still doing here?"

Cactus Blossom continued forward and stopped in front of Lisette and Gil. "I was looking for you and your woman, Long Legs. I have fixed a meal and coffee, and it grew cold while we waited for you."

"My wife does the cooking for the Four Aces crew."

Actually, Lisette rather enjoyed the idea of having a break from all those ghastly cooking smells. *You should be ashamed of yourself. Meals are your responsibility, and Gil depends on you.*

"You'd rather have your woman cook than warm your tepee?" Cactus Blossom was saying. "You are a strange man, Long Legs."

"Mrs. Hatch, if you've eaten, I suggest you be on your way."

"Gil, we can't send her off on foot."

"Go see Fritz Fischer, Mrs. Hatch. Tell him I said to give you a horse from the remuda."

"I am not Mrs. Hatch. I am not *wife* to anyone."

"It figures," Gil groused. "Take Hatch with you. Take two horses and be gone."

"My man doesn't want to go. He wants to work for you."

"If he wants to be with you, he'll go." Gil slapped his hat atop his head. "Come on, Lisette. We're wasting good daylight hours."

Lisette wasn't in the mood to argue about anything. Yet as she walked past the calf, as Gil strung a rope around the mother's horns to lead her back to the herd, Lisette stood her ground.

"If Cactus Blossom wants to go along with us, I think we should let her."

The Comanche woman beamed at this.

Gil did not.

He motioned to Cactus Blossom. "Go back to camp. And right now, God damn it."

She turned on the ball of a moccasined foot and disappeared in the direction of the campsite.

His face set in a hard line, Gil asked Lisette, "Are you trying to tell me how to run my cattle drive?"

Lisette scowled. Gil wouldn't even want the Madonna along on their journey. Qualifying her statement, she said, "I'm telling you I could use some help."

"Yates and Pigweed can do it."

"That crabby old man and that slow-witted boy?"

215

she asked, and disliked herself for playing dirty and skewering two men who'd treated her as if she were some sort of duchess. Nonetheless, she wasn't contrite enough to back down. "You know I haven't been feeling well, and Cactus Blossom would be a comfort to me."

"Don't do me this way, Lisette."

"I've been given to understand most trail cooks have assistants to help them."

"You need help, ask for it. In the meantime, please don't appeal to my sympathies."

"All right, fine. I'll just go on being lonesome, and you can go on being the big cattle baron, making his own rules. And the Lord help anyone who gets in your way."

"What do you mean, lonesome? You've got your work, you've got more than a dozen cowboys at your beck and call, and you've got *me*. How can you be lonesome?"

"I miss having another woman to chat with."

"Then you should have stayed back in Fredericksburg. There're a lot of women there."

Irritated at his cut-to-the-bone remark, she stepped back, and her annoyance turned to a wish to get even. She huffed over to the mother cow, took the rope from its horns, and wound it around the calf's neck. The babe gazed up with trusting eyes; his mother threw back her mighty head to bawl a protest before tipping a horn at Lisette.

"What are you doing?" Gil asked.

"Oh, I don't know, making mincemeat pie?"

Thrusting her nose in the air, Lisette urged the wobbly calf along. She might not have any control over whether Cactus Blossom stayed, but she, by darn, wasn't going to leave this poor little baby for the buzzards.

Babies had special meaning to her.

Gil grasped the strongbox and tucked it under his arm. "If you're wanting to make mincemeat we've got plenty of suet in the chuck box."

"Don't take my words so damned literally!"

"Watch your mouth, woman. It isn't becoming, your cursing."

She didn't dignify his comment with a reply. Head held high, she walked the calf to camp. The mother followed along docilely. Lisette heard her husband's footsteps behind her. The hoodlum wagon in sight, she called out to Pigweed Martin, "Unload your wagon. Put some hay on the floorboard. Then help me pick up this newborn cow. We're—"

"We're what, Lisette?" Gil asked, danger in his tone.

He ground to a halt in front of her and dropped the strongbox. The boom of steel hitting the hard ground caused her and the baby calf to jump.

"If you'd let me finish, you'd know. We're taking the calf with us."

With his loose-jointed gait, the skinny wagon driver walked toward the trail boss. A thumbnail picked at his protruding teeth before Pigweed asked, "That be okay with you, Chief?"

Lisette held her breath.

Chapter Nineteen

"Hell, no, it's not okay." Gil's hand chopped the air. "We're not hauling any dead weight to Abilene."

Disappointed, indignant, and vexed beyond reason, Lisette muttered through clenched teeth, "I might have known."

Well, she wasn't going to let any mule-headed, callous-hearted husband of hers stand between right and wrong as she saw it. The calf wasn't going to be left behind; he *would* ride in the open-air hoodlum wagon. And in her husband's favorite terminology, that was that.

Tugging gently on the rope fastened to the newborn calf's neck, Lisette guided it—no, him—to the chariot of his salvation.

The little fellow lifted his snout to cry for his mother. The magnificent beast, her muscles moving like waves beneath the tan-and-white hide, trotted over to her offspring. She reared her broad head to moo before lowering it to nudge the babe to an udder. He found breakfast again. *This is what life is all about,* thought Lisette . . . *a loving mother taking care of her own.*

Just as she would be doing . . . someday in late autumn.

At the crest of her thought, Gil ordered, "Yates, put the strongbox away."

Lisette wound the slack end of the rope around a wheel, then proceeded to climb aboard the hoodlum. The wagon was piled high with crates and bedrolls. The crates would have to stay. The bedrolls—it was back to the chuck wagon for them. Guided by the careening emotions that had plagued her for days, she started to make room for the bullock by dumping a bedroll on the ground.

Gil hurried over to the wagon and clamped his fingers around the wooden sideboard. Sunlight glinted in his furious eyes. "You'd better not be doing what I think you're doing."

"If you think I'm clearing this hoodlum for the calf, then you know exactly what I'm doing."

"Lisette, get down from there. We are not, absolutely not, taking that bullock with us."

"Oh yes, we are. He'll ride from here, and in this very wagon."

The mother cow lowed; her great horns turned in Gil's direction.

He ordered, "Rope this cow. Get her to the herd." The mountaineer Attitude Powell rushed forward as Gil bellowed to Pigweed Martin, "Get all this bedding back in the wagon."

His overlarge gray eyes protruding, Pigweed protested, "Your missus might hit me with one of 'em bedrolls, Chief. She's powerful mad. Can I wait a few minutes, till she gets her dander down?"

Pigweed got no response, and every man still in camp was watching the McLoughlins with absorbed attention. Cactus Blossom watched, too. Frank Hatch seemed to be hiding a smirk.

Eli Wilson rode up. "Are you all right, Mrs. McLoughlin?"

"Get lost, Wilson."

The preacher looked at his boss, then at the boss's wife. "Are you all right?" he repeated.

"Yes. Now, please do what he said."

From the corner of her eye, as she continued to pitch bedding from the wagon and the preacher rode out, Lisette spied her husband reaching for the rope.

"Don't you dare untie it," she threatened.

His arms akimbo, Gil glared. "Get down from that wagon. And I do mean now."

"Don't tell me what to do!" She tossed a bedroll at him, missed. "I'm not budging until I'm finished with these."

She launched another bedroll; it struck his chest. If she thought there had been murder in his eyes before, she was certain of it now. She had pushed him too far. *You've been acting like a child.* Her temper abated, but what could be done to rectify the situation?

Turning to Cactus Blossom, Gil asked, "You know how to drive a wagon?"

"Yes."

"And you're wanting a job?"

"Yes."

"You're hired."

"Now, McLoughlin, don't be hasty," Hatch inter-

220

jected. "Cactus Blossom and I neither one want to bring trouble on y'all, nor injure you in any way. You were rather adamant about not having her along."

"Hatch, do you or don't you want this squaw of yours?"

Hatch nodded.

Rubbing the stump of his arm under his chin, and riding a black cutting horse, Wink Tannington returned to camp. He said and did nothing.

Johns Clark, on the other hand, inquired, "Ma'am, do you need some help?"

"No, Johns—thank you."

He shot her a look of sympathy, as did Deep Eddy Roland, who said to Gil, "What's the harm in taking the bullock along?"

"When you're the goddamn boss, I'll tell you!"

Deep Eddy raised his hands in a gesture of I-give-up, and like Johns, went for his mount.

Gil whipped around. "Pigweed, fetch my sorrel from the remuda."

Pigweed set out at the same instant Lisette bent to toss the last bedroll on the ground. All remaining in the hoodlum were crates of supplies and a woman who dreaded owning up to her fit of temper.

"Herd 'em up," Gil ordered the cowhands. "Cactus Blossom, round up these bedrolls. Put 'em in the chuck wagon. Hatch, give her a hand. When the two of you get through, Hatch, get riding. Cactus Blossom, set that chuck wagon in motion."

"Albino, come on." The tiny Comanche woman

looked up at her and extended a hand. "We leave now."

"She is not going with you," Gil announced, his words dangerously even, all of a sudden.

"Albino . . . ?"

"Go on, Cactus Blossom," Lisette urged, shaking in her boots. "Do as he says."

The Comanche, wariness in her gaze, accepted the orders.

And just where does *this leave me?* Lisette asked herself as Hatch and his woman scurried about and the campsite cleared out. She didn't have to wonder long. Gil parked his foot on the wagon tongue, swung a leg into the bed, and lunged toward her. As if she were a sack of potatoes, he heaved her onto his shoulder, debarked from the conveyance, set her to her feet. He dusted his hands, riveting a look of total disgust into her eyes, and stomped toward the approaching sorrel.

He intends to leave me here, she concluded.

Desert the mother of his unborn child, right here in the middle of nowhere.

"What about me?" Lisette asked, her voice weaker than she would have wanted.

"Way I see it, you got your choices. You can behave and ride with me on Big Red. Or you can stay here and caterwaul till kingdom come. Do whatever strikes your fancy."

Once before he'd ordered her to abandon the outfit. This time his suggestion didn't cut as deeply. Once she thought about it, she knew he wouldn't leave her here. Not over so little as a calf.

She decided to call his bluff. "I choose to walk this baby to civilization."

"Like hell you will."

Tight-lipped, he wheeled around, and with long and hurried strides, returned to grab the calf into his arms, its mother lowing a protest from the distance. Gil set the calf to its feet on the floorboard.

Thankfully he wasn't deserting the baby.

"I'll ride in the hoodlum," Lisette said courageously.

Gil shook his head. "It's the saddle or the soles of your shoes. Take your pick."

"I choose to walk. I don't fear the wilds," she lied.

"Good. Glad to hear you're not scared. You've learned the first lesson in survival."

The hoodlum driver returned, leading the mighty Big Red. Pigweed's eyes nearly popped from his skull as he caught sight of a hairy, bovine face peeping above the hoodlum's sideboard.

"Boy," Gil explained, "you're dragging this calf along."

"Chief, I don't reckon I hanker to smell his poop all the livelong day."

"Where's your head, boy? All you've gotta do is stop every once in a while and muck the wagon out."

Pigweed shrugged a thin shoulder. "Ifn that's what you want, Chief."

"That's what I want."

"What about your missus?" Pigweed asked, screwing up one side of his face.

"She makes her own choices."

"Missus, reckon you wanna ride with me?" The

223

driver raked a hand into his crop of straw-colored hair and waited expectantly.

She shook her head.

"All right, I guess, missus."

Nothing appeared too right with Gil McLoughlin.

Pigweed meandered to the hoodlum wagon, got aboard, and clicked his tongue as he snapped the reins. The wheels were set in motion. The mother cow broke loose from Attitude Powell. She trotted to the wagon, following along as if she were a donkey chasing a carrot.

"I couldn't help her getting away," fretted Attitude as he hurried forward.

Gil tossed his arms wide. "Just get on your horse, then. Ride out."

Attitude went for his mount, and Gil glared at Lisette. She didn't know how to make amends with her husband. And right then she didn't know if she wanted to.

MORE PASSION AND ADVENTURE AWAIT... YOUR TRIP TO A BIG ADVENTUROUS WORLD BEGINS WHEN YOU ACCEPT YOUR FIRST 4 NOVELS ABSOLUTELY *FREE*
(AN $18.00 VALUE)

Accept your Free gift and start to experience more of the passion and adventure you like in a historical romance novel. Each Zebra novel is filled with proud men, spirited women and tempestuous love that you'll remember long after you turn the last page.

Zebra Historical Romances are the finest novels of their kind. They are written by authors who really know how to weave tales of romance and adventure in the historical settings you love. You'll feel like you've actually gone back in time with the thrilling stories that each Zebra novel offers.

GET YOUR FREE GIFT WITH THE START OF YOUR HOME SUBSCRIPTION

Our readers tell us that these books sell out very fast in book stores and often they miss the newest titles. So Zebra has made arrangements for you to receive the four newest novels published each month.

You'll be guaranteed that you'll never miss a title, and home delivery is so convenient. And to show you just how easy it is to get Zebra Historical Romances, we'll send you your first 4 books absolutely FREE! Our gift to you just for trying our home subscription service.

BIG SAVINGS AND FREE HOME DELIVERY

Each month, you'll receive the four newest titles as soon as they are published. You'll probably receive them even before the bookstores do. What's more, you may preview these exciting novels free for 10 days. If you like them as much as we think you will, just pay the low preferred subscriber's price of just $3.75 each. *You'll save $3.00 each month off the publisher's price.* AND, your savings are even greater because there are never any shipping, handling or other hidden charges—FREE Home Delivery. Of course you can return any shipment within 10 days for full credit, no questions asked. There is no minimum number of books you must buy.

Chapter Twenty

The hoodlum, the calf aboard and his mother trotting along, drifted out of sight. The sound of longhorns moving to north and the dust from beneath their hooves began to fade.

Lisette and her husband were alone at the now deserted campsite. Big Red, fretful as ever, pulled at the reins held in Gil's hand. His long mane drifting like wash on the line in a breezy day, he shook his massive head. His master quieted the stallion, then wound the reins around a tree trunk.

From over his shoulder, Gil said impatiently, "Wife, I am not going to stand here all day, waiting for your answer."

Just moments ago she had thought she didn't want to make up with Gil, but that wasn't so. Since "guilty party" fit her like a second skin, he deserved an apology.

"I guess we should talk," she said hesitantly.

"No. I'm doing the talking."

He wouldn't talk, he'd yell, she decided.

She was in for a surprise when he rounded on her and said in an evenly modulated voice, "I won't put

225

up with your undermining me in front of my men, Lisette."

"I'm sorry. I—"

"I told you a good while back, 'sorry' doesn't work with me. If you and I are going to get along, you're gonna have to think before you act."

"I was upset over Cactus Blossom. It would've been terrible, sending her off alone, and—"

"I don't see how she relates to your snit over that calf." He rubbed a finger across the scar Blade Sharp had left.

"It's bothered me since the first day I joined this outfit, the way you abandon the sucklings."

"They have to be left behind. We can't slow the drive to let them poke along or take time to nurse."

"You spend hours herding their mothers back to the fold."

"Not as much time as we'd spend babying those calves along. This isn't a ranch or a farm, Lisette. This is a cattle drive. A drive that depends on moving and moving fast. We need the spring waters and the best grasses. Soon summer's going to be here. The water and grass will be scarce. You know the first cows at the railhead get the best prices."

He grimaced. "And I'd have appreciated it if you'd had the courtesy to speak with me about your obsession with calves before you took the matter into your own hands."

"I was afraid to." She studied the toes of her shoes. "I figured you'd find me weak for even mentioning the matter."

"I would've. But no matter how I might have reacted, you had no call to take the reins as trail boss." He took a step toward her. "Nobody, nobody tells me how to run my cattle drive."

Still shaking from the morning's events, she bristled at his high-handedness. "You've got a cold heart."

"When it comes to business, yes."

"I don't see how you can sleep at night, with all those dead calves in our wake."

Exasperation set his whisker-shadowed features. "Let me tell you something, Lisette McLoughlin. I sleep pretty damned well, thank you very much. Want to know why? I've been to hell and back. I'm thankful I survived."

"I thought you had a conscience."

"Conscience has nothing to do with it. Ours is the game of survival. I've made this trip before—three times. And what I didn't know about enduring, I learned up this very cowpath."

"They teach cruelty to animals somewhere along the way?" she asked crossly.

"You're better suited to the drawing room, woman."

"You would have made an excellent executioner."

"Thank you, wife." His eyes got dark. "Appreciate it. I love being so compared."

Contrite, Lisette licked her lips and contemplated the ground once more. "Forgive me. I was being cruel."

His voice lost its sharp edge as he said, "Don't apologize for a trait that might just get you to Kansas and back. This land demands cruelty. And it

227

could get worse before we reach Abilene—especially in the Indian Territory. There's neither a town nor a lawman between Texas and Kansas."

Catching on "Indian Territory," she shivered, thinking of savages, arrowheads, tomahawks. And guns.

"Comanches are up there, too, aren't they?" she asked.

"In some areas. Mostly around here. Lisette, I can't say I blame the Comanche for trying to protect the land we whites are taking from them. They want to live and prosper same as us. They fight to keep their way of life; we fight to capture the land we need. And we'll keep fighting until one of us wins."

Borrowing wits from somewhere, she jacked up her chin. "What do Indians have to do with baby cows?"

"What I'm trying to make you understand is . . . nothing—neither man nor beast—has an inherent right to life out here. Either you survive or you don't. We've been lucky so far, honey. We've had good weather and only one Indian attack. Let's pray that holds, because no one—no one—will make it unless he or she is tough as ten-year-old pemmican."

"You're certainly that."

"Right." He nodded. "But even the fittest don't make it sometimes. Some of us are going to die, some of us are going to live. Some of those will be cattle, some will be man. It's as simple as one-two-three."

"You paint a grim picture."

"I speak the truth." Gil collected Big Red's reins.

"You've got two choices. You can toughen your hide and go on with me to Kansas. Or you can stay in Fort Worth till I get back to collect you."

"You want," she began in German, then spoke in English. "Y-you want to leave me in Fort Worth?"

"I'll rent you a place in town, hire you some help. You needn't concern yourself, I'll leave plenty of money for you to live on."

She swallowed, then met his determined gaze. "It sounds as if you've been thinking about this awhile."

"I don't deny it. I think your settling would be for the best. You said yourself you're lonely for women-folk. And the work's getting to be too much for you."

"I can handle my work."

"You won't be able to handle it a few months down the line."

"Not true," she protested.

He closed the distance between them. His fingers locking around her shoulders, he said, "Why don't we stop the pussyfootin' around. You haven't admitted it, maybe not even to yourself, but you're with child."

"I . . . I've admitted it to myself."

His voice quiet, he asked, "Why didn't you tell me?"

"I was waiting for the right moment." Rubbing her suddenly aching temple, she said, "If you won't be back till no telling when, you might miss the birthing."

"There's a chance of that. A slight one. But a chance."

All her old feelings of loneliness and fears of abandonment struck anew. Nerves lurching like an out-of-control wagon, she took a step backward. Her knees almost buckled.

"Lisette," he said patiently, "it's best for the cattle drive if you stay put. I can't have anything holding us up."

"You could have put it in more personal terms."

"Then think of all those heads of cattle as gold pieces, giving us security. Delays could mean losses."

"You've no right to assume I'll cause delays. Anything could happen to slow the procession."

"You're right about that." A grim set to his mouth, he added, "You'd have no business in the middle of it. You are going to stay in Fort Worth, keep your sense and sensibilities in check, and bring our child into the world. That's more important than me being there for the birth."

Maybe it wasn't important to her husband, but it was very important to Lisette. She was on the verge of telling him all the things she'd decided this morning: she wasn't some delicate flower in need of pampering; she was as healthy as a horse, and babes had come into this world under far worse conditions.

He wouldn't want to hear that, she figured. Why? Because she'd become a hindrance rather than an asset to the Four Aces undertaking. He ought to have a sign painted on the sides of the chuck wagon: *No Sentimentalists Need Apply.*

"I don't blame you," she said, filled with the self-pity she believed was deserved, "wanting to be free of a teary-eyed female who's muddying up your trail drive."

"You're putting it bluntly."

She read "but truthfully" in his eyes. If he loved her, he would want her within sight. Nothing would keep him from being with her when their child drew his first breath.

But he had never said anything about love. Never.

Tears burned her eyes; her throat tightened; her stomach knotted . . . and threatened to roil. *I'm not going to be sick again. I've shown too much weakness already.*

He offered his hand. "Come on, honey. Let me help you up Big Red. We need to catch the herd."

"And get on to Fort Worth."

"And get on to Fort Worth," he echoed.

"I have no say in it?"

"Lisette, will you stay there of your own accord?"

"I'll do whatever is best. For you, for the child."

"It's best for you, too."

This wasn't what she wanted. They were nowhere near Fort Worth, yet the ache of her lonely prospects doubled. She wouldn't beg, though. She would *not*. Settled behind him on the saddle, she let him lead her toward Fort Worth.

Nonetheless, she wasn't above having the last word. "If you don't return in time for my lying-in, should I have Hermann Gilliegorm McLoughlin christened?"

"Don't you dare name him that."

"Guess there's not much you can do about it. You'll be on the trail, and I'll be in Fort Worth."

"Damn you." His words were profane, yet he laughed and reached behind him to pat her thigh.

"You're a spiteful lass."

"Agreed."

"Lisette," he said quietly, "I guess I ought to tell you something. I wouldn't have left you here. Not for over five minutes or so."

"Thank you for telling me."

Her faith wasn't misplaced. She wrapped her arms around him, leaning her cheek against his back. Gruff and dogmatic he might be, but Gil McLoughlin was a good man.

"Liebster, thanks for letting that baby calf ride in the hoodlum."

"Damn it, don't remind me."

Matthias Gruene was away from camp, rounding up cattle that had strayed during the night, when the set-to about the bullock occurred, but he heard about it the same day. Attitude Powell enlightened him. Dinky Peele added his two cents. At a rest stop, Jackson Bell had a few words to say on the subject. Wink Tannington spoke floridly on a woman "knowing her place."

Setting his spur rowels to spinning, Matthias headed his mount toward the chuck wagon. Lisette needed help.

The Indian woman was wandering around the wagon, Lisette nowhere in sight.

"Where is Mrs. McLoughlin?" he shouted.

"Shhh." Cactus Blossom brought a finger to her lip. On quiet feet, she walked to Matthias. Tossing a braid over her shoulder, she looked up with wide-set black eyes. "Albino sleeps in the wagon."

"Is she all right?"

"As fine as a woman can be at a time like hers."

Suspicious, Matthias asked, "What 'time like hers?' "

"She needs her rest. She's going to have a papoose."

The announcement hit Matthias with the force of grapeshot. He squeezed his eyes shut, his head dropping almost to his chest. Lisette, a mother. No! Not darling Lise, sweet as a peach, tart as a lemon. He pounded the heel of his fist on the pommel. He accepted that Lisette belonged to her husband, but the trail boss getting a baby on her added a finality to the marriage Matthias was loath to embrace.

Since the night she'd shown up and wanted to be part of the outfit, he'd had fantasies about the girl he loved with a purity of spirit. Those fantasies, his new feelings—they were sinful. Sinful!

And she loved her husband. Any fool could see it. *She'll never be yours. Accept it, Gruene. Accept it.*

He couldn't. He yearned for her love, for her passions, and for *him* to fulfill her every want and desire.

"You're in love with Albino."

His head shot up to meet the beautiful Indian's wise eyes. "Leave me alone," he muttered.

"You need a woman, Mouth That Beckons."

"Not just any woman."

Cactus Blossom laughed. "You speak with a forked tongue."

"I didn't lie. I spoke a simple truth."

233

He turned his mount and rode away. Rode away as if demons were chasing him. Matthias Gruene had always been a loner, and he clutched solitude around him. He was glad for the loneliness of the trail with only cows for company. That evening he avoided the campfire, took supper on a piece of jerky and deep quaffs of the schnapps he kept in his saddlebag. That night he laid his head on his saddle, with grasses and twigs his mattress. He closed his eyes to blank out the stars above, but mostly the vision of Lisette.

Then it came to him, a slight whiff of lilac water, Lisette's cologne. Fingers touched his cheek. Lisette? He grabbed the hand. This wasn't the woman of his dreams . . . but there was nothing wrong with the way she looked or smelled.

"What are *you* doing here?"

"I'm here to warm your night and chase away the bad spirits."

"What are you doing, wearing *her* cologne?"

"Don't question too deeply, Mouth That Beckons."

Her scent enveloped him, and challenging her statement became impossible. Yet Matthias mustered a modicum of reason.

"Where's Hatch?"

"He sleeps."

"Won't he miss you?"

"As I said, he sleeps." The woman unfastened the buttons of Matthias's britches. "And you agonize. I saw it in your face. I like your face. Much is written there." Fingers wrapped around his manhood; a thumb played with the tip of him. "Don't suffer over

234

what you do not have, Mouth That Beckons. It is not practical."

He tried to push her fingers from him. "You'd better go back to Hatch."

"You do not listen. I told you, he sleeps."

"And he'll wake up wondering where you are."

"He knows I pleasure other men. Tonight I give you pleasure, Mouth That Beckons."

Her lips replaced her fingers. Matthias shuddered with need. His fingers combed through the Indian's coarse black hair, then canvassed her back. She felt so tiny against his big Teutonic frame, and the feeling was more than good.

He didn't give a damn whose woman she was. He was tired of stepping aside for other men.

"Give me pleasure, pretty lady," he moaned as Cactus Blossom's tongue stroked him.

She raised her head. "I am not Albino."

"I know."

He ripped the laces of her dress to clamp a big hand on her breast. He felt the crest swell beneath his finger. His *männliches Glied* hardened even more, and he shoved the woman to her back. His mouth descended as he positioned himself between her beckoning and spread legs. Lunging into her warmth, he seized her lips in a bruising kiss. Quivering, she clamped her knees on his hips. And her words encouraged him to plunge again and again.

"*So gut,* so good," he groaned at the end.

The woman's palms made a chalice around his jaw. "And you know I am not Long Legs' woman?"

"*Ja,* I know. You are Cactus Blossom."

The agony had vanished. Lisette was lost to him, but this woman filled a need. From the moment he'd first seen Cactus Blossom, Matthias had admired her spirit and serenity. Now he had more to admire about the black-haired, bronze-skinned beauty. Maybe all he'd needed was attention such as he'd craved from McLoughlin's wife.

"Come here," he murmured.

"I am here already."

"*Ja*, you are," he conceded and smiled. "Stay with me."

She did.

And each night, past midnight, Cactus Blossom found him. It was no longer Lisette he coveted. The petite Comanche woman was the one he wanted to roll in the grass with.

One dark midnight, as the pads of his fingers skimmed over her belly, he asked, "What happened to you? Why do you have scars?"

"Don't question too deeply, Mouth That Beckons."

"I am. Tell me."

An owl hooted from a nearby tree, a cloud covered the moon, and Cactus Blossom was gathering her thoughts. At last she replied, "From mourning my daughter. The spirits were not kind to my Weeping Willow. When she came into the world, there was no hope for her to grow tall and strong. When she died, I mourned her in the way of my people." She rose and pulled the buckskin sheath over her head. "I took a knife to my flesh."

Before he could say anything, she started away.

"Don't go."

"I will be back." There was a tear in her voice. "Tomorrow night."

The poor woman, he thought. Obviously she still mourned her dead babe. And Matthias adored her all the more for her sensitivity.

Five nights after their first coupling, Matthias had a visitor and it wasn't Cactus Blossom. McLoughlin sought him out.

"We haven't seen you around camp," the Scotsman said as Matthias set his saddle to the ground for the night. "Are you sick or something?"

"No."

"Lisette's been wondering about you."

"You hired me to be strawboss." Matthias frowned at McLoughlin. "I've been earning my keep."

"Your keep includes meals."

"I eat jerky."

"When you could be eating from Lisette's table? Seems peculiar to me." The trail boss slapped at a firefly that landed on his jaw. "She's learned how to make chili. I think you'd like it."

"Too spicy."

"How do you know if you haven't tried it?"

"I hear it's too spicy."

"Matt, what's bothering you?"

"I'm tired and I'm wanting to sleep." Sleep was his last consideration. Cactus Blossom would be here. After midnight.

"I did have another purpose in seeking you out," McLoughlin said. "I want you to double back to Cleburne, buy a couple more hoodlum wagons, then meet up with us, pronto."

237

"What for?"

"You know what for. To carry calves in." McLoughlin cleared his throat. "I don't have to tell you, when we cart the new calves, the mother cows are following along agreeably. We're spending a lot less time keeping those cows in line."

Matthias laughed. "You've finally seen the reward in Lise's idea, I take it."

"I have." McLoughlin spoke in a sheepish tone. "Hers was a smart plan. I told her so, but she's too kind to be vindictive about it. Says she didn't have any idea of the positive outcome. Good woman, that wife of mine."

"You're not telling me anything I didn't already know." Matthias's thoughts turned to another woman. He didn't want to be separated from Cactus Blossom, and he said, "Send Hatch after the wagons."

The night got quiet. Crickets and cattle made noises, and Sadie Lou barked in the distance, but nothing else. He knew the boss didn't like his decisions questioned, but he'd done it and wouldn't back down.

McLoughlin asked, "Why would I want to send Hatch?"

"He's new. Let him take the menial tasks."

"No task is menial if it benefits the drive."

"Send him anyway."

"Matt, you got something against Frank Hatch?"

"No. He does a day's work." Matthias pulled the flask he hadn't touched in five days from its hiding place. "Want a drink?"

"You know I don't allow liquor on the trail."

"Rules about liquor are for the other men. I'm not just one of them. Which is why I resent your sending me on a petty errand."

"You may be strawboss, but I'm in charge, and I'm tempted to fire you over that remark."

While Matthias had great respect for McLoughlin's abilities to get cattle up the trail, and while his loyalty was to none but the Four Aces and its owner, he wasn't going to be threatened. "If that's what you're wanting to do, do it."

Another stretch of silence.

"All right. I'll send Hatch."

"Thank you."

McLoughlin started to walk away, but he stopped a half-dozen paces in the distance and turned around. "I need your advice on something."

After their difference of opinion, it cheered Matthias, the Scotsman's show of confidence. His loyalty to the brand wasn't misplaced.

"Matt, I get a peculiar feeling about Hatch. Sometimes I think he's trying to chouse me. Other times, I get the inkling I've seen him somewhere before. It's craziness, I know."

"Have you asked if he knows you?"

"You know the unwritten law. If a man doesn't offer anything about himself, another man doesn't ask."

"Then forget your suspicions."

"No, I don't think that'd be smart. Better send Tannington with him to Cleburne, just in case he can't be trusted." McLoughlin slipped a thumb behind his gunbelt. "I can tell you one thing I'm not only suspicious about. Cactus Blossom is sneaking off at night, and if she's not letting one of the men at her, my name's not McLoughlin." His eyes hardened, visible even in the moonlight. "Wouldn't be you, would it, Matt?"

Matthias took a swig of schnapps, then reminded the trail boss of his own words. "You know the code of the West. If a man doesn't confide, another man shouldn't pry."

Chapter Twenty-one

Gil had a dilemma. Matthias might have told him to mind his own business, but the answer spoke for itself. He was poking Hatch's woman. Watching Matthias take another plug from the flask, Gil shook his head in disgust, then studied the stars above. Matt was drinking and poking; no telling how Hatch would react to the latter; and if he sent the trouble-makers packing, Lisette would throw one of her tantrums.

She didn't need to get upset, not with the babe on the way.

"Put the sauce away, Matt. You're not above rules just because you're second in charge."

The strawboss imparted a dirty look.

"Something else," Gil said. "If you don't keep your hands off that woman as well as the corn, you're out of a job."

"I'll quit the drinking, but as for Cactus, no, I won't stay away from her. If it means you and I part ways, then so be it."

"This late in the season, you'll have a hard time

finding another strawboss job. If she's worth starving for, go to her."

"She's worth it. And you're nothing but an—" Matthias lowered the flask. "You've got Lise, but to hell with anyone else who wants their own woman."

"Lisette is my wife, not my whore," Gil replied. "And I am the boss. What I say goes."

"Look, you said you're sending Hatch for the wagons. That means he'll be out of the way for days on end. Cactus and I will be discreet. And it won't be long after Hatch returns that we'll be in Fort Worth. I can find some sort of work there. Let me stay on till we reach town."

"I'm not running a brothel, Matt. Not now, and not between here and Fort Worth."

"This has nothing to do with whores. This has everything to do with me and my woman."

Gil shoved his thumbs behind Thelma's belt and stared at the ground. What was the most important issue here? Matt Gruene was the best cowpuncher he'd ever met, and he kept the cowboys in line, which freed Gil to be the trail boss. The drive would suffer if Matt left. And Gil decided the Cactus Blossom situation would run its course between here and Fort Worth. Then Matthias would see the light.

"All right," Gil said. "You can stay on. But you better have meant what you said about discretion, or you're out once we hit town."

He stomped to Big Red. Climbing into the saddle, he muttered a "damn." During his previous drives up to Abilene, all he'd had to worry about were Indians, the elements, and keeping the cattle from stampeding. This drive had been snakebitten from the beginning. He might lose Matt Gruene. And he'd lost control of the outfit.

Ten days had passed since Wink and Mister Hatch had returned to camp with a pair of extra hoodlum wagons, and Lisette was thrilled at the success of carting the newborn calves along. She was not thrilled about Cactus Blossom. Something was wrong, very wrong.

And now, as she put the finishing touches on the midday meal with the Comanche woman's assistance, Lisette was more worried than ever. The usually conversant Cactus Blossom hadn't uttered a word all day, her stoic face set in an unreadable mask.

Pouring coffee into the grinder, Lisette asked, "Are you not happy?"

"I am happy."

"But you could be happier."

"Everyone could be happier, Albino."

Lisette agreed on that score; she'd be much happier without the prospect of reaching Fort Worth and saying good-bye to her husband. They expected to reach the cowtown by late afternoon.

She just couldn't think about it, especially not now, when Cactus Blossom was in need of a friend.

"Are you having problems with Mister Hatch?" Lisette placed her hand on Cactus Blossom's arm; it was much too cold for this warm noon of mid-May. "Is there anything I can do to help?"

"No." Cactus Blossom took knives, forks, and spoons from the chuck box drawer. "But I do

243

admit . . . I have found a man to give me the love I missed with Dung Eyes."

Gott in Himmel. It would be stupid even to ask if she'd been sleeping with one of the men. Reading the meaning between the lines and the smile now brightening that bronzed face, Lisette knew it was true as the blue sky above.

"Who is the man?" Lisette asked.

"Mouth That Beckons."

"I beg your pardon?"

"Albino . . . how do you feel about Matthias?"

Lisette should have known he was the Mouth in question. She'd seen his eyes on Cactus Blossom, and she'd fretted over the attentions that could rain trouble on the entire trail drive. At last she answered, "He's been my friend for many years."

"If you did not have your man, would you want Matthias for your own?"

"Blossom, that is a question which is ridiculous to address. Gil and I do have each other, and we'll stay that way until death parts us. He is my heart, my soul . . . my breath, my life."

"I believed that to be so, but I had to ask." Cactus Blossom tossed a black braid over one shoulder. "You see, I love Matthias. We will be married in Fort Worth."

Her suspicions confirmed, Lisette sighed. What happened to his feelings for that "one lady" he'd mentioned before reaching Lampasas? Evidently, absence made his heart grow colder. Well, it was his life, and she wouldn't be judgmental.

"I wish you the best, Blossom. But you must be careful, extremely careful. There's my husband's reaction to consider, but he's not the real problem. Once Mister Hatch discovers all this, there will be a lot of trouble."

"I have already told him."

"And he didn't object?"

Cactus Blossom looked her in the eye. "No."

Lisette opened a can of tomatoes—always a special treat to cowboys—and recalled her friend's earlier strange look. "Is there something you're not telling me?"

"I fear Mouth That Beckons will have no use for me if—"

"If he discovers your profession?"

"He knows about that." Cactus Blossom turned away. "I have changed my mind. I do not want to speak of my troubles."

Lisette sighed. "If he loves you, Matthias will forgive you anything."

"To the Great Spirits, I pray this." Cactus Blossom sliced the large roast, then said in a change of subject, "This meat is much favored by Mouth That Beckons. What do you call it?"

"Sauerbraten." Lisette paused. "What about Matthias's job? Will he go on without you? You'll need his salary."

"Long Legs says he cannot go with him to the land above the Territory."

Lisette, her brow tightening, said, "You misunderstood. Gil wouldn't fire Matthias. He wouldn't."

"He did."

"Surely not. You've taken something out of context."

Lisette, needing to get the matter straight, her ap-

245

prehensions building with each passing moment, hurried over to the triangle and rang it to announce the midday meal. But Gil didn't appear; she untied her apron. If Cactus Blossom wasn't confused, Matthias was not going to be dismissed, not if Lisette had any say whatsoever.

Frank Hatch eyed Lisette as she rode off on a dun mare from the remuda. Good, she was gone. And he was glad the heathen bitch was out of sight, too. The last thing he wanted was his former squaw's flapping mouth. He was truly glad she wanted to tie up with that slow-talking German.

And he, Charles Franklin Hatch, late of Charlwood, would come out smelling like a rose.

His only regret where she was concerned had to do with her sin at Dead Buffalo Bluff. She would, however, pay for it. In good time, when it would best serve him.

He scanned the luncheon gatherers. Thankfully, none of the Yankees took the first shift. The old man, Yates, was griping about his "rheumatiz," while Jackson Bell, Toad Face Walker, the Mexican, Ochoa, and Wink Tannington squatted close to the chuck wagon and shoved food in their mouths.

Hatch watched Tannington. Going back to Cleburne had been a boon. The Mississippian had come over to his side in the war against Major McLoughlin of the Union Army. It hadn't taken much to get Tannington's help, just a few comments about the trail boss's autocratic ways, plus some well-placed reminders of Yankee abominations against the South.

And Tannington had assured him that Jackson Bell, a young man of robust health and good Virginia lineage, would be easy pickings, if the cards were played right.

Hatch needed allies in his quest for revenge.

"Say, Mister Bell, I understand you were with General Lee at Appomattox." Hatch glanced at the Virginian. "How do you feel about lining the coffers of a Yankee major?"

Jackson Bell's fork stopped midway between his plate and his mouth. "What do you mean?"

Hatch turned to Toad Face. "I understand you were with General Beauregard. You gentlemen had it rough, didn't you?"

Yates, his bones creaking, got up and hobbled over to Hatch. "What're ye getting at, Hatch?"

"I'm just thinking how things would have been different, had the Bonny Blue flag not been lowered." Hatch shook his head in a show of dejection. "Who would've thought, back in '61, that the Confederacy would lose so much . . . that we—fine gentlemen of the South—would be employed by a damnyankee?"

"Ain't that the truth," Tannington interjected on cue.

Toad Face Walker took a plug of tobacco into his mouth. Chewing thoughtfully, he spat a brown stream. "Far as I'm concerned, the war's over."

He huffed off, which was fine with Hatch. Toad Face, who was aptly named and whose crudity rivaled the vilest of human amphibians, was just too ragged and filthy for Hatch's taste.

"War ain't over for me. My brothers died at

Vicksburg. And I lost this"—Tannington raised his stump—"at Shiloh. And what did we get for it?"

"Why don't ye shut yer traps?" Yates hitched up his britches. "The cap'n, he ain't answerable for what go'd on afore."

Curling his lip, Hatch asked, "Tell me, Mister Yates, were you a part of any campaign?"

"Naw. But me nephew Homer done sided with Jeff Davis."

"Unless you're taking your kinsman's side, I suggest you shut *your* mouth and finish filling your face."

A hush fell over the campfire, the pop of a flame the only sound, and Hatch itched to set the chuck wagon aflame.

"Since when do you give the orders around here, Hatch?" McLoughlin stepped out from behind the chuck wagon.

Once before, Frank Hatch had seen that look on McLoughlin's face—the day Charlwood had gone up in smoke. It was a look of supremacy and bedamned-to-you. Major McLoughlin would suffer for it, and soon.

"I was simply speaking with my fellow workers," Hatch replied. "Surely you don't seek to take away my right to free speech . . . as set out by your Constitution."

Right then Lisette rode up on the dun mare and dismounted. "What is going on here?" she asked, not looking too pleased.

"Find something to do." McLoughlin scowled at her, then turned back to Hatch. "Since you don't want to 'fill the coffers of a Yankee major,' I suggest you pack your gear and ride out." His eyes cruised over the others. "That goes for anyone who doesn't ride for the brand."

Her hands on her hips, Lisette watched as her husband gave those orders. She glanced worriedly at the men, then took a step in McLoughlin's direction. "Maybe—"

"I told you to find something to do," the trail boss said to her.

Jackson Bell, his shoulders hunched, shouted at McLoughlin. "You're acting like a typical Yankee. Why don't you quit picking on the lady? She's done nothing."

Ochoa and Tannington agreed. McLoughlin's face looked like thunderclouds, black and dangerous, and the expression intensified when Lisette shook her finger at the men and said, "Now listen here, all of you. Leave my husband alone. And if you don't like him or the way he runs this outfit, I suggest you do as he suggests. Pack up and ride out."

She turned on the toe of her shoe and went over to fiddle with the chuck box. McLoughlin's fingers made fists at his side as he glowered at her. And Hatch hid a chuckle. Evidently there was one thing McLoughlin disliked more than disloyalty from his cowboys, and that was his wife wearing the pants.

Hatch grinned at his men who *would* become his allies, by the grace of the Bonny Blue. The second phase of his plan for retaliation was proceeding even more smoothly than imagined.

Chapter Twenty-two

Now what have I done?

After defending her husband against the Southerners, Lisette followed as he stomped away from the noon meal-camp. She called over her shoulder, "Oscar, take the chuck wagon," then rushed on. "Gil!"

He deigned not an answer; he climbed into Big Red's saddle, heading north, and Lisette collected the dun mare she'd left ground-tethered only minutes ago.

She looked to the rear, seeing that all the men, including Hatch and his compatriots, were peaceably taking their places with the herd. What might have been a disturbance had been put down, whether by Gil's threat or by her defense of him, she didn't know, but she was thankful for the outcome.

Across the prairie south of Fort Worth, she rode forward, catching her husband five minutes later. "We need to talk," she said, the mare prancing beneath her. "Gil, talk to me."

One hand on the saddlehorn, he replied, "I have nothing to say."

"I do. Gil, what is the matter with you?"

"I warn you, Lisette. Don't push me."

From the distance she heard the longhorns passing through the mesquite grove. Eyeing her husband, she said, "You're treating me as if I'm nothing more than one of your hirelings."

"You are the cook."

"I'm your wife, too. That should count for something."

He maneuvered Big Red toward her mount, leaning his face toward Lisette. Through clenched teeth, he answered, "Maybe we do need to powwow, since I thought we got the chain of command straight after you pulled that snit over packing calves along."

Somehow she felt as if pointing out the success of her idea wasn't the best thing to do. She dismounted to wind the mare's reins around a mesquite trunk, and faced her husband's disgust.

He had secured the sorrel, was standing not five feet in front of her, murder in his eyes.

"I don't appreciate what you did." His voice pitched in a dangerous level, he added, "I won't have my men thinking I hide behind apron strings."

"All I did was leap to your defense."

"You fight your battles and I'll fight mine."

Should she try to apologize for overstepping her bounds? No . . . he didn't like apologies, for one thing. And for another, she didn't feel as if she'd been in the wrong, flying to his defense. Any good wife would defend her husband.

She watched him keep a distance between them; his body spoke the language of separation—of body and spirit. He just couldn't let go, could he?

Hoping that a good, honest talk would open his eyes, she asked, "Is that what marriage is all about?

251

Two separate beings, going through life without working through the trials and tribulations together?"

"I'm not talking about marriage." His hand sliced the air. "I'm talking about a trail drive."

She crossed her arms under her breasts. "Let me tell you something, Mister McLoughlin. When our marriage became a lifetime agreement instead of a temporary arrangement, I gave up my dreams of freedom. I set a new goal for myself. I made up my mind to make a success of our marriage, and it wasn't just for my own benefit. Your successes became equally important to me. And we depend on the cattle drive for our *mutual* success. If you can't handle that, you're not the man I married."

"If I disappoint you, so be it."

"You're exactly what I was running away from."

"Meaning . . . ?"

"I've worked myself ragged trying to please you, but you're an autocrat and a tyrant, just like my brother, and I could have stayed in Fredericksburg—with a roof over my head—and gotten the same treatment."

"You'll have a roof over your head. By tonight. And you can do whatever you please for the next few months."

"How easy it is for you, getting rid of pesky baggage," she replied tightly. "You'll be rid of me . . . and Matthias will be gone."

"Matthias isn't going anywhere, except to Abilene."

"I've been told you fired him."

"Only if he didn't get shut of that Indian woman by the time we reach Fort Worth."

"Then he's as good as fired. He and Blossom are going to be married."

"Damn." His mouth flattened into a tight line. "Does Hatch know about it?"

Lisette nodded.

"No wonder Hatch was rabble-rousing." Gil blew out a heavy stream of air. "Damn it, I thought Matt would've had enough of her by now."

"Maybe *some* people aren't so eager to dispose of their loved ones." Lisette wheeled around. "Personally, I'll be glad to be away from you."

She was tired of trying to please Gil. She was sick of his domination. And she was at her wit's end over the prospect of being dumped in Fort Worth. Yet . . . even though he had told her over and again that it was best for the cattle drive if she stayed behind, even though he treated her as if she were nothing more than an underling, she loved him. But she'd be left to the Comanches before she'd engage in another spat with Gil McLoughlin.

Her attitude didn't change as they reached Fort Worth and rented the three-room house to the rear of Mrs. Ruth Craven's two-story clapboard boardinghouse.

Annoyed by her silence and bossiness, Gil left Lisette at the boardinghouse to do her stewing and set out to take care of business — the business of Matt Gruene. He searched through the crowded streets of Fort Worth, futilely. At a small chophouse near the Trinity River, he found a lone diner. Jakob Lindemann was devouring an apple pie.

"Have you seen Gruene?" Gil asked, straddling a chair.

Lindemann wiped his mouth with a linen. *"Ja.* He is with Cactus Blossom. They have rented a house from Frau Two Toes."

Gil knew the place as well as the woman. Bertha Two Toes, white wife of a Crow from the Territory, had a shack on the banks of the Trinity. Big, young, and meaner than a rattlesnake, Jimmy Two Toes was the sort of no-good who made even the Comanches look good.

But now wasn't the time to ruminate over Two Toes.

"You reckon Hatch knows about Matt?" Gil asked.

"Ja." Lindemann cut another spoonful of pie. "At the Panther Saloon I heard him talking with Tannington. Hatch said he was glad to be rid of 'that heathen bitch.' "

"I've long suspected Hatch cared nothing for her, but I find it surprising any man would have such a casual attitude about losing a woman to another man."

The Fredericksburger shrugged. "She is only an Indian."

"She's more than that to Matt." And Gil got the uncomfortable feeling that he and Lindemann might be making too little of Hatch's reaction. "See you later, Lindemann."

Gil left the chophouse and hurried through the darkened streets to Bertha Two Toes's rental house. It took several knocks on the weathered door to rouse the occupants, and when Matt answered the summons, Gil knew from the strawboss's tousled appearance that he'd interrupted sex.

I ought to be making love. I ought to be with Lisette, settling that latest fight of ours. Tomorrow I'll be leaving, and—

"You want something, McLoughlin?"

"A few minutes of your time."

Arranging her buckskin sheath around her hips, Cactus Blossom stepped to her lover's side to say, "Come in, Long Legs."

Gil entered the modest quarters furnished with a single pallet. "I understand you're going to be married," he said without preamble.

"That is right." Matthias nodded and put an arm around Cactus Blossom's shoulders. "Tomorrow."

"I'd like to talk you out of it. The strawboss job is still yours, Matt, if you'll get back where you belong."

"You didn't think twice when you took Lise's hand."

"We didn't have someone like Hatch after us."

Cactus Blossom lifted her chin. "Do not talk out of both sides of your mouth. Let us have our happiness, and go back to yours. We do not need you, Long Legs."

"You don't. But I can't imagine Hatch taking this lying down." Gil grimaced. "I don't think you've heard the last of him."

"Don't concern yourself in our business." Matthias scraped his fingers through his hair. "As I told you before, I'd rather we didn't part on bad terms. Can't you accept that you have no say in this, and go on? On good terms."

"Yeah, that's exactly what I can do." Gil turned to leave, but his former strawboss's voice stopped him.

"If we're parting with no hard feelings between us, Gil, then I'd be honored if you'd stand up for me at the wedding." A moment of silence passed. "Will you do it?"

"No, I don't think so."

Gil left.

In a private room of the Panther Saloon, which was a fairly clean establishment catering to cattlemen rather than their drovers, Hatch sat at a felt-top table and played stud poker. A pile of gold coins rested in front of him, a trio of gamblers flanking the table. *Better let them win or I'll have Hitt and his boys against me.*

Hatch needed the Hitt gang.

He lost the next three rounds.

"You gentlemen are too good for me."

"You ain't givin' up, are ya?" asked Asher Pierce.

"Of course not."

Two more rounds lost. Hatch's pile of coins declined to a handful. His eyes swept across his fellow players. None were youths, each had the etching of trouble in his harsh features. Two were Confederate veterans.

The bald Asher Pierce, shuffling the cards with his meaty hands, puffed on a cigar. Rattler Smith sucked on a toothpick and studied his newfound riches. The last of the three, Delmar Hitt, was a carpetbagger from Ohio.

Hatch had long known of Hitt. After General Lee's surrender, when the Yankees had arrived to collect taxes in Georgia, Delmar Hitt had been among them. Within a year, the carpetbagger had absconded with the proceeds, had beat for Texas. If not for the taxes on the charred remains of Charlwood being a part of that booty, Hatch might have admired Hitt's deviousness.

Hitt, like McLoughlin, like Cactus Blossom, would pay for crimes against Charles Franklin Hatch. All in good time. For now, though, Hatch had plans for the infamous Hitt gang, and quarreling would gain him nothing.

"Are you gentlemen interested in a deal?"

"Yep. Ante up." Rattler Smith tugged on the large mole that grew from an earlobe.

"I don't refer to cards. I refer to big money."

Smith took the toothpick from his mouth; Pierce set the cards aside. Hitt leaned his chair back on two of its legs, and lifting a graying brow, he fingered his cravat. "If you have something to say, say it."

"I want your help rustling a herd of cattle."

"If we're interested in stealing cows, why would we want to help you?" Hitt came back. "We could do it for ourselves."

"You could. But you'd be going cold into an outfit. And you'd have to think of the dangers involved." Hatch paused. "I understand you lost some of your men last time. And you yourself took a bullet, Hitt."

Rattler Smith put the toothpick back in his mouth, rolled it to a corner. "How do ya think ya could make it easi—?"

"Shut up, Rattler. I'll do the talking," Hitt cut in, then eyed Hatch. "Answer him."

"I've been riding with an outfit out of Fredericksburg. Big herd. Three thousand head plus a few calves. I know the ins and outs, and I've got three of the cowpokes on my side."

Hitt scanned Hatch's natty attire. "You're trying to chouse us. You haven't been on any cattle drive."

"On the contrary. I've been with the Four Aces outfit."

"McLoughlin's company?" Asher Pierce asked and ran hand across his shiny pate. "I never did like that Yankee son-of-a-bitch."

"That makes two of us," Hatch replied.

He told the Hitt gang about McLoughlin being in charge of Charlwood during the latter part of the war, about his mother and stepsister being jailed for defending the Bonny Blue flag, about the plantation burning. "You saw the ashes, Hitt. Don't you remember me?"

"I remember. Of course, you weren't such a dandy back then."

"No, I wasn't."

By the time the carpetbaggers had arrived, Frank Hatch had been in considerably better shape than when McLoughlin and his soldiers had occupied Charlwood, and he had been shaved and clean upon appearing at the Tax Collector's Office, a meager pile of coins in his hands.

Speculatively, Hitt placed a forefinger across his upper lip. "I seem to recall you were somewhat undone at having 'damnyankees' in Georgia."

"Think about how you would've felt had the tables been turned."

"That's why I don't trust you. I think you're out to get me."

"I bear no grudge over your vanishing with the tax money," Hatch lied. "Matter of fact, that's why I sought you out, once I heard you were in town and were in the—shall we say—cattle business. I know you're as mean as I am vengeful. You see, I want nothing more than to wreak havoc on McLoughlin's livelihood."

"Why him and not me?" asked Hitt.

"After McLoughlin burned the fields as well as our home, I would have lost Charlwood anyway. I was try-

258

ing to keep the property for Mother and Mary Joan, but I knew it was useless, what with ruined fields and no money to pay darkies."

Again Hitt fingered his cravat; the diamond stick-pin twinkled in the lamplight. "The story goes Charlwood was the abomination of the south. Your mother and stepsister had starving slaves chained to—"

"Enough!" Hatch rose to his feet, toppling his chair against the wall. In Georgia, neighbors—supposedly loyal Confederates—had tried to shame him over their acts. Never again would he allow anyone to defame anyone connected to Charlwood. "I'll not having you criticizing my kinswomen!"

"Don't raise your voice at me, Hatch. I'm not deaf. And sit down. I don't fancy looking up at you."

Settle down. Remember your purposes. He sat down again. "Hitt, are y'all with me or not?"

"We are." Smith and Pierce nodded, and Hitt leaned forward to say, "Jimmy Two Toes is up in the Territory. We'll pick him up along the way to Kansas."

"What do you mean, Kansas?" Hatch asked Hitt. "I've been up to my eyeballs in filth for weeks." He shuddered. "What's wrong with stealing the herd now?"

"For one thing, Texas lawmen would be on us. And second, what would we do with three thousand long-horns? Use your head, Hatch. There's no market for cattle here in Texas. Let McLoughlin have the head-ache of getting them through the Territory and close to the railhead. Then we move in."

Hatch didn't like having to depend on others for help, but what could he do? He couldn't handle the job alone. Moreover, Hitt's advice made sense. He must suffer the road. "All right, we take them in Kansas."

Rattler Smith mused aloud, "Three thousand head. Thirty, maybe forty dollars each. That's a tidy sum, even divided up."

"Now you're whistling 'Dixie.'" Appeased at his own conclusions as well as the bean counter's, Hatch laughed. "And there McLoughlin will be. His cowboys looking for pay. No cows to sell. Stuck up in Kansas."

Hitt prompted, "Tell me about these men you've got on your side."

Grinning smugly, Hatch recalled the previous night. After another parlay with the Southerners, the allegiance had been expanded to include two more.

"There's a Mexican, Ochoa. He's in it strictly for the money. The other two are Confederates. Jackson Bell, out of Virginia. Wink Tannington has been with me for weeks."

"Are you sure we can trust them?"

"Most positively."

"Good." Hitt squinted at Hatch. "And we divide the money up. Nice and even."

Hatch had no intention of letting anyone but himself leave Kansas with Four Aces loot. No one.

"Right, Hitt. Nice and even."

Now it was time to make other plans. Cactus Blossom must pay for tossing his precious bundle over Dead Buffalo Bluff. This corner of revenge he could handle on his own, but not now.

Tonight he would revel in his dreams of getting even with that Yankee dog McLoughlin.

Chapter Twenty-three

"Lisette . . . talk to me. Let's not waste our time together. I'll be leaving on the morrow, and I want to spend tonight in your arms."

She didn't reply, and Gil frowned. For the last half hour she'd been sitting on that horsehair sofa, right here in the house behind Ruth Craven's boarding-house, not paying a damned bit of attention to him. She continued to sew lace on a baby bonnet.

"I'm sorry for upsetting you out on the trail." He wasn't one for apologies, but it came easier than he had imagined. "I don't want you upset."

She snipped a thread with her teeth, picked up another piece of lace, and began to hum some damned song. Annoyed that he'd apologized for nothing, he crossed the sitting room to pick up the half-gallon jar of beer he'd bought after leaving Matthias and Cactus Blossom. He poured himself a glass and set another on the table next to his wife.

"Thirsty?" he asked, and might as well have been asking the wall. *Okay, fine, let her be that way.* He kicked off his boots. Entering the bedroom and exaggerating a yawn, he called over his shoulder, "Sweet dreams."

Silence met him as he yanked off his clothes. He pulled back the covers and slid between the sheets, naked. The bed was set to an angle where he had clear view of the horsehair sofa. The lamp adjacent to it illuminated Lisette.

His annoyance vanished. Mesmerized, he watched the shadows as she lifted her arm to make stitches in the baby bonnet. In six months' time, their child would be wearing that bonnet. Gil smiled, trying to imagine the babe. Would it be a girl or a boy?

His eyes went to Lisette. The material she stitched was blue. "Hoping for a boy?" he asked.

"All men want sons, so I pray for a male child."

Thank God. She was talking.

"Wouldn't bother me if it's a girl." Gil rolled to his side, leaned on an elbow. "I fancy the idea of a little blond lass with big cornflower-blue eyes—just like her mother's."

"Go to sleep, Gil."

Damn. He thought he'd made headway. Here they were, on the verge of being separated for months, and they weren't making love. Hellfire, could he do anything to please her?

"I want to make love to you, darlin'."

"Gil, go to sleep."

He wished his bagpipes weren't with the chuck wagon; a serenade might prove advantageous. Then again, he got the impression bagpipes wouldn't have worked tonight. He reached for the glass of beer next to bed. Draining it, he continued to watch Lisette.

She stood, stretching her arms above her head, her breasts straining the material of her simple calico dress. His blood warmed. When Lisette moved to a sideboard and its pitcher and bowl to splash her face with water, his eyes moved with her. And then she was unbuttoning her dress; it pooled at her feet to leave her garbed in her chemise alone. The lines of her back enthralled him. His breath in short supply, he felt his shaft elevating the sheet.

She dipped a washrag into the bowl, lifted it to wash beneath her arms. He got a ripe view of one proud-crested breast. Again she moistened the washrag . . . but this time she hesitated before putting it to her flesh. He caught the tiny movement of her head. *She knows I'm watching her.*

It wasn't distance she wanted.

She lifted her chemise to cleanse the apex of her thighs, and he could take no more. Quickly he was out of bed, through the doorway, across the parlor. Still, she presented her back. Stopping close enough to get a whiff of lilac-scented soap blended with the warm scent of his woman, he settled his hands on her hips. Sliding them up and down the swells, he inched closer.

"You feel good to me, Lisette—like silk. Warm, smooth silk. And your hair—you must have washed it while I was out. It smells like lilacs on a warm spring morning." His nose circled through those locks. "I love the way you look. And smell. And feel."

"Your silver tongue matches your silver eyes."

"My tongue is capable of many things. Shall I show you?"

"You mean there's something we have yet to do?"

"Yeah. Lots of somethings." Even more blood swirled to his shaft. "Let's talk about it."

Her arm moved backward, her fingers scooting between them. "Old Son is especially randy tonight," she murmured.

"Every night, for you."

"What . . . what will you two do while we're apart?"

"Dream of you. Night and day." His fingers spread across her lower abdomen. "And I'll be thinking of our babe. She'll be growing where I'll long to be."

"He, Gil. He."

"She."

Lisette chuckled, and Gil nuzzled her neck. His palms smoothed to her waist and higher, his fingers pressing her breasts. Her head eased back, her hair tickling his shoulders and chest. She trembled. He kissed her hair, her ear, the long column of her throat. He turned her, pulled up her chemise, then lifted her atop the table.

"I want you," he whispered. "I want you right here in this sitting room. I want to suckle your breasts as if I were your babe. And I want to kiss every inch of your body."

Stepping between her legs, he lowered his head to her bosom. Her fingers spread at the back of his head as he cherished the place where their child would be nourished. Yet she pushed him away.

"Gil, we mustn't settle our differences like this. When we make love, it should be with harmony between us."

"What better way to harmonize than this way? I want you. You want me. Let's don't deny ourselves."

"I . . . I don't need you to want me. I want you to need me."

"I need you."

"Not just for *this*."

264

"I need you, Lisette. For this . . ." His hand swept slowly to the top of her thighs, his fingers to the sensitive nub. "And for everything else."

She fought against her desire, saying, "If you insist."

"You act as if you're performing a duty."

"You ask for much, Gil."

"Yeah, I do." He scooted her closer and placed her legs around his hips. Surging upward, he groaned as her tightness enveloped him. "Put your arms around me, honey. That is, if this is something more than your just letting me have husbandly rights."

It was, and she did.

Gil wasn't too specific about the *everything* he needed her for, not that night nor the next morning, and Lisette decided not to make too much of it. They had the rest of their lives to settle their differences; she'd had enough of the silent treatment. Beyond that, she wanted to make the best of their last hours together. They had made the most of the night. The musk of their loving hung heavy in the air. Her breasts and thighs remained tender from the rasp of his jaw. Did other husbands do that to their wives, lave the most tender part of their women?

As she left the bed, a rooster crowing from Ruth Craven's coop, Lisette turned to her husband and asked, "What would you like for breakfast, *Liebster?*"

"You."

"Don't you ever run out of energy?" she teased.

"I do not."

"Well, you'll have to settle for food. We've a wedding to attend, and you've a herd to take north."

265

He said nothing, and she eyed him. Gil lay on the bed, the top sheet tangled around the lower reaches of his hirsute form. His eyes were half lidded, his mouth half parted.

"Come back to bed, wife."

She wanted to comply; her veins throbbed with desire once again, but . . . But! "Gil, we have to eat a meal, and the wedding is at noon, and I must buy a new dress beforehand."

"Your clothes have gotten snug." He perused her naked form. "I'd say you're showing a lot."

She laughed nervously. But why? Did it have to do with the odd way Gil was looking at her? She didn't care for that unreadable look.

"You look beautiful to me," he said. "You always have."

He wasn't one to compliment, and his remark surprised her, pleasantly. She stepped to the bed, sat down, and leaned toward him as he said, "I'll never forget the first moment I laid eyes on you. You were strolling out of the Lutheran Church. Fall leaves were drifting into your braids, and you were laughing and slapping them away while you chatted with some woman. From your description, she must've been your friend Anna. My eyes weren't on her. All I saw was you. You and your pretty blond braids and your sweet smile of laughter. I knew right then I had to have you."

"I wish I'd known you were watching me." A delicious shiver climbed up Lisette's spine, compelling her into more of her own admissions. "I'll never forget that morning I approached you. All I wanted was a job, but when I looked at you, I knew you were all man. And I was a woman appreciative."

"Did your feelings have anything to do with why you chased after me and my cows?"

"I'll admit, I didn't think so at the time." She blushed. "But thinking back on it, *you* must have been more attractive than the job prospect. I could have stolen Adolf's gold or something, hidden in some cart on its way to a stage line, and gotten to Chicago on my own."

He leaned forward, taking her hand. "Lisette, it pleases me, your saying that."

"I'm glad. Because I . . ." Should she say it? Yes. "I love you, husband. Love you with all my heart."

They went into each other's arms, and her feelings soared when he admitted, "You're wonderful, my darlin'. Wonderful! And I want you to know something. I feel as you do. I never put too much stock in love, but that's got to be what I feel for you." His fingers splaying across her hips, he whispered, "I love you."

Had she heard right? She jiggled her head to make certain her ears were working. Fastening her eyes to the silver and blue of his, drinking in his smile, feeling the warmth of his touch, she added her own smile. This was the moment she had yearned for.

"Tell me again," she whispered, her finger tracing his night-roughened jaw.

"I love you."

"Oh, my darling Gil. Oh my."

She laughed with glee, with heart, with pure pleasure, then arched against her beloved husband. Two hours passed before they stopped admitting, and acting on, their love. This was the best way to ease the pain of his departure.

Sated, she leaned above him and kissed his lips. "We had best get dressed. We have much to do before the wedding."

"I won't be attending."

"You can't be serious." She straightened. "Matthias and Cactus Blossom are my friends."

"Your friends, not mine."

"So, we're back to yours and mine."

"Don't start in, Lisette." He climbed out of bed, grabbed his britches. "I want the herd past the city limits by noon. Oh. Did I tell you? Oscar Yates has agreed to be strawboss; I don't trust Tannington with the job, even though he's the best cowhand I've got left. I've put Cencero Leal in charge of the chuck wagon. The boys like spicy food."

"I'm sure everything will be just fine."

They won't miss me in the least.

What was the matter with her? Yes, Gil would be leaving and the outfit would do just fine without her, but she should be ecstatic, after his admissions of love. What was love without understanding? And she didn't understand her husband. Not at all.

Again, Lisette fell to silence. She washed and dressed, fixed a breakfast, and watched as her husband ate bacon and eggs, but she didn't say another word. At the cookstove, she watched from the corner of her eye as he scraped the leavings from his plate into a pail, then rinsed the earthenware in the wreck pan.

"Lisette," he said, "I know I'm a tyrant at times, and I may be too old to change my ways, but I'll work on them."

What more could she hope for? And did she want

him to change? If he did, he wouldn't be the man she'd fallen in love with.

Maybe she'd never understand him. Maybe it wouldn't matter.

Closing the space between them, she replied, "If we never argue, think of all the excitement we'll miss in making up. Aren't a few disagreements worth that pleasure?"

"That's right. Turn my words around on me." He laughed. "You never cease to be amazing."

"As long as you keep loving me, think whatever you please."

"Nothing could make me stop wanting you."

Even though he was leaving — she wouldn't see him for months on end — Lisette reveled in his words.

And then Dinky Peele and the quiet Northerner, Deep Eddy Roland, called on them. "It be time to leave, Mister Mack," said Dinky. "How you doin', Miz Lisette?"

"I'm fine" — *as can be expected*. "How are you, Dinky? And you, too, Deep Eddy?"

The Northerner nodded and fiddled with the lariat that was never out of his hand. Dinky, on the other hand, smiled broadly and elaborated on his good health, as well as on his excitement at getting back on the trail.

"Miz Lisette," Dinky said, "we sure gonna miss you. Dat ole trail, it ain't gonna be right wit'out you."

Hearing this from one of the cowhands, especially one who was so special to Lisette and to her husband, fashioned a smile on her face. She stepped forward to hug the diminutive black man. "Thank you for saying that, Dinky. I'm going to miss you, too."

269

"Well, I be seeing you 'bouts, um, well, I don't know 'zactly when, Miz Lisette, but whenever Mister Mack be back, I be wit' him."

"I'm counting on that," she said.

Dinky and Deep Eddy waved, then exited the house. Gil, a bundle of belongings under his arm, hesitated at the door. "How about a last kiss before I leave?"

"You weren't going anywhere without one."

He extended his free arm; she walked into his embrace. After a long and lingering kiss good-bye, he winked and said, "Be good while I'm gone."

"At what?" she teased.

His hand snaked around her behind and swatted it, then he joined his men and rode away.

Missing her husband already, even though he'd been gone but a few minutes, Lisette set out for a dress shop, selected several dresses in a larger size, had her packages delivered to Ruth Craven, then walked through the midday heat to the river. Matthias, Cactus Blossom, and a black-suited official wearing a gunbelt waited on the banks.

Struck by what a handsome couple they made, Matthias so tall and Cactus Blossom so petite, and both of them young, attractive, and having many wonderful years ahead of them, Lisette smiled and offered greetings.

Taking her place at the bride's side, she learned the third person was Cartwright Knowlton, justice of the second district of Tarrant County. He was tall, gaunt, and appeared to be in his later middle years.

Justice Knowlton said, "We'll need another witness."

Matthias corralled a stranger to step in. The marriage vows began. At the end, Justice Knowlton said, "You may kiss your bride."

The moment's poignancy touched Lisette. They were so obviously in love . . . and she recalled her own wedding. It seemed as if years had passed since Gil had vowed to "keep her for as long as ye both shall live."

He'll be back. You haven't lost him.

"Wait. Hold up."

Placing Frank Hatch's voice from the distance, Lisette turned her head, as did the others. Matthias uttered a German swearword; Cactus Blossom sucked in her breath; the witness made an X on the marriage license, then offered congratulations before departing.

Hatch advanced on the riverbank; he wore a crisp white suit and an equally crisp Panama hat, and carried a silver-handled walking stick. An ugly look plastered his face.

"Am I too late to make a protest?" Hatch asked.

"You are," answered the justice.

"By the Bonny Blue." Hatch dug the cane tip into soft ground. "I'd hope to spare Mister Gruene before it was too late."

What in the world could the Georgian be referring to? Lisette wondered, uneasy, then recalled Cactus Blossom's vague comment of yesterday.

"Leave," Matthias demanded succinctly of Frank Hatch.

"But I am here for your benefit. You have married a—"

"Dung Eyes, cease!"

271

Hatch smiled nastily at Cactus Blossom before cutting his attention to Matthias again. "Did you know you've married a murderess?"

Cactus Blossom chanted something in Comanche; Matthias stepped toward her accuser. "You lie."

"Do I?" Hatch brushed his lapel. "Cactus Blossom, the mother of my infant daughter Weeping Willow, had no use for the child of her body." His normally flat eyes moistened. "She tossed my daughter over a cliff. Alive."

Shocked, revolted, yet believing his charge couldn't be true, Lisette turned to the bride. Tears cascaded down the tortured, bronze face.

Matthias, stricken, said, "Cactus, he couldn't be telling the truth."

"It is true."

Lisette took a step backward. She had taken a baby killer to friend!

Chapter Twenty-four

How could any mother murder her own child?

This thought rang through Lisette's head as she watched the tiny Cactus Blossom Gruene plead for understanding with her new husband. His shoulders were stiff, and Matthias's square face went a shade lighter than ash.

A gust of hot wind lifting the brim of his Panama, Frank Hatch said to the justice of the peace, "I suppose you're not interested in doing the right thing by a papoose, but keep in mind, Weeping Willow was half white. This savage must be punished."

"Absolutely," agreed the official.

Her eyes wild, Cactus Blossom retreated from the threat, her moccasined feet muddying with river water. Even though she was horrified, Lisette stepped over to put a comforting hand on the unnerved Comanche woman.

Cartwright Knowlton addressed Hatch. "Where did the incident occur?"

"South of Lampasas. At Dead Buffalo Bluff."

"I'll have to report this to the marshal."

"Do that." Hatch tipped his hat—as if he had offered no more than a weather report—and turned to saunter from the banks of the Trinity. "I'll be back in time for the trial."

"*Gott.*" Shoulders slumped, Matthias swerved away from the scene of his wedding. "*Mein Gott!*"

Cactus Blossom's chin fell forward as her bridegroom stumbled toward the street.

"Matthias, come back," Lisette called out. "You cannot leave."

But he left.

And Justice Knowlton closed in. "You're on your way to jail, savage."

"You do not understand, white man." The beads on the buckskin dress rattled; Cactus Blossom's teeth chattered. "It was for Weeping Willow that I took her life. She was not right at birth. Her body was twisted. I could do nothing for her. The Medicine Man could do nothing." Shoulders drew in like the closing of a flower. "Her cries of pain shredded my heart. I could not allow her to suffer."

"Save your sorry excuses for the jury." Knowlton went for his pistol while scanning the riverbank. "You going with me peacefully? Or do I need to yell for help?"

For a frozen moment Cactus Blossom stared at him, but realizing the import of his words, she ducked. Knowlton aimed and fired at her departing form.

With a cry of "Stop!" Lisette tackled him from behind, and the bullet plopped into the Trinity.

By now a cluster of citizens were running for the riverbank. Someone grabbed Lisette, pulled her

274

away. Cactus Blossom disappeared into a stand of pecan and oak trees. And Lisette McLoughlin was hauled to the sheriff's office, where she faced assault charges.

"Lock her up," said the sheriff.

Two deputies escorted her to jail. Iron bars clanged shut, echoing through her ears, and the pungent odor of long-dried urine and vomit assaulted her. This was an awful place, cramped and dank. A tiny, barred window above her head gave the only light. No one shared her cell, yet she heard the catcalls of male prisoners from the next cubicle.

Shivering despite the heat of May, Lisette clutched her arms. Yet her concerns were for Cactus Blossom. How terrified she must be. How alone she must feel, deserted by her husband at a moment of great need.

Poor Blossom. Where are you?

Sitting down on the hard cot, Lisette peered through her iron cage and caught sight of an obese Manx cat snaring a rat. As the rodent was caught between the feline's teeth, Lisette turned from the sight and shuddered anew. She dropped her chin. *No one or nothing has an inherent right to life out here.*

Weeks ago Gil had said those words, and she had been righteous in her protest against his theory. She still believed in the dignity of life and would never harm anyone, least of all her own child. She told herself she ought to hate Cactus Blossom for the heinous act, but somehow she couldn't.

All afternoon, all evening, Lisette fretted over the terrible situation. Supper arrived, but her appetite had left her. Two hours later, a deputy took the bowl away. She spent a fitful night on the jailhouse cot, heard roosters crowing at daybreak. Again she refused a meal. By now another question had formed: How was she going to get free?

A modicum of ablutions finished, she sat down on her cot. She needed to get word to Gil, but how?

"Miz McLoughlin?"

She lifted her head to see Cartwright Knowlton, Justice of the Peace.

"Nice white lady like you, I thought someone would've put up bail by yesterday afternoon." His hands on the bars, his eyes on her gold ring, he asked, "Where is your husband?"

"What do you want, Mister Knowlton?"

"I'd like to know why you defended that savage."

"She is my friend." Lisette left the cot. "Do you know her whereabouts?"

"Not yet." Knowlton shifted his weight from one foot to the other. "Miz McLoughlin, I hate to see nice white folks get in trouble, so I've decided to drop charges against you."

You bigot!

Arguing would gain no end, though.

"Thank you, sir." Once she was free of her bonds, she could find Cactus Blossom and provide a comforting shoulder — and money. She would help out, since Gil had deposited a considerable amount in the bank for her use. "Mister Knowlton, I hope you'll be considerate if my friend is captured."

"Can't promise that. The law is the law."

Then, hopefully, Cactus Blossom was miles from

here by now. No doubt she was far away. No money, no hope, nowhere to go. Alone, lonely, and betrayed by the men she had trusted.

The justice stepped back from the bars. "By the by, there's a fellow over in the sheriff's office. Before I dropped charges, he had arranged to post your bail."

Gil? Matthias? Who? It couldn't be Gil, since Knowlton had asked after him.

"Stay out of trouble, Miz McLoughlin," the justice of the peace said as he receded from sight.

The jailer unlocked her cell.

And she met the angry glare of her brother.

"How did you find me?" Lisette asked Adolf time and again, but he didn't deign to answer. Hobbling along, his fingers cutting into her arm, he forced her down the dusty streets of Fort Worth. Somehow he knew where she lived; he took her there; the door slammed behind them.

In the sitting room, limping toward her, he raised his hand. *"Hure!"* He started to slap her but pulled back his hand. "Disappearing from your family, going off on a cattle drive, taking up with a disgraced man. Have you no shame?"

"How do you know this? Did Anna tell you?"

"No." He pulled an envelope from his pocket. "Herr McLoughlin informed me."

She traced her finger over Gil's bold script, then read the letter. It was brusque, even curt. And it was traitorous.

How many times had she tried to impress upon Gil the importance of secreting her whereabouts from Adolf? How many times! Yet on the night of their wedding he had betrayed her.

Gil, who had demanded so much.

His face set in a determined cast, Adolf said, "I will take you back to Fredericksburg now. Pack your belongings."

She shook her head. "No. I won't go. When I return, it will be with my husband."

"Don't lie to me about any husband. You couldn't have been married. Not on a cattle drive. Herr McLoughlin was no doubt trying to cover an illicit affair."

"You're wrong. One of the drovers is a minister of the gospel." She placed the letter aside, then rushed into the bedroom to search through a bureau drawer. Pulling a piece of blue paper from its depths, she thrust it at her brother. "Here is our marriage license."

Leaning against the sideboard where she and Gil had made love, Adolf read the license. "It seems to be authentic."

"Of course it is."

Adolf placed the document atop the McLoughlin Bible, which centered the table in front of the sofa. "So, you have married and have been left in this town."

"Only until *mein Mann* returns. Together we'll return to Fredericksburg."

"No. You will go back with me."

She raised her chin. "I will not."

278

"You must, sister. This town is no place for a woman alone, especially in your condition." Scratching his yellow beard, he looked her up and down. "You are with child, are you not?"

Was it that obvious, this soon? "I suppose you've been around Monika enough to know the signs."

"From the looks of you, I'd say you were involved with Herr McLoughlin before you left the farm."

"Not true."

"Even if you speak honestly, you have brought disgrace on the family. The whole town knows you left, and"—he flushed—"Monika was indiscreet. She told the ladies at church that you had taken up with Herr McLoughlin."

Before she had escaped the farm, Lisette would have been mortified over such gossip. Now she had her husband's love, albeit at some distance, and it was a strong buffer against anything outsiders could say or do.

"I find I'm quite comfortable with myself and my deeds."

"You have changed for the worse."

"I don't think so." Imagining the quilting circle, she added with a laugh, "Since my husband is quite handsome and virile, I'll wager the ladies are jealous of my good fortune."

Adolf's face turned maroon, and hunching his massive shoulders, he advanced on her. "He must please you well to have turned a lady into a wanton."

Four drumming knocks beat against the door. "Mrs. McLoughlin, are you in there?"

"Ignore her."

"I will not. She's my landlady." Lisette answered the summons. "Good day, Mrs. Craven."

The elderly lady stepped inside. "Where have you been? I've been worried sick. Then one of my roomers said he'd heard you were in jail. Put a stop to that kinda talk, I did. I told your husband—nice man, that husband of yours—anyway, I promised I'd keep an eye on you, and . . ." The wrinkles on her face deepened. "Who is this?"

"My brother, Adolf Keller of Fredericksburg."

"Oh. How d'ya do?" Ruth Craven pursed her mouth and said to Lisette, "You look a mess, as if you haven't been eating or sleeping right." She lifted her hand; it held a linen-covered basket. "I made steak and okra for lunch. Here's your share. I think there's enough for the both of you, provided Mister Keller isn't too greedy."

"I am not here to eat. I am here to collect my sister and return home."

"She's in no shape to go anywhere, mister."

Lisette pulled back the linen. The batter-fried food smelled delicious, and her stomach growled. A few weeks ago, such smells would have been gruesome, but thankfully her body had adjusted to little Hermann's presence.

"Thank you, ma'am."

"I'll have my serving girl heat some water and bring over the hipbath. You eat, wash yourself, then get some rest." She pointed at Adolf. *"You* are going with me, big boy."

Amazingly, he left with Mrs. Craven—but not before warning, "Do not try to escape, sister. I will

280

keep an eye on this house."

Lisette knew his wasn't an idle threat. Escape ought to be her foremost consideration, but to tell the truth, she was too weary and too pregnant for anything but the landlady's suggestions. Once she had washed away the grime of jail and had given her body a rest, she could better deal with Adolf.

Then she must find Cactus Blossom.

The sun had set by the time she woke from her nap. The moment she lit the hurricane lamp in the sitting room, Adolf barged through the door. "Are you packed?"

"There's something you don't understand, brother. I am no longer under your control. I will not return to the farm and be an unpaid servant to you and your wife."

He lumbered across the room, his limp more noticeable than ever, and settled heavily on the sofa to extend his bad leg and rub it. "Lise, I don't want your efforts. I want to know you're all right."

"Excuse me, but I find myself skeptical."

"You never did like me, did you?" he asked, hurt in his voice as well as his blue eyes.

"It isn't necessary to like while loving."

"You love me?"

"Of course I do." She sat in the rocker next to the sofa. "You're my brother."

"If you love me, then why did you leave without so much as a message to ease my mind?" Leaning forward, he covered his eyes with a hand. "Before I received Herr McLoughlin's letter, I was out of my mind with worry. I feared you had met Olga's fate."

"*Ach du meine Güte!*" In remorse over her thoughtlessness, she moved to the sofa and hugged Adolf. "I'm sorry, so sorry. I never meant to trouble you. I never thought I mattered."

"You matter—more than you think." He patted her arm. "You were always a good girl. A little thoughtless, perhaps, but good and kind. We have missed you. The boys ask for *Tantchen.*"

"I have missed Karl and Viktor and little Ludolf."

"Perhaps you are nostalgic enough to allow me to escort you home?"

"Allow you? Adolf, that's the first time you've ever asked rather than demanded—for anything."

Her eyes met her brother's, and his were . . . Why, they were kind! Never had she and Adolf been close. And he'd stolen what should have gone to Gil McLoughlin. The dowry money was the least consideration, she decided. Her husband had accepted her as she was.

Yet Gil had had no right to be choosy, since he was no paragon. The end result of his manipulation wasn't settled, and the facts remained—he'd written to Adolf and had never told her. That was deceit. And it was betrayal, since he knew how much she worried over Adolf's finding her.

She itched to confront him, and ask *why*. And why did he expect her to be as virtuous as Caesar's wife? When it would take almost a Caligula to throw her back into the clutches of Adolf Keller.

What was the matter with her? Gil in no way resembled an evil Roman emperor. Yet it hurt, that letter.

282

Her brother lifted her chin. "You haven't answered, sister."

"I'll be home in the new year, and Gil and I will bring a cousin for your sons to play with." She hesitated. "If Monika will allow them to fraternize."

"You were like two cats, fighting with each other, but in your absence Monika has grown to appreciate you." Adolf chuckled. "She complains loudly that she has no female relatives to talk with."

Lisette eased against the sofa back. "Most likely she misses the fruits of my labor."

"Not at all. We have hired a black couple. There are so many former slaves who beg for work, and a few have found their way to Fredericksburg. Mose and Hattie Mae have taken over your responsibilities." Adolf smiled. "Monika misses *you*." "I am touched," Lisette replied honestly, and anger at her husband receded in a slight amount.

And the strangest realization hit her: she longed to be in Fredericksburg again. To cuddle her nephews, to chat with Anna, to make peace with Monika. There was church. She missed the verdant hills and the cool streams. She yearned to see the Four Aces. She was homesick.

"It will be a nice homecoming, when Gil and I return to Fredericksburg."

"Haven't you heard what I'm trying to say? I cannot leave you alone, none of your family within weeks away. When you have your lying in, you must be with us."

Perhaps Gil wouldn't return in time for the birthing. If he encountered no problems, it would take a minimum of two to three more months to reach Abilene; he'd have to sell the longhorns; there was his return with the cowboys, the saddle horses, and Tecumseh Billy, which would take another six or eight weeks. If a problem arose on the cowpath—and that could happen, since no rain had fallen in more than three weeks and they had yet to trail through Indian Territory—his return could happen well after his child drew a first breath.

Maybe she should be with her family. No; Gil might return. And even if he didn't, she wanted their quickest reunion. If nothing else, to get a certain matter straight between them: the letter.

Another thing . . .

"Adolf, there's more than me to consider here. Do you know why I was jailed?"

"*Ja,* for attacking a magistrate over an Indian woman."

"Not just any Indian woman. She is my friend. And she's Matthias Gruene's wife. Oh, Adolf, she is in great danger. I must help her. And I have tarried precious hours." Lisette swallowed. "Adolf, I hope Matthias is with her."

"Don't count on it. I understand he was seen at the edge of town this morning, alone."

"Then he didn't go after her. Poor Blossom." Lisette quit the sofa to traverse the sitting room, twice. "Adolf, I think you should leave now. I must do my own leaving. I've got to find Blossom."

"Not without my help."

"What?"

284

"If you seek the Comanche woman, I will go with you."

Nonplussed, Lisette stared. Today had certainly been a day for discovering new facets to the brother she had long thought cold and heartless.

"Adolf, you can't. You've the return home. And your leg . . . If I can't find Cactus Blossom in town, and I doubt I can, I must ride after her."

"Your condition is more serious than my lame leg."

"I am fit. I am not a hothouse flower. And I can ride like the wind."

"Sister, we are bred of the same blood." He stood straight. "I may be lame, but I can still 'ride like the wind.' If Matthias has not seen his way clear to find his bride, then the Kellers will find her. Get packed."

"I never dreamt you would make me this happy." Lisette took Adolf's hand. "Dear brother, let's find Cactus Blossom."

Chapter Twenty-five

Cactus Blossom ran through the woods north of Fort Worth. The full moon guided her to the old shack Dung Eyes had used last year. Stopping to put an ear to the ground, she heard the hooves from his mount, plus three more ponies. She followed the sound; her aching legs picked up speed. Before this night was over, she would confront him, would make him understand why she had taken Weeping Willow's life.

This she had to do for their daughter.

But her instincts shouted, "Be careful."

By the time Cactus Blossom stopped, Dung Eyes and his companions had unsaddled their mounts and had made a fire in front of the shack. She hid from them, listened.

"You're not too bright, Hatch," said the smartest-looking of the four. "You should've ridden out with McLoughlin. He'll be suspicious, your showing up in the Territory."

While the other two tended the fire, Hatch waved a dismissive hand. "I'm not taking up with him again. I have plans to bring misery on his undertaking."

"You do anything to mess up this deal, and I'll personally make a gelding out of you."

"You worry too much, Hitt. We'll have those cows under our control, easy as pie." Hatch pranced around the orange flames of the fire. "Then I'll have my revenge against that damnyankee."

"You're crazy, Hatch — crazy as a hunting dog." The one called Hitt shook his head. "You ought to keep your mind on the money rather than revenge. Okay, McLoughlin burned Charlwood, but there's nothing you can do to get the place back."

All of a sudden the pieces came together. Cactus Blossom knew why Dung Eyes wanted revenge. For all the seasons she had known him, he had ranted and raved about the "damnyankee" who'd burned his tepee in Georgia. *Long Legs* was the "damnyankee" he had long hated.

She must get word to Albino's man.

Or she must stop Dung Eyes.

Both . . . she must do both.

But she was outnumbered. She eyed each man, noting that each wore Irons of Exploding Furies. Her knife was no match for their power — unless they slept. Then she could disarm them, could . . .

She backed away, slowly, quietly, but her ankle connected with a tree stump; she fell backward and sprawled to the ground.

"What was that?"

As she tried to right herself, Hatch and the others advanced.

"You bitch."

She scrambled away, but not before a knife whizzed through the air. The blade caught her back, pain bursting. The ground came up to meet her; she tasted dirt and leaves. Before falling unconscious, she thought, *I must not go to the Great Hunting Ground before making peace with my husband. And I must warn Albino's man of danger.*

Night fell on the River Trinity. A couple of miles in the distance, Matthias saw the lights of Fort Worth. He wished a thousand miles separated him from civilization.

He'd been here since yesterday, when he'd needed solitude to deal with the awful truth about his bride. *"Mörderin!* Murderess!" he yelled, clenching his fists. "Why? Why? Why?"

He had thought he'd found heaven with Cactus, but hell had seized him.

It was dawn before he pulled himself together. He had to go back, had to find out *why* she'd taken her daughter's life. He trudged back to their rented house, but she wasn't there. He searched the town over, his efforts in vain.

They found her two days after Adolf appeared.

Lisette and her brother had combed Fort Worth and its surrounds, finding neither Cactus Blossom nor Matthias. Bertha Two Toes had given the best clue: she'd heard the squaw was headed up the Chisholm Trail. And that was where they found her, in a farmer's soddie a few hundred yards from the Trinity.

288

After discovering Cactus Blossom on the edge of his cornfield, the kindly sodbuster had administered aid to the best of his ability. Eldon Bird led Lisette and her brother into the mud home. On a narrow bed, Cactus Blossom shivered beneath several woolen blankets.

"Albino." She lifted an arm from under the covers. Her voice held a faraway quality, her eyes the glaze of pain. "Dung Eyes was wrong. It hurt me to take my Weeping Willow's life."

Lisette soothed the waxy hand. "I know."

"I will soon be with my papoose."

"Don't give up, Blossom."

"Do you hate me, Albino?"

"No."

"I am glad. You are much in my heart." Cactus Blossom closed her eyes. "I have made peace with the Great Spirits over my Weeping Willow, but my Mouth That Beckons will never forgive me. Just as Dung Eyes could not. Lisette"—this was the first time she'd used her friend's true name "—there is something you must know about Dung Eyes. He is—ohhhh."

She tried to scream, tried to clutch her wounded back, and squirmed on the straw-filled mattress. Lisette attempted to calm her, touched the poker-hot brow. Cactus Blossom began to ramble in her native tongue, then fell unconscious. Lisette kept a vigil at the bedside.

What had she tried to say about Frank Hatch? Lisette wondered over and over.

The sun waned outside the soddie. The farmer—a single man in his mid-twenties—prepared a pot of chicken soup over an outdoor cookfire. A tray of bowls in his hands, he offered food. Cactus Blossom stirred, and Lisette tried in vain to coax her to eat. Once more, her friend fell comatose.

Adolf demanded that Lisette take nourishment, and she understood his concern for her condition. She emptied her bowl, set it aside.

Wetting another washrag in a basin of water, Adolf placed the cloth on Cactus Blossom's forehead. Lisette knelt at the bedside, and for hours on end, she prayed—to God and to Cactus Blossom's Great Spirits.

As dawn broke, Lisette realized all efforts were in vain.

Cactus Blossom was dying.

"Mouth That Beckons?" was the plaintive appeal as Cactus Blossom opened her glassy eyes.

"He's on his way," Lisette lied.

Huddled next to the bed, she turned to her brother and whispered, "Go back to Fort Worth. Ride fast. Make one more try at finding him. Bring him, *if* he wants to be with her."

Adolf set out. He returned at midnight, Matthias beside him. Matthias rushed to his wife, begging forgiveness and holding her in his arms.

Although Lisette drew comfort in his appearance, she said to her brother, "This might have been avoided if he hadn't deserted her on that riverbank."

"Be careful of your words. Bitterness isn't like you."

"Always, I thought Matthias too noble to abandon a loved one. Even for a moment."

"Humans are frail, sister."

"And I am only human." Wondering if she'd ever be the same about anything, she glanced at the repentant Matthias. "Odd, how we don't appreciate what we have until we're in jeopardy of losing it."

"*Ja.* I understand." Her brother squeezed her shoulder. "I did not know how important you were until you were gone."

Eldon Bird entered the soddie. He carried a pot of coffee and another tray of food. "Anything more I can do to help?"

"Pray."

Prayers went unanswered. As the sun rose on the sixth day after Cactus Blossom had become Mrs. Matthias Gruene, she drew her last breath.

Kneeling beside the corpse, Lisette took the rigid hand of her friend who had suffered much from life. Sadness held her in its grip as her finger closed the lids of those beautiful dark, dark eyes for the last time.

"Go in peace, find your Weeping Willow," she murmured, the words pushed past a closed throat. "I'll never forget you, rare friend."

They buried Cactus Blossom beneath the shade of an elm tree, shovelsful of earth thudding on the simple coffin fashioned by Farmer Bird and Adolf Keller. Matthias stood motionless. When the last bit of soil topped her remains, he fell on the grave. And cried.

Eldon Bird crossed himself. Adolf put a comforting hand on the widower's shoulder, saying, "I'm sorry."

Cloaked in sorrow, Lisette hung her head.

Adolf pulled her aside. "We'd better find your husband. He needs to know what she had to say at the end."

"You're right."

"We must speak with the sheriff in Fort Worth before we set out."

"Mister Bird can go back." As soon as she said those words, she decided they weren't such a good idea. "No, I can give a firsthand description of her killer."

But, once they had finished at the sheriff's office, could they find Gil? He had a week's start on them, and it would take another day just to circle back to town. They could catch up with the outfit, provided they didn't spare the horses.

Horses were the least of her concern. Cactus Blossom had warned them about Frank Hatch's evil designs against Gil.

What should they do about Matthias? In his grief, he was in no shape to go with them, and might not want to, anyway.

Lisette went to the grave, put her arms around him. "You made your peace with Blossom. And she wouldn't want you to grieve. Let's go in the house, *mein Freund*. I will make some coffee."

"Coffee isn't what I need." He turned his tortured eyes to her. "I must see that Frank Hatch pays for his crimes."

Lisette replied, "Then you are welcome to leave with us."

Matthias jackknifed to his feet. "We mustn't tarry."

* * *

A fortnight had passed since Gil had ridden away from his wife. Troubled days, abysmal nights on the plains of north Texas. Grasses were brown; creekbeds had run dry. Rain, there had been none of it, and finding water to slake the cattle's thirst had been nearly impossible.

During each of those fourteen nights, dry lightning had skittered through the heavens like fingers of hell. A week ago the sounds had sent the herd on stampede. A hundred longhorns had been lost — and two cowboys were trampled to death in the melee.

Dinky Peele and Fritz Fischer had joined Willie, Ernst, and José as casualties of the trail. Fischer had been a hard-working wrangler, an asset to the outfit. Dinky had been more than an asset. Gil mourned the death of the little black man who, after being found half starved in Vicksburg, had become a trusted and dependable cowhand.

Life had a way of not playing fair.

There was another problem, one that had him worried, but with so many other problems, Gil hadn't spent too much effort mulling. And wouldn't, unless forced to.

Right now, the outfit had made camp for what looked to be another chaotic night. Astride Big Red, Gil kept an eye on the herd, kept them corralled between a bluff and a dry creekbed. While the majority of his men rallied around the chuck wagon, he rode along the cattle's perimeter, Deep Eddy Roland taking the other side.

Sadie Lou trotted alongside her master's mount, occasionally barking and feinting a recalcitrant cow into line.

As they were wont to do, Gil's thoughts turned to his wife. While he had promised her that fantasies would keep him going, they were no match for the real thing.

The drive missed her touch as well. Gil turned his line of sight in the chuck wagon's direction. Cencero Leal was no Lisette where cooking was concerned. His overspicy food had sent several cowboys running for the bushes on a regular basis.

Manpower was a problem, period.

Oscar Yates, though an acceptable cowpuncher in spite of his advanced years, had been plagued by aches and pains, and he'd done little to inspire his underlings. Thus, Gil had had to act in the roles of boss, strawboss, and occasional cowboy.

On horseback, Deep Eddy Roland approached him, Sadie Lou running to him. She had taken to the quiet man from New Hampshire.

The normally taciturn cowboy asked, "Shouldn't we be halfway to Red River Station by now?"

Gil didn't take the question as criticism. Over the past few days, he had grown to appreciate the New Englander and had given consideration to making him second in charge.

I'd rather have Matt on the job.

"We should be nearing the crossing," Gil answered, "but the Red River is weeks in the future."

Deep Eddy squinted at the night sky. "Better we should get there in all haste." He exhaled. "I found another cow. Her throat was cut."

"Damn. That makes ten since we left Fort Worth." Gil crushed Big Red's reins in his fist. "Wish we could blame it on Indians. But they wouldn't be

294

wasteful enough to leave meat for the buzzards."

And Gil had his ideas on the culprit's identity: Wink Tannington.

He couldn't prove his theory, but all fingers pointed to Tannington. The Mississippian had sided with Frank Hatch prior to their entering Fort Worth, and here lately his attitude had been bad.

Jackson Bell's hadn't been any better.

Gil trusted neither man at this point.

Night winds whistled across the prairie as he spied the second shift of night guards riding away from camp, riding toward him and Deep Eddy. Ochoa and Preacher Eli Wilson halted their mounts close to Gil.

"Keep a close eye on the herd," he said to Wilson.

The preacher rubbed the back of his hand across his mouth. "Don't worry, we will."

But Gil did worry.

"Ochoa," he shouted, "take your post."

Without a word, the Mexican toed his mount and disappeared into the herd. Like Deep Eddy, Ochoa was the quiet sort. But he was too quiet as far as Gil was concerned, since his wasn't the confidence-garnering silence of the New Englander.

"I don't trust that one," he said to the night sky.

"I don't either," Deep Eddy replied. "McLoughlin, about that cow . . ."

"Show me."

The New Englander led him to the site. Trying to find something good out of something bad, Gil said dryly, "Looks like we'll have fresh meat tomorrow."

He returned to camp, ordered extra men to keep watch over the herd. ". . . in case the throat-slasher is still in the vicinity." Cencero and Attitude set out to butcher the cow. And he faced a plate of spicy beans and yesterday's tamales. The weary cowboys gobbled the fare. Their boss ate nothing.

As the midnight hour approached, Gil spread his bedroll, stretched out and tucked the blanket beneath his arms. Sweat pooled on his back and on his leg, and he threw back the cover. He waited for Sadie Lou.

Where was she? With the exception of the start of this drive, the collie had been loyal, had been adoring, had curled at his feet when sleep had called.

Go to sleep.

He couldn't. And Gil began to feel sorry for himself all over again. He didn't have his wife; the trail was the worst he'd ever encountered; he didn't even have his dog at the moment.

Lisette, he could account for, and it was best that she had stayed in the safety of Fort Worth. No doubt she'd linked up with the Lutheran Church by now, had taken Ruth Craven to bosom friend, had fashioned a dozen baby bonnets. This stretch of the cowpath was no place for a woman, especially an expectant one.

His mind was at ease where she was concerned.

That wasn't the case with Sadie Lou. Uneasy, Gil got to his feet. Preacher Wilson approached. In his arms was a large, shrouded bundle.

Gil's heart stopped. "Sadie Lou?"

Eli Wilson nodded. "We found her at the edge of the herd. Her throat is cut."

"Shit."

Taking his loyal friend and helper into his arms,

296

Gil pulled back the cloth and crushed Sadie Lou to his chest. He wasn't one to cry, but a tear slipped. His grief went above losing a canine pal; he grieved for Dinky and for all who had gone before him.

Could matters get worse?

They did.

As Gil finished burying his loyal Sadie Lou, a woman's voice called out to him, and the night wasn't playing a trick.

"By the Holyrood," rumbled past his set teeth.

Lisette was here. *Here.*

Chapter Twenty-six

It was in the moments before daybreak that she appeared in this hell. Blue-hot emotions sparked through Gil McLoughlin when he caught sight of Lisette leading a horse, walking toward him. Damn it, she had no business on the trail . . . but seeing her was a most welcome sight. Was there such a thing as being happy in a river of woe?

Happiness ought to be the least of his concern.

He had three choices, as far as he was concerned. He could gather his wife into his arms and kiss her soundly, which he yearned to do; he could pull her across his knee for the paddling she richly deserved for leaving the safety of Fort Worth; or he could shout at her. He chose the latter.

"What in blue blazes are you doing here?"

"Seeking you. Why else?"

She didn't appear too pleased at meeting up with her husband, which made two of them. By now, Gil was nothing but furious that she hadn't stayed in Fort Worth, yet—damn it—it was good to see her.

He threw down the shovel he'd used to bury his

faithful cowdog, stepped over her grave, and hurried to his wife. And stopped short.

He stopped and got an eyeful of her companions. "Good God."

What else could go wrong?

Matthias Gruene, looking like he'd licked woe's riverbed, was with her. And descending the saddle was her brother. Good God.

"What the devil is going on?" Gil asked.

"I intend to tell you. I intend to get several things straight." She turned to her brother and Matthias, who were unsaddling the trio of winded horses, and said, "You two help yourselves to food. I'm sure you'll find some jerky or dried fruit or something to snack on in the chuck box."

They took themselves off.

His feet wide apart, Gil crossed his arms over a chest filled with conflicting sentiments. "I'm waiting, Lisette."

"I bring news of Frank Hatch."

She gave details on the spoiled wedding, on Matthias's abandonment of Cactus Blossom, on how the Comanche woman had died as a result of Frank Hatch's knife.

"On her deathbed," Lisette said, "she told us that Hatch has been after you for years."

"She was wrong. I never saw the man before Lampasas."

"Not so. You burned his plantation in Georgia. I believe it was called Charlwood."

Charlwood? Gil stood stock-still. Then Hatch had to be the son of Irene Morgan . . . and brother to Mary Joan Morgan. Gil remembered the scruffy, dirty man who had claimed to be their relative; he in no way resembled the dandy Frank Hatch. But the story was too absurd not to be true.

And it made sense of a lot of things.

"Lisette, you're making too much of the Hatch threat," he understated on purpose.

"I don't think so. I think you're trying to spare me."

"Spare you? Spare the woman who'd ride after a cattle drive, twice? Not on your life."

If he made her privy to his true sentiments—and fears—about Charles Franklin Morgan or Hatch, late of Charlwood Plantation, there would be no way to send her back where she belonged. This he sensed. And his senses were excellent.

Something else. He suspected he hadn't heard the whole story.

He glanced at the distant form of Adolf Keller, then said to Lisette, "I never expected to see you with your brother. What is going on?"

"You're trying to change the subject."

"Right. The subject of Frank Hatch is closed."

With a blistering look, she said, "I'd think, given Matthias's bride died at the hands of the man who's sworn vengeance against you, that you might show concern over him."

"I've just buried a female who meant more to me than a thousand Cactus Blossoms." He motioned to the rear. "That's Sadie Lou under that mound of dirt."

Instead of rushing to her husband and offering solace, Lisette's fingers covered her mouth. "Oh, Gil, no."

Okay, she hadn't seemed pleased to see him, but she could have tried to put her arms around him,

300

and that hurt Gil, especially when she hurried to the grave instead of to him.

"She was such a dear little *hund*." Ducking her head, Lisette whispered, "A good while back you told me that many could die before we reach Abilene. I wonder who will be next."

Before Gil could form a reply, something flashed by him, and that something was Jackson Bell.

"Where are you going?" he called suspiciously.

Bell stopped for a split second, clutching his stomach and answering, "Sick!" before streaking out of sight.

What was one sick man became two, then three, then three more by the time ribbons of dawn brightened the sky. Cencero Leal's Mexican plates had finally gotten to them in a big way.

And from the moment Jackson Bell had announced his malady, Lisette had gone into action and had taken charge of doctoring. With six men unable to ride today, there would be no taking the herd up the trail. Furthermore, Gil got no chance to reason with Lisette on her leaving, much less a chance to question her about Adolf Keller.

Cencero offered to cook breakfast, but to a chorus of protests from healthy cowboys, he withdrew the offer. Surprisingly, Adolf Keller limped over to the cookfire and proved a better hand at the skillet than Cencero or Yates ever had.

Gil pulled Matthias aside. "You and I need to talk, but with so many men out, I've got to take up the slack. Will you go with me? I need your help."

"All right."

"Saddle a horse from the remuda and let's go."

By now the sun emitted waves of heat, sending

rivulets of sweat down Gil's back as he sauntered over to Big Red. He doffed his shirt, shoved it in the saddlebag, then swung atop the sorrel. A couple of minutes after he started riding around the herd of thirsty cattle, Matthias caught up with him.

"Matt, I'm sorry to hear about Cactus Blossom." *Damn it, a lot of trouble would have been avoided, had Lisette left that squaw where we found her in the beginning.* "My condolences."

"I'm not here for empty sympathy."

"Why are you here? The job's yours if you want it."

"I meant more than just the job, McLoughlin. With Hatch after you, you're my best chance to find him."

"Does that include working the strawboss job again?"

"Yes."

"Then you're hired." Gil parked an elbow on the saddlehorn. "Matt," he said quietly, "as much as I want and need you with the outfit, you might be better off as a lone wolf. There's no guarantee Hatch will show."

"You know better than that."

"Yeah, I do. But don't go saying anything to Lisette. It would be best to keep her in the dark about trouble."

"How long would that last?" Matthias asked.

"Long enough for her brother to take her back where he found her. Or better yet, back to Fredericksburg."

By evening, Lisette remained in camp. Weary beyond imagination after a day of tending the sick,

302

cooking dinner, and standing under the broiling Texas sun, she ached to sit down and relax. But for now, she and Gil had unfinished business—the business of his deception over that letter.

Further, she needed to tell him about her scrape with the law. To avoid giving fuel for a fire of "you've kept something from me yourself," she needed to head him off at the pass.

The broth kettles put away, the medicines stoppered for the evening, the poisoned cowboys resting, she rubbed the small of her back and looked around for her husband.

Noticeable in their absence were Fritz Fischer and Dinky Peele. Preacher Wilson had been the one to relay the grim news. Lisette glowered. While he'd kept mum about the two deaths, her husband had told her about a dog's demise. Sadie Lou had been special, of course, but there was something odd about a man who mentioned dogs rather than humans.

Back in Fort Worth, she had decided she might never understand him. Now she wondered if she ever would.

"Have you seen Gil?" she asked Attitude Powell.

"I see'd him talkin' with your brother." The mountaineer ran a comb through his long beard and motioned with his free hand. "They're over at the remuda."

She walked toward the rope corral, catching sight of her husband and Adolf. With Fritz dead, everyone had been taking turns seeing after the saddle horses. Tonight was Gil's turn. He and Adolf were rubbing down a couple of geldings; neither noticed her approach.

They were talking about her, naturally. She ought to make her presence known, but curiosity got the better of her. Hiding behind a tree trunk, she wanted to hear what they had to say.

Gil took a curry comb from an equipment bag. "Keller—"

"Why don't you call me Adolf? Since we are brothers by law."

"I don't have a problem with it, if you don't have a problem calling me by my given name."

Pleased that they were being civil, she smiled. Although she was raring for a fight, she wasn't so angry she didn't want peace in the family.

Gil said, "I've got to protect my wife from trouble, Adolf. Here and everywhere else. Fredericksburg will be just as important as the Chisholm Trail. I don't want any trouble out of you and yours, so I'd like to know how do you feel about my taking your sister to wife."

"I would not have picked you. Otto Kapp was my choice."

"Otto . . . Kapp?"

"Since I had no choice," said Adolf, "I have made up my mind to accept you."

"Which brings up another subject. What *are* you doing with my wife? How did the two of you link up?"

Lisette, her feet aching, sat on the ground as Adolf related his trip to Fort Worth and his discovery of her incarceration.

"Jail?" The curry comb dropped from Gil's grasp. "What are you talking about?"

In brief terms, Adolf told him.

"She said nothing on the subject." Gil slapped the

304

rump of a remuda horse. *"Nothing.* Damn. It must've been terrible for her. But I won't abide any deceptions on her part."

Hypocrite! Lisette's teeth clenched so fast that she bit her tongue.

"She's not meaning to deceive you," Adolf said quickly. "And if you will think on it, brother-in-law, you will realize she has had no chance to speak with you."

Gil took a cigar from his shirt pocket, lit up. Lisette could hear the respect in his voice as he said, "I'm glad to hear you're taking up for her, like a good brother should. I never figured you had it in you. But as I said, I'm glad to hear it."

"I have, many years, been blind to my sister. But that is in the past."

"I'm even gladder to hear that." Gil took another puff of cigar. "Because I need your help. You've got to get Lisette away from here. Before something happens to her."

"You are referring to Frank Hatch?"

"I am. Adolf, I know you're a veteran of the Confederate forces, but I hope you'll be understanding about what I'm fixing to say. The man who's stalking me is part of the most unbalanced family I've ever run across. Hatch's mother and stepsister used their barns as ammunition dumps for the rebels."

"Many people did that sort of thing."

"Yes, but most people didn't starve and chain their slaves. The Morgans, Hatches, whatever their names—they tortured those poor people, then left them to die in their bonds. The day we found them . . . Damn. If I live to be a thousand years old, I'll never forget the smell, the inhumanity. It

305

was the worst thing I've ever seen in my life."

Why hadn't he told *her* these things? He was confessing his soul to *Adolf*. Lisette had been hurt by his deception; she was furious at this latest facet to him.

"We jailed the women, with the rebels' wholehearted consent," Gil was saying. "And I ordered torches to the plantation and its fields. Never regretted it. And never will."

"I don't blame you. I never believed in bondage, but a lot of folks treated their slaves fairly, so I didn't mind fighting for the cause. God knows we're all slaves to something." Adolf blew out a breath. "But how wretched it must have been for the people under those women's control."

Gil said quietly, "I've been given to understand you kept Lisette in a miserable situation bordering on slavery. What's more, I understand you took what was hers. Her dowry."

"I'll repay you, if you are bothered."

"That isn't what I want. I could buy and sell you a dozen times."

"Das ist Richtig." Adolf gave a horse a pat on its rump. "What happened to the women you referred to earlier? The ones who are related to Herr Hatch."

Gil crouched down, rocked back on his heels. Resting a forearm on his knee, he replied, "I've heard . . . It was after I left, but I heard 'Charles Morgan' gained entrance to their cells, killing several guards in the process, and freed his kinfolks."

"Wouldn't you do the same, were you in his place?"

"I wouldn't want to speculate on that, Adolf. But I can tell you . . . It was after I left Georgia, you understand, but I heard he murdered them both."

306

"Gott in Himmel."

So rocked was she that Lisette didn't know whether Adolf had said those words or she had thought them.

Adolf spoke. "You didn't recognize this Lucifer? You were with him for weeks, and you didn't make one comparison?"

"I . . . I didn't. I must say, I'm amazed that the two are one and the same."

"Rest assured, there is no question of identity." Adolf took a couple of uneven steps, then tugged on his beard. "I am glad my sister was not with Matthias's wife at the time of the stabbing. Maybe it was good Lisette ended up in jail instead."

"You've got a point." A moment lapsed. "Maybe it isn't such a good idea, your taking her home. The way she is, she might find another way to get in trouble, and I wouldn't be there to save her."

The arrogance of him!

"It seems I cannot trust my wife."

Lisette had heard enough. She left the ground, and huffed back to camp. At that moment she didn't like Gil McLoughlin—not at all. How dare he think so little of her? She would not be counted as weepy or untrustworthy or as a blight on the outfit. And there was one way to start her change.

Hitching up her chin, she returned to camp, cornered Cencero Leal, and demanded, "Show me how to use a pistol."

307

Chapter Twenty-seven

"Planning to shoot me?"

Ignoring her husband and sitting atop his trunk in the chuck wagon, Lisette loaded the revolver. When or if Frank Hatch showed up, she needed to know how to use a gun.

Gil eyed the revolver barrel. "Since you told me you've never pulled a trigger in your life, don't you think you might want to put that thing away before someone gets hurt?"

"Someone like yourself?" she taunted.

"Figure if you put a bullet in me, I won't question you about your visit to the Fort Worth lockup?"

"I have nothing to hide over it."

Gil looked up at the canvas roof, then back at her. "Little girls shouldn't play man-games, so you'd better put that gun away."

"I hadn't *better* do anything," she shouted, taking offense at his high-handedness. "Unless I damn well please to do it."

"Watch your mouth. Profanity doesn't become you."

"Don't tell me what to do."

"You're tired. We're both tired." He unbuttoned a shirtsleeve. "Let's go to bed."

"That's your answer to everything, isn't it? 'Let's go to bed.' But I guarantee you, Mister McLoughlin, this argument won't be settled by sex."

"That wasn't what you said in Fort Worth."

"This isn't Fort Worth."

"Fishwife," he grumbled under his breath. The lantern swayed, the floorboard creaked as he stomped toward her. "Put that goddamn gun down and get in bed. Don't worry, I won't be touching you. I'll be outside."

He brushed by her, thrusting back the flap to start over the spring seat, but she stuck the barrel between his ribs. "You aren't going anywhere, husband. Not until my mind is settled."

He froze. Slowly moving his head downward, he raised a brow. "You haven't got the guts to kill me."

Of course she had no intention of harming him, but . . . "I said, you aren't going anywhere. Sit down."

He eased toward the rear of the wagon. "Mind if I get comfortable?" he drawled.

"Do as you please, as long as you're willing to talk."

"Wanna help me with my boots?"

"No."

"Wanna put down that gun?" At her refusal, he said, "Wouldn't take much for me to take it away from—"

"*Ruhig!*"

"I don't suppose that means, 'Yes, my darling, I'll stop pointing a loaded weapon at you.' "

"Richtig."

He shrugged, then kicked off his footwear. He shucked his shirt, and she tried to muster her wits against the sight of him. She wouldn't be seduced by his appeal, not when she was totally angry with him.

It didn't help, his sliding those britches down his long legs and stepping out of them. Slowly. Reaching to a hook, he hung his trousers up. His naked form, all those sensual movements . . . Maybe they ought to settle this argument in each other's arms. No. Not tonight.

"I overheard you talking with my brother," she stated.

"Figured it was something like that."

Gil sat on the spread bedroll, easing his back against the rear of the wagon. He brought a knee up, rested his wrist on it. The view left nothing to her imagination.

Her blood warming, not with anger, she found it difficult to hang on to the pistol. "I was angry even before I heard you telling him all the things you should have been telling me."

"Figured as much."

"You deceived me, Gil."

"How do you reckon?"

"By writing to my brother."

He shrugged again. "I had every right, if not my duty, to let him know we were married."

"You shouldn't have done it behind my back."

Gil grinned. "All's well that ends well."

"Is that how you look at this? As ending well?"

"It will if you'll put that gun down and come here."

"I can see you're ready. Ready and randy—as usual."

"Yeah." He ran his hand across his chest. "And your armor isn't as intact as you'd have me believe." His lids went halfway down on his eyes. "I see your nipples puckered through your shirt. I'd like to play with them. Lick them. Suck on them. And a few other choice places as well."

At his bald words, she refused to allow herself to be swept into his seduction, but the gun shook nonetheless. Two weeks without his lovemaking had made her very ready for it; her yearnings had nothing to do with reason.

Don't be a *Tropf*, she told herself. She was not going to be easy prey, not when . . . "We need to get something straight between us."

"We've got something straight going for us. Old Son."

"Is that all I am to you? Someone to sleep with?"

"I told you in Fort Worth—I love you." He closed his eyes, leaning his head against the back of the wagon. Catching her off-guard, he asked, "Who is Otto Kapp?"

"A man in Fredericksburg."

Gil opened one eye and scowled. "I thought you haven't had any suitors since that Thom character jilted you."

This wasn't the direction she wanted the conversation to lead. "We need to discuss the now and the future. I won't have you going behind my back, such as writing letters without my knowledge, nor will I allow you to confide in others. Just as it's my place to be at your side for better or worse, it's

311

my place to hear your troubles."

"I won't allow you to own me, Lisette. And I won't let you wear the pants. Not here, not later."

"I don't want to be the boss. All I want is to be privy to your hopes and fears."

His mouth flattened. "I hope you'll stay out of the long arms of the law, as well as Frank Hatch's path. And I fear that if you don't, on either score, you'll put yourself and the child in peril."

"Gil, I am healthy as a horse."

"Even horses fall at times."

"I won't. And I intend to stay with you. As a partner instead of a handicap. A long time back you said when we next saw Fredericksburg, it would be together. Well, that's the way it's going to be with Abilene. When you next see that town, it's going to be with me at your side. If you fight me, it couldn't be good for our child."

"I've got plenty of fight. But not tonight." He exhaled a tired breath. "Lisette, can't we discuss this in the morning? I'm worn out, and you must be too. Come here, honey, and let's make like married people."

"Oooh!" She picked up one of his discarded boots and threw it, catching Gil on the shoulder; this opened his eyes. "You exasperate me."

"Your timing is poor, sweetheart." The boot stayed where it had fallen: at the base of his stomach. "I'm fresh out of hearts and roses, so get in bed. Now."

"Hearts and roses? I know nothing of either."

"If you'll give me till after this drive is finished, I'll teach you about them."

Without a word, she stared at him. He looked

tired and weary. Who wouldn't be that way, what with all that he had gone through? And what had she done? Chip at him, over and over again.

The floorboard creaking under her feet, she went to him and knelt down. Placing an arm across his chest, she braced on her palm. "Gil, I'd like to know all about hearts and roses."

He lifted a brow, and she blew an arousing stream of air on his throat. "I've noticed a couple of things about you, *Liebster*."

"And what would that be?" he asked on a crooked smile.

"You need my help. You're short-handed again, you're having trouble with the drive, and I can free Cencero Leal from the chuck wagon. Which might just keep your cowboys healthy enough to get our longhorns to the railhead."

"You'd make a good cadger, Lisette. You aren't above any means of persuasion."

"If I was, we wouldn't know the joys of being in love."

He laughed. A hand snaked around her waist. "You win. We're partners to Abilene. But under conditions. You're going to take care of the baby. And stay out of trouble, you hear me?"

She grinned at her victory. "That's the second-best offer I've had all night."

"What's the first?"

"Mmm, curling up with you and Old Son."

The next day, Adolf Keller left for the return trip to Fredericksburg. He objected to his sister staying with the Four Aces outfit, but Gil gave his assurances. The longhorns didn't move out, though. A handful of cowboys were still under the weather. It was four days later that they started up the buffalo-dotted Chisholm Trail again.

Hatch made no appearance during that time, and Gil was relieved. He had enough problems as it was. The heat, the lack of water, the menace that didn't go away.

Someone continued to slaughter cattle.

And Gil came to the conclusion that someone couldn't be Wink Tannington, since the one-armed cowboy had been in camp when the latest incident occurred. Hatch wasn't around; so, who among the men was disloyal?

It ceased to be a major problem. The occurrences stopped.

Luckily, the outfit reached the Red River without more trouble than nature allotted. The longhorns basked in the glory of the river's water, water, water. Thankfully, the herd got across without loss. Fortunately, the Territory Indians gave little trouble beyond begging for a cow or two as the herd passed over the land between the Red and the Washita.

The hell of it was, it was slow going. Too much heat, not enough water, and a major stampede caused by the boys getting into an argument and firing guns into the air. To a man, the cowpunchers were tired and weary and ready for Abilene.

Still, they didn't see hide nor hair of Frank Hatch.

Gil began to believe they wouldn't. A major relief to both him and Lisette.

On the flip side of the coin, Matthias was afraid Hatch wouldn't show. He wanted to face Cactus Blossom's killer, and he grew more impatient each day.

Two months had passed from when Lisette and Matthias had rejoined the outfit until now. Late July was hotter and drier than ever. On top of that, Lisette was getting bigger and bigger, way bigger than she ought to be at this stage of her pregnancy. And Gil worried about her. Her pale, drawn face caused him to miss sleep.

Each time he ordered her to rest, to take it easy, she got her back up, saying, "I will do my part for our common goal, husband."

She was one mule-headed German girl.

Tonight, as Gil rode through the fractious, thirsty herd, he kept his bandana over his nose. Dust whirled, making visibility nearly impossible. But he heard noises, suspicious noises from an area around the horse corral. His spurs digging into Big Red, he hurried in that direction.

The dust storm abated; he got a clear look at the trouble.

A youngish Indian—gigantic, brawny, wearing a feather in his black felt hat—had a revolver at Pigweed's head. He was a familiar redskin from the Crow tribe—the ladies' man of a sort, Jimmy Two Toes.

And Frank Hatch had a rifle pointed at Gil. "Throw down your gun, McLoughlin."

Tossing Thelma to the soil, Gil took a survey. A half dozen horses lay inert, their throats slashed. Deep Eddy Roland had his hands in the air. So did

Attitude Powell, Toad Face Walker, and Preacher Wilson.

Two Toes and Hatch had them. And they had allies.

"All along, I've suspected the traitors in this outfit," Gil said, glaring at the three. "Thank you, Tannington, Bell, Ochoa, for your loyalty."

Hatch fired his rifle; the noise caused Big Red to rear. Gil righted the stallion, and he saw the right in getting down from the saddle. If he didn't, his loyal men might pay.

For Charlwood.

Chapter Twenty-eight

Rubbing her back and blinking away grit from the dust storm that had just ended, Lisette stood alone in front of the campfire when the commotion began. She heard voices across the prairie and the bang of rifle fire. She grabbed her pistol. Running as fast as her burdensome stomach would allow, she wended her way through the herd, but pulled up short when her shoe sank into something soft. Manure.

"Verdammt."

By the time she'd found a clump of grass and had wiped away all traces of cow leavings, the sounds of trouble had stopped. Nonetheless, she continued on under a canopy of stars, the area close to the remuda her goal.

Nearing the horse corral, she cursed again, this time to herself. Dead horses, men in trouble — Gil among them! *Dear Lord, don't let anything happen to him. Not to him or his men.*

What could she do to help?

Making her presence known would be a hindrance. Slowly, determined not to call attention to herself, Lisette moved behind a cow, putting a barrier between herself and the scene. She saw the backs of outlaws. One of them was Frank Hatch.

And then she recognized more.

Wink Tannington, Ochoa, and Jackson Bell—traitors all—were aligned with Hatch and a young, muscle-bound Indian wearing a black hat with a feather in the band.

"Hatch, let my men go," Gil said. "They're not part of the trouble between you and me."

"You pay, they pay. Too bad."

Gil spoke quietly. "This isn't Georgia. As I said, what happened there is between the two of us."

"Georgia. Interesting place. I remember you—quite well. Of course, I remember the first Mrs. McLoughlin, too. Whatever happened to Elizabeth?"

"I haven't the slightest idea."

"Do you suppose she took up with Elmo Whittle? He used to be my overseer at Charlwood, in case you've forgotten. He and Madame McLoughlin had a hot affair going in the stables, I remember *quite well.*"

Although she was some distance from her husband, Lisette could tell that a layer of ice descended on his face.

"I don't think all of this is over my ex-wife," Gil said.

"Seems you have a propensity for the same type of woman, McLoughlin. Why, I seem to recall a gentleman in Lampasas, Blade Sharp. Before I put him out of his misery, he said he and your new wife had almost been—shall we say—close."

Gil's hands balled into fists. "That's a lie."

"Is it?" Hatch went on, "I've had an opportunity or two with the sweet Lisette myself."

318

That was another lie!

And Lisette almost blurted a protest. It took slapping her palm over her mouth to stop it. Gil, meanwhile, was trying to advance on Hatch.

"Stay where you are," the Georgian demanded.

Lisette heard a sound from behind and nearly jumped out of her skin. Thankfully, she didn't scream. It was Matthias, Cencero Leal at his side. She exchanged looks with both, and pointed to her pistol. They showed their firearms. Matthias and Cencero also had lariats in hand.

The unspoken question was, now what were they going to do?

It was three against seven, and Hatch and his fellow rustlers had their guns trained on Gil and the rest of the Four Aces' crew.

Hatch said, "Pick up the damnyankee's gun, Two Toes. Get the other ones, Ochoa."

The Indian thrust Pigweed Martin at Tannington. With his single hand, the Mississippian caught the wagon driver by an arm.

The Mexican stepped forward, grabbing weaponry from Attitude, Toad Face, and Deep Eddy. The one called Two Toes lunged at Thelma.

Just as the brave neared Gil, a long leg kicked out, catching Two Toes. The Indian teetered, his feathered hat tumbling to the ground and rolling in the dust. Gil pushed him and yelled to his men, "Hit the ground."

They did.

Two Toes struggled for footing. Deep Eddy Roland tossed a rock, striking the Indian's head; he fell.

Cencero and Matthias urged a couple of cows forward. Jackson Bell tried to get around the cattle, to

319

no avail. Gil grabbed Thelma, then turned her on Ochoa. The Mexican dropped his rifle.

Matthias rushed forward, swung his lariat, divested Wink Tannington of his hold on Pigweed, then lifted his own pistol. Jackson Bell dropped his revolver, begging, "Don't shoot," but a steer rushed him; he fell under the onslaught; hooves came down.

Sick at her stomach, Lisette saw Bell's head being crushed under the steer's weight.

But Hatch was moving in on her husband.

Sucking in her breath, Lisette lifted her arm, aimed at Hatch. And fired.

Frank Hatch pitched forward.

All of it happened in a blink of an eye.

But, thank God, the scuffle was over.

Jackson Bell was dead. Gil and his men tied up the outlaws. Hatch was not dead, his injury nothing but a flesh wound in the arm.

"Hang 'em. Hang 'em all!" chorused the loyal men of the Four Aces.

"No." Gil pleaded for reason. "We'll let the law take care of these brigands."

"What law would that be?" asked Oscar Yates.

"The one you and Matt are going to take them to, up in Kansas."

It went without saying there was no law between here and there. Lisette knew his meaning: with Matthias in charge of Cactus Blossom's murderer, Frank Hatch wouldn't make it alive to the authorities.

So be it.

Foiled, I've been foiled.

This thought ate at Hatch as the damnyankee's men tied him in the hoodlum wagon's hold, along with the others. Amidst a night grown black as a dungeon—at least in his estimation—the wheels rolled over. Hatch would have kicked himself had his legs been free, had his upper arm not throbbed from Lisette's grazing. Foiled by a woman's lucky shot. What was his world coming to?

Hell, that was what.

For two months Hatch had toed Delmar Hitt's line, had kept a distance from the outfit, but had been thirsty for a corner of vengeance, had thought killing a few of the horses plus Tecumseh Billy would bring satisfaction.

Slaughtering animals had seemed simple at the onset; his allies had agreed and had even taken care of most of the gruesome deed. The collie dog, though, had been his own work. It had felt good. And earlier tonight—mmm!—hearing those horses scream and seeing them fall had felt even better.

Oh, revenge had been sweet.

Had been? It wasn't over.

"You've not seen the last of me," Hatch yelled to the damnyankee. "I will return!"

Gruene leveled a six-shooter on Hatch. "Be quiet."

"Shoot me. If you have the testicles to do it."

Gruene didn't.

Ochoa said, "You should have leestened to Señor Hitt."

"Shut up, greaser."

"Ain't you the one, giving orders like you knew what you was doing!" Tannington taunted. "You messed us up, Hatch."

"You didn't have to go along with it."

Jimmy Two Toes didn't speak, simply bestowed one of those ugly Indian looks.

May the devil take him. Hatch sneered. May the devil take all of them. But he needed the Crow Indian, plus the two Southerners.

He eyed his fellow captives. "I feel good about tonight, all things considered. We didn't get that lead steer, but we made a dent in the horse herd."

"And got ourselves caught," grumbled Tannington.

"Chief kill you for stupid," Two Toes said to Hatch.

"I've gotten out of worse trouble than this. I've escaped a Yankee prisoner-of-war camp, I've slipped through enemy lines, and I got free of a Georgia jail." All right, it took killing Mother and Mary Joan, but so what? "Delmar Hitt doesn't scare me a bit." He smiled. "This is no hill for a stepper."

Gil watched the hoodlum wagon disappear over a rise, then turned to his wife. Big, big eyes waited for his reaction. He took her hand, led her to an area beyond the cowpath.

Shoving his thumbs behind Thelma's belt, he stared at the uneven ground. "Do you think—?"

"Gil, was I wrong to shoot Hatch?"

"No." His only regret? That the bullet hadn't caught Hatch between the eyes. "Was I wrong in not hanging him?"

"You're asking my opinion?"

Looking up at his wife, he smiled. "I am."

"Thank God."

"No. Thank *you*, honey." He removed his thumbs, took a step toward her. "Lisette, thanks for sticking up for me."

"No thanks needed."

"I think there are. I guess I do need you to help fight my battles from time to time." At her radiant smile—as radiant as the orange glow of the campfire, as bright as stars above—he added his own smile. "I finally understand what you've been trying to drum in my head. Helping each other is what marriage is all about."

"My sentiments exactly."

"I'm a lucky, lucky man, having you for a wife."

"I'm glad you think so." She swallowed. "Gil, I heard what Hatch said, and I want you to know—he lied. I never encouraged him along any lines."

"I know." He caressed her cheek. "Honey, let's get some rest. Tomorrow is a big day. We've got to get our cattle closer to the railhead."

Chapter Twenty-nine

When Delmar Hitt discovered that Frank Hatch
had defied orders and had ridden unsuccessfully into
the McLoughlin camp, he curled his lip and muttered to Asher Pierce and Rattler Smith, "It figures."

"We shouldn't've trusted that feller," Rattler
groused. "He's too dad-blame crazy to keep his mind
on the dollar sign."

On this hot-as-a-firecracker afternoon in early August, the last of the Hitt gang assembled behind a
stand of trees. Instead of watching McLoughlin have
the headache of getting their cows closer to the railhead, the three saw a wagon—filled with Hatch and
hïs *compadres*—cross the low waters of a brackish
stream.

"I have no use for stupid men," Hitt said to no
one in particular. "I count Hatch and Two Toes
among the stupidest."

"What are we gonna do now, Delmar?" asked
Pierce.

"Follow their wagon."

"Then what?" Rattler asked and scratched his ear.

"I'll let you know when I decide." Hitt took little

notice of a half dozen buffalo drinking from the Salt Fork. He put a foot in the stirrup and settled atop his buckskin mare. "C'mon, men, or we'll lose sight of that hoodlum."

They caught up.

A grizzled oldster drove the wagon, a youngish fellow on the seat beside him. The younger one carried a rifle. Thankfully, Hatch and Two Toes didn't make fools of themselves by acknowledging their partners; the others had never seen them.

"Hold up there," Hitt called out. "Got a minute?"

"What fer?"

"Since you have four men tied up in the back of this wagon, I assume you've had some trouble." Hitt reached into his pocket, extracting a badge he kept handy, and handed it to the whiskered old codger. "Sheriff Waldo Prothro of Abilene, Kansas, at your service."

"Ye be right smart south o' yer area, ain't ye?"

Waiting for an answer, the four men in the back of the wagon watched intently. So did the driver and his shotgun rider.

Hitt smiled the smile that had hustled hundreds of Georgians out of their tax money. "We heard there were some rustlers in the vicinity, so my deputies" — he gestured to Rattler and Pierce — "and I decided we must ride down and help out."

"That be plumb nice o' ye. 'Cause that be just exac'ly what these varmints are: outlaws. They been cutting the throats o' the cap'n's dogies."

"An abomination." Self-proclaimed Sheriff Prothro, a master at deception, summoned a frown of indignation; the "deputies" did likewise, Rattler tugging

325

on his ear. Hitt said, "My deputies and I will see that these blackguards face the full force of the law."

The shotgun rider finally spoke, a German accent evident. "Don't trust them, Oscar."

"Aw hush, Matt."

The squarehead had to be Matthias Gruene, husband to Cactus Blossom. Hitt got uneasy. If that squaw wasn't dead—

"I will not hush. I want to know if—"

"We could use some help," the codger said, interrupting his companion. "It be a fur piece to Kansas, and I ain't hankerin' to smell these here varmints all the way up there."

"I do *not* smell," Hatch piped up.

You will after the sun gets to you for a few hours, thought Hitt.

"Let me see that badge." Matt reached for the silver star, turned it over in his hand. "Looks authentic."

"I assure you it is," Hitt said smoothly. Actually, he'd gotten it off the chest of a sheriff last year, right after he had put a bullet in the back of the lawman's head.

"That man—the one in the corner—is a murderer." Matt's fingers tightened on the gun stock. "He killed my wife. And I intend to see he pays for it."

It was good to know the woman was fair and truly dead.

Hitt compelled menace into his features as he glanced at Frank Hatch. It wasn't difficult, since that he was out to teach a lesson.

He cut his eyes back to Gruene. He emitted

feigned sympathy now. "He'll pay for his misdeeds, sir. As will all the rest." He honed in on a particular miscreant, who fidgeted on the floorboard. By the look on that face, Delmar Hitt figured Hatch was smart enough to know that he was hearing the truth on this score. "I guarantee you, sirs, he *will* pay."

Indecision and reason fought in the German's face, and Hitt figured there would be trouble: Gruene wouldn't turn the captives over.

No problem.

Hitt would kill Gruene and the codger.

But he didn't have to.

The squaw's widower rubbed a hand down his face, then said, "Take them."

What a fool.

"Sleep easy tonight, sir," Hitt said. "You've made the right decision."

Within minutes, the stupid side of the gang was sprung, the Four Aces duo on their way south. Delmar Hitt found himself as amazed as he'd been in Georgia. People were so gullible. And this time, it had been almost too easy.

Oscar Yates behind him, Matthias rode the pinto mare that one of the deputies had traded them. Necessity had forced an exchange of the wagon for this mount. How else would Sheriff Prothro and his deputies have gotten Frank Hatch and the others to jail?

"Never thought ye'd let ole Hatch outta yer sight alive."

"It was your idea to turn them over."

"Yep, but 'tweren't my wife what was killed by

him. Iffn it'd'a been Susie, I'd a—"

"Why don't you be quiet, Oscar?"

"I ain't gonna. I wanna know why ye let him go."

"There's too much lawlessness in this land already." Matthias paused. "I'll let the law . . . and God . . . take care of Frank Hatch."

They had even turned over the hoodlum wagon.

Gil McLoughlin shook his head in disgust and rolled his eyes at his wife, who lifted her shoulders as well as her palms in a gesture that said, "It puzzles me, too."

In the fading light of day, Matthias Gruene and Oscar Yates stood next to a pinto mare that any tinhorn with a lick of sense could tell had had a running iron put to its original brand.

Giving up a valuable piece of property such as a wagon was secondary to Gil's suspicions about the situation. He demanded, "Describe the lawmen."

"They was three o' them. The sheriff, he was the Yankee type, sorta smooth talkin'. Them other two didn't have much to say. One kept scratchin' his ear. Had a big mole on the end o' it, he did."

"Was the other deputy bald?"

Yates nodded. "He were. I could see he didn't have no hair, even beneath that hat o' his. 'Tweren't a wisp of it where his sideburns oughta be. My Susie used to say, 'bald as an egg.' "

"You didn't give Hatch and his cohorts over to any Sheriff Waldo Prothro." Gil turned to the big German. "What was the matter with you, Matt? Why the hell weren't you suspicious enough to figure out you turned them over to the Hitt gang?"

Matthias paled. "They'll be in cahoots in no time."

"They are already," Gil corrected. "Actually, it wouldn't surprise me if they weren't from the beginning. Delmar Hitt wouldn't have gone to any lengths for a stranger, much less give up a horse."

Hatch on the loose with the Hitts, the wagon gone. *Damn.*

His shoulders slumping, Matthias beat a fist against his dungareed leg. "If I had it to do over again . . ."

Lisette waddled toward Matthias. Lately she'd been using an apron to cover the too-tight shirt she'd borrowed from the largest man in the outfit, Attitude. She still looked beautiful to Gil.

"We don't know for certain about this Hitt gang," she said to Matthias.

Gil scowled. "I am. And—"

"A lawless land demands taking the law into one's own hands," Matthias said. "Frank Hatch deserves to die."

He wouldn't get an argument out of Gil. Hatch's mother and stepsister might have been as vile as their kinsman, but they hadn't deserved to perish at his hands. And Cactus Blossom . . .

Don't start getting tender-hearted.

Gil turned from the Comanche woman's widower, and made his way toward Tecumseh Billy. Lisette followed behind. The steer lifted his lengthy horns, his bell tinkling, and small black eyes wide-set in a curly white face stared blankly into the night . . . until he caught sight of Lisette.

His tail twitching, T-Bill lumbered over to her.

Her hand went to her apron pocket, and she pulled a carrot from it. The steer, fond of such a treat, chewed on the vegetable.

Gil said to his wife, "I've got two choices. We can get on up the cowpath, or I can ask for volunteers, then ride after Hatch and the Hitts."

Her eyes widening in alarm, she put a hand on his forearm. "If you ride out, Gil, you could get hurt—or killed."

"If I find them, *they'll* be the ones to suffer."

"You'd have to leave some of the cowboys behind to watch the herd, even if they all wanted to go. Wouldn't it be better if you could outnumber them?"

"You're trying to outmaneuver me, woman."

"Possibly. But shall I remind you of something? You said you'd had enough of killing during the war."

"I did." Gil paused. "But Matt was right. A lawless land calls for lawless measures."

She sighed in exasperation.

Drool slipped from Tecumseh Billy's mouth as he opened it to chew the air. Gil scrubbed his knuckles across the space between the steer's eyes. Right then he caught sight of a calf; he pulled his hand away.

The bullock loped by without any spark of recognition. But Gil knew him. He was the calf Lisette had rescued the morning after they had met Cactus Blossom. Cactus Blossom . . .

There was no use trying to forget she'd ever existed.

Gil's memory ran fresher than ever before. As if it were right now, he saw her hand poised to make the now departed Sadie Lou "roast for dinner." The Comanche woman could have just as easily thrown a knife at him or his wife. Damn, how he had hated having her tag along, but she had been a help to Lisette. And Matthias—a good man, a great strawboss, despite his lack of judgment with "Prothro"—had grown to love her.

Never had Gil felt even a tad of regret over losing her. Until now.

"Gil? You're not thinking about riding out, are you?"

He swung to that softly spoken feminine voice.

"I'm thinking I need a hug." He opened his arms, and when his wife was there, somewhat clumsily, he buried his face in the coronet of her hair. "Sweet darlin', I've just come to realize something. Cactus Blossom should have been mourned."

"She is. By Matthias. By me."

Gil stepped back to brush his hand across his mouth. "If Matt wants to avenge Cactus Blossom, I'll help him."

Lisette's shoulders stiffened, then slumped as she sighed. "If you go after Hatch, take care of yourself. The babe and I need you."

"I know."

A bell tinkled as Tecumseh Billy plodded over to Lisette. He lowed to draw her attention, as if to say, "Why are you paying attention to him? I want another handout."

Gil and Lisette looked at each other and chuckled. In this, there was communication that needed no words. And it helped to ease the tension.

"Better find another carrot, darlin', or he'll get testy."

She took the steer by a horn. "T-Bill, time to eat."
The trio walked back to camp, Lisette to fulfill
her promise of carrots, Gil to seek Matthias out.

Chapter Thirty

He could get himself killed.

Lisette may have acquiesced in her husband's decision to let Matthias make the choice in the Hatch debacle, but her nerves skittered like lightning in a midnight sky as she and Gil returned to camp, the lead steer in company. With her shaky knees, it was all she could do to find another carrot for T-Bill.

Feeding the lead steer, she never let her eyes stray from her husband as he spoke to the two cowhands lounging around tonight's campfire. Gil asked Preacher Wilson and Deep Eddy Roland to find Matthias, send the strawboss to camp, then make themselves scarce.

Gil motioned at T-Bill. "Take him with you."

Men and beast set out.

"I'll fix some coffee," Lisette said.

"Why don't you sit down, honey? Do some relaxing for a change."

Relax? At a time like this? "How can—never mind."

She closed her mouth, since Gil had enough on

his mind without wifely naggings. After collecting a couple of bedrolls, she settled them against a wagon wheel. Her back to the spokes, she sighed. It did feel good to rest; never had she felt the burden of her stomach so profoundly.

Gil dumped enough Arbuckle's Coffee into the huge tin coffeepot to brew a barrelful. He filled the pot with water, set it on the cleek above the fire trench. Crouching back on his heels, he stared at the fire, an elbow on his knee, keeping his own counsel. Every once in a while he squinted at the stars.

By the time coffee bubbled, Matthias trudged toward them.

Gil looked up at the approach of those boots. "How about a cuppa?"

"That sounds good."

Gil poured three. Their fingers touched when he handed Lisette's over; she felt his tension. While she was a wreck, thinking about him stalking Hatch, he, too, was very much uneasy.

Sitting cross-legged, Matthias eased down in front of the fire to drain the mug. The dancing flames reflected each line of his haggard face.

"Matt . . . how 'bout a plug of snakebite medicine?" Gil asked.

An eyebrow quirking, Matthias cocked his head. "You're offering me whisky?"

"Every once in a while it's called for. I could use a shot, and you look as if it would do wonders for you, too."

"I won't argue."

Gil collected the Scotch whisky from the chuck

wagon. "How 'bout you, honey? Want a shot of Snake Bite?"

Though it sounded like just the medicine to ease the pain of her anxieties, she shook her head. Young Hermann was doing enough gamboling already.

Her husband poured generous portions of whisky into Matthias's cup as well as his own. He took a sip; the strawboss quaffed his, then held up a hand for another portion.

The bottle neck at the rim of Matthias's cup, Gil said, "There's something I should have said before, but in all honesty, I didn't feel . . . until now. Matt, I am truly sorry about your wife. She was a good woman."

"*Ja*, she was." Her widower ran a hand down his face. "I don't know if I'll ever quite understand about Weeping Willow, but you don't know how I miss my wife."

Tears burned Lisette's eyes.

"We all miss her, Matt. You, me, my wife." Gil took another swallow of liquor. "That's why I called you here." He set the cup aside. "Way I see it, we've got a couple of choices. We can leave the herd in camp and ride out looking for Hatch and the others. Or we can try to evade them." A second passed. "What do you think we ought to do?"

"What if I say, 'Let's string Hatch up'?"

"We ask if any of the boys want to go along. Whether they do or not, we saddle our horses, tonight—before Hatch gets farther away."

"How would we know where to find him?"

Gil reached into his vest pocket and pulled out a cigar. For a moment he studied it. Then, taking the burning end of a campfire twig to the end of his cigar, he dragged it toward his mouth. On a cloud of expelled smoke, he closed one eye and studied his second-in-command. "I don't imagine we'll have too much trouble finding Hatch. The way I see it, Delmar Hitt is after my cows. That's why he tied in with Frank Hatch. Hitt and his boys are hiding somewhere along the Chisholm Trail, waiting for us."

Standing, Lisette hugged her arms rather than going by the instinct to cover her ears against the deep meaning of Gil's words.

Matthias asked, "You'd put yourself and your men in jeopardy, in memory of Cactus Blossom?"

Another puff from the cigar. "Partially."

"What do you mean, partially?" Matthias asked, echoing Lisette's thoughts.

"Your wife is gone and there's nothing that'll bring her back." Gil's words were slow. "But we—you, me, my wife—live on. We can't let that Georgian take another life."

"What about *your* wife?" Matthias asked. "Are you willing to jeopardize Lise?"

"She stays right here till we get back."

"*If* we get back." Matthias reached for the whisky bottle. "For Lise's sake, I think we should try to make Kansas before confronting Hatch."

She watched her husband's reaction, seeing that he was in agreement, even before he tossed the cigar into the fire, and said, "We'd better stay off the Chisholm's established route. Even so, it'll be hard to cover our tracks, but we've got to try. Before first light, let's beat for Abilene."

336

Matthias Gruene left the campground; he was glad the trail boss had listened to reason. Their hunting down Frank Hatch would have put a strain on Lisette, which Matthias was wont to do. He still loved her, but his affection had returned to the pure kind.

If something happened to McLoughlin, she would suffer as he suffered for his dead wife.

Oh, Cactus, you'll always be the great love of my life.

Recalling his boss's words of heartfelt sympathy, he took comfort. Gil McLoughlin was a hard, cruel man at times, but at others he proved more considerate.

As a man racked by regrets where his own wife was concerned, Matthias hoped the Scotsman would continue being decent to Lisette, but somehow he wasn't convinced that would happen. He had nothing specific in mind, nothing but instinct.

The next morning, before sunup, Matthias saddled up, and before riding out, he took a sidelong glance at Lisette. In all haste she was packing the chuck wagon. Her husband wouldn't be going after Hatch, yet Matthias could see worry and concern in her features. He yearned to go to her and offer his shoulder, but he didn't. It was her husband's place to offer reassurance.

Tapping his heel to his mount's flank, Matthias took off to help her husband get his herd to Abilene.

The Scotsman changed course, veering off the Chisholm Trail. Through the hot summer days, into the equally stifling nights, each man worked extra shifts. From way before dawn until far after nightfall, they pushed through the Territory, Tecumseh Billy at the lead.

They encountered a few buffalo — very few — but little else beyond desolation. The outfit neared the Kansas border, and everyone began to think they would make the state line without trouble. They were wrong. But trouble didn't come from Hatch and the Hitt gang.

A quarter hour earlier, they had pulled away from the afternoon rest stop. At a stand of cottonwoods and blackjacks to the east of the rounded hills, T-Bill stalled and refused to go on. Trouble appeared atop a rise.

It took the form of a half-hundred Indians.

Chapter Thirty-one

While fifty might not seem a horrendous number, it appeared as if the whole Indian nation was upon them.

Trembling, Lisette manned the chuck wagon—the reins frozen in her hands—when those warriors surfaced over a hill to the north. Somehow she brought the team to a halt.

The Indians, astride ponies, were too far in the distance for her to get a close look at them, but below the clotted clouds on the horizon she saw the outline of feathered headdresses, rifles, war clubs.

Her head seeming to move on a ratchet rather than a neck, she faced her husband. A dozen or more paces separated the wagon from him and Big Red, but he was inching the stallion in her direction.

He pulled alongside her. "They may not be on the attack."

"I don't think we should trust them."

Gil chuckled. "It's too late to worry about that. We're surrounded."

"It wouldn't hurt to pray, then."

Asking God's mercy, she watched the leader ride forward. A feathered war club in his grip, a rifle in a scabbard at his side, the brave stopped in front of her husband. Naked from the waist up with the exception of metal armbands and a silver medallion on a leather chain around his neck, he appeared young enough to take scalps with a flick of his wrist.

And the tattooed dots on his torso gave him a fierce look that beat his Comanche neighbors to the south for menace.

Raising one hand, he said in almost flawless English, "I am Iron Eagle of the Osage."

"I am Gil McLoughlin of Texas. I consider you and yours my friends."

What a lie, thought Lisette.

Iron Eagle cut his eyes to Lisette. Her scalp prickled; would it soon be decorating his tepee?

He turned his attention back to Gil. "You trespass on our hunting ground."

"We mean you no harm, Iron Eagle. All I seek is to take my cows to market."

"You have scared the buffalo. We have few to spare."

In fact, Lisette hadn't seen a buffalo in days, and she decided Iron Eagle was out for revenge. Whatever the case, the Osage land had been infringed upon; the welcome mat certainly wasn't out.

"Why do you not take your beeves along the trail of your brothers?" Iron Eagle asked.

"We have had trouble with the white man," Gil answered.

The Indian laughed. "You have a saying in

English. I believe it is, 'It serves you right.' "

"I don't claim to be perfect, Iron Eagle. I'm just a fellow trying to make a living, just as you're trying to keep meat on the spit." Gil leaned forward in the saddle. "Wait a minute. Don't I know you?"

"My memory is stronger than yours, Gil McLoughlin of Texas. I know I know you." The Osage placed his war club crossways on the pony's back. "Twelve moons ago you culled ten beeves from your herd to feed my people."

"I didn't powwow with you. I spoke with Crooked Finger."

"Chief Crooked Finger has gone to the Happy Hunting Grounds."

"I'm sorry to hear that." Gil appeared genuine in his sympathies. "Good fellow, that Crooked Finger."

"Yes."

"How is his wife? I remember eating a fine meal—"

"Red Dawn is my mother."

"No fooling?"

"I do not make jokes." The Indian led his pony abreast of Big Red. "Gil McLoughlin of Texas, your beeves appear thirsty. Will you trade ten head, and some coffee and tobacco, for water?"

"The United States agents don't keep you in them? Even if you are a state line south of where you're supposed to be."

Indignation fought insolence as Iron Eagle replied, "The white chiefs in Washington speak with forked tongues."

A quarter minute stretched before Gil replied in

an cheerful manner, "I'd consider your requests a good trade for water."

"White brother, I invite you to my village."

"I would like to give my regards to Red Dawn."

Lisette's fright diminished. The conversation between her husband and the Indian had turned to a chat implying no attack. *Don't get overconfident.*

Gil turned the sorrel and rode back to speak with his cowboys, and Iron Eagle put a moccasined heel to his pony's flank. He rode close to the chuck wagon — and seemed to be taking an overlong look at blond hair.

"Are you the woman of Gil McLoughlin of Texas?"

"Ja. Ich bin Lisette McLoughlin."

He cocked his head. "Has your tongue been wounded?"

"I beg your pardon?"

"Hmm. You speak clearly now."

Funny things for him to say.

"What are you called?" he asked.

Why hadn't he picked up on her name? Oh, dear, she'd probably spoken German. In hopes familiarity would breed friendliness, she said, "Please call me Lisette."

She was glad when Gil returned. Within a few seconds he was tying Big Red to the rear of the chuck wagon. He told her to scoot over, he would drive.

"Gil, you hate Indians," she said as the wheels began to turn. "Are you up to some sort of trick?"

He shook his head. "The Osage aren't bad Indians, not like the Comanches. I'm not wild about giving up ten head of cattle, but it'll be worth it, *if* Iron Eagle comes through . . . which I think he will."

The Osage chief did make good on his promise. The cows smelled water even before Lisette caught sight of a gurgling stream; they rushed it, thankfully bypassing a browned cornfield.

Cornfield? She hadn't known Indians farmed.

Most of the cowboys and a goodly number of the braves stayed with the herd when Gil and Lisette followed Iron Eagle down a rutted lane. Lisette, accustomed to seeing Comanches, was surprised to note that the Osage Indians were a tall lot, their height rivaling her husband's and Matthias's.

A buxom woman wearing a cotton dress sewn in the native fashion walked toward them. From a distance she appeared to be in her middle years. Up close, and with the exception of her straight black hair, she didn't appear as Indian as her Osage brethren.

"Red Dawn!"

"Gil McLoughlin?" Showing education, she spoke in unaccented English. "Is that you, Gil?"

"It is. And this is my wife, Lisette." He turned on the seat and winked. "C'mon, honey. Everything's going to be fine."

It did begin well.

Gil and Red Dawn renewed their acquaintance, she offered friendly greetings to Lisette, and teased him about the expected "papoose."

"If you will bring your tobacco," said Iron Eagle, "I will provide the pipes."

Gil nodded.

After kissing Lisette's cheek and patting her arm, he walked, the Osage chief at his side, over to the chuck box. Matthias met them there.

"Come to my lodge," Red Dawn offered and took Lisette's hand. "I will give you buffalo to eat."

Any offer of food that she didn't have to prepare enticed Lisette.

They passed over a rounded, wooded hill, and when they did, Lisette caught sight of Red Dawn's village. It surprised her. Why, it was almost the same as any township in the civilized world!

She approached Red Dawn's home, and it wasn't a tepee; it was oven-shaped and covered with earth.

The interior was not only roomy; it was decidedly and lusciously *cool*.

And there were no scalps on the wall, thank goodness.

The lodge smelled of herbs and woodsmoke, had buffalo skins decorated with Indian designs stretched across its walls, and had a pair of platform beds. Several bolts of cotton stood upright near an accumulation of pottery dishes.

And . . . why, those were *books* stacked against a wall.

Lisette honed in on a feathered headdress that hung from one wall. It was a glorious thing, had some of the finest needlework she'd ever seen, and she said so.

"I made it for my Crooked Finger," Red Dawn explained. "He wore it on ceremonial occasions."

"You made it? How fascinating. I, too, am interested in millinery. Would you teach me how to work beads into leather?"

"Of course. But wouldn't you like to rest for a while?"

"That does sound appealing."

Yet Lisette continued to peruse the lodge and the hostess. Red Dawn seemed quite civilized. What had she expected? Despite her friendship with the deceased Cactus Blossom, Lisette had held a myriad of notions where Indians were concerned. Before now, if someone had asked her to describe her fate in Indian hands, she would have shuddered, recalling Olga.

And the awful description her husband had given of Indian habits—heavens! All the while he'd known Red Dawn and her family. Now that she thought back on the day he had proposed marriage, Lisette realized he had been exaggerating for his own benefit.

So be it.

Red Dawn and her son, plus the people she had seen as they journeyed into this village, had been kind and cordial. Their customs were different, of course, but it had taken some time for the *Mädchen* Lisette to grow accustomed to the Texan way of life. Strange did not mean bad.

Pardon me, Olga. but I like these *Indians.*

"What do you think of my lodge?" asked Red Dawn.

"It is quite interesting. I've never been in an Indian home before."

Red Dawn chuckled. "Neither had my father, until he met my mother. And neither had my daughter-in-law, until she came west and met Iron Eagle."

"Oh?"

"I am a halfbreed. My father—pompous son of Virginia—was a student of the classics. He yearned to write about the heathen." She chuckled. "He learned to like our ways. But he insisted his young ones learn to read and write his language."

"I agree with him. One's heritage shouldn't be lost."

Lisette decided young Hermann must learn her native language along with the customs and traditions of his father's homeland, though when it came to wearing skirts—kilts, as Gil called them—she would draw the line.

Red Dawn said, "My son's wife is white. She is from Maryland. Ah. Here is Laurann now."

At that moment a lovely redheaded woman stepped into the lodge. On her back was a cradleboard, and in it, a sleeping, black-haired child. Red Dawn introduced Iron Eagle's wife, then scurried about. Laurann took the cradleboard from her back and rocked the sleeping child in her arms.

Staring at the baby, Lisette felt a rush of emotion. The little one was beautiful, all black wispy hair and plump cheeks. "A boy? Or a girl?"

"A girl." Laurann smiled with motherly pride. "We call her Amy Sleeps Sweetly."

"When she wakes, may I hold her?"

"I'd be offended if you didn't want to."

Lisette's curiosity ran wild. What had happened to

346

bring a gentle white woman to the Indian Territory?

"No, I was not captured," Laurann said, as if reading Lisette's mind. She hung the cradleboard on the wall. "I met my husband when my father went to Kansas as an agent for the United States government."

"I'll admit I was curious."

"Sit down, both of you." Red Dawn swept her hand in the direction of the beds. "Better yet, lie down. Young mothers and expectant ones need to relax at times."

Lisette followed the redhead's lead to recline. A featherbed it wasn't. But it was the most comfortable mattress that had touched her back since she'd left Ruth Craven's rent house.

The apron strings were uncomfortable, so she loosened them, but did not take the masking garment off, since her stomach showed through the shirt's buttonholes.

Red Dawn must have sensed her predicament, for she said, "We must make you a dress while you are guest in our village."

"Oh, I—I couldn't accept."

"You will insult me if you do not."

"Red Dawn, I'm sure we won't be here long enough for dressmaking, but I do appreciate your thoughtfulness."

"We will see. Maybe you will find yourself surprised." A tray in her hand, Red Dawn offered a plate and a goblet from it. "Have some pemmican. And some elderberry wine to wash it down with."

The jerked buffalo proved to be tough chewing, its

347

taste much stronger than beef, but it had a good flavor. The elderberry wine—she ought not to drink it. But she was thirsty, so maybe just one sip . . . The goblet was empty in no time.

A young boy, probably six or seven years of age, charged into the lodge. Gripping a miniature tomahawk, he glared at Lisette. Despite his stance, he was a handsome boy with blue-black hair brushing his shoulders.

"My son, David," Laurann announced proudly. "David Fierce Hawk."

"Hello, David."

He grunted, and Lisette looked him over. He was sturdy and tall, his skin several degrees lighter than the Osage seen so far, with the exception of Red Dawn. And he was not happy. Running to Laurann, he pointed at Lisette. In his language and displaying a gap where a baby tooth had been, he shouted to the redhead.

"You are impolite," Laurann chided.

Again he spoke in a tongue foreign to Lisette, and received a swat to his rump. Disgust and humiliation shooting from his light brown eyes, he asked in English, "What are white people doing in our village?"

"David." Laurann blushed. "Don't speak in such a way. Mrs. McLoughlin and her entourage are our guests."

"We do not need the buffalo slayers!"

"David!"

Red Dawn waved a hand. "Pardon my grandson. He listens too closely to our Pawnee neighbors."

While Lisette had given up her qualms about the Osage Indians, she understood the boy's misgivings. Anything new was daunting.

"David," she said warmly, "that is a fine tomahawk. Would you show it to me?"

Warily he assessed her. But a moment later he shuffled forward. "My grandfather made it for me."

"It's very nice. Have you slain many buffaloes with it?"

"Buffaloes! I will kill white men!"

Lisette knew the boast of youth when she heard it; she'd do nothing to break his spirit. "You appear to be a very strong young brave, David Fierce Hawk. I imagine you will be a great warrior when you grow tall as your father."

"I will." His face lit. "You are very nice, for a white woman."

"David," said his mother, "go play."

"I do not play! I prepare for war!"

"Prepare for war, then, but leave us be."

Pulling a face, he answered, "Yes, Mother."

Lisette smiled. David Fierce Hawk, she surmised, would grow to be a fierce man, stalwart in his beliefs, yet acquiescent when the moment was right.

As the sturdy young brave left his grandmother's lodge, Red Dawn took down the headdress. "Lisette, I believe you asked me about this. Would you like to know how I made it?"

"Oh, yes, ma'am."

For the next several minutes, Lisette and Red Dawn bent their heads in concentration. Yet Lisette couldn't get her mind off David Fierce Hawk. It was as if something settled in her, saying, "Your family hasn't heard the last of him."

How ridiculous. David was a mere child!

Amy Sleeps Sweetly began to bawl. With her mother's approval, Lisette changed not only the girl's clothes but also the moss lining the cradleboard. The infant widened her big, green eyes and gurgled.

"It's lovely, tending a baby," Lisette murmured.

"You are sentimental because of your own babe." Laurann smiled. "Such a nice trick nature plays on women, making us love babies so."

"That is right." Red Dawn refilled the goblets.

By the time she'd finished the second glass, Lisette felt light-headed, almost giddy, and she and the other women were chatting as if they had known each other for years. It was only natural to mention Blossom, to tell them of her tragic end.

"Such a shame," said Laurann. "And her poor child. Weeping Willow must have been deformed awfully."

"I hope nothing like that happens to my baby." Lisette touched her belly. Little Hermann rolled and tossed. "I pray he'll be healthy."

A pensive look on her face, Red Dawn brought her forefinger to her upper lip. "This white man called Frank Hatch. I wonder . . . No, I make too much of it."

Laurann cocked her head. "Make too much of what, Mother?"

"Didn't Iron Eagle tell you? When the moon was last high, a scouting party found the tracks of seven horses. Most Cold Morning and Wind on the Trees

350

have stayed on their trail. Our braves should return shortly. They will bring word. It might be of Frank Hatch and his brothers."

Seven mounts? Lisette did some mental addition: if those horses had been ridden by the Hitt gang, someone was missing. She hoped that someone was Frank Hatch. Better yet, she hoped none of those seven horses was topped by either him or the men who had taken charge of the hoodlum wagon.

That would be too good to be true.

She sensed trouble on the horizon.

Chapter Thirty-two

Edgy, Lisette waited for her husband. To the west, the sun had faded to spokes of tangerine behind the gray sky. Cooking fires blazed in the Osage village, women preparing meals, braves loitering around. One lodge past Lisette, she saw two men from the outfit, Pigweed and Deep Eddy, relaxing by a fire. A trio of Indian maidens giggled and fed them from pottery plates.

Lisette smiled. Pigweed and Deep Eddy were going to become spoiled.

She spotted Matthias, his stance bespeaking a widower's grief, watching the men and the maidens. The girls had to remind him of Cactus Blossom, and Lisette started to offer comfort, or at least a cheerful diversion, but he turned and left, leaving her to wonder, *Where are Gil and Iron Eagle?*

"White lady."

Lisette spun to the sound of that young male voice. "David, how are you?"

"Do not call me David." He stood tall . . . for a boy only seven years of age. "That is a white man's name."

"It's a wonderful name. Very old. From the Bible. And your parents chose it for you."

He pulled a face, the gap in his teeth showing. "My mother picked it, not my father. Call me Fierce Hawk."

"All right. Fierce Hawk."

"What are you called?"

"Lisette."

"Is it a Bible name?"

"Yes. In English it is Elizabeth."

"I do not like Bible names. I will call you Woman of Great Stomach."

She chuckled and smiled at the sturdy boy, hoping that young Hermann would turn out as healthy and hardy. But maybe not so opinionated.

"Fierce Hawk, do you know where your father and my husband are?"

Nodding once, he sat cross-legged and ran a thumb across the ridges of his child-sized tomahawk. "They powwow with Most Cold Morning and Wind on the Trees."

They were the ones who had been trailing the seven mysterious horses.

"Da—Fierce Hawk, are the braves discussing a white man called Frank Hatch?"

He shrugged. "I do not know. When they saw me, Father sent me to 'play.'" A small, bronzed hand beat against his knee. "I wish he and my mother would not make fun of my war practice."

Lisette was on pins and needles to find out what was going on with Gil and the others, but she put that subject aside to ruminate over the young brave's wounded tone. Remembering what it was like to be

353

a child not taken seriously by adults, Lisette sat down beside him.

"Grown people can be thoughtless at times, Fierce Hawk, but that doesn't mean they seek to belittle."

He eyed her prominent belly. "When you have your papoose, will you . . ." Those quizzical eyes, an intriguing shade of brown, lifted. "I know you will be kind to your papoose. You are a nice white lady."

"So is your mother."

He nodded vigorously, but obviously his mind wasn't on Laurann. "Someday, can I play with your papoose? It will be a boy, won't it?"

"I think so. I shall call him Hermann."

Fierce Hawk frowned, and for all his big-man talk, he was a typical youngster, much like Viktor and Karl. "Hair Man? Yuck. I don't like that name. Is it from your Bible?"

"No. It's from my father. But it goes back to my homeland, and before that, to Roman times. In Latin, it is Arminius."

"I like that better than Hair Man." Cocking his head, Fierce Hawk inquired, "What about the Romans? I do not know of them."

"They were mighty warriors."

"Really?" His eyes became saucer-round. "Will you tell me more about Romans?"

"I wish I could, but to tell the truth, I don't know or remember everything, and they were too great for me not to do them justice. You see, I should've listened more closely to my parents." There was a hint for him in this. "But your grandmother has many books, and I'll bet there are one or two that will bring the Romans alive for you."

"I don't want to read." He rolled his eyes. "Red Dawn wants me to."

"Well, if you want to learn about the Romans . . ."

"When your papoose gets big, will you teach him to read?"

"He will go to school."

"Eeeck."

"My Hermann will like school," she said positively.

"Maybe you will have a girl. Like my mother did." He scrunched his nose. "Girls are no fun."

"You'll change your mind. Someday you'll find them quite attractive."

"That's what my father says. He says I will grow strong and tall and will want a squaw." Fierce Hawk placed the tomahawk on the ground, settled an elbow on his knee, and rested his chin on his knuckles. "I do not think I will grow to like the girls in my village. They giggle too much. If your papoose is a girl, maybe I will like her. If she does not hide her giggles behind her hands."

Lisette grinned, then turned serious. "Fierce Hawk, my husband and I live very far away. I don't think you'll have a chance to see my baby, be it a girl or a boy."

"When we hunt buffalo, we travel very far." Fierce Hawk straightened his back. "If your girl does not giggle, I will make her my squaw."

Instead of chortling at that determined remark, Lisette got the strangest feeling. That afternoon she'd thought she had not heard the last of David Fierce Hawk, and this conversation didn't seem to count against that premonition.

"Maybe we will see you again one day," she said,

patting his smooth arm. "But, Fierce Hawk, don't be disappointed when you find my baby is a boy."

"No. You will have a girl. She will be mine. You will see." Turning shy, he admitted, "I hope she is as pretty as you."

"She'd better be," Gil said, standing above them and drawing Lisette's attention. "She had better look just like her mother, boy, or I will be disappointed."

He stood smiling down at her, and Lisette answered with a smile of her own, one that faded as she wondered what news he brought, especially when Iron Eagle appeared.

"David, go play."

The boy grumbled at his father's orders, but waved to Lisette. "I will see you again someday, Woman of Great Stomach."

Iron Eagle disappeared into his mother's lodge as Lisette got to her feet, Gil's steadying hand giving her support. His fingers pressed against her elbows, and he said in a tease, "You amaze me. Be they young or old, you always charm the menfolk."

"I think it was the other way around in this instance. Fierce Hawk has me completely charmed."

A growl rumbled from Gil's throat. "Good thing he's a wee lad."

"Enough of this nonsense. Gil, what word did Iron Eagle's men bring?"

He stepped back, doffing his Stetson and rubbing his brow with a forearm. "Hatch and the others are camped a few miles to the east. Apparently Delmar Hitt isn't with them."

"What do you think?"

"Later tonight, we ride after them."

"Oh, Gil," Lisette murmured on a sinking feeling. "Oh, no."

"Oh, yes. So we'd better enjoy the evening while we can."

"I wish you wouldn't go."

"Lisette, we've no choice. We can ride after Frank Hatch, and have Iron Eagle and his braves on our side, or we can strike out alone."

"I . . . I understand."

"Good. And don't be fretting over it, honey. We have them outnumbered—greatly outnumbered."

She took some solace from his statement.

From the corner of her eye, she saw Iron Eagle leaving Red Dawn's home. He walked to them. "Lisette, my mother and wife would like to see you."

"Better go on, honey. Iron Eagle and I have a few more plans to make."

Her mind on the events of much later tonight, Lisette headed for the lodge. *You must stop worrying. Everything will be all right. Be calm. Put it out of your mind—that's the best thing.*

She made her way inside. While the Osage woman and her daughter-in-law had promised a surprise—and she'd expected some sort of frock—Lisette was more than astonished at the result. It helped to take her mind off the evil Hatch.

"These are for you." Two bell-shaped cotton dresses, plus a couple of underskirts, dangled from Laurann's fingers. "Since you're interested in beadwork, we thought you'd want to do that part yourself."

Red Dawn presented a pouch. "Beads."

To be free of Attitude Powell's shirts . . . To have

357

loose, comfortable clothing . . . But most of all, she was touched by these women's kindness. *"Danke.* I mean, thank you."

"Sew on the beads," Red Dawn ordered softly. "Soon we make ceremony."

"And I must leave." Laurann collected her daughter, and waved a hand. "See you later."

Lisette borrowed a bone needle and cotton thread from her benefactress and put her fingers to flying. Within an hour beads decorated the scooped neck of one dress, a sleeveless creation of turquoise blue. With Red Dawn's assistance, she stripped out of her clothes and pulled the new frock over her head.

"Mmm, I feel free. And *comfortable.*"

"And you look beautiful. Would you like a necklace to wear, and some feathers to work into your braids?"

"My husband likes for me to wear my hair loose, so I'll brush it that way. But I wouldn't mind borrowing a bit of ornamentation."

"You will find feathers in that box beside my platform." Nodding her head, Red Dawn rifled through a pouch. "Ah. Here they are." She lifted a string of turquoise beads trimmed with copper medallions. "I traded with an Apache for these, many moons ago."

"I—I'd better not borrow that. If something happened to it, I'd feel awful."

"Do not worry, Lisette. Beads are only beads. Friends are something to cherish."

"You are a friend I'll never forget."

"You had better not!" Red Dawn shook a finger. "Now, let us finish making you ready for your handsome husband."

Red Dawn provided luxuries such as Lisette hadn't seen in weeks, if ever. Water and soap. A pair of soft moccasins to replace her scuffed lace-up shoes. A jar of extract from herbs and flowers to dab behind her ears, on her wrists, and between her breasts. Of course, the necklace. And then Red Dawn held up a silver-handled hairbrush.

"I haven't seen one of those since I left Germany." Lisette ran the bristles through her hair. "Where did you get it?"

"My daughter gave it to me when she married Iron Eagle."

"You and Laurann are fortunate to have each other."

"I think so. She is a fine daughter."

Never had Lisette missed her own mother so.

From outside the lodge, she heard the tattoo of drums, the voices of Osage Indians gathering around the fire. She eyed Red Dawn. "What is the occasion?"

"Our braves will dance for rain."

"Would that we should all dance for it. And for peace."

Red Dawn offered a hand. "I am not too old. And you are not too with papoose." She paused. "Maybe you are too far along. I would say your time will come in less than a moon."

"Oh no. Three months."

"I have borne seven papooses. And I have watched the growth of many more from other women. I say, one moon."

Lisette glanced at her stomach. She felt Hermann

move within her. Her hands closed over the mound. "Three months."

Red Dawn clicked her tongue in the motherly fashion. "You do not know how to count the moons."

Maybe I have lost track of time, Lisette thought. It seemed as if an eon had passed since that day she lay with her husband for the first time. Again she surveyed Hermann's keep. God in heaven, she appeared ready to pop.

No wonder Gil hadn't touched her in days.

Who would want a grimy woman wearing a tight shirt and tighter britches? Well, she was rested, freshened, and looking her best, thanks to Red Dawn. She'd *make* him want her—tonight.

Before he rode after Frank Hatch.

"Red Dawn, let's celebrate . . . rain." Oh, how nice it would be to make love with the rain beating down. Throwing back her head, Lisette laughed. "I love . . . the rain."

"Come. We dance."

Lisette loved to dance; it had been a wonderful pastime in her younger days. All of a sudden, despite her love of it, she felt self-conscious. Here she was, big as a barn . . .

"I shouldn't," she replied. "I am too unattractive. People will laugh. My husband will think me—"

"We dance for rain, not for men. And no one will laugh."

"When I dance, I'd rather it be for my man."

"That is all right, too."

When his wife emerged from Red Dawn's lodge,

Gil handed Iron Eagle the pipe he'd been smoking. A phalanx of braves, cowpokes, and Osage women were gathered in a large circle around a fire, Gil sitting next to his host. He had the urge to make a spectacle of himself by charging to his feet and hauling Lisette into his embrace.

Her sleeveless, low-cut dress would have drawn dropped mouths in white society. Gil was pleased they weren't there, since the dress showed Lisette's long and graceful arms to their best advantage. And the soft skin of her chest was enough to make him want to yank her into the woods.

Firelight caught on the metal of her necklace, and Old Son took notice.

Soon as we hit Abilene, I'm buying her some jewelry. And I'll expect her to wear it—and nothing else!—to bed.

Gil gave himself a mental shake after that thought. By the time they reached the railhead, her pregnancy would be too far advanced for bedchamber frolics. But he'd overheard Red Dawn say—*Forget it!* Once their daughter was a few weeks old, Lisette would be clothed in nothing but baubles.

She was near him now, moistening her lips and lifting her fingers. Desire coiled through him as she tossed that heavy mane of hair over her shoulder. Her big eyes were welded to a spot below Thelma's belt. Her gaze cruised up to his face, and she murmured his name.

She's trying to seduce me. He liked it.

Too bad he'd be riding out after Hatch as soon as the rain dance was over.

Over the beat of drums, he patted the ground, stood to take her hand, and said, "Sit down, honey."

361

"Not yet. First I dance."

In a line to Gil's right, a dozen or more braves, each wearing nothing but loincloths and headdresses, along with arm and ankle bands, approached the circle. Chanting and singing, they danced to the fire.

Red Dawn appeared out of the shadows, her fingers lacing with Lisette's. "Come," she said. "We dance."

Lisette and the Osage woman took their places between the performing braves. Gil's eyes didn't leave his wife. Within moments, despite her girth, she caught the rhythm of drums, the cadence of the beat. When she neared him, he heard her chanting in a mixture of German and English.

Bending low, then arcing her arms toward the heavens, she sang, "Rain. *Regen*. Rain."

Mesmerized, Gil leaned back on an elbow, extending a leg in front of him. Again she raised her arms. Again her feet skipped around the fire. This time his wife stopped in front of him. Curling her fingers, one at a time, she bent low over him. He got a whiff of herbal perfume. And wanted a big taste of his woman.

"Will you dance with me and our son, husband?"

"I'll embarrass myself if I do," he whispered. "Old Son is on the prowl."

"No one will laugh."

He danced, and no one laughed—or if they did, he didn't notice. All he knew was the feel of Lisette in his arms. They weren't dancing in the Indian fashion; they held each other in an embrace that would have been shocking in white society. It would

362

have been much closer, if their unborn daughter wasn't expanding her mother's stomach.

They hadn't made love in days. On the trail, he'd known she was tired, but she showed no signs of weariness tonight. He had to have her. There wouldn't be time to do it leisurely, but he got the impression she was just as ready for him.

"Old Son is wanting to pay a visit," Gil murmured into her ear. "What do you think?"

"Why don't we find a quiet spot?"

"Excellent idea." Yet he didn't act on their lusts. "Honey, there's something . . . I overheard Red Dawn—you do look awfully pregnant. I wouldn't want to hurt the baby."

"Red Dawn may be a wonderful Indian, but she doesn't know what of she speaks."

"Then it's okay, at six months to . . . ?"

"More than okay."

He danced his wife from the circle. Behind Red Dawn's lodge, he kissed her parted lips. Sweet, so sweet, they were tinged with elderberry wine.

"No wonder you were dancing, honey," he whispered in a tease. "You're drunk."

"And I'm thirsting for another sip of something good."

"What'd that be?"

"Another one of your kisses, husband."

"Happy to accommodate."

His fingers furrowing through the mass of her hair, he took her lips again. He tried to press her to the outer wall of Red Dawn's home, but her girth rendered his actions inefficient. He wouldn't quit.

He grasped and pulled up the hem of her dress.

His mouth descended to the cotton-covered bosom that captured his attention. Breasts full and hard-tipped met his questing tongue, and he laved them, each in turn. Lisette's hand tried to scoot between them; he stopped her movement.

"Tonight, my darling wife, you simply enjoy."

Scooting downward, he placed the back of her right thigh on the top of his left one . . . and moved in. As usual—thankfully!—she wore no pantaloons to impede his fingers. His palm caressed her belly, moved lower to the thatch of silky pubic hair he knew to be the color of cornsilk, and he heard her moan of approval. God, she felt warm and eager and good.

His tongue flicking over her arm, he murmured, "Been a long time, honey."

"Too long."

Playing on their words, he drawled, "Oh, I think Old Son is just the right size."

"And how do I know that?" she came back saucily.

Gil growled. "Want me to prove it?"

"Mmm. Yes."

"In time, honey. In time."

Making circular motions, his middle finger delved between her feminine lips to find the flashpoint of her sexuality. It was there for him, swollen already, and slick with her juices. "Ah, honey," he groaned, and continued to caress the place that was his alone. Her breath was coming in short rasps, her moans intermingling with his growls of approval.

And he had his own heightened reaction. While he had been stiff for her, it seemed as if he would burst, so spurred was his arousal. Over and again, he expressed his love. And he told her how much he wanted to be inside her . . . at the moment she reached her climax.

"Do it, Gil. Do it."

"Help me."

Her fingers undid Thelma's buckle, the six-shooter and holster falling to the ground. Just as Lisette began to fiddle with the buttons on his britches, he heard a voice. Iron Eagle's. Quickly, he stepped back and adjusted Lisette's dress.

Damn. He hurt to step away from his wife—in more ways than one.

"White brother, the ceremony has stopped." Moonlight mirrored warpaint. "Now we find Frank Hatch."

Chapter Thirty-three

West of the Osage village, Frank Hatch slept on the ground and dreamed of his greatest triumph to date.

Under the broiling Territory sun, Delmar Hitt had stopped the hoodlum wagon, had ordered Rattler to untie the captives. "Leave Hatch to me," he had said.

Ochoa, Wink Tannington, and Jimmy Two Toes were released from their rope bonds, and after stretching their cramped muscles, they jumped to the ground. Tannington bestowed a look of loyalty at Hatch before accepting a revolver from Asher Pierce. The Mexican did likewise.

Two Toes simply grunted, unharnessed the team, and grabbing a hank of mane, leapt onto a paint's bare back.

Rattler and Asher rode to the Indian's side.

Turning those beady Yankee eyes toward the sole occupant of the wagon, Hitt peered over the sideboard and curled his lip. "You stupid bastard, you may have ruined our chances of rustling the Four Aces' herd."

"I don't share your pessimism."

A knife in his grip, Hitt climbed onto the wagon bed. In one upward movement, he sliced through the binding on Hatch's legs. A fatal mistake. Hatch kicked a leg, catching the gang leader in the groin.

Hitt screamed, dropped his knife, and clutched himself. He fell to the side and rolled over.

In that same instant, gunfire cracked. Rattler Smith rode toward the wagon, but Tannington shouted, "Stay where you are."

Frank Hatch's tied hands grabbed for Hitt's knife, and quick as lightning, he swung his arms. A jolt shot through him as knife connected with bulk.

"Awwwwwgh!"

Blood spurted onto Hatch's face. The feel of it was revolting, but he couldn't let anything stop him. Delmar Hitt tried to turn. Using all his strength, Frank Hatch yanked the knife out of the carpetbagger's back, then plunged again.

The force of his efforts reverberated through his bones as the life went out of Delmar Hitt.

"You won't be calling me disparaging names again."

A dead quiet took over, a silence as dead as Delmar Hitt.

Hatch yanked the back of his hand across his mouth, wiping smears of blood onto his sleeve. Triumph surging through his veins, he stood. "Are you men with me, or not?"

They were.

Ah, what a glorious day.

In his sleep, he yawned. Again something tapped against his mouth. Over and over. Frank Hatch recoiled against the blood. He spat. He shook his head, the motion cutting short his dream of triumph.

Lying on the ground, he awoke and opened his eyes. Someone snored; another broke wind. He spied Jimmy Two Toes milling around the spent campfire. Again Hatch slashed the back of his hand across his face, but he wasn't wiping away blood.

Rain. It was raining.

The best part was, his wonderful dream had been true. Delmar's bones were bleaching somewhere on the Chisholm Trail, and his henchmen—along with Tannington and Ochoa—had become the Hatch gang.

Such a pleasant sensation, even better than watching Elmo Whittle pump the first Mrs. McLoughlin.

Frank Hatch spread his arms on the ground, and rejoicing in his luck and the cooling rain, he fell asleep again. This time nightmares attacked him. Cactus Blossom throwing their deformed baby off that damned cliff. She didn't even cry, little Weeping Willow. Not as she tumbled over the precipice, not when her father lowered himself to the canyon floor to wrap his arms around her poor, twisted body. He had tried to shake life into her. There was no use. She didn't breathe.

For once, she didn't cry in agony.

Her father sobbed, for he had loved but two things in his life: Charlwood and Weeping Willow.

In his sleep, Frank Hatch became almost human. Almost. For his dreams turned to yet another triumph: the one of beating Cactus Blossom at the art in which she had trained him—the knife.

368

* * *

Through the pouring rain, Gil spied him — sleeping on the ground. Back in Lampasas he hadn't recognized Frank Hatch as being the son of Charlwood, but there was no way he could be mistaken now.

He and his fellow raiders circled the campsite. His eyes cut from side to side, counting a half dozen forms on the ground. Damn it, where was the seventh?

Iron Eagle and his braves advanced on four men; Deep Eddy and Matthias pulled guns on a form that had to be Tannington. Gil slipped Thelma from her holster, cocked her hammer, and put the barrel against Frank Hatch's forehead.

His finger froze, unable to pull the trigger. During the war, he had promised himself not to take another human life. But if he didn't kill Hatch . . . given the Georgian's background of violence, he might turn on Lisette.

"Wake up, Sleeping Beauty."

His eyes flashing open, Frank Hatch clutched the ground before grappling for his knife. "I'll cut your heart out, McLoughlin."

"No. You're through murdering. I won't fault you for Blade Sharp. But this is for your kinswomen. And Cactus Blossom." He pulled the trigger. "And especially to protect my wife."

When Gil put an end to Hatch's evildoing, Lisette slammed closed her eyes and retreated farther into

369

her hiding spot near Hatch's encampment. Sickened by the goings-on around her, she thought about the events that had led her to chase her husband.

She had ridden a Four Aces' gelding and found the scouting party as they neared the blackjack brake. Of course, Gil had ordered her to stay in the safety of the village, but despite her earlier confidence, she wouldn't let him out of her sight.

She had feared if she did, she'd never see him alive again.

Then something moved behind her. She started. An arm reached around her, pulling her backward; a hand closed over her mouth.

"You die."

It was the voice of Jimmy Two Toes.

Where the hell is my wife?

When Gil found the chestnut gelding bearing the Four Aces' brand as it meandered around the trees lining the death site, he knew Lisette hadn't stayed in the Osage village. Damn her! And Jimmy Two Toes had to have captured her.

He was the only one not accounted for, the only one of the seven not dead—eight, actually. Tannington had lived long enough to say that Delmar Hitt had been dead for days, at Hatch's hands.

Rain—the rain Gil had wished for a thousand times—beat like needles onto his upturned face. It would cover tracks. And darkness, eerie darkness, enveloped the night; it would be hours before daylight. *Hours.*

"We'd better split up," he said to Iron Eagle.

"I do not think he will go to my village. You and I, white brother, should travel toward the setting sun."

Gil nodded. "The obvious place to search, since Jimmy Two Toes is no great thinker. He'll probably head toward the cowpath. Matt, you and Deep Eddy scour the woods to the north. Pigweed, Johns, Eli — take the area south of here."

Iron Eagle assigned braves to both groups.

Never more scared in his life, for he feared losing Lisette, Gil searched the boggy woods, Iron Eagle at his side.

Dawn broke. Gil found a turquoise bead, a copper medallion. They had been part of the necklace she'd worn the previous night. His heart slammed against his chest.

"White brother, look."

The relics in his tightened fist, he turned in Iron Eagle's direction before studying the ground. Water pooled in deep horse tracks. Tracks leading to . . .

"The Valley of Many Buffalo."

He was going to kill her.

Lisette knew this to be so of the enormous Indian Jimmy Two Toes. Furious upon witnessing his partners' demise, he shoved a bandana in her mouth and pushed her, stomach forward, atop his mount. He jumped up behind her. His revolver stayed trained on her back.

Within an hour, his paint pony fell under the extraordinary weight. He left the horse, rain falling on its carcass.

Urging her on with the point of his revolver, Two Toes led Lisette through the night. Shivers from the wet and from her fear racked her body. Her teeth could not stop chattering.

As the red sun lightened their path, rain ceased. Two Toes clamped a hand around her wrist. "Halt. We go there."

With the gun, he pointed to a steep embankment leading down to a wide fissure in the earth. Her heart stopped. This was where he would leave her . . . dead.

"Go, Yellow Hair."

His hand pushed her shoulder; she stumbled but he caught her, jerking her upright and shoving her toward the canyon. She fell on the muddy decline, her stomach thudding against the steep ground. The baby didn't move. *Hermann, don't die on me. I'll get us out of this, somehow* . . .

Jimmy Two Toes loomed above her.

"Get up, Yellow Hair."

Pushing her sodden and tangled tresses out of her eyes, she struggled to her feet and descended to the valley floor. Two Toes limped next to her. The vale was spongy from last night's downpour, and littered with mud-flecked buffalo skeletons and arrowheads. Her moccasins were no match for those sharp objects. Pain shot up her legs, pooled in the center of her aching back.

"Sit, Yellow Hair."

A knee-high boulder jutted out of the ground. Huffing and puffing, she eased onto it and took a look at her captor. In spite of his limp and the drop to the valley, he didn't even appear winded.

She glanced down and saw her beautiful new dress in damp, clinging tatters. It shouldn't bother her, not when she and Hermann were in jeopardy, but it did. Thankfully, Gil's son moved within her.

"My dress is ruined," she murmured aloud, but certainly not to Jimmy Two Toes.

"Take it off."

"I . . . will . . . not."

"White women look good without dresses. Nice white titties. Make prick hard. Take off dress, now."

Under no circumstance would she quail under his leer; she sneered at the Indian. He epitomized all she had once hated in his race.

"Me young and horny. Many white women like. You will like, too."

Never would she give herself willingly to his lusts. And she would not let him murder her unborn son. Never. What should she do? Her attention riveted to the revolver. If she could get possession of it . . .

But how?

"Pull up dress." He waved the pistol. "Me want see nice white legs."

Maybe she could shame him into sense. It was doubtful, but she had to try. "What would your wife think if she heard you saying these things to me?"

"Bertha my woman, but she in Fort Worth. You with me. She not know about it. Take off dress."

The shame angle wasn't working; maybe stall tactics would.

"I'm too tired for sex."

"Me not care if you have headache. Bertha have headache all time, but me not care. She have titties down to here." He turned his palms up at the line of his waist. "I like big titties."

"My breasts don't reach my stomach."

"They plenty big." He took a step toward her. "Me see for self."

No one was going to see her breasts but Gil McLoughlin. No one. She placed a hand over her bosom. "I will not allow you to molest me."

"Do not know word 'mollusk.' "

"Neither do I."

"Yellow Hair, you want see my prick? It very big." He unbuttoned his pants to display the prize. "Make good scr—"

"You aren't as big as my husband," she said haughtily, swallowing the gorge in her throat.

"It soft now. Get bigger if white mouth kiss it."

"That is disgusting."

"Do not know word 'disgusting.' "

"Think of yourself, then you'll know the meaning."

" 'Disgusting' bad word?" At her nod, he went on. "You not think disgusting later. White women call me 'ladies' man.' "

As far as Lisette was concerned, Two Toes had nothing to recommend him. "How much did you have to pay them to say that?"

"Yellow Hair have tongue like war club."

He planted his crippled foot on the boulder; Lisette reared back from his presence as well as his odor. Suddenly it was all she could do not to laugh. What a ludicrous sight he made, all mud and ugliness and waving revolver, standing with his privates exposed.

"You have mean tongue, like Bertha," he said. "You change if want be Two Toes's woman."

"I am Gil McLoughlin's woman, and I carry his son."

"I make my son." His chest puffed. "Teach him Crow ways. He grow tall as tree, proud to have good Crow name."

If he considered raising Hermann as his own, Lisette decided, then he wasn't going to kill her.

Maybe if he *thought* she would submit, she'd have him at a disadvantage. He couldn't perform his dirty deed with a pistol in his grip, could he?

"Maybe I have been mean-tongued," she said. "You really aren't that bad." *As compared to the bubonic plague, maybe.*

"Now you talk nice. I like." Shoving the gun behind his vest and into the waistband of his britches, he ran his thumb across the prize that would win no contests. "Take off dress."

"Jimmy—do you mind if I call you Jimmy?—I'll undress, but if we're going to be man and woman to each other, shouldn't we make it interesting?"

Gil heard his wife say those words about being "man and woman to each other." At first he figured hers was a stall tactic to get away from the brawny Indian. But as she talked on, he changed his mind.

What the hell was she doing, making sex talk with that Crow of dubious repute? Gil was here to rescue her, and he had figured to find her cowering in fear, but she had destroyed him.

He might have known Lisette would never cower.

Jealousy conquered the last of his reason. Always, she had some man fawning over her. Always, she made excuses. Never had she been so brazen as now.

At least not within Gil's line of sight.

He motioned for Iron Eagle to stay back; the last thing he wanted was for anyone to hear Lisette seduce Jimmy Two Toes.

Drawing his gun, Gil crept forward and kept cover.

Now that he got a closer look—God damn it, that Indian had his equipment exposed!

"What you want me do, Yellow Hair? You very pretty. Me want to make happy."

"Oh, I think you can." Eyes that had once been demure looked with heady longing at the Crow. "Take off your clothes."

"Why you want me do that?" He shook his head. "I make good screwing with clothes on."

"Jimmy, Jimmy, Jimmy, where's the excitement in that?"

Gil's hand tightened on Thelma's handle.

Lisette laughed throatily and left the rock. Combing her fingers through her hair, she tossed the mass of it over a shoulder—just as she'd done last night, for her husband. "When I'm with a man, I like for him to be naked as the day he was born."

"That make headache go away?"

"Oh, yes."

Two Toes lifted his brows and nodded. "Okay. What you want me do?"

"Take off your clothes, *Liebling.*"

Liebling? What the hell did she mean by that? There she stood, pregnant with Gil McLoughlin's child, calling a hatchet-faced Injun an endearment . . . an endearment that had a lot nicer ring than *Liebster.*

376

Meanwhile, Two Toes shucked his moccasin; a mutilated foot poked from a holey sock. His equipment bobbed in the air.

"See. Big now. Bigger than last man?"

"It certainly is."

It was not!

"You kiss now?"

"Not until you take off your trousers."

"First, you take off dress."

Enough! Gil raised Thelma, pointed, and fired. A blotch of red suddenly appeared on Jimmy Two Toes's shoulder; the Indian fell backward.

Lisette screamed, ducking behind the rock.

"Needn't worry," Gil called out. "It's just me — your lawfully wedded husband."

The lawfully wedded husband who, in a fit of jealousy, had just shot a man over his wife.

Chapter Thirty-four

"Gil, thank God you found me!"

Leaving Jimmy Two Toes moaning on a pile of buffalo bones, Lisette scrambled up the hill and tried to fall into her husband's arms, but he stepped back. His face closed, he replaced his six-gun in the holster. Surely he hadn't overheard . . .

"Gil, you don't think I was serious with that Indian, do you? I did *not* mean those things!"

"Let's go," was all he answered.

She stood frozen, her eyes glued to the anger and disgust in her husband's face.

Iron Eagle rushed past them, rifle in hand, shouting, "Two Toes gets away."

"Leave him be," Gil said.

Lisette turned slightly to see the Crow hobbling across the valley floor, clutching his injured shoulder.

A question in his eyes, Iron Eagle stood halfway down the grade as he asked Gil, "Do you not want me to kill him?"

"No." He turned and marched toward Big Red.

"Gil, hold up," Lisette shouted as he put distance between them. "We must talk."

There was no response. Not then; not when they returned to the Osage village; not when she changed into the last of her two dresses, nor when they said their thank-yous and good-byes to Iron Eagle, Red Dawn, Laurann, and the others. Lisette couldn't even enjoy her farewells to Fierce Hawk.

If anything could be found to rejoice in, it was that Frank Hatch was no more.

When they left, she clutched a package under her arm, another gift of clothing from Red Dawn and Laurann. How wonderful it had been, that afternoon and evening in their village. How awful, the leaving.

Onward to Abilene the Four Aces' company journeyed. August became a thing of the past. Early September sweltered. Lisette's stomach grew larger, until her skin stretched to the breaking point. In fact, silver lines trailed her flesh.

Her husband didn't see her changed skin; he made his bed under the stars.

She was beginning to think he didn't love her.

Each time Gil looked at his wife, it was a mirror into the past. He saw Betty, her stomach large with some man's child, luring Whittle between her legs. The evening Hatch had mentioned Betty's affair with the scruffy overseer, he hadn't been telling Gil anything he didn't already know, yet it had been a strong reminder of what a fool he'd been to trust a woman.

And now Lisette—who had made like a whore for Two Toes.

What about all the trouble it had taken Gil to get between her legs? Damn it to hell, it had taken every bit of his persuasion to get there, and she'd never been so bold as she'd been with that Crow. Maybe she liked the hatchet-faced type.

Another demon arose. Adolf Keller had mentioned a certain Otto Kapp. Did he have a hatchet face?

And Gil recalled a tidbit he'd overheard in the Osage village. "Your time will come in one moon," Red Dawn had said, nearly a month ago. Of course Lisette had made denials, but Gil began to agree with Red Dawn. Never had a woman looked so very pregnant at just less than seven months.

Could history be repeating itself? Could it be that her child did not belong to him? That was just too absurd to consider, but . . .

He hated himself for not trusting his wife.

Tomorrow they would reach Abilene, and Lisette would be glad for the journey's end. She was weary from the cowpath, from the burden of Hermann, from the heat of late summer . . . and from her husband's cold shoulder.

Furthermore, she would be relieved to get off this hard wooden seat. She put a foot up on the splashboard as Pigweed clicked his tongue and headed the team to their final campsite. As usual, Gil rode ahead of the wagon. Finally, he raised an arm to signal an acceptable site. As usual, he had little to say.

But he did allow, "I'm riding into town to hire a

couple of men to watch the herd. That'll free up my cowpokes to eat a last meal together. Make it a good one."

He left, and Lisette prepared a feast for dinner: steak; mashed potatoes; canned tomatoes doctored with onions; ears of corn bought from a farmer that morning; sourdough biscuits; vinegar pie. And gallons of coffee.

By the time the meal was ready, Gil returned with a cadre of townsmen. The locals took their places in the herd, allowing all the cowboys to gather around the fire.

Gil kept his distance, saying, "I'm going to make a final tally of the cows."

All the other men were here, except for Matthias and her husband. Oscar, Deep Eddy, Pigweed, Preacher Wilson, Jakob, Johns, Attitude, Toad Face, and Cencero loaded their plates.

Attitude tugged on his long beard and said, "I want to thank you, Mrs. McLoughlin, for being a good partner in this drive. You're the best damned cook"—Oscar kicked him for cursing—"'scuse me. You're the best cook in the world."

"You are," the others chorused.

"Thank you."

Lisette was aware that once the herd was aboard a Chicago-bound train, the majority of her husband's cowboys would backtrack with the saddle horses and Tecumseh Billy to the Four Aces ranch. She did *not* know her own plans.

Would Gil wait in Abilene for Hermann's birth before returning to Texas? A few weeks ago, this

381

question hadn't been pertinent, but now it couldn't be ignored. Surely he wouldn't expect her to stay here alone while he returned to Texas. But he was not only practical about their livelihood, he was not himself in the matter of Jimmy Two Toes.

Her eyes sweeping over the men, she said, "I guess I won't be with you next year. I'll be at the ranch, taking care of young Hermann."

Deep Eddy put his plate on the ground, and the others nodded agreement when he said, "We'll miss you."

Pigweed Martin shuffled over to her. "Missus, I been aiming to tell ya: you sure is sweet and nice."

Sweet and nice. The evening she'd first appeared in the Four Aces encampment, Willie Gaines had said the same thing. Poor Willie. Presently, she paraphrased her words of that fateful night. "I'm rarely sweet and nice."

Pulling his upper lip above up his bucked teeth, Pigweed clasped his fingers together. "Well, missus, I think you is."

"Thank you, Pigweed."

He traipsed to the opposite side of the fire.

"Mrs. McLoughlin, could I fix you a plate?" Preacher Wilson asked, smiling.

Too tired to eat, Lisette declined his offer. She looked up at the minister and recalled how he'd been opposed to her working in the outfit. Yet he hadn't been sanctimonious about her presence in a long, long time. Furthermore, she recalled his reason for signing on to begin with.

"Eli," she said, using his given name for the first

time, "why don't you ride on into town? I know you're anxious to be with your family."

"Mister McLoughlin hasn't released me. And there's my salary . . ."

"I'll pay you, if you'll get the strongbox from the wagon."

He did and she did. Cash reserves were low, she noted—not a problem. The cattle would bring money in, no doubt by tomorrow afternoon. She went for an additional stack of currency.

"Eli, I know you're wanting to start a church, so take this." She pushed the bills into his palm. "A first offering."

Folded money in hand, he tipped his hat. "Thank you, Lisette. May the Lord be with you." He started to walk away, but stopped. Turning, he said, "You're a fine woman, and I want to apologize for calling you a Jezebel."

"That was quite a while ago, Eli. I haven't thought of it since. And even if I had, I wouldn't hold it against you. I understand your misgivings."

"Forgiveness is the Lord's . . . but I appreciate yours."

He disappeared into the night.

Lisette sat down, rested her back against the wagon wheel, and sipped a cup of coffee while watching the cowboys devour the food. Tecumseh Billy lumbered over to her; she pulled a carrot from her apron. He ate the treat and backed away.

"Give us a song," Johns suggested to Cencero.

Long ago, Johns had said those words to José. Long ago.

The grinning Mexican lifted his guitar. "Thees song ees for our Señora McLoughleen."

All the men cheered; she smiled. She would miss the loyal men of the Four Aces outfit.

Cencero began to strum the guitar, started to warble a lovely Spanish song. When the tune had ended, he began another. For once, the cowboys weren't squabbling among themselves. Could it be that they, too, were sentimental on this last night of the cattle drive?

Tears stinging her eyes, she set her empty cup aside.

"Juanito, *mi amigo*," said Cencero. "Join me."

Johns produced a harmonica; the musicale continued.

Oscar, walking bow-legged, set his plate in the wreck pan, and stopped in front of Lisette.

"You ain't et nothin', girl."

"I'm not hungry."

"Ain't good for yer little one, goin' wit'out chow. Susie always said, 'A wuman's gotta take care-a herse'f as well as her babe.' " His rheumy eyes moistened. "Sure do miss that wuman o' mine."

"I know you do." Lisette took his leathery hand to squeeze it gently. "You had a good marriage, you and Susie."

"Sure did. Never was blessed wit' no younguns, though." He winked away a tear. "Ye and the cap'n, why, ye don't know how lucky ye be, startin' a family right from the git-go. Ye'll have a lotta good years, ye and the cap'n and yer youngun. Be lotsa years fer more o' them."

384

"I certainly hope so."

"Why don't ye let ole Oscar fix ye a plate, Miz Lisetty?"

Now that she'd had some time off her feet, food did sound appealing, and she accepted his offer. A few bites were enough. Standing, she departed the campfire. Away from its warmth, the night air brisk, she attempted to hug her arms. Hermann got in the way.

"You're a nice get-in-the-way, my son."

She scanned the horizon, seeing the outline of cattle, cattle, cattle. Where was her husband? She wanted a moment alone with him. She needed to find out, *had* to have an answer to the question: For herself, for Gil, for Hermann, what would the next few months bring?

Chapter Thirty-five

"Meine Liebe, where are you going?"

Irritated that Matthias needed her when she sought her husband, Lisette nevertheless stopped in her tracks. For a friend, Matthias could be as pesky as Tecumseh Billy.

"I'm looking for Gil," she answered.

"He has gone back into town."

"What for?"

"Lise, he doesn't confide in me. How would I know his purpose?"

Why had Gil left the herd again? There was no reason she could imagine, unless he wished to visit a saloon and cry in his beer. *Verdammt!* What did he have to cry about? The cattle drive was at an end, Hatch was no longer a threat, and he would become a father in a little over two months.

Yes, she had been coarse and deceptively receptive to Jimmy Two Toes, and Gil didn't want to hear her reasons, but her husband had many things to be happy about.

The saddle creaking, Matthias dismounted, and reins in hand, he walked toward her.

"Excuse me," she said, trying to step around him. "I fancy a walk—alone."

"He hasn't been good to you, has he?"

"Matthias, respect my wishes."

"Except for my few days with Cactus Blossom, I've always wanted to be by myself. But I—" He paused. "There's a pond not far from here. It's a nice place to be with an old friend. Will you share it with me?"

She lifted her hand to brush the hair from her temple—Gil hadn't noticed that she had combed it loose for him. "I will," she answered at last.

Matthias leading his mount, they found the pond. The horse drank from the water while frogs and crickets made noise. Lisette settled on the soft grass, with Matthias to her right.

Rather than have him pose questions, she asked, "What will you do, now that the drive is at its end? Will you rush back to Texas with the remuda and T-Bill?"

"It depends."

"Depends on what?"

"My choice depends on what your husband does. I fear he'll leave you in Abilene, Lise, and if that comes to pass, I intend to stay and make certain you're all right."

"Gil will take care of me."

Recalling her husband's promises of a honeymoon in Illinois, of introducing her to his grandmother, Lisette choked down the lump in her throat. How long had it been since he had mentioned anything of the sort?

"You're blind where the Scotsman is concerned," Matthias commented. "I don't think you even know that he has a chip on his shoulder."

"I . . . I know he has problems, but it's not your place to worry over them."

"I do—because it affects you. All I want is your happiness. And Gil isn't making you happy. If I knew why, maybe I could help."

"I don't need help."

"You're wrong there." Matthias drummed four fingers on his knee. "Lise, as long as I've known Gil, he's been a man possessed by some ghost."

"His divorce hurt him a lot," she replied after a minute.

"And you're paying the consequences." When she said nothing in response to his comment, Matthias pressed her. "Talk to me, Lise."

Feeling traitorous, yet gaining a bit of peace from bearing her hurts, she admitted the awful truth about Jimmy Two Toes and the buffalo valley. ". . . And Gil took it all wrong. He won't listen to me." Her throat tightened. "How could he ever think I'd want that horrible Indian?" She hesitated. "I guess it's because he equates me with his former wife."

"She was unfaithful?"

"More than simply that."

She told him about Betty, and when she finished, Matthias said, "If he could forgive her, he could forget her."

"A simple concept. A difficult thing to accomplish." Lisette's hand moved backward to massage the small of her back.

Matthias scooted closer, his fingers pressing against her ache. "Your husband should be rubbing your pain away."

The sole time Gil had taken such action had been in the meadow—the place where Hermann had been conceived. Did he have any understanding how difficult it was to be with child, especially one so large as his son?

There was a lot about Gil beyond her understanding.

Matthias' hand closed around a hank of her hair. "Remember when I used to tug on your—"

"Get your hands off my wife."

Gil. She sprang away, catching sight of her husband and Big Red. "I . . . I thought you were in town."

"Obviously."

"I wanted to take a walk."

"Did you, now?" Not waiting for her reply, Gil hoisted his arm and jerked a thumb across his shoulder. "Beat it, Gruene."

Matthias pushed to stand. "You'd like it if I would just *get lost,* wouldn't you, McLoughlin?"

"I wouldn't shed any tears."

The strawboss, his fist balled, said, "The night you married Lise, you promised to be good to her. You haven't been."

"You have a problem with English? I said shove off."

With pleading eyes, Lisette looked up at her old friend. "Go. Go now."

"Is that what you truly want, Lise?"

"Yes."

When Matthias was out of earshot, Lisette stood; it took an ungraceful effort. She closed the distance between herself and Gil. "What do *you* want, *mein Liebster?*"

"Answers." Grasping the pommel, he swung a leg over the saddle. His boots on the solid ground, he slapped Big Red's rump; the stallion galloped toward the remuda. "Lisette, why do you want other men to touch you?"

"The only hands I want on me are yours."

"Don't give me that. Discounting Matt, you were acting the whore for Jimmy Two Toes."

"I was trying to get an edge on him, and—"

"You would've gotten an edge on him, all right."

She didn't think; she acted. Her arm arcing, the air resounding with the whang of her palm against jaw and bone, she slapped his face.

Gil moved not a muscle. The moon shadowed the set lines of his face.

"Damn you, Gil McLoughlin, I am tired of your brooding silences. I am sick of your acting the wronged husband. And I won't abide your innuendoes!"

"That so?"

"Yes. And I want you to know something. When I was in that valley with Jimmy Two Toes, I was scared to death. He had a gun pointed at me, and I thought if I could get hold of it, I could save our child's life."

"Sounds convincing, but I'll never know if you speak the truth, since you don't have his 'revolver' to prove your claim. And I never saw it. I know one thing for sure." Gil's jaw tightened. "Since the last time I've known your abundant charms, I've caught you with two men. So, what am I to think?"

"When was the last time you wanted my 'abundant charms'?"

"You don't want to know."

An invisible knife slashed her chest and twisted in her heart. She whirled around, making for camp. Before she'd taken five steps, her feet quit moving. Her chin dropped. If the tables were turned, she would be just as angry as Gil, provided she'd twice happened on him in compromising positions.

Pivoting, Lisette asked, "Do you still love me, Gil?"

"I'm not sure."

His answer hurt, but if pride kept her on the path to the campsite, they might never clear up his misconceptions, he might never express his love again. And mean it.

She wouldn't ask if he still wanted her. The answer, no doubt, would cause more pain. How long had it been since . . . ? The last time he'd wanted her, in the Osage village, their lovemaking had been cut short. He had to be just as frustrated.

Tonight, right here, right now, she would *make* him admit his longings, make him act on them. In each other's arms, they would chase away ghosts.

He wanted to be as cold as his heart, yet it had been a long time since they had been together. He stayed put. Reaching back and walking toward him, Lisette untied her apron. It fell to the ground. She wore the last of the two dresses Red Dawn had sewn. Damn it, he ought not to want her.

Yet she was still the woman Gil had fallen in love with, was still the woman he had taken to wife, was still the woman who crowded his thoughts, but what was wrong with him that other men's leavings held appeal?

What was wrong? For weeks, jealousy had eaten at him. If he'd been thinking right, he'd have known she hadn't set out to seduce that Indian, and he damned himself for not listening to her pleas. From the beginning. Yet . . . Two Toes was only part of the problem.

He had to do something. Gil's eyes lowered to her belly. "Give your child a break. Our coupling could bring its birth."

"I'm not that far along. Monika told me that she and my brother were comfortable with lovemaking well into her seventh month."

"Good for them."

Her palm flattened against his chest, her fingers arousing his nipples. "It will be good for us, too, *mein Liebster.*"

From somewhere, he marshaled restraint. "Why

don't you call me *Liebling?*" That's what you called Jimmy Two Toes."

"Do you forget that is what I also called Sadie Lou?" His wife pressed her stomach against his. He felt something move as she said, "I call animals by that endearment. You are my only beloved."

Chapter Thirty-six

Her heart strummed against her chest, against their child, as Lisette waited for her husband's response. "Gil, do you understand how much you mean to me? It's you I love and adore. And you've told me you love me, and you're not a man to lie." Her blind faith faltering, she added, "Are you?"

"You ask too much, Lisette."

The pain of his rejection washed through her when he shoved her hand from his shoulder, yet not ready to give up, she said, "I have been, and will always be, faithful to you."

"Talk is cheap."

"Then let's not talk," she whispered. "We should . . ."

What could she do to heat her husband's blood to the degree of hers? She knew he enjoyed aggression; in the past she'd been rather clumsy at it. What could she do that would be different?

Unbidden, her mind wandered back to the morning in the buffalo valley. Did men really enjoy being kissed on . . . ? It seemed shocking, yet when Gil had pleasured her, his actions had been anything but what should be expected of marital relations. Perhaps he would like her lips on Old Son. She certainly enjoyed it when his mouth caressed her flesh.

Her fingers worked on freeing him of his gunbelt, then she tugged the tail from her husband's shirt and released his britches' top button. When she touched her lips to the hair of his chest, her passions increased. She loved the feel of his taut form, the taste of his salty skin, the scent that was solely her husband.

She had to speak. "On our wedding night you made me take your boots off. Tonight I want to."

"If you've got something to prove by stripping me, think again. I'm not interested."

He could speak a million words, and if she let them, each would hurt her, so she buffeted her heart against anything but his bodily reaction. And her own.

"Old Son speaks the language of lovemaking." Using her husband's arms as a crutch, she got to her knees. Gil tried to step back; she gripped his wrists. "I can't get your boots off unless you lie down."

"Stop it, Lisette. I won't have you getting warmed by Matt, then . . ."

"You stop it, Gil. Matthias is my friend. You are my lover — my only lover. And that's the way it'll always be."

"Promise?"

"I already have. At our marriage. And I'm true to my promises." Her palm cupped the warm place of him. "Lie down, *Liebster*. I will take your boots off."

"Damn," he muttered, yet he reclined on the grass.

It was a small victory for Lisette, but she took it.

Her back to him, she straddled his legs. "Put your arms around my waist, as you did on our wedding night."

His fingers curled around her sides, and she felt the tension in his grasp, yet there was something else in it. She felt the passion he wanted to deny.

Her palm smoothed over his knee. "Do you want to know what I was thinking the first time we touched this way?"

"I reckon you'll tell me, whether I want to hear it or not."

"You're right, my beloved. Nothing could stop me from telling you how much I wanted to turn around and kiss you. I wanted your lips on mine . . . I ached for the lovemaking you sought on our wedding night."

"But you wouldn't say so, since you didn't want me to find out you weren't pure."

"You're right. But you'd fired my passions, Gil. Fired them from the first moment I approached you in Fredericksburg."

"Just take off my damned boots and be done with them."

She slid them off his feet, sent them flying. The fingers of one hand wound around five toes. The strangest thought assailed her: Would Hermann have such big feet? Heaven above, why think of their son at a moment like this?

She turned, aligning herself with her husband's muscular form. Despite his reluctance, he shivered with desire. Her lips pulled into a ghost of a smile; at least he wasn't totally insensitive to her "dubious charms."

If only she could make him forget the past . . .

She unfastened his Levis. "Let me love you." Unschooled in this new art of lovemaking, she took his shaft in her hand, then put pursed lips to the tip of it. The musky odor of his sex aroused her even further. Yet Gil tried to push her away.

Again she placed a kiss on him. "You don't like this? Have you not had other women do this to you?"

"For Christ's sake, you *are* innocent." He chuckled, and she breathed a sigh of relief. "That's not how you do it."

He taught her the art of pleasuring him, yet only a few moments passed before he groaned. "Stop. Stop now."

She raised her head. "You still don't like the way I—"

"Damn it, honey, don't you understand? I'm near my peak." He lifted her away from him, turning her to her back. "There's only one way to end what you started. And I pray God I don't do anything to hurt our child."

A hum of pleasure escaped as Lisette felt him enter her. He was so big, so hot, so *hers*. This coupling lacked the intensity of their previous ones; she knew his caution had to do with her condition. She gained as much satisfaction, though.

"Are you all right?" he asked huskily, and cupped her jaw with his hands.

"I am." Her fingers tightening around his hands, she looked up at him. His eyes were closed, his mouth set in a grim line. "But you're not."

"You got that right. I'm thinking how neither one of us has an ounce of pride. You don't know when to back off, and I don't have the strength to keep you at arm's length."

"Maybe that will keep us together until death parts us."

"Maybe you're right." He pulled her close. "I hope so."

Nestled against him, she said, "I'm sorry I let Matthias get too familiar. And I want you to realize—I'm not Betty. You think about her a lot, don't you?"

"No."

"Gil, I think you're not telling the truth."

He disengaged himself from Lisette's arms, stood, and picked up his clothes. A light mist began to fall. "Come on, honey. We'd better get back to camp. Get dressed. You'll catch your death if you don't get your clothes on."

It was chilly. But the cold part came from realizing that her husband spent too much time thinking about the past. Well, she could only do so much at once.

She pulled her dress over her head. "What will we do, now that we've reached Abilene?"

"Sell cows."

"I mean, what are you planning for me and Hermann?"

He put his arms around her, kissing her temple.

"I'm planning to make sure you don't name him Gilliegorm."

"Does that mean you'll stay with me for the birthing?"

"Absolutely."

Laughing in relief, she patted his taut buttock. "Oh, Gil, everything is going to be wonderful!"

Arm in arm, they returned to camp.

Attitude Powell called him away, though.

She climbed into the chuck wagon, spread the bedroll for the last time, and ran a brush through her hair. She counted twenty strokes before Gil thrust back the flap. Tension shot through the air, and her arm dropped as he climbed over the seat, anger in his motions.

"What's this about you paying off Preacher Wilson?"

"He was wanting to be with his family, and I didn't think you'd mind if I released him."

"He could've gone to his family and gotten his money later."

"I gave him his salary a day early. What's the wrong in that?"

Gil slapped his palm on the trunk holding his kilt and bagpipes. "Because I don't pay my men until *I* get money in my hands."

"Surely you don't expect your saddle-weary cowboys to ride broke into Abilene."

"They *were* going to get an advance on their pay. That's my policy. Now they'll have to wait upwards of a week for so much as a dollar."

She turned up a palm. "You'll have plenty of

money after you speak with the cattle broker."

"Money doesn't change hands that quickly, Lisette. As I said, it could be days before I sell the herd." Hunching his shoulders, he pointed a finger. "And you've just depleted our resources."

Her mind's eye painting a picture of the depleted strongbox, she shuddered and muttered, "Oh, Lord."

"Right. Oh, Lord. Since you like being the boss, do you want to be the one to 'fess up there's no money?"

"Maybe I could ask Eli for some of it back."

"Right. I want to be a fly on the wall when you tell him, 'Mister Preacher Man, could I be an Indian giver and take back some of my offering money? You see, my cowboys are wanting to spend it on booze and whores.' "

She grimaced, but couldn't helping chuckling when she considered saying those things to Preacher Wilson. "Oh, Gil, we *are* in a fix."

"Not we." He crossed his arms over his chest. *"You* are going to do the talking, boss lady."

"Can I—Should I wait until we're in town?" she asked in a small voice.

"Do as you please. You always do."

At first light the longhorns crossed the wide and shallow waters of Smoky Hill River, following the east bank of its tributary, Mud Creek. Shivering despite the warm morning, Lisette sat next to Pigweed and dreaded owning up to her mistake.

"We near 'bouts there, missus. Just a couple more hills."

Because she'd given his salary away, she couldn't look at the chuck wagon's driver. Her eyes turning to the right, she got a first glimpse at the tracks of the Kansas Pacific Railroad. Like twin silver ribbons decorating green velvet, the rail line meandered up and over the eastern horizon. Something swelled in her chest, side-tracked her great anxiety.

"Oh, Pigweed, would you look at that. Isn't it beautiful? I've never seen railroad tracks before. Have you?"

"No, missus, I ain't. Do be purty, though."

"It's the jewel at the top of our crown," she whispered in awe. "After all these months, to finally see it . . ."

"It be nice, missus. But me, I'd rather see the inside of the saloon. I got a powerful thirst, I have."

"Y-yes. Yes, of course."

The wagon rolled over the tracks, the motion strange and jostling. Her limbs vibrated from it as well as from dread; she faced forward and got an eyeful of Abilene's outskirts.

A herd of longhorns were being corralled into a holding pen near the rail line. Beyond there, people and animals—horses, chickens, dogs—lined the streets of log houses and several buildings. The tallest, a three-story clapboard structure, had words painted across the top floor: Drovers' Cottage Hotel.

While she always had looked forward to a soft bed, this time she wasn't so eager. Besides, until Gil could sell the herd, they might not have funds for any bed, be it soft or hard.

Her husband rode up. Doffing his hat and run-

401

ning his forearm across his brow, he said, "Leave the chuck wagon at the blacksmith shop — tell Pete Miller to put the charges on my account. The boys and I will meet you there — later."

The blacksmith's shop. The place where she must own up to giving Preacher Wilson . . . Once more she shivered. But collecting as much composure as possible, she squared her shoulders and sat straighter on the wooden seat. "All right. I'll be waiting."

"Pigweed, you come with me."

Hours passed. Late afternoon shadowed the street in front of Pete Miller's smithery. Perspiring in the summer heat, Lisette sat on a ladderback chair on the porch. From behind, she heard the forge's roar and the ping of metal striking an anvil. Each ping advanced her dread.

She wished Gil and the cowboys would hurry with penning the cattle so that she could get on with her admission.

Restless, she stood, walking up and down porch's creaking boards to observe the surroundings. Most of the activity centered at the stockyard. The street crowd had lessened, only a handful of people in view. There were, of course, quite a collection of horses tied to hitching posts fronting the town saloon, Ma Pinter's.

A skinny brown dog padded in front of her, his head lowered, his tail tucked. He lifted his nose, then wagged that tail at Lisette before going on his way. The mutt was the first canine she'd seen up close since Sadie Lou. Poor Sadie Lou. One casualty in a long list of them.

A stately woman exited the Drovers' Cottage, her step brisk. A cream-colored straw hat, fashioned in the bird's wing style and trimmed in blue velvet, sat at a jaunty angle atop her wealth of upswept silver hair. She marched down the street, toward the stockyard. A reticule clutched under an arm, she swung the other. Definitely, she was a woman with purpose.

Lisette found her infinitely interesting.

The woman neared her; Lisette guessed her to be about fifty.

Nodding politely and regally, she kept to her pace, saying, "Good day t' you."

"Good day."

The brisk steps slowed, picked up again, then came to a halt, the hem of her skirt swaying to display shoes of brown leather. Turning on the toe of one gaiter, the woman marched back and ground to a halt below the porch.

There was something familiar in the bright eyes and in the set of her mouth. Could it be possible that she—? Of course not. This woman was too young to be—

"Are you German, lass?" the stranger asked.

"I am."

"Thought so from your accent." A winged brow lifted as she studied Lisette's hand, especially the ring finger. "You wouldna be the wife o' Gilliegorm McLoughlin, would you?"

"I am. And you amaze me. I expected you to be older." Lisette smiled, knowing exactly who was

403

standing at the bottom of the porch. She went down the three steps to stand eye to eye with the woman. "This is a pleasant surprise. Gil and I had no idea you'd be in Abilene." She paused. "Grandmother."

"You'll make me feel old if you call me that." She opened her arms. "Come here, lass. I've been waiting for weeks t' see you. Give Maisie a hug."

Chapter Thirty-seven

Gil's grandmother proved to be wonderful and warm, though a character unlike any Lisette had ever met before. In no time at all, Maisie led Lisette across the street to the hotel "for a spot o' tea." As they settled in the comfortable but deserted dining room, hot tea and shortbread cookies were delivered to their table. The matriarch of the McLoughlin clan gingerly opened the drawstring of her reticule and eyed the waiter.

"How much do I owe you?"

"Two bits."

"Kind o' high." Slow as molasses, she pressed a quarter into the man's hand. "With prices like yours, lad, you won't be getting a gratuity, or my name wouldna be Margaret McLoughlin."

"I know your name, Mrs. McLoughlin. And your habits." He rolled his eyes. "You've been here three weeks."

Lisette bit her cheek to keep from laughing. Gil had mentioned his grandmother's thriftiness. Matter of fact, he'd told her that if Maisie were to die as a result of grabbing for a penny from beneath a stampeding herd, her death would be attributed to natural causes.

"Eat every bite o' those shortbreads," Maisie ordered. "Waste is a terrible thing."

"Yes, ma'am." Lisette bit into the delicious buttery cookie, her taste buds blooming like morning glories at first light. "Mmm, worth every penny of it."

Maisie stirred her tea. "Lisette, you wouldna be a woman t' waste money, would you?"

"I never had any to waste." Was it wasteful to give to the church? Never mind about that.

Lisette blushed as the older woman accessed her boldly.

"A bonny lass, you are."

"So are you," Lisette replied honestly. "Your grandson much resembles you."

" 'Twas always my thought." An eyelid dropped over an incredibly bright eye. "Had my share o' admirers as a lass."

"I imagine you did."

"Had no eyes for any o' them, except my Sandy. Now that was a lad, I must tell you. Strong as an ox, pretty as a Bobby Burns poem." She winked again. "He would o' kept me in your condition, if I'd let him. The McLoughlins are a lusty clan. But then, there's no need to be telling *you* that."

An eon ago, Lisette would have been uncomfortable with such frank talk. "I don't know about the others, but Gil meets your description," she bragged.

"Weel, don't make it too easy for the lad. Keep him guessing." She paused. "How is Gilliegorm?"

"Fine."

"I'm glad t' hear that. I've spent years o' sleepless nights worrying that he'd never find happiness again. You do know about that Betty, don't you?"

Lisette nodded. "He, uh, he still has a problem where she's concerned. I've begun to wonder if he still

406

loves her." Heavens! Why had she said that? "I—I . . . Never mind."

"Lass, he doesn't love that Betty. He never did. If he's still hurting, it's his pride, not his heart." Maisie clicked her tongue. "Damned shame it is, since she's straightened up and made a new start for herself. After she lost the bairn and Gilliegorm, too, she came t' her senses. Married a nice man, and they've got a bairn. Looks just like him."

"How nice for her." Lisette's fingers tightened on the teacup. "I'm still paying for her mistakes."

Maisie patted her hand. "I'm sorry, lass. Truly sorry."

"Oh, enough of this. Let's discuss something positive."

"All right. How old are you, lass?"

"Twenty-two. Twenty-three tomorrow."

"Is that so? We'll have to have cake and coffee in celebration. Mebbe a wee dram or two. My treat."

"That won't be necessary. Birthdays aren't special to me." She studied the barely wrinkled face. "How old are you?"

"Seventy."

"Unbelievable."

"You're flattering me, lass. Don't stop, though. I'm seventy, I can assure you. My poor departed Angus— Gilliegorm's faither—would o' been fifty-four." Maisie finished her cup, ran a finger across the cookie plate to gather the last crumb. "Are you wondering what I'm doing here, lass?"

"Actually, I am."

"The lad wrote me, said he'd married, would be bringing you up here, so I had t' get a look at you for myself."

"I look a mess."

A sincere and pleasant smile lifted the beautiful old face. "You look fine t' me, you do."

"You, Maisie McLoughlin, are doing the flattering now."

"Weel, I've got t' get on your good side. I'm not getting any younger, I haven't seen my grandson in years, and I'm wanting t' be around for the great-grandson."

"It's too bad your property is in Illinois, or you could be closer when little Hermann is growing up."

"Hermann?"

"Yes, that's the name I've chosen. After my father."

"What does Gilliegorm have t' say about that?"

"Nothing. Or he hasn't in a long time."

"You wouldna give consideration t' naming the wee lad after my Sandy, would you? Alexander."

"The *wee lad* doesn't feel like an Alexander. He feels like a Hermann."

"Could I . . .?" Maisie's face turned pink. "Would you mind if I had a feel o' the bairn?"

"Of course not." Lisette glanced around, confident of privacy. No diners, no sight of the waiter. She stood and walked to the other side of the table. "He's moving now."

Maisie put her palm atop the mound of Lisette's stomach. Hermann, disrespectful tyke, kicked his great-grandmother's hand.

Grinning broadly, she looked up, her eyes moist. "Oh, lass, he'll be a fine Hermann."

Lisette's throat closed. Maisie was mother personified—opinionated, concerned, open. "You remind me of my *Mutti*," she whispered. "Not in every way— she was more reserved—but I think I'm going to

408

love you, Maisie."

"I already love you."

And they belonged together. Several times Gil had said he wished his grandmother would settle in Fredericksburg, and Lisette agreed with those wishes.

If only she didn't have to go home to Illinois.

"Maisie, would it be asking too much . . . Do you think you'll ever make it down to Texas?"

"Weel, yes, if you're certain o' the invitation."

"I'm certain."

"Good." Gray eyes twinkled. "You see, I've sold the apple farm, and I intend t' make your town my home. Don't you be worrying, I won't live at the ranch. I'll buy my own cottage."

"You will not. You'll live with us. Little, um *wee* Hermann will need you."

"Waiter! Bring champagne!" When he didn't appear immediately, Maisie grumbled something about not being able to find good service. "He must be English."

"We'll have champagne later, after Gil—Gil! Goodness, I forgot. I'm supposed to meet him at the blacksmith shop."

Maisie scoffed. "Abilene is a wee town. He'll find you. Is the lad at the holding pen?"

"He is."

"I thought so," Maisie commented on a nod of head. "I was on my way there when I found you."

"Maisie, I must leave. I've some apologizing to do. I gave the church the advance money Gil intended for his cowboys. And I've got a lot of explaining—"

"The kirk always has its hand out. Be careful of empty-handed ministers."

This was no time to discuss church stewardship.

409

"Gil will be furious if I'm not where I'm supposed to be."

She was supposed to be here. She wasn't. Nine thirsty, penniless cowpokes behind him, Gil hurried into the blacksmith shop. "Pete, have you seen my wife?"

"Not since I started repairing this wagon wheel."

Damn.

Gil did an about-face. On the porch, he met the eager stares of his men. While he had made Lisette believe she'd have to do the talking, he had figured simply to shock her into thinking before acting. Whatever his motives and intentions, he had expected her to be here.

"We've got problems," he said, his words slow. "I can't pay you until after I've signed a deal with McCoy and Brothers."

"We didn't figure on all of it, just drinking and womaning money," Attitude said.

"I can't make good on my promise."

Mouths dropped, then the men began to shout.

Oscar didn't shout, but he frowned and said, "It don't be fair, expectin' us to do wit'out."

"That's the way things turned out. But, I assure you, I'll be talking with Joseph McCoy as soon as I leave here. I'll have your money as soon as possible."

"How soon is possible?" Attitude asked.

Never had Gil McLoughlin had to grovel over money before. *I could shake her.* "As soon as I can get it."

One man climbed the three steps. Deep Eddy stuck his hands in his empty pockets before turning to the others. "Cool down. This isn't McLoughlin's fault.

410

You see, Lisette—"

"Ed!" Gil wouldn't have the men turning against their adored Lisette.

"Wait!"

The assemblage turned.

A reticule in her hand, Lisette waddled across the street. "Here's the money."

Where had she gotten it? Knowing Lisette, there was no telling. But she made the men happy, turning over a fair share to each, so Gil wouldn't pitch a fit. Soon, though, she *would* explain herself.

Like longhorns on stampede, the cowboys rushed the saloon.

She beamed. "I have a surprise for you."

"I'll just bet you do." His upper lip twitched. "Where did you get that money?"

"I borrowed it."

"Who from? And what did you have to promise in return?"

"Gil McLoughlin, you are really a cynical person. You should work on your attitude. Children learn from their parents, after all, and I don't want little Hermann forming bad habits."

Shaking his head, he groaned, "God help me."

"God has your money. I'll tell you who did help us, though. In a few minutes." She looped her arm with his. "Come on. We're going to the hotel. Your surprise awaits."

Dragging him along, she swept by the desk clerk and entered the dining room. There was no one in here, except for an elderly woman, her back to the door. Wait. That wasn't just any elderly woman.

"Maisie!"

" 'Bout time you showed up." She scooted the chair

411

from the table, got to her feet, and spun around. Mirth in her features, she said, "Lad, you owe me five hundred dollars."

"*You* loaned my wife money?"

"I dinna stutter."

He threw back his head, opened his arms, and laughed. "C'm'ere and give me a hug," he said in the accents of his homeland. She did, and he held her closely, kissing the crown of her silver head. "How much interest will ye be charging?"

"Hundred percent."

"Oh, Maisie, me love, you never change."

"Aye, I do not. And that's a hundred percent per day."

"Whew." He reared back, loving the teasing. "Then I'd better get to McCoy and Brothers, post-haste."

"Good. Afterward, you can buy dinner."

"Fine. But I've got business to take care of first."

Bussing his grandmother, then lingering a bit over a kiss with Lisette, he left. He called on Joseph McCoy. It took some cajoling, but the cattle broker offered for all two thousand nine hundred longhorns. A bank draft rested in Gil's breast pocket. The amount came to almost six figures. It would have been more, if not for the delays and losing a hundred head.

Well, he couldn't complain.

Gil walked to the stockyard to take a last look at the herd.

Tecumseh Billy was sulking.

"Just a few more days, old boy," Gil called out from the other side of the fence, "and you'll be back on the trail."

The lead steer backed away, unimpressed.

412

Gil spied Deep Eddy Roland walking toward him.

"Thought you'd be at Ma Pinter's Saloon," he said to the New Englander.

"A little of that place goes a long way."

"You got something on your mind, Ed?"

"I heard a rumor Matt Gruene is quitting on the outfit."

That would be fine with Gil.

"If Matt quits," Deep Eddy said, "I want his job."

"It's yours, *if* it becomes available." Gil bent an eye. "If you're up on gossip, do you know if the other men are threatening to quit?"

"They aren't. They'll all ride for your brand."

"That's good, since I'll need all the help I can get for herding the saddle horses and T-Bill back to Texas. And Big Red. He's going back, too. When I return to Texas, it'll be with a wife and a newborn. Maybe with my grandmother, too. I won't be needing the sorrel."

"Rest assured, I'll look out for him."

"I know you will, Ed. I know you will."

Whether or not Matthias bailed out, Deep Eddy was a man to count on.

That evening, dinner was champagne, fine food, and family togetherness. Gil enjoyed watching Maisie and Lisette act as if they had been kin forever. And they all celebrated success.

He glanced at Lisette. *We're rich, honey. We're rich.*

That was not the sort of thing he'd say in front of Maisie — or she'd hold him to the interest rate. By now the dining room had cleared out, the only occupant besides the McLoughlins was the waiter, who dozed on the straight-backed chair in the far corner.

Maisie finished off a slice of cherry pie. "Would it

be time t' be thinking about plans for our trip to Texas?"

"I've got it all figured out." Gil pulled a cigar from his pocket. "Looks like we'll be here in Abilene for several months. I've decided the best course for us is . . ." He smiled at his wife. "Soon as Hermann is big enough, we're going to take a train to Chicago. My wife and I have honeymoon plans."

"I'll take care of the wee one. You two can enjoy yourselves that way."

"Maisie, you are a jewel," Lisette said.

"Now listen closely, ladies. We're going to take a paddlewheeler down the Mississippi, then catch a ship for Corpus Christi. Which means we'll have the least amount of time riding in wagons. Sound agreeable, honey?"

"More than agreeable." Lisette wiggled on her chair. "If I never sit on another spring seat again, it'll be too soon. By sea is the only way to travel."

"Nay, lass. The only way t' travel is in your man's arms. All the way upstairs." She gave her grandson an arch look. "Better keep those muscles built up."

Figuring all this frank talk would embarrass his wife, Gil told Maisie to hush. Lisette, though, didn't appear uncomfortable with the conversation; in fact, she was taking an overlong gander at his arms.

"Would you like a drink, honey?"

"No thanks. Better not." She yawned and patted her mouth with her fingers. "I think I'll retire to our room."

"I'll have another, lad."

He pushed back his chair. "Help yourself. I'm *carrying* my wife upstairs."

"You will not," Lisette protested. "You stay right

414

here and visit with Maisie. I made over a thousand miles in a chuck wagon. I can make it to the third floor under my own steam."

There was no arguing with her, but he did walk her to the stairs and take a kiss before returning to the dining room. Maisie had poured herself a couple of fingers of brandy.

He settled opposite to her again. Rocking the chair back on two of its legs, he said, "I'm pleased you and Lisette are tight as ticks."

"You couldna done better."

"Glad to hear that, since you'll be living with us."

"Got another one of those cigars, lad?"

"Maisie," he drawled. "I thought you gave them up."

"Don't you be chiding me, sitting there with that stogie stuck in your mouth, looking like the cat that ate the canary. Gimme a smoke, lad."

He reached into his pocket and did as ordered.

Maisie squinted past a trailing ribbon of gray. "Your letter was dated seven months ago, in February."

"That's true."

"Frae the looks o' your wife, you dinna give the right story. You said she was a reluctant bride. That you'd be having t' coax her into your bed."

"It took a lot of coaxing."

"You're not too old t' take a switch t' your ankles for lying. I'd say you jumped the gun on the wedding ceremony."

There was no accusation in his grandmother's words, but Gil took umbrage; they confirmed suspicions he'd had for weeks. Lisette was just too big to be two months from term. Shock waves jolting through him, he defended his wife. "There was no gun-jump-

415

ing. The child is due in November."

Maisie reached across the table and took his hand. "Frae where I sit, I don't mind when the wedding took place. Or the month the wee one starts squalling. You need someone like Lisette t' heal your pain . . . if you'll let her."

The pain of Betty was nothing compared to this blow.

"Did I say something wrong, lad?" Maisie brought her fingers to her lips. "I dinna mean to. Gilliegorm?"

He drained his snifter. "Let's call it a night."

"A wee bit early, isn't it?"

It was about seven months too late—for the truth.

Chapter Thirty-eight

Who the hell was Hermann's father?

Determined to find out, Gil took the hotel stairs two at a time, rushed down the corridor, and jammed the key in the lock. The door reverberated on its hinges as he pushed it open.

A single lamp provided low light. In her sleep, moaning, Lisette turned from side to side. Gil crossed the rug, stopped at the edge of the bed. She wore nothing; he didn't figure it a repeat of last night's invitation.

She was nude out of necessity, didn't have any clothes; how could she dress in night gear? A man ought to keep his wife properly attired. There had been a time when Gil had wanted to bedeck her in the best. Furthermore, he'd promised himself to buy her baubles and beads.

What was the matter with him?

Let her lover drape her in finery and frippery.

Who was the man?

His hands moved to shake her awake, but the nearby lamp illuminated the shadows under her eyes. No matter whose child she carried, she was his wife. And his conscience wouldn't let him disturb her. She needed rest.

He retreated to a small settee, sat down, and pushed

off his boots. Within a couple of minutes, he wore nothing but britches. Now what was he going to do?

He didn't particularly want to sleep with her. He couldn't rent an extra room, since the hotel was filled, owing to the three Texas outfits in town. And if he left, there was sure to be talk. Gossip didn't bother him, but he wouldn't put a Kansas mark on the McLoughlin name, not with his grandmother in town. There had been enough of that over Betty.

Be honest. You don't want to shame Lisette, either. Who gave a hell — ? *You do.* He refused to heed his conscience . . . or was it his heart?

He got in bed, turned away from Lisette. Pulling the sheet up, Gil tried to sleep. He couldn't. Minutes that seemed like hours passed. He felt the mattress move, heard her as she rolled over. She sighed and put an arm around him; her stomach pressed against his back. He tried to deflect her touch, but something thumped his spine. Gil clenched his teeth against the feel of her bulk.

Thump, thump, thump.

Reaching to the rear, he pressed his palm against her flesh, meaning to push her away. Her stomach felt lumpy. What was that? A village idiot's question, he supposed, but he'd never put an examining hand to a pregnant woman's stomach before.

He jiggled the lump. It moved with him. That was an arm, maybe a leg. Wonder upon wonder, that was a real babe in there. Not a concept. Not a monster. Not solely a less-than-appealing Teutonic name. And Hermann was a rowdy little tyke.

No wonder Lisette had circles under her eyes, what with lugging her son around all the day and night long. Last night . . . Old Son had invaded Hermann's realm.

Last night.

Gil swallowed, recalling the pleasure he had taken and the realm he had invaded. Her son tumbled.

"Behave," she mumbled in her sleep.

Hermann answered with more thumps.

A short snort of laughter escaped Gil's nose. *If you were here already, lad, I'd box your ears for not giving your mother her proper rest.*

He wished he could rejoice in the new life. How wonderful it would be, someday holding Hermann in his arms and making the boy understand right from wrong. Gil yearned to see something in that small face: a likeness to the McLoughlin clan, a resemblance mingled with the Germanic race.

There was no accounting for sense.

Gil eased onto his back, his arm falling off the side of the bed. Lisette edged closer. If he left his arm like this, it would be numb in no time.

"You and I need to talk, Hermann." Placing his palm on Lisette's stomach, he whispered, "Go to sleep."

The motions stopped. Yet Gil didn't remove his hand. He closed his scratching and burning eyes, but tears escaped anyway. He wasn't a man to cry. He couldn't recall ever crying, not since he left childhood.

Tonight he cried.

A rooster crowed, light streamed into the room, yet Lisette didn't leave the bed. Who in their right mind could leave this heaven of soft mattress, softer pillows, and real sheets?

Besides, she had neither the reason nor the energy to go downstairs for breakfast. Her hand reached for her husband and came up empty. Swallowing her disappointment, she clutched his pillow to her. It smelled of bay rum and Gil.

Then Hermann awakened, shoved her bladder. "Naughty boy, won't you leave me any peace?"

He would not. By the time Lisette used the chamberpot and had freshened herself with the water from a pitcher, she heard a knock on the door. It was Maisie.

"I've brought you something." She produced a trio of boxes. "Maternity dresses and all the gear t' wear with them."

Three Mother Hubbards, all of gingham and roomy enough for Hermann, though none would win a contest for appeal. A pair of kid slippers—oh, they were lovely. A tent of a chemise, very practical. At the bottom of the third box, pantaloons.

Lisette blushed upon holding up a pair. "I haven't worn these since I left Fredericksburg."

Maisie plucked them from her fingers. "Then you won't start. My grandson will be expecting you to stay as you've been, and I won't be starting any family feuds."

Lisette laughed. "Oh, Maisie, you are a card."

"My Sandy used t' say I was a whole deck."

"I think Sandy was a very observant man." Lisette put an arm around Maisie's shoulders. "Thank you for shopping. How much do I owe you?"

"Owe me? Lass, this is your big day. Happy birthday!"

"Thank you for remembering. And for your generosity."

"Don't you be telling a soul! I won't have it bandied aboout that I am fast with my coin." Maisie tapped a finger against her face. "Now give me a proper thank you."

"Gladly." She kissed that dear cheek.

"Get into one of those dresses, m'lass. The train will be here in a couple o' hours, and you don't want t' miss it."

420

"You are right there. I've never seen a train."

Maisie walked to the door, kept her hand on the knob. "I will meet you downstairs. I told the cook t' hold some food."

"Is Gil in the dining room?"

"At this hour? Good gracious, no. He's been over at the bank since it opened for business." She winked. "He's gotta get me my money, you know."

"Of course," Lisette came back with a wink of her own.

Thirty minutes later, she and Maisie were in the sunlight. The two women strolled down the street to stop at the Kansas Pacific depot, a small building.

"Train gonna be late?" asked Maisie.

The attendant, a nonchalant fellow of middle years wearing a visor and a white shirt with yellow galluses above tweed trousers, stood behind the window and made a notation on a piece of paper. "Train's on time." Giving a cursory look at the two women, he craned his neck and said, "Next?"

A skinny matron elbowed Lisette out of the way. "One ticket to Chicago."

Following Maisie to a bench that hugged the depot's outer wall, Lisette sat down. "There was a time when I thought I'd be buying a ticket to Chicago. Gil changed all that."

Maisie remained quiet. Too quiet. At last, she said, "There's something I need t' tell you. Last night I popped off to Gilliegorm, and I want t' apologize for it. I shouldna hinted the two o' you were intimate 'fore marriage."

"We weren't, well, you know, until after the wedding."

Maisie looked over at her stomach, saying, "Aye. If that's what you're wanting people t' think. But you

421

needna be shy around me, lass. I can tell you, I've a se-cret or two in my past. Sandy and I, we got a head start on the Church o' Scotland. Never regretted those times in the heather."

"Maisie, Gil and I did *not* know each other in the Bib-lical sense until *after* we were wed."

With lips pursed, the woman's wise eye assessed her. "Then I'd say you carry two instead o' one."

"Twins?" Lisette squeaked. "Surely not."

"Any o' them in your family?"

"No."

"None in ours, either. But there's always a first time." Maisie patted Lisette's stomach. "Twins."

God in heaven, **what** would they do with twins, should Maisie's **prediction** become fact?

A whistle, faint in the distance, came from the east and drew Lisette's attention away. She was on her feet in a split second, was saying in wonder, "Oh, Maisie, it's the train."

"Be a while 'fore it arrives."

"Good, then I'll find Gil. I want him with me when I see a train for the very first time. And you, too, of course."

"You go find your **husband**, and I'll keep the bench warm."

He was nowhere to be found. Dejected, she returned to the depot. "I couldn't find him," she said to Maisie.

"He'll be along. Just sit tight."

"I prefer to stand."

By now she could see the train engine, a plume of black smoke puffing into the air, leaving a trail across the bright sky. More than a score of slatted boxcars followed behind the engine, as did a couple of passenger cars.

People collected on the platform, each craning to get a

closer look at the pride of the Kansas Pacific. Seeing the train had lost its significance for Lisette. Gil wasn't with her.

With nothing else to do, she turned her attention to the tracks again. The engineer leaned out of his window, waved to the appreciative crowd, and pulled the whistle in quick succession. The cow catcher was the first to reach the station, nothing on its grids. Looking up at the engine, Lisette couldn't help but be awed.

"Oh, Maisie, it's so big. And powerful."

Someone walked up beside her. "And as soon as it loads up my cows, it'll be turning back for Chicago."

"Oh, Gil, I'm so glad you're here! Isn't it wonderful?"

"Lisette," he said, taking her hand and emitting a whiskied breath, "Let's go back to the hotel."

Something was wrong — very wrong.

"All right," she whispered in reply.

Husband and wife returned to the hotel.

In their room, Lisette asked, "What's the matter?"

"Plenty."

She dropped down on the settee and studied the rug, figuring he had plenty to say. He placed an envelope on the seat beside her.

"Your pay," he announced.

She eyed the fat white envelope. "I don't expect *pay*."

"That's what you're getting. And I'm going to get the truth about you."

She sighed in exasperation. "Now what?"

His fingers dug into his palms. "Sometimes I wonder if you're naive, stupid, or just plain conniving."

Shocked and appalled that he thought so little of her, she asked and pulled out each syllable, "What are you talking about?"

"That child in your belly." He took a backward

423

step. "It couldn't be of my making."

She flinched, horrified that the man she trusted with all her heart and soul could even think, much less speak, such a horrible charge. She surged to stand, pushing his chest and sending him another step backward. "That is a lie!"

"Is it?" His eyes cold as ice, his mouth slashed with rancor, he looked her up and down. "I don't think so."

"How can you stand there—reeking of liquor!—and denounce your child?" She rushed across the room to close her arms protectively around the child and to keep her back to Gil's cruel, cruel eyes. "Damn it, when are you going to get over the hurt of Betty?"

"The day Fate proves me wrong about you. Which I doubt will happen."

Lisette whirled around. "Time will prove you wrong. You wait and see."

"Brave words. But then, you've had to be tough." He walked to the window, placing his hand on the top casement and leaning into it. "I've done a lot of thinking, and I've come up with the truth. You showed up on the trail and said you were in desperate straits. You wasted no time in huddling with Matt, if you'll remember. Tried to pawn it off as friendship, but the wool is off my eyes. Another thing: your brother isn't such a bad fellow, and you couldn't have been unhappy enough to the point of striking out, unless you were in desperate straits. Such as knowing you wouldn't have a name for your baby."

Her teeth chattered as she said, "For a smart man, you haven't a brain."

"You'd like to think so. But I've got enough gray matter to figure out you were sick too soon, Lisette. And you got big too soon."

She tried to make sense of insanity. She could mention

424

the twins theory, but somehow she didn't figure it would carry too much weight. "You've had too much to drink."

"Not nearly enough, sweetheart. Not nearly enough. There isn't enough booze in Kansas to drown my troubles." Pushing away from the window, he marched over to the dresser, poured a large quantity from the bottle atop it. "Who's the papa, Lisette? Otto Kapp? Perhaps the squaw man Matt Gruene? Maybe you don't even know."

The blood drained from Lisette's face, and she ached to slap him, but tried one more time for reason. "And you believe there's no chance this child is yours?"

"There's a chance all right, but I wouldn't put money on it." He drained the whisky-filled glass. "If you give birth short of term, I'm divorcing you."

Divorce. Once before he had threatened it. Once before he had done it. Words came back to her, words hurled at her in a Texas meadow. "I'm capable of doing it again." Her heart went as bleak as his eyes. This was the man she'd thought noble and good? She saw him in a whole new light.

Always, she'd excused his rotten behavior. No more.

"I think you'd better leave," she managed to say.

"When I'm damned good and ready. After you've told the truth."

"I said—leave!"

"I don't follow your orders."

"Well, then, follow this!"

She reached to the rear and grasped a hard object. All her hurt giving strength to her motions, she pitched the lamp at Gil. As it connected with his shoulder, she felt a strange sensation in her stomach. Not a pain, just a feeling that everything had changed.

She laughed at her ludicrous thought. Of course

everything had changed. Nothing would ever be right again.

Liquid gushed down her legs, pooled at her feet. *Gott in Himmel,* she had embarrassed herself by urinating. Was there no end to today's humiliations? Clutching her knees together, she saw her husband raking a hand across his shoulder. Crimson blotched it as well as the sleeve of his shirt.

He glanced down at the floor and muttered a base oath before advancing on her. "Lisette, the birthing has started."

"Stay where you are."

She withdrew a step, the back of one knee connecting with the bed; she fell and landed hard on the mattress.

A voice from the corridor shouted, "What's going on here?"

At the same moment, pain — as brutal as that of being kicked by a mule as a child — clamped like the fist of Satan in her stomach. The devil hadn't called her; it was . . . *"Mein Gott, das Baby."*

The desk clerk barged through the door. "What is going on here?" he repeated.

"Looks like we need a doctor."

"You do look pretty messed up, Mister McLoughlin."

"Not for me, damn it, for my wife. She's in labor."

"I'll get Doc Koch." Rushing away, the clerk closed the door in the dust of his promise.

Depleted, Lisette turned her face to the damnable pillow that held the scent of her husband. Her tears wetting the linen as the fluid of birth had stained the carpet, she cried, "It's too early for Hermann."

She heard Gil moving toward the bed. "I'd better get Maisie."

Thrusting the pillow aside, she looked up at his ashen

426

face. "Tell me, Gil, will you fetch her before or after you file for your precious divorce?"

"One or the other."

She tossed the pillow to the floor. "If you do any-thing—*anything*—to deprive our lawfully conceived child of his father, I'll make your life a living hell."

"Calm down, Lisette. Calm down."

She barely heard him; agony—was it physical or from the heart?—clutched her again. Whatever it was, it grabbed from her womb to the top of her head and seared to the ends of her toes. Her bodily torment re-ceded, but the one in her heart did not.

She and the baby didn't need him.

"Forget I threatened you." Her voice seemed as if it were outside her body. "I want nothing of you."

"Lisette, calm down. You need your strength for Her-mann."

"Go to hell, Gil McLoughlin." She put her arm over her child. *Her* child. "If you want a divorce, fine. If you don't file, I will. You no longer mean anything to me."

He picked up the pillow and placed it beside her. "I'll get Maisie."

He left. The door's closing resounded in Lisette's ears. She wept. Life was not hearts and roses. Death would be preferable to this hell called earth.

I'm sorry, Hermann I have no more strength. For his father, she had no regrets. About anything.

Chapter Thirty-nine

With the local physician in charge, Maisie McLoughlin, sat praying at her granddaughter-in-law's bedside. The light from the window faded; she lit the lamp and saw shadows on the chalky features of the unfortunate Prussian girl. Maisie ran a finger under her tired eyes and choked back tears.

"It doesn't look good," Wilhelm Koch, doctor of medicine, announced on a blown-out breath. "This should've been easy for her, what with her height and wide hips. The child is breech."

A noise from the bed drew Maisie's attention. The dear lass's eyes rolled, the whites showing as she reached unsuccessfully for the bed post. A weak cry issued. When the convulsion passed, she dropped her hand.

The physician placed his stethoscope on the bedside table. "Do you know if she's Bavarian? They're Catholics, you understand," he whispered. "Where is her husband? He should know if her religion demands a priest."

Maisie ground her teeth. "I doona know where the bloody fool is. If I did, I'd crown him for not being here. And I will, when he shows his face."

"Search for him. I have done all I can. We need God at

this point. God, and the husband of this woman."

"I'm not a great believer in the Almighty, Doctor Koch. And right now, I doona have much faith in my grandson, but I will find one or the other."

On a barstool in Ma Pinter's Saloon, Gil McLoughlin avoided a tall glass of Scotch. Smoke, whores, and cowboys filled the tavern. A piano player pounded the ivories. Someone approached Gil: Matt Gruene. Bile rose in his throat.

"Give me a beer," Matthias ordered the barkeep, then said to Gil, "You look like hell."

Looks were not deceiving; Gil was in hell.

Matthias lifted his beer, took a slow sip, and lowered the glass. "I won't be leaving with T-Bill and the remuda."

"That's what I heard."

"Why aren't you with Lise?" Matthias asked.

"You tell me."

"I'm not a mind-reader. What are you getting at?"

Every muscle in his body hankering for a fight, Gil abandoned the bar stool. Glaring, he asked with a grate, "How many months have you been sleeping with my wife?"

Brown eyes hardened. The glass got set aside. "If Lise hadn't told me about the trouble you'd had with your former wife, I'd beat the living hell out of you, McLoughlin, for a remark like that. Lise—"

"Give it a try." He raised his fists. "Come on."

"Sit down, McLoughlin."

"Like hell I will."

With all the fury of damaged pride, he charged Matthias. But the big German was lightning quick, and Gil was slowed by his injured shoulder. Matthias hauled back and struck his jaw. Pain exploded. Another punch caught his stomach, drawing a groan. He tumbled, but righted himself. Thrusting his left elbow into Matthias's gut, he plowed a puny right hook into his opponent's face.

"Out," the barkeep shouted. "No fighting in Ma Pinter's."

Two customers grabbed Gil from behind. Another couple of them seized Matthias. The brawlers were tossed outside, the former strawboss into the dirt street, Gil into a horse trough.

Spitting water, he tried to heave himself to his feet. A heavy board whapped against his right arm, sending him sprawling onto the saloon's porch, barely missing the window.

Matthias tossed the board aside and stood above him. "Are you ready to listen to reason?"

"Y-yeah."

Gil swiped mud from his face and followed after his ex-strawboss. They crossed the street to the depot, and sat down on opposite ends of the bench.

Matthias spoke. "This morning I had a few minutes with Lise. She told me you're divorcing her. And I'm glad to hear it. You see, once she's free, I'm going to marry her."

Jealously, Gil said, "A little soon after Cactus Blossom, isn't it? Or was she just a diversion while you couldn't get to Lisette? Tell me, Gruene, are you the baby's father?"

"Not yet."

"What the hell does that mean?"

"Being a child's blood father means nothing. It's the rearing that makes a father. I will do that for Lise's child."

Gil took a long look at Matthias. "You're serious."

"Never more so in my life. I appreciate, love, and respect her, and—"

"So do I."

"No, you don't. You may love her, but you don't appreciate or respect her." Matthias leaned back against the bench. "And you'll never be able to . . . unless you quit fighting yourself over that first wife of yours." Matthias pointed to the right. "There's another horse trough. Clean yourself up, Gil McLoughlin. Inside and out."

Matthias left the bench, disappeared into the night, and Gil studied the ground. Thoughts tumbled over and over in his brain, but he sorted them. And tried to clean his soul.

Now that he thought about it, he realized that he should have never suspected Matthias of cavorting with Lisette. The German loved her all right, but his feelings were honorable. And Gil got the impression that he had been tricked over that marriage business . . . tricked to open his eyes.

They were open.

Now what should he do? What was it Matthias had advised? To quit fighting himself over Betty? How could he do that? By washing away the past, forgetting it ever existed. Impossible. *Learn from the past.* That would work, provided he concentrated on the positive.

His time with Betty had been hell, but they had had a few good moments. There, that felt better. He hoped she was doing all right, had found peace. This felt even better still.

He hoped he could give Lisette peace. With all his heart, he loved her, and that made the difference between her and Betty. It was, and always would be, Lisette in his heart.

Yes, she could have been in the family way when desperation had driven her to him, but she had proved to be a good and dear wife, supportive and loving. And Matthias had been right: it was the day-to-day that made a father.

Gil recalled two nights before, when he'd had a chat with young Hermann about disturbing his mother. The lad hadn't heeded Lisette's pleas, but he'd behaved when Gil had put in his two cents. A child needed a father.

"I'll be that for Hermann."

If Lisette would give him another chance.

He walked to the horse trough. Almost there, he caught sight of his grandmother.

"How is my wife?" he asked worriedly.

"Gilliegorm, it's . . . I'm sorry." Maisie dabbed her eye with a handkerchief. "She's not going to make it."

"Noooo!"

A light from the end of a tunnel. It was hazy here, calm and peaceful. She floated through the channel. A specter appeared, clothed in a gossamer gown. A gentle breeze soughed, ruffling the hem of that fabric. *"Mutti."*

"Daughter, if you give up, the child will die with you."

We have no one; it would be best if he is with us.

"You have Maisie McLoughlin. You have Matthias Gruene—he could make a good father to your child."

It was Gil I wanted.

"If you still want him, fight for him."

I tried.

"Don't give up, my little one."

I am not little, Mother.

"You are not. You could expel a child with no problem."

Another form floated forward. Olga. Olga, as beautiful as she had been before the Comanches had taken her. Lisette tried to reach for her sister, her hand drawing empty air. *I've missed you, sister.*

432

"You will have eternity to miss your husband," the young girl chided. "The Scotsman's resting place won't be with us."

He's going to hell?

"Yes. Unless he heals the chasm of his heart, which I'm thinking he has ideas to." Olga sighed. "Lise, you must save your child."

Mother drifted closer. "Listen to your sister, Lisette."

But I have no more strength.

"Yes, you do. Draw in your breath — and push!"

"It's a girl!"

Smiling despite his fears, Gil lifted his head from the bedside. "A girl. I always hoped so."

Doctor Koch handed the squirming mass to Maisie, then bent to cut the cord. "Luck's given your wife a second chance. Pray it holds."

"I've been praying."

"You need to leave, Mister McLoughlin." The doctor shooed him away. "You're in the way."

"I'll go. But first," Gil leaned over his wife, "if you'll give me a chance to prove my love, you'll never regret it. I don't care who gave you our daughter — she's mine. And I'll raise her as such."

He felt the tiniest movement against his hand. "Don't make promises you can't keep," his wife whispered weakly.

"Lisette, my darlin', I will never again let you down."

"Get out, man!"

Turning to the doctor, he asked, "May I hold my daughter first?"

"Later."

He kissed his wife's forehead. "I'll be downstairs."

She convulsed.

"What is it going to take to get rid of you, man? We've got a problem. When you get to the lobby, send up the manager's wife, Mrs. Hocker."

It took all Gil's strength to leave that third-floor room. No . . . to leave his wife. He trudged down the corridor and descended the staircase. What was the problem that had turned the doctor's face ashen?

The desk clerk brought a cup of coffee; Gil didn't drink a drop. The hotel manager's wife answered Doctor Koch's summons, then returned to fetch supplies. Three times she made the trip.

Gil collared her on the fourth. "How is my wife? How is my daughter?"

"Haven't the slightest idea," Mrs. Hocker replied. "Your grandmother cracks only the door when I go up there."

A grandfather clock by the front desk ticked away the minutes, one turning into sixty of them. One hour turned into three, then four. They seemed like forty. Gil could stand it now longer. Damn it, Lisette had delivered the baby. What was the delay? Why wasn't Maisie giving him reports?

"Why can't I hear my daughter crying?"

"You're out of hearing range," replied the yawning desk clerk.

A few moments later, Dr. Koch descended the staircase, black bag in hand. "Your wife is recovering."

Gil pushed the air out of his lungs. "Thank God."

"I'd say He had something to do with it. Your wife says it was angels, though."

"May I see her?"

"Not now." With one of those stern physician scowls, Koch said, "She had a mighty rough time. She's going to

434

need a good deal of rest to get over this."

"My daughter? Is she all right?"

"Doc, you want a cup of coffee?" the desk clerk asked.

"Yes, Roscoe, that sounds good. Pretty it up with some of that brandy you've got stashed in the desk."

"Damn it, you can think about drinking after you've answered me. How is my daughter?"

"Couldn't be better, all things considered. Ah, thank you, Roscoe." The physician accepted the steaming cup and took a large swallow. Once again giving attention to the new father, he continued his discourse. "Awfully small, and they'll need extra attention for a while, but I think they'll make it."

"What's this 'they?' " Gil asked skeptically.

"They've got your midnight-black hair." Wilhelm Koch waved a finger at Gil's head. "Black Celts, just like you and your grandmother, if I'm any judge of lineage, which I am. They were born a couple months too early, but their lungs are pretty strong. I've got hot water bottles around them."

Gil stared up at the ceiling, wishing he could see into the third floor room, to the rear of this hotel, where his family had struggled so. "What's this 'they?' " he repeated.

"Didn't I tell you? Mister McLoughlin, you're the father of triplet girls."

Triplets? By the Holyrood. *Three* of them. Gil felt the floor climbing up to meet him. Triplets! For the first time in his life, Gil McLoughlin fainted.

Chapter Forty

"I've been thinking of names . . ."

Bending over their common crib in the bedroom of the house Maisie had rented, Lisette gazed at heaven's precious gifts. She turned her attention to the man who stood on the far side of the bassinet. Preacher Eli Wilson, wearing a black suit and a broad smile, murmured oohs and aahs at the infants.

"Good idea," he said, "putting them in the same crib. It gives warmth as well as comfort."

"I think so."

Smiling with motherly pride, Lisette looked at her daughters. As yet unnamed, they were sleeping — for once, at the same time. How wonderful it was simply to gaze at them. My, they were beautiful. All perfectly formed, all raven-haired and wing-browed, all decidedly Celtic. Like their father.

Their father, who had denied them. Their father, who stood below the bedroom window each night and played his damned bagpipes — and disturbed his daughters' sleep.

The preacher clicked his tongue. "They're growing by leaps and bounds. I can almost see them gaining weight."

At six weeks of age, they were big enough to travel.

"They're the spitting image of their pa," Eli said.

"Yes." Lisette fingered a wisp of black hair. "They look so much alike, I think they should have different-sounding names. In keeping with their personalities."

Eli frowned. "Shouldn't you ask Mister McLoughlin's opinion? Why won't you speak with him? I know he comes by here several times a day."

"Gil did his talking in the Drovers' Cottage." At one point, hurt would have tightened her chest. There was nothing for him in her heart but the emptiness of broken dreams. She tightened the belt of her heavy wrapper. "Anything more would add insult to injury."

Lisette settled in a nearby overstuffed chair and looked up at Eli. On the afternoon she'd awakened from that third birth, she'd asked for him. For not the first time, she wondered if she'd made a mistake, taking the man of God into her confidences. Weren't they enough, Maisie's pleas? Both had urged her to hear what Gil had to say.

Even Matthias, before he'd left for California, had mentioned that Gil might be worthy of a second chance.

Phooey.

"Your husband comes to see me." Eli retreated from the crib, and picked up a straight chair to set it beside Lisette. "A more repentant man, I've never counseled. It wouldn't take but a minute or two to ease his mind."

"His peace of mind isn't my concern." Her fingers curled over the top of the wicker bassinet. "And I must save my strength for my daughters. They are my life now. We leave tomorrow for Chicago. I'm going to open a millinery shop."

"The Lord be with you." Eli rubbed his forehead.

437

"Will the old Mrs. McLoughlin go along?"

At that moment Maisie opened the bedroom door that had been left cracked. "I am not *old!* But aye, I *will* be living in Chicago with my girls. All four o' them. Never had a daughter, never had a granddaughter. Lucky I am, though 'twould be nice t' see my grandson with a settled look on his mug."

Standing between Maisie and Gil was Lisette's only regret; she ducked her head. "I . . . I'm feeling rather spent, Eli. Maybe we could say our good-byes?"

They did.

"Good luck with your new church," she said in parting.

"God is with us." He smiled. "We break ground next week. And rest assured, Lisette, I'll always remind the congregation of your generosity."

"All I want is your prayers for my daughters."

Maisie walked the preacher to the door; Lisette turned to her infants. One opened eyes certain to stay blue, and gazed up at her mother. Lisette's heart expanded. Her time with Gil hadn't been a waste, not by any means. She had her girls.

"Hello, Miss Shy Eyes," she whispered, set on not waking the others until she had some time with this one, and obtained a coo in reply.

Lifting the babe from the crowded crib, she parted her wrapper and held the child to a breast. Little fists balled, pushed against the soft flesh as those precious little cheeks moved in and out.

"My darling, I'll never let you down." *Not like your father did—I'll never speak ill of him to you, though.* "We'll have a good life. I promise."

Lightly, Lisette pressed her lips to the top of the tiny dark head. She heard the door hinges creak open and close, then the sound of boots moving slowly across the room. It didn't take looking up to recognize the encroacher. And she felt his eyes on her as surely as if he were touching her face.

"You two look more beautiful than I ever imagined."

"Don't. Please don't."

"I've missed you, Lisette. I want you with me. You and the girls. Forever and always."

"Go away," she whispered, refusing to lift her head.

"I won't until I've held my daughters."

"Shhh. You'll waken them."

"I intend to. I damned sure want to hear them cry before you take off for Chicago. And not from outside a window."

"So, Maisie told you we're leaving."

A slight shuffling of boots. A paper sack rattled. "Never fear. The Society of McLoughlin Women is intact. She didn't say a word. Eli Wilson told me."

Wanting to be angry with Eli for betraying a trust, Lisette found it impossible. Maybe, deep in her heart, she'd wanted a last word with the man who had given her these girls.

At last she lifted her head to see a dark suit, a white shirt, and a string tie . . . and the tormented visage of Gil McLoughlin.

Oh, God in heaven, she didn't hate him. The urge to ease his agony fought with the memory of the hurt he had inflicted. Damning herself, she wanted to revel in this moment . . . of a father seeing his children for the first time.

Oh, God in heaven, she still loved him. But what was love if she would always be in fear?

Stepping to the side, Gil bent over the bassinet. Into the arms that had held Lisette and had given her heaven on earth, he lifted a blanketed child. A measure of his visible agony diminished when he held the girl up for inspection.

"Lisette, she's beautiful." There was wonder in his voice. "She looks just like you."

"I won't argue the beautiful, but everyone—" No! She wouldn't tell him what everyone, including herself, thought. "Yes, she looks just like me."

Miss Shy Eyes had had enough milk; she relinquished the nipple and sighed. Gil's eyes stroked the exposed breast, then the small face, and Lisette not only pulled her wrapper across her bosom, she scowled at him. "You have no right to gaze at us that way."

Whipping his notice to the child in his hands, he said, "You know, she's a dead ringer for you, except for my hair. And there's no mistaking these eyebrows. They're mine."

It ought to be heartening, his admission of paternity, yet Lisette could not forget the insult he had placed on that child when sheltered in the womb.

"Put her down, Gil."

"Yeah. I'd like a gander at her cribmate." Gingerly, he placed his daughter beside another. "Good gracious, I can't tell the difference."

"There's a difference, all right. You've been holding The Scamp." A smile escaped, though Lisette tried to hide it. "I think she'll be the one for troublemaking."

Gil chuckled. "There's one in every family."

No comment passed Lisette's lips. She settled her fed daughter on her shoulder, rubbed the sweet little back, and received a loud burp.

"Just listen to that," Gil said, awe in his tone.

"I think you should leave. I've more nursing to do."

From the look on his face, Lisette knew he wanted to

stay and watch. He'd given up that right in the Drovers' Cottage.

"Must be burdensome," he murmured, "three of them at your breast."

"It's a burden of love."

"You've been burdened by a lot of love in your life."

Her teeth set, she replied, "It's my life, and you have no say in it. Especially after our divorce is granted."

"I don't want one."

Pushing to her feet, Lisette carried Miss Shy Eyes to the marble-top dresser. Her fingers shaking, she pulled away the wet wrappings and reached for a clean diaper. From the corner of her eye, she saw Gil picking up another daughter.

"Have you tagged a moniker on this one?" he asked.

"I call her The Thinker." Lisette paused. "I swear, Gil, she studies everything as if she's forming an opinion."

He carried the child over to the dresser, placed her beside her sister, then stepped back to study the result of his seed. The Thinker met his gaze, and he laughed. "Wife, I think you're right."

Lisette fastened the diaper. "I don't lie."

"I know." He scooped the two girls into his arms, turned, and put them both in their crib. A trio of cries filled the bedroom, and waving his finger, their father demanded in a soft voice, "Hush."

Amazingly, the howls ceased.

"They need proper names, Lisette."

"Actually, I have come up with two. Shy Eyes, I'm going to call Olga, after my sister. The Thinker—she'll be Margaret, after Maisie. And The Scamp . . . well, I don't think she'd appreciate sharing a name. I haven't decided what to call her."

His brows furrowed, he gazed down into the crib. "Hmm." A finger went to his upper lip. "I've got it." He swiveled around. "Let's give her a name that *might* make her think before she gets into troublemaking. Let's call her Charity."

"Maybe." Lisette, her back to the dresser, clutched the marble of its top when Gil stepped over to her. "You've heard them cry," she whispered. "Now go away."

"I have another demand."

One of his hands settled at her waist, the other moving to her nape. "Don't," she murmured, but he stepped closer. His body heat enveloped her, as did his presence. Lowering his head and parting his lips, he kissed her. *Ach du meine Güte!* He tasted so wonderful, so familiar. It was all she could do to break the embrace.

"I said go away," she bit out, hugging the arms that yearned to tighten on him.

Disappointment sifted in his eyes. "I'll leave, but before I do, I want to leave these for the girls." He reached for the paper sack. In it were three miniature hobby horses. "I whittled them."

"I . . . I'm sure the girls will enjoy the toys."

His fingers reached into a breast pocket and extracted a small velvet box. "This is for you."

"I don't want anything but a divorce."

He opened the box. Three diamonds set in a heart-shaped pendant winked up at her.

"Our time together wasn't hearts and roses. I wish it could have been, but it wasn't. But the heart is mine — it's a symbol of my love, Lisette." He paused. "And the diamonds are for Olga and Margaret and Charity."

He lifted the pendant as if to fasten it around Lisette's neck, but she moved away.

Unfazed, he continued. "Couldn't find any roses.

442

None to be had in Abilene. But if you'll go back to the Four Aces with me, I'll plant you a thousand rose-bushes."

"The only gift I ever wanted was your loving trust."

"I can't undo the past. If I could, I would. But I can't. But if you'll give me a second chance, Lisette, I promise you'll never regret it."

She said nothing, and one side of his mouth pulled into a grimace. "I am awfully, awfully sorry for not trusting you. Back then, it was because of my past—"

"Betty will always be your first wife."

"I've forgiven her. And I've gotten over her."

If only I could believe you.

He took Lisette's hand. "I know you're leaving to-morrow. You've got a night to think on us. If you'll give me another chance, be wearing my heart when the train pulls in. If I see it on your chest, all of us are get-ting aboard to make good on our plans for the future."

"I won't be wearing it."

"In that case, I'll turn in the opposite direction. But remember something. You're the only woman I'll ever love—well, except for our girls—and if you have anything in your heart for me, you'll give me a signal."

"How nice it would be for you, were I still so gullible."

He blinked. "You have until tomorrow, Lisette."

A night to think about Gil. And it was a miserable, indecisive one. When dawn broke, she didn't know whether or not to trust him. There was no way to fore-see the future, and Gil might well prove untrustworthy. But . . . if she turned her back, would the past always haunt her as it did her husband?

By noon, she had dressed in a traveling suit, and with Maisie's help, they bundled the girl up, then settled all three in a perambulator. She said to Maisie, "We'd better hurry, or we'll miss the train."

His wooden trunk at his side, Gil had been waiting on the platform for hours. Yesterday filled his mind's eye. Lisette, nursing their daughter. Lisette, unwilling to accept his apology. Lisette . . . If she had been able to forgive, she would have been here minutes, if not hours, ago.

Damn, he hurt.

For six never-ending weeks he had hurt. He supposed he deserved losing out on a second chance at happiness, but — damn it — he was only human. He wanted his wife and daughters. Where were they?

With uninterested eyes, he watched a herd of longhorns being packed aboard the eastbound Kansas Pacific. Smoke belched out of the engine. More than a dozen eager travelers climbed the steps to the passenger car. Lisette wasn't among them.

From across Texas Street, two women and a baby carriage headed this way. Gil held his breath. The moment of reckoning was at band. With a cape buttoned under her chin, he couldn't tell if Lisette wore the pendant.

"Damn."

Quickly he closed the distance between them. Nothing adorned the cape. Nothing!

He took his wife by the shoulders. "Don't guess I can talk you out of your decision, can I?"

"Absolutely not. I don't know whether I can trust you. And you don't know what I'll do in the future. Or even today, as far as that is concerned. But —"

"I trust you, and I was a fool not to trust you from the

beginning," he replied, his heart breaking all over again at her rejection. "If you had decided to give me a chance, I would've proved worthy of your love. And I would've done my damnedest to do right by you and the girls."

"That is what love is all about."

"All aboard!"

The whistle blew. While the conductor helped Maisie with the perambulator, Lisette scooted around Gil. He saw his world leaving for Chicago.

"Lisette, I love you. I'll always love you."

"I know."

The big wheels of the Abilene-to-Chicago rolled over once.

Her back to him, Lisette put her foot on the step. "Gil, what's keeping you?"

She whirled around and the cape came unbuttoned. Hot damn! She was wearing his heart.

Author's Note

I hope you've enjoyed Lisette's and Gil's love story. In some ways, this story had a personal side for me. Because my husband's family came to Texas from Germany during the Republic Days, I have long been interested in the Germans, like Lisette, who settled this state. Matter of fact, I borrowed the name Lisette from Carl Hix's great-grandmother, Lisette Hof Tampke. And Gil McLoughlin, the Scotsman from Rock Island, mirrors my bit of background. My mother's father (my sole ancestral link to north of the Mason-Dixon line), David Jamerson, came to Texas from Illinois after serving in the Spanish-American War.

The blending of Scots and Germans held me so enthralled that I haven't been able to put Gil and Lisette away. Not at all. Their daughters will continue the McLoughlin story in my next two novels. And they have a son, too. . . .

Martha Hix
San Antonio, Texas
December, 1991

DISCOVER DEANA JAMES!

CAPTIVE ANGEL   (2524, $4.50/$5.50)
Abandoned, penniless, and suddenly responsible for the biggest tobacco plantation in Colleton County, distraught Caroline Gillard had no time to dissolve into tears. By day the willowy red-head labored to exhaustion beside her slaves . . . but each night left her restless with longing for her wayward husband. She'd make the sea captain regret his betrayal until he begged her to take him back!

MASQUE OF SAPPHIRE   (2885, $4.50/$5.50)
Judith Talbot-Harrow left England with a heavy heart. She was going to America to join a father she despised and a sister she distrusted. She was certainly in no mood to put up with the insulting actions of the arrogant Yankee privateer who boarded her ship, ransacked her things, then "apologized" with an indecent, brazen kiss! She vowed that someday he'd pay dearly for the liberties he had taken and the desires he had awakened.

SPEAK ONLY LOVE   (3439, $4.95/$5.95)
Long ago, the shock of her mother's death had robbed Vivian Marleigh of the power of speech. Now she was being forced to marry a bitter man with brandy on his breath. But she could not say what was in her heart. It was up to the viscount to spark the fires that would melt her icy reserve.

WILD TEXAS HEART   (3205, $4.95/$5.95)
Fan Breckenridge was terrified when the stranger found her near-naked and shivering beneath the Texas stars. Unable to remember who she was or what had happened, all she had in the world was the deed to a patch of land that might yield oil . . . and the fierce loving of this wildcatter who called himself Irons.

Available wherever paperbacks are sold, or order direct from the Publisher. Send cover price plus 50¢ per copy for mailing and handling to Zebra Books, Dept. 3718, 475 Park Avenue South, New York, N.Y. 10016. Residents of New York and Tennessee must include sales tax. DO NOT SEND CASH. For a free Zebra/ Pinnacle catalog please write to the above address.